PETER LAWS is an ordained Baptist minister with a taste for the macabre. He writes a monthly column in the *Fortean Times* and also hosts a popular podcast and YouTube which reviews thriller and horror films from a theological perspective. He lives with his family in Bedfordshire.

peterlaws.co.uk   @revpeterlaws

By Peter Laws

THE MATT HUNTER SERIES
Purged

a&b

PURGED

PETER LAWS

Allison & Busby Limited
12 Fitzroy Mews
London W1T 6DW
allisonandbusby.com

First published in Great Britain by Allison & Busby in 2017.

A CIP catalogue record for this book is available from
the British Library.

First Edition

ISBN 978-0-7490-2078-1

Typeset in 11.25/16.25 pt Sabon by
Allison & Busby Ltd.

The paper used for this Allison & Busby publication
has been produced from trees that have been legally sourced
from well-managed and credibly certified forests.

Printed and bound by
CPI Group (UK) Ltd, Croydon, CR0 4YY

For Joy, who kept the light going.
This book is for you, and for the bridge in the rain. xxp

'Therefore go and make disciples of all nations,
baptising them in the name of the Father
and of the Son and of the Holy Spirit'

Matthew 28:19 (The Great Commission)

CHAPTER ONE

He was about to push her under for the fourth time, the final time.

Then something snapped in his fingers. In his heart. Just a sudden jolt that he might finish this way too quickly and wouldn't log it all in his brain. To rush stuff is to forget stuff, his mum once said. So he clicked a quick pause on the world and looked up at the lake. Just for a second or two.

Night had turned the water black but a fat moon was hanging. The sky was cloudless and close. He even saw a star moving slowly, the tiniest dot. The International Space Station maybe, or perhaps a full-on, sent-from-the-heavens sign. The latter, he decided. At the far edge of the lake the waterfall was still moaning in agreement, pounding hard into a cloud of spray. Even the jet-black pine trees swayed happily to its hiss. But the best and most magnificent sight was at his feet.

One more push.

He looked down at her, in awe. She lolled in his arms, water slapping at her shockingly skinny shoulders. The fused wet rope of her blonde hair had curled onto the surface of the lake, but her body . . . it was glowing. Wow. The Holy Spirit was bubbling under her bony skin, changing her and letting him watch.

She giggled, just then.

Her eye flicked open, just the one, deep in its socket. 'So are you gonna let me up or what?'

It was wrong and he knew it was wrong. He was stalling and stretching it out; shirking his cosmic responsibilities. But she looked so . . . well . . . angelic. Besides, what sort of ungrateful lunatic would go all Speedy Gonzales through an actual, bona fide miracle?

But as he pondered all this, she had got her footing again on the lake bed and was up. She waded quickly to the shore in noisy sloshes, calling for him to follow. Then she turned and her skull face was beaming. His breath quivered. He glanced quickly around the lake and noticed that the sound of the waterfall had changed. There was a tapping sound in its drone now. A *tut-tut-tut*. He hurried and dropped next to her on the lapping shore, her dripping bare feet still touching the lake's edge. He flicked the sacred water from his fingers.

'I absolutely love it here.'

He winced at how loud her voice was.

When he picked her up earlier, she'd said her name was Nicola Knox. It was probably the most ridiculous name he'd ever heard. She described anorexia as 'an insect eating her from the inside'. A disease, she said. *Riiiight*. He knew that stuff. He'd seen those shows. The phrase 'eating disorder' was just a fancy pants way of saying vanity. Only fourteen years old and she was already hooked on idols. Still, though, as he ran his eyes down her arms, wasn't she just a little plumper than before? Healing already?

'I should thank you,' she sniffed, a little weepy now. It made her voice quieter, which was good. 'I feel . . . nice.'

He smiled at that.

'And it all changes from now? I'll eat better?'

'Oh, you'll feast. You're a new creation. There's no more suffering.'

'Sounds so . . . I don't know. Crazy.'

He stared at her.

'I mean, I believe it, but it just comes across a bit—'

'A bit brilliant. Because you're not crazy. You're baptised . . . you're God's adopted child.'

Tut-tut-tut – you're losing control of this.

'You *do* look different,' he whispered.

'Do I?' Her unpleasantly thin neck extended a little. It reminded him of the part in *E.T.* that had always repulsed him. The long raising of the head, the telescopic throat.

'Yeah . . . you look healthier.'

She threw her hands over her mouth and laughed nervously through them. Guffawed, in fact. 'When I get home I'm going to rock up to the dinner table and eat like a maniac. Mum's going to freak. And she'll cry. God, we both will. We'll *bawl*.' Her eyes glistened with water, then she spotted a shift in his face. She prodded him with a genuinely sharp finger and for a second he saw that glow under her skin start to flicker and fade. 'I won't go back on this.'

'You'll stick with Jesus?'

'I'll never go back. Ever.' The mechanics of her face peeled back a smile, which only emphasised the frightful bones in her cheeks. It made him sad, because he'd seen this before. People insisting that once they'd had a divine experience they'd never move away from faith. It offended him to hear that sentiment again, and it hurt him too.

Because she wouldn't stick with this.

The self-inflicted slashes on her arms were proof of that. Nicola Knox was a girl of extreme hot and colds. When the hard times came, when she caught reflections in the butcher's window of her furious 'fat' teenage self, glaring back, she'd see insects again. She'd lose the faith that was burning in her right now. And really, if that was to happen, then why bother? Why give someone the Holy Spirit and the promise of eternal, blissful life, if He would just end up dribbling right out as she walked back to the car? Fact is, she was going to die at some later date. No question about it. Maybe next year in a bus crash, or maybe when she hit eighty and was all obese, sipping soup through a straw on a cruise ship. The time didn't matter. Either way she'd have

11

lost this moment and be tumbling overboard. Straight into hell.

He'd help her.

She smiled at him, but really it was more of a grin. And he knew grins are different. There was something about her that he didn't like any more. Something old. It flashed in her eyes. For the first time he noticed one of her nipples pushing and rising under her wet summer shirt.

His eyes lingered on it, willing the shadow to rise. Astonished at how quickly sin can spread from one person to the next. Like fleas. Or the plague. He had to look away. He stood up and stretched out his arms behind his back, elbows popping. He could hear the blood pulsing through his ears, like the wings of a huge invisible bird. But through it all he could hear—

Tut-tut-tut – you're losing this.

'I know it sounds childish,' she said, fingers stroking the grass, 'but I honestly feel like singing.'

'Then sing.'

'You won't laugh?'

'Never.'

She started. They were quiet drawn-out notes, high-pitched and tinny. No words, just humming. It sounded like 'All Things Bright and Beautiful'. Hearing her choose such a song showed a hint of beauty about her again, which meant it wasn't too late.

She leant back, arms locked, hands in the grass and feet in the water. She closed her eyes and started swaying her head from side to side like this was a musical. She stopped humming and frowned. 'Do you know the actual words of this song? I can't—'

He stepped right up behind her. Leant over and looked straight down at her upside-down face, gazing back up. 'All things bright and beautiful . . .' he sang. His tuning was far better than hers.

'Oooo, that's it,' she said. 'That's the one.'

'All creatures great and small . . .'

Her eyes closed. She smiled again. 'Mmmmm. Keep going.'

'All things wild and wonderful, the Lord God made them all.'

There was a rock right by them, just next to where she'd stuffed her socks into her trainers. He'd noticed it earlier as they waded in. He leant over and grabbed it. It was a heavy, jagged thing, big enough to hurt his fingers as he stretched his hand around it. And it was very cold against his skin like it had been dropped there from very high up, chipped off the moon. The waterfall wasn't tutting any more.

'Don't stop singing,' she said. 'You sound lovely.'

'Each little flower that opens. Each little bird that sings . . .'

A tear caught in her eyelash and he heard her say, 'Oh my God, I'm forgiven,' under her breath. He logged that moment. Put it in his 'Things that I've Seen That are Glorious' file.

His own voice trembled as he sang. 'He made their glowing colours. He made their tiny wings.' Then he clenched his hand around the sharp rock. His eyes darted left and right. Then he raised it. No time to ponder now. It was all about speed.

He could hear her crying. 'I feel . . . so . . . clean . . . I feel—'

The rock made a sharp cracking sound when he hit her with it. The loud snap raced out across the lake. At first he thought it was the rock itself cracking but that was as solid as ever. Maybe anorexics had weaker bones. Or there was just less flesh to cushion a blow. Either way her forehead had pretty much caved in, first time.

He watched her stick legs jerk out, the hollows of her knees splashed hard into the water. He saw her freaky long toes clench like old ladies' fingers grasping for stuff. Her elbows gave way and she fell backwards, hard against the grass. He crouched next to her. Watched those deep eye sockets wincing. Lids tightly shut in pain, quickly covered in black-looking blood. She said, 'Ow. What did? Ow. Ow.' Each word getting louder.

'*Shhh. Shhhhhhhh*. Little flower.'

Suddenly, two white balls flicked open in her face and they were instantly swamped by the black blood. Then the mad, wobbling howl of shock began and became a scream.

Panicked, he snapped his head round, just to make sure nobody was taking a random stroll at three in the morning. He looked back across the field towards the barn where they'd parked. His white Astra glowed blue in the moonlight. He looked up at the Healing Centre at the far edge of the lake, then up the hill where the black silhouette of the church looked on at what he was doing. In his mind's eye, he could imagine applause coming from up there. From some late-night congregation, praying for his ministry. But it was the hiss of the waterfall, or rather creation itself, that was clapping its hands. The best part was that there were no dark figures on the hill, no flashing eyes in the woods. The village of Hobbs Hill was fast asleep, like he'd planned.

He must have been looking for longer than he thought because by the time he turned back Nicola had turned onto all fours and was starting to crawl away. She moved very slowly, he noticed, as if he might not actually see. It was very silly of her, really. For a moment he just observed the weird jerks of her skinny limbs, the fluids falling from her face. She was like some freaky animal person; one of those feral kids. And he saw urine flooding the backs of her legs.

Help her!

He grabbed the rock and raced up behind her, jamming his knee into her rib-lined back with all his weight. They both plunged into the grass. When her chest hit the soil her scream vanished in a thump of air and he leant in close. He placed a whisper in her ear, as tenderly as he could manage: 'You're going to be healed. You must let me finish.'

His hands clenched around his rock.

Arms high.

Aaaaand down.

This time the sound wasn't a crack, it was a moist thud. Someone dropping a watermelon on kitchen lino. It went deeper this time, right into the back of her skull. He had to yank and pull at the rock just to get it out of her sticky blonde hair.

'I've just got to get you to the water. You'll never be fat again. Okay? *Okay?*'

She was twitching like crazy underneath him, face down. Her legs, her arms, her fingers all jerked. For one horrible second he thought she really might be full of insects, just like she'd said. And now he was being tricked into making little doors for them to get out.

But there was a little glow left. Just enough.

He didn't want to look at her, honestly he didn't, but he always wondered. When you snuff out the light, does it burn brighter just at the end? He'd just baptised her and her soul was in that delicate stage of freedom. Maybe he'd see this agony flash into wonder; terror into awe. Perhaps he'd spot a reflection deep in her eyes, of a tunnel opening up – a long white, strobing runway. Maybe she'd gasp something like, 'I can see God, and he's reaching out his hand.'

He had a little Mag-Light torch in a velcro pouch on his belt. He grabbed it and eagerly flipped her over onto her back. He clicked so that the beam would shine right into her face. But he didn't see heavenly bliss looking back. It was a frantic ghoul stuck with blood and soil, looking right at him. There were bits of grass on her face too, like the earth was wriggling its fingers around her, keeping her in the ground and the dust. But the world would have no claim on her now, he'd see to it.

Help her!

He grabbed her feet and started pulling her towards the water in hard frantic yanks. In the moonlight he could see her biting and chomping at the air, eyes rolling upward. He wouldn't be filing *that* memory away. No way. That was going straight into the brain bin. At one point she spasmed and her back arched horribly. A bubble of vomit raced up into his mouth so he had to swallow it.

He could see those two golden teeth of hers, at the back. The ones she'd shown off about before. They both flashed under the torchlight as she bit at the air, like there were two glowing eyes in her mouth. Someone hiding inside her. But he wasn't worried about it. He'd brought his tools. He'd sort that out, afterwards.

The waterfall. The roaring, jealous waterfall was now raging and calling out. It kept saying *bring her back, bring her back to me. Let's help her!*

It was just as he started to drag her into the cold water again that he noticed her lips peel apart, making thick bubbles of blood. She was saying something and he shivered when he heard it. At first it sounded like 'please'. It hurt him to think that she was still pleading for it to stop. That she hadn't realised that what was happening was the fulfilment of all they'd prayed for in the water only ten minutes before.

Yet when she said it again, it sounded less like please and more like *yes*.

Not a delirious 'yes', not a sexual 'yes', and definitely not a 'please', but *yes*.

And he felt a tear fall from his eye. Just like that.

Every sound blended: her screams, his breathing. The cows in the next field had even woken up, excited by the new smells. But it was the song of the constant waterfall that pulled it all together. And he knew that he was listening to the portcullis of heaven rattling open.

Chains swinging, angels singing.

God on this throne clasping his hands together in watery-eyed delight as another latchkey prodigal finally skipped her way down the front path. And a nod of appreciation from the Lord to him, his willing servant who gritted his teeth and did what other Christians would talk about but never dare do. To actually guide the lost ones home. A home that would never perish, spoil or fade.

Just before he pushed her under for the third and final time, he grabbed her wet, tiny hand and he kissed it gently. It was still glowing. Just a little, but enough to reflect on the quaking surface of the lake.

'Nicola . . . you are beloved.' He wiped a tear away with the palm of his hand, and checked his watch. 'So let me sing you in.'

He sang the hymn again and was pleased to hear that she was singing too. Muffled and wet, but definitely there. He pushed her down and stood on her while he looked up at the stars. At all those little windows.

CHAPTER TWO

Professor Matt Hunter had never seen this before, but a chunk of Oxford Street was empty. This was a hot summer Sunday, warm enough for people to leave their jacket at home with cavalier abandon. Sunny enough to suck a Callipo on the way to work and stride the pavement, enjoying being *out*. But here it was, looking desolate. It was weird and kind of cool. Like he was about to drive his little car through the opening scene of a zombie movie.

A policeman he recognised was hovering outside a Starbucks, kicking dirt just near a plastic cordon. When he saw Matt's car he snapped into life and dragged the fence apart.

'Head on through, Professor.'

Matt leant his head out of the window, tapping the brake. 'Where am I going? . . . and it's Craig, isn't it?'

'Memory man!' he said, impressed. 'Yes, I'm Craig Mills.'

'So . . .'

'Oh. Head for the noodle bar, first right.' He jabbed a finger at a side street about ten doors down. 'It'll be really obvious.'

'This isn't a bomb or something is it?'

'They thought it was but it turns out it isn't. Which is good. That's why they called you in. It's one of your things.' He glanced down at what Matt was wearing. 'Love the outfit by the way.'

Matt tried to laugh. 'Well, that makes one of us.'

The pavements were empty. Shop doors lay open, cars were lurched up on kerbs with nobody inside. The only faces he could see were shop dummies tilted at jaunty, bad-for-the-spine angles. They looked depressed and disturbed about this season's outfits. He totally sympathised. When he turned the first right it really *was* obvious. Three police cars were parked in a little arch with a huddle of officers around them. All of them were staring at a noodle bar across the street called *Shangri-La!* Which according to the sign was: *Where East Meets Best!* Cute.

He took one last glimpse of his reflection in the rear-view mirror. He leant towards it, looking at his neckwear and groaned. It was the sort of sound he used to make as a teenager, before he left for school, on the day of an apocalyptic acne breakout.

Heads turned and eyes widened when he got out. He only knew one of these officers, the really lanky one. He just gawped back at Matt and nudged one of the others, nodding at the black trousers, the black shirt; clocking the white clerical collar and trying not to chuckle. He'd have felt less conspicuous in a dayglo mankini. He walked up, glancing across at the noodle place. He figured he should probably whisper. 'Where's Sergeant Forbes?'

One of the car doors instantly clicked open and DS Larry Forbes shimmied his heft out, making the car shake. He had a mobile pressed to his head but he jabbed it into silence without saying goodbye and rushed over. He slapped a sweaty hand into Matt's. 'Look, mate. Thanks for coming down, and sorry for calling you out on your holiday.'

'Sabbatical.'

'Right . . .' he sniffed. 'That book finished yet?'

Ah . . . the question Matt heard maybe thirty times an hour. Mostly from his own nagging brain. He shook his head. 'Larry . . . why am I here and why am I wearing this?' He tapped at his neck.

'Did it take you a long time to fish one of those out?'

18

'Wren found it. Inside a box of VHS tapes in the loft. Which should give you an idea how long it's been.'

'You're quite the Dapper Dan.'

He leant in and whispered again. 'I feel like a dick. Now what's this about?'

A huge chunk of an officer suddenly loomed out of nowhere and stood by Larry's shoulder, dwarfing them both and blocking out the sun. His Buzz Lightyear head looked so big, the black and white cap on it probably had to be sledgehammered into place each morning by a team of four. 'So is this him?'

'U-huh,' Larry bit his lip. 'Matt, this is Sergeant Bob Gerard. He's heading up the Tactical Support Team.'

Matt held out his hand. Hovered it in mid-air. Gerard just looked at it for a few seconds.

'This is where you put your hand out and we shake,' Matt said. 'Then you tell me why I'm the only one in fancy dress.'

He grabbed it and Matt felt the crush. 'I hope you're aware, Mr Hunter—'

'Professor Hunter,' Larry butted in. 'He's writing a book.'

'Isn't everyone?' Gerard pursed his lips. 'You do know, Professor Hunter, that hostage negotiation is a very . . . very . . . delicate business.'

Matt's jaw dropped open. He turned to Larry. 'You've got to be kidding.'

'Hardly . . .' Gerard said. 'We've got a Nigerian male in the noodle bar. Says his wife's possessed by Satan. He's got a knife to her throat and he's getting very tired and very jumpy. He says that he'll kill her if we don't . . .' he raised his fingers in air quotes, '". . . send a vicar in".'

'And you called *me*?' Matt said. 'I jacked that in years ago.'

'Larry says you know the spiel. The religious stuff.'

'He does. He's a walking Wikipedia page.'

Gerard leant in. 'You don't have to get close. We just need you to talk to the guy. You've worked with Larry before and he trusts

19

you. He says that you've got a way with these . . . spiritual types.' It sounded almost like an accusation, not a compliment. Like telling someone they had a natural, high-five rapport with paedophiles. 'We need someone fluent in all that religious shit.'

Matt suddenly laughed at how well Gerard had just summed up his career these days. In fact, he should get them to carve that on his office door at the university. Stick it on his business cards. Type it at the bottom of all those articles or on the cover of this new book – if he ever finished it. Professor Matt Hunter: writer, researcher, police consultant and speaker on various flavours of weird religious shit. It had a certain pop to it.

'Obviously, I'd much rather go in there myself,' Gerard said.

'Hey, by all means you can borrow it. Keep it, actually,' Matt went to grab the collar, 'because me and my family are going away this afternoon and right now I'm supposed to be helping my wife pack.'

Gerard shushed him with a Hulk-sized hand. Facial muscles turned a few degrees less tense. 'Take a look behind you. About five'o'clock.' Some policemen seemed incapable of just pointing and saying 'over there'.

He worked out where five o'clock was and saw a young black boy through the glass window of a shoe shop. England top, tracksuit bottoms. He was nine, maybe ten years old. He had one palm pressed against the glass. A policewoman was holding the other.

'That's Adowa,' Gerard said quietly. 'All I'm saying, is that we'd appreciate it if you didn't let his dad slit his mum's throat today.'

The kid's teeth were showing and his eyes were glazed with fright. Like he was another shop dummy, only this one was reliving something. Something bad. Matt turned back and looked back at the noodle bar. His favourite was always Schezuan chicken, which Wren and the kids hated, meaning he never had to share. He noticed it was on special here but he suddenly felt sick. 'Fine. I'll try. But I'd appreciate it if you don't let him slit my throat either.'

'Then don't get too close. Stay by the door, even. And remember we'll be in there in a shot if it kicks off.' Gerard nodded at some officers who hurried over with a small silver flight case. Then he finally reached out his hand to shake. 'Act holy.'

CHAPTER THREE

Matt turned his head to the side and caught his reflection in the glass window to make sure the earpiece was well hidden. A ghost of the vicar he used to be made exactly the same move. Then that vicar stared back at him. Glaring at him. Judging him. This ancient version of himself sometimes did that, cropping up in the middle of some cool dream or thought process. He was sorely tempted to flip his old self the finger but that would have looked extremely unhinged to the officers behind him.

Instead he just blinked and took a long deep breath in through the nose, out through the mouth. The type singers do before a TV audition, or divers before a jump. Or more to the point, prisoners before the guillotine slices their entire bloody head off. He pressed a finger against the stab-proof vest again. Damn, these things felt thin. He pushed through the open glass door of the noodle bar, trying to keep the tremble in his hand to a minimum.

It was a mess inside.

Bowls of noodles lay strewn across the long wooden benches, dangling like exposed veins off the edges. Bottles of soy sauce had rolled to the floor and were forming sticky brown pools on the white tiles. It was chaos. It absolutely stank, too. Like really stank.

Considering Matt was such a flag-waving, prawn cracker-munching fanboy of Chinese food, it was surprisingly nauseating.

On the wall a golden cat winked and waved its paw while a James Bond medley (in Chinese) seeped out from the speakers. He even spotted a child's toy, which looked like Elmo from *Sesame Street*, probably abandoned in the screaming rush. Now Elmo lay face down in a puddle of sweet and sour sauce, grinding his animatronic limbs back and forth like he was slowly screwing the spring roll wedged into his crotch.

Gerard's voice crackled in his ear. '*Alright, Professor. No stupid risks. You're just calming him down and that's it. So keep your distance. Now . . . call out his name. Nice and gentle.*'

Here we go.

'Mr Adakay?' Matt called out, his posh voice sounded like the squeak of a dog toy. He cleared his throat and said it again, more macho. 'Mr Adakay?'

The speaker on the wall said '*Goooooooldfingaaaahh!*' It was the only response.

'*Again,*' Gerard said.

'Kwame Adakay? Can I call you that?'

Just the tinny brass stabs of the music. And Elmo's little sex groan.

'Kwame. I'm a pastor. You asked for a pastor?'

Silence. He took another step.

'Kwame? Are you there?'

Another.

Gerard whispered, '*You're moving too fast.*'

'Would you like me to come round, Kwame? To where you are?'

'*Slow down!*'

A whisper, disembodied, suddenly hissed itself from behind a wall of glowing fish tanks. It was Kwame. 'Slow. Come slow.'

'*Okay. Do as he says.*'

'No problem. I can do slow.' Matt lifted his empty hands up. *Nothing up my sleeve.* Then he turned the corner. Kwame was on the other side, surrounded by a tableaux of fish tanks, shapes swirling and diving with neon streaks. The water looked pretty dirty.

Kwame was one of those uber-hairy guys. Fur on the face and forearms, a tracksuit-wearing Sasquatch of a man. His hand was pressing his wife's forehead back. Her eyes were shut tight, chin high, sweaty neck exposed. A long strip of wet green lettuce hung out of her mouth like an alien tongue. For some reason she'd decided not to swallow it. The knife's tip rested almost directly on the quivering cord of her jugular vein.

'I'm here to help. My name's Matthew Hunter.'

Kwame's bauble eyes moved slowly up and down him, checking out the black shirt, the dog collar. 'Are you qualified to wear that?'

'I am.'

It wasn't a total lie.

'You look a bit too young to be a pastor.'

'Wow, Kwame, I like you already. I'm actually thirty-four. And is this your wife? Is this Arima?' His words had a nervous hint of jolly about them, like he was making chit-chat at a summer barbecue. This was either a clever or suicidal tactic, he had no idea which.

'Used to be my wife, Pastor. But Satan got her now.'

'How so?'

'I mean he crawl inside her body. While she sleep. Slithers in through her mouth. And when she wake, she . . . she a foul thing.'

'I see. Just take your time.'

Gerard: '*Good. That's good. Keep that tone.*'

That tone . . .

Matt stepped out of his body for a minute and listened to himself slipping into the smoothy ministerial voice he once used to soothe the dying or depressed or doubting. Or in Kwame's case, the demented. It was that patent *hey-I'm-just-your-fellow-metaphysical-traveller* voice. How quickly it came back after all these years.

'. . . I tell her, say Christ, say his name, and she spit and cough and can hardly speak.'

24

'So what's with the knife? Why not just get her help?'

'*Don't challenge him, idiot!*'

Matt considered pulling out the earpiece and plunging it into the nearest bowl of noodles.

'My pastors at the church . . . they already try to help her. They pray, they sing, they read the word.'

'And?'

'It never work.'

'Why the knife, Kwame?'

Kwame's face started to wrinkle and crease.

'I'm not going to judge you, okay? But come on. Let's stop messing about. Tell me straight about what's just happened here.'

'*For God's sake, Hunter. Don't harass the—*'

A loud pop of malfunction shot through the earpiece, making Matt wince. Then silence. Dead batteries maybe, or interference. Whatever the case it meant no more Gerard. Panic and relief flooded Matt, both at the same time. He wanted to push his finger into his ear to give the thing a wiggle. Didn't bodyguards do that in films? But he wasn't about to do something so obvious in front of Kwame.

'Okay . . . I tell you. We were eating dinner just now and she say . . . she say she going to kill our son. She gonna give little Adowa . . . brain cancer . . .'

'But how could she do that? It's impossible.'

'Oh, she crafty. She can say a prayer to Satan and the boy get it just like that. She done it before. Gave her sister a stroke last year. Just by *prayin'* it.' His chest was starting to bulge now with deep, heart-squeezing breaths. The Umbro sign moved up and down in quick jerky movements. 'Had to stop her. Had to, cos I love my boy.'

'Of course you do. I saw him outside and he looks like a fine young man.' Matt paused. He gave a gentle tilt of the head and said, 'You've been through a great deal, haven't you?'

'Oh, yes.'

'And the pastors' prayers did nothing?'

Kwame just looked at the floor, bewildered.

Matt didn't speak, just earnestly nodded like he was pondering the spiritual pain. Actually he was just wondering what the hell Gerard would be suggesting right now. Then an idea instantly flicked up inside his brain.

'Okay. Kwame, answer me this. Did your pastors fast before they did it?'

'What?'

'Did they avoid food?'

'Why you ask this?'

'Jesus said some demons only come out with prayer and fasting. Gospel of Mark. Chapter Nine. Did they fast?'

The constant quiver in Kwame's lips suddenly stopped. 'I can't remember. I don't know . . .' he shrugged. 'Maybe, no.'

'Well, it's not rocket science, is it? I reckon they probably didn't. But *I've* been fasting, Kwame. You hear that? Which means I can exorcise her right now. If you want me to.'

If Gerard could still hear the audio feed on his end, this would probably be the point that he'd put his head in his hands.

'So, shall I do it?'

Kwame pushed his tongue against the inside of his cheek. 'You lying to me, mister?' Maybe he could smell the cheese and chorizo wrap Matt had scoffed an hour earlier.

'You know what?' Matt said. 'I'm not asking you to trust me.'

'Pardon?'

'You don't know me. I don't know you. I don't even know what noodles you ordered.' Matt pointed in the general direction of the heavens. A bead of nervous sweat trickled down his temple. 'But you've got to trust Him. Because that's what this is about, Kwame. Not me, not you. Not Adowa. It's not even about Arima. Because in the end this isn't about flesh and blood. It never was. This is the heavenly realms we're dealing with. So are you going to let Arima come over here so I can get started?'

The three of them stood without speaking for a moment, Kwame's lips moving in silent prayer. The James Bond medley slinked into a pathetic synth version of 'For Your Eyes Only', like a demo on an insane child's keyboard.

'Do it then,' Kwame said finally. 'Do the exorcism. But I'm going to hold her. And I won't let her go until the demon comes out. That should work.'

No numb-nuts, that won't work.

Matt felt a sudden fury at Larry for suggesting he dig this damn vicar collar out from that fossil of a box in his attic. But then he found himself flicking through the files in his mind, found a drawer, pulled out a folder. Ah!

'Set her on the floor,' he said. 'Over there. Kwame, I'm going to have to lie on her.'

'Excuse me?'

'I need to lie on top of her.'

'What you talking about—'

'You remember Elisha, don't you? When he brought the little boy back to life?'

Kwame thought for a moment, began to nod.

Matt quoted the Old Testament text, as close as he could remember. He was almost, almost, tempted to say it in a Charlton Heston voice to give it *gravitas*. But he didn't. '"*As Elisha stretched himself out on him, the boy's body grew warm.*" Kwame. Do you want your wife back today?'

He was already moving her into position, knife held close. It was amazing how a few Bible quotes could get people to fall in line. Arima moved with him, upright and stiff in his arms. Like a kooky version of one of those shop dummies outside. The only movement came when she slowly sucked the lettuce up. It slithered through her lips, almost all the way up. Like she hadn't sucked it in at all, but it had just crawled in, all by itself. A piece of religious trivia suddenly popped open in his head. Something his brain often liked to do. He could see himself reading about medieval Christianity on a Tube ride and how Gregory the Great reported nuns eating unblessed lettuce and getting possessed. He remembered laughing at that, when he read it. Leaning over to Wren and saying '. . . can you believe this? Satan via the veg aisle?'

He saw the wet green tail vanish between her lips and it didn't feel quite as funny.

Ffffft.

Kwame lay his wife softly on the floor and with his spare hand he cleared the wiry afro fringe from her eyes. He wiped away a single white bubble of spit from the corner of her mouth. Even with the blade at her throat there was a tenderness to his movements.

Matt crouched down and just did it. He slowly crawled on top of her, ignoring the ghost of Gerard's voice (or maybe it was his own common sense) saying in a steady, frantic whisper, over and over again . . . *what the hell are you doing? What the hell are you doing?*

Maybe this would be a funny story he would tell in lectures or in radio interviews. Maybe he could include it in his book. That hilarious Sunday he dressed up as a vicar and lay flat out on top of a possessed Nigerian, who had a knife at her throat. But the closer he got to her face, he had a sickly throb of dread, real and sharp, that maybe people would tell this story in hushed tones, at his funeral. What a tragically bizarre way for a fella to die, they'd say, trying not to laugh into their cucumber sandwiches.

She smelt very strange and thoroughly unpleasant, like the food scraps bin he had at home under the kitchen sink. When he put them out for collection each week, when they were moist with decay – she smelt of that and maybe a little vinegar. And she was cold beneath him.

For the first time she started making a noise, a quiet moaning while her cold hips started to push against his.

Slowly at first.

Up and around.

Up and around. Dirty Elmo style.

A subtle, sexual writing that Matt hoped to hell Kwame wouldn't notice. She was humming a melody. 'Amazing Grace'.

'You'll need to move the knife from her neck. Just for a few seconds, okay?'

Kwame narrowed his eyes. 'I tell you, Pastor, that I'll stab you if this don't work. I'll cut your bloody throat.'

The indentation in Arima's neck sprang back as Kwame pulled the knife away.

Matt started to pray aloud, something in Latin. This time he *did* get a little Heston with it because, frankly, he was nervous. It was a harmless blessing prayer that he'd learnt a million years ago in Bible college but he could already see Kwame starting to relax, clearly thinking Matt was legit. Oh, Bible verses make you look holy but pray in Latin and everyone thinks you're Max von Sydow in *The Exorcist*.

After a minute of this, Kwame even took a step backwards, up against the swarming fish tanks. He sank onto one of the benches so he could watch. There was distance between him and his wife, finally.

'I need you to pray, Kwame. Pray the Lord's Prayer . . . right now. And pray loud.'

Hairy hands slapped together, wedging the knife blade between his palms. His eyes closed tight and became a black spiderweb of wrinkles. Arima kept humming the melody of Amazing Grace.

How sweet the sound . . . that saved a wretch like me.

Okay. This is it.

'It's really hot today,' he whispered towards the earpiece. The agreed code for 'she's clear'. Hopefully, the malfunction was only one way and the army of police could still hear him outside.

No response.

He wiggled his face, felt the earpiece shift. 'It's *really* hot today.'

He waited for the doors to burst in.

Nothing.

'Pray it again, Kwame. Keep going and don't stop.'

Kwame nodded, closed his eyes again.

Matt took in a breath. New plan.

Just as Kwame's lips circled to form the 'ow' of 'Our Father' Matt hollered out as loud as he possibly could. *'She's clear!'*

It took a split second.

To look back and see the slip of a grateful smile start on Kwame's face, he must have thought the mystery pastor's sudden announcement meant he'd actually cleared out the demon and set his wife free. Matt even heard the guy shout hallelujah. But then those huge eyes flung themselves open like two iron doors on a cage and his sweat-soaked face crumbled into confusion. A line of police crashed through the glass front doors and scrambled toward the fish tanks, filling the place with a disorientating rugby team roar, skidding through the soy sauce, barking and shouting, 'Police! Police! Drop your weapon!' But they still felt quite a distance away.

Matt went to push himself off Arima so he could get clear but her icy hands suddenly clamped round his wrists. Stronger than she should be, she locked him there for a second. A very long, drawn-out second. Kwame threw himself toward him with a squeal.

He felt a sudden ripple in the back of his neck.

It could have been a draught of air from the now open door, or Kwame dropping onto him with the knife. The tip of the blade plunging at the part the stab vest wasn't covering.

Oh shit.

The bones in his spine automatically locked themselves into position, like he was a Transformer bracing for impact. He had a sudden flash of an image of himself sitting paralysed in a high-backed chair sipping carrot soup from a spoon from his weeping wife's trembling hand. So real that he heard his breath shudder.

'Iiii,' Kwame from behind, 'kiiiilll.'

Time slowed the syllables. The officers' roar was loud, but he could tell it was too far away. The sound of them bent into a low dinosaur growl, every sound dragging, sinking as though the batteries of the world were finally running out.

Instinctively Matt pulled up his knee, wound it like a spring and hammered it backwards. The sole of his shoes (the ones he wore for lecturing and funerals and vicar impersonations) slammed into something – Kwame's leg, most likely, from the horrible cracking sound. Like a branch snapping underwater. It was followed by frantic crackling as the officers deployed their Tasers. The knife clattered to the floor followed by the jerking crunch of his electrified body. Like all that hair was about to burst into spontaneous combustion.

'You're clear, Hunter.' It was Bob Gerard, panting, laughing. 'You mad little shit. You're clear.'

Matt yanked his wrist out from Arima's hand. But then he stopped.

For the first time her eyes began to open. She did it gradually and, it seemed, with some discomfort. Her lids tore as though they'd been stuck shut with surgical glue. Her lips pressed forward to speak and a black hole slowly split into an open seam between them. What she said made some of his strength drain away.

'Mama neeeeeeeed.' Her dry voice crackled like old paper.

'Mrs Adakay?' he said.

'Mama neeeeeeeed.'

It was the strangest thing. He'd never met the woman, never seen her face, never even knew the name Arima *was* a name before today. But those words hung in the air like a shared secret between the two of them. And when he saw her lips form the shapes and sounds he closed his eyes, as if it might block out the syllables. It didn't. Arima's pleading just threw up the image of his own mother against the back of his eyelids. Her matted hair sticky, face down at the kitchen table, voice bubbling into liquid.

Some sadistic little neuron fired in his brain: bet she said that, too. I bet you, I bet you, I bet you . . .

He shook his head quickly and opened his eyes as Arima said it again. 'Mama neeeeeed her boy.' Then a manic look of excitement animated her face.

He ripped his wrists from her hand and sprang to his feet,

brushing himself down. Arima was still on the floor but now she started to reach out both hands to him, as though she was pleading for him to crawl back on top of her. Then her eyes grew wide and she opened her mouth to hiss, low and long. He could see the piece of unswallowed lettuce, rattling like a second tongue right at the back of her throat.

'Mama neeeeeeeeeeeeeeed.'

Why the hell was she smiling?

The medics were shuffling down the corridor, swooping around her.

'Help her, will you?' Matt told them, eyes fixed on Arima's arching back. It was so high that he half expected to hear each vertebrae snap as she contorted, cracking like the flick of a pack of cards.

He needed some air. He dug the earpiece out with shaking fingers and, holding it in his fist, marched through the glass doors and back out onto the pavement.

He spotted a van in the street that hadn't been there before. Then a TV camera was thrust into his face as soon as his foot touched the tarmac. The street suddenly echoed with sound. It took him a moment to realise it was the officers applauding. They stuck up their thumbs, whistled with delight.

'Great work, Reverend!' the reporter said and from somewhere, he heard a woman wolf-whistle. But what he mainly heard was Arima still crying out, even through the glass. *Mama, mama, mama neeeeeed.* He reached up and yanked the dog collar off his neck, then tossed it into the bin, like a fourteen-year-old hiding a cigarette from his mother, and hurried toward his car.

CHAPTER FOUR

Her smell was on him. Especially, Matt felt, on his face. Like he'd put the recycling out and ended in a comedy slip of carrot ends and onion skins landing on his head. When he breathed in a certain way, he could taste her too.

Arima Aroma, he thought and smiled for what felt like the first time in hours, finally free of the eternal debrief to the police and reporters, who dragged him back before he'd even reached his car. He buzzed the window down. London air, thick with the Thames, whistled in.

Mama neeeeeeeeeed . . .

He blinked hard and grabbed one of his CDs for a distraction. *Star Wars: The Original Motion Picture Soundtrack*. Yeah, that was nerdy enough to do it. He pushed the disc in. The orchestra's main theme tore into life, rattling the car. He bobbed his head as he drove.

He checked his watch and winced at the time. Almost three. Crap, he was *so* late. He pushed his foot into the accelerator and sped for all of five seconds until the next traffic light blinked onto red: ye shall not pass.

'Damn it.' As he waited he noticed the little angry breaks in the skin in each of his wrists, caused by Arima's fingernails. He called out above the music, 'I think Mama neeeeeeeed a good psychiatrist.'

It didn't sound as funny out loud.

Even though he'd torn that clerical collar off, he could still feel it pressing around his neck. Those things often used to do that, when he wore them professionally. He'd take it off at night for a shower and still feel it gripping. Like when you wear a hat for a long time and it still feels like it's there. A phantom frigging limb, that's what it was. He felt pretty stupid but even now he had to check in the rear-view mirror just to make sure he really had dragged it off.

Dog collar. Whoever thought that name up had an excellent grasp of irony.

There was a time in his life when he'd worn one constantly.

Back in his early twenties, when he'd been the obedient, house-trained minister of Bewley Hill Independent Evangelical Church (a long-winded name for a long-winded church). He'd unlock the doors at 9 a.m. at least, setting out chairs because there were no pews. There wasn't any art (cos that was evil and sensuous), no golden candlesticks (cos that symbolised greed) and no altar to put them on (cos that was . . . heaven forfend! . . . too Catholic). Bewley was village hall-style spirituality. It was No-Frills, Everyday Value, Waitrose Essentials Protestantism, thank you very much.

What that church *did* have was a Godzilla-sized version of the King James Bible on a folding wooden table, surrounded by canvas chairs with cold metal frames. Oh, it was the very cutting-edge of spiritual expression, in around 1692. He'd set those chairs out only after battling with the temperamental heating system, which never worked cos God's saving his heat for hell!: the hilarious recurring joke of the church secretary.

Then he'd have to figure out the angles on the stubborn/Satanic overhead projector. He'd be slipping newssheets into Bibles and stacking them neatly. Shivering in the rain while putting up laminated A-board posters of that morning's sermon title. And picking up the cans and used condoms strewn around the church steps, paranoid that he'd feel the prick of a syringe.

Then the service would begin and he'd be up there for an hour, preaching a thirty-minute sermon and belting out four hymns. Two modern, two traditional, always trying to keep the balance. While he tried to seem approachable and authoritative, unique and ordinary all at the same time. And throughout it all, he'd be praying for the healing of the world.

He shuddered in the car at the thought of it. Literally shuddered. In the same way Terry Waite probably freaked out if he ever accidentally woke up in some deep dip of the night and thought he was back in his hole.

Matt touched his fingertips to his bare neck one more time and smiled. Nothing there. And there was no creepy cross hanging from the rear-view mirror, like he used to have. No little hand-held Eucharist box stuffed in his glovebox so he could take communion to the shut-ins, with bite-sized bread and a tiny bottle of wine for pensioners who liked their gluten-free Jesus to go.

He pushed the car into gear as the lights turned green. As good a symbol as any that he really was free and life was good. And while his writing and speaking and teaching at the university showed that religion was still his bread and butter, there was now a crucial difference. He didn't have to actually eat that bread. Sniff it? Yeah, why not? Prod it a bit, like an interesting mushroom growing on a tree? Fine.

But consume it? Uh-uh. Cos that stuff did things to people. Bad things.

He could tell he was getting nearer to his house because gangs of youths started to shimmer out of the concrete, with hoods up like medieval monks with ASBOs, then he pulled into his turning. It was called Cropsy Road, a Victorian terrace of three-storey houses. His had a bright-red door, which he'd painted last November on a Turner Classic Movie-inspired whim. The sort where Ebenezer Scrooge might swing his head out of the windows and shout Merry Christmas.

Only Scrooge didn't walk fifty yards to the end of his street to a nightclub called Hedonism and a strip of sticky-floor pubs and kebab shops. These delights had appeared about six months after they'd bought this house and sunk all their savings into it. Bad timing, that.

Turns out that when you stick a few prostitutes on the corner and a gang of hoodies by the front gate it works a dark magic on a house's price tag. Add the fact that Wren might be redundant from her architects' firm in three weeks, they'd probably be stuck here for another year, despite his own income.

One day, if the finances were right, the Hunter family would keep on driving and push through the outer force fields of London. They'd live in one of those Buckinghamshire villages that Wren kept bugging him about. He'd finally finish the book he was writing and work for a leafy college somewhere. Life would involve picking the kids up from school and drinking obscure ales with Wren each night at quaint pub quizzes, where he'd floor the competition on the Bible and Star Trek rounds. Not sports, though. Never sports. But maybe he'd take up running again.

Yeah, that'd work just fine.

He parked and headed up his path, his little souvenir NASA key fob dangling from his hand. When he stepped into the hallway he saw Wren was halfway down the stairs, dragging a huge suitcase behind her.

Thud. Thud! Thud!

'Whoah.' He rushed over. 'Let me help.'

She aimed a palm at him, stopped him dead. Then she yanked the case down the final step and curled a lock of her bright-red hair behind each ear. She looked at him. Or rather, she aimed her eyes at him. Both barrels.

'Well, would you look at this. I figured I'd go all trad and do the packing by myself.'

'Wren, I'm sorry I'm so late.'

'And we all know how much Wren Hunter loves packing.' She held a finger gun to her head and pulled the trigger. Then she hooked a thumb at her face. 'Best. Wife. Ever.'

'Undeniably.'

'Stop smiling.' She pulled a long breadstick from her back pocket and chomped down hard on it. She often carried them around like that, and he could never fathom how they didn't snap. 'I called ahead. I told Seth that we're going to be late. Great start to my business pitch, this is.'

'Look, I'm really sorry. I got called in on something. Police stuff.'

'*Again?*' She snapped the stick theatrically between her teeth. 'Book writing getting tedious, is it, Professor?'

He took a step closer. 'I saved a woman's life today.'

Her shoulders dropped and she started dragging her suitcase down the hallway. 'Don't tell me that.'

'Seriously. I saved an actual person's actual life today.' He grabbed a couple of cases and dragged them with her.

She let out a long, lip-flapping breath as she dumped it by the door, 'And how the heck am I supposed to complain about that?'

'You can't. That's the genius of it.'

She gazed at the black shirt and trousers. 'And how come you're dressed like a waiter?'

'I'll explain later.' He checked the clock on the wall. 'Look, I'll quickly get changed and then I'll start loading up.'

Wren nodded, cupped her hand around her mouth and called up the stairs, 'Girls. We're going.' The obligatory pause. Then both of them called up at the same time.

'*Girls!*'

Muffled music suddenly stopped upstairs.

'Crud,' Wren said. 'I haven't locked the windows. I'll do that and you load up.'

He nodded, and she sprang off on her usual pre-holiday security detail. Windows locked, timer lights set, Radio 4 on low but constant – so burglars pressing their ears to the windows would think the house was occupied . . . by posh people discussing garden weeds and Klimt.

As she headed into the kitchen Matt went to grab the final case and saw Lucy at the top of the stairs, looking down at him. She had the usual expression whenever she deemed him worthy of a glance. One raised eyebrow, a horizontal line for a mouth. Sixteen years old and already a master at the cold glare shut-out.

'Hi, Lucy.'

She clomped down the stairs, then when she was sure her mother wasn't in earshot she tilted her head. 'Hello, Matthew.'

The sound of his first name dangled on a string between them. And she smirked at whatever power she thought it gave her. He'd read a magazine at the dentist's once that said the 'first name gambit' (sounded like a chess move) was often used against stepdads. Goes with the territory, so to speak.

'Come on. Help me load up the car.'

'What's with the black get-up?' She nodded at his clothes. 'You been serving at a pizza restaurant or something?'

He laughed. God, her and Wren were alike. 'Actually I've been puppeteering for local orphans.'

She looked at him like he was a maniac.

Another voice suddenly squeaked from upstairs and he felt his heart lift. It was Amelia: 'Can we take my telescope?'

She was leaning over the bannister with a box under her arm, beaming a smile and nodding her head like an eager dog. She waved her hand across the air for a Jedi mind trick. 'You *will* take the telescope, Father. It is . . . your destiny.'

He laughed. 'Bring it down. If there's room, we'll take it.'

'Yay!' she rattled down the stairs.

'You two are geeks,' Lucy said.

'I'd rather be a geek than a freak,' Amelia jabbed Lucy in the ribs with her finger.

For a moment his two girls stood next to each other on the bottom step. His kids. Amelia at seven years old was so clearly a little version of him, that even the dumbest of passers-by would guess they were flesh and blood. Lucy, on the other hand, seemed to take every opportunity (at least lately) to remind Matt that they were nothing of the sort. Maybe he'd understand it if her 'real' dad was some top bloke with a heart of gold or bottomless credit card. But Eddie Pullen was a violent piece of dirt who'd been clicking his fingernails for the last ten years in Durham prison. For beating Wren very nearly to death. You'd think the laws of comparison would make Matt come out better. You'd think!

He smiled at them both. 'Shoes on.' Then he nipped upstairs to quickly get changed into jeans and a T-shirt. They all dragged the cases down the front path.

It was just as he popped the boot that he noticed the group of local teenage boys across the road. They were, sadly, a common feature of this street. As much a part of the concrete as the potholes and the Sunday morning piss puddles. They'd climbed up on their usual metal-framed bench over the road and were glaring over. It was lunchtime. and one of them already had a bottle of cooking sherry in his hand. A quarter full. Stay classy, Cropsy Road.

Matt started bundling cases into the boot, making sure there might be a telescope-shaped gap somewhere, while Wren bent over to put a pile of her building specs and plans into the front seat.

'Hey, sexy!' One of the teenagers shouted at her, then followed it with something as grammatically efficient as it was offensive. 'Tits out!'

'Nice one, Reece,' one of them said. 'Nice one.'

Matt moved too quickly and smacked the back of his head on the boot lid.

The rest of the boys roared with laughter.

'You want to say that again, you little git?' Matt called over, refusing to rub his head. Then he saw Wren was already marching over.

'What did you just say?' She had her hands on her hips, chin pushed forward.

'I said,' Reece stood up on the bench and grabbed his crotch, 'get your dirty titties out.'

Cackles and whoops. Fingers slapping thumbs. Matt hurried over.

'And tell me, Reece, why would you want me to do that?' Wren shouted. 'You idiot babies need your milk?'

They stopped laughing.

Then Wren hollered, 'Grow some pubes!'

'Oh, my God, Mum,' Lucy called out from the back seat. 'Get in before you get us stabbed.'

Matt stomped toward the boys and was about to pass Wren when she grabbed his elbow. 'Don't.'

It didn't matter anyway. They'd seen the look on his face and were already nervously slipping away.

'Go on. Get lost.'

He watched them as they were swallowed by the shadows in the alley across the street. But just before Reece vanished he cupped his hands around his mouth, glaring at Matt. 'Control your beeeeeaaaatcch!' Then he vanished in a scamper of giggles and trainers.

'Leave it,' she said, as Matt stepped toward the alley. 'Let's just get going.'

He glanced at the shadows, shrugged, then they both got back in the car. 'Little buggers.'

Wren's voice was quiet as she pulled the seat belt across her. 'Sorry. But boys can't just speak to women like that.'

In the rear-view mirror Matt could see a tiny, impressed smile on Lucy's face.

'What's a *beeaaatch*?' Amelia said.

Wren pulled her seat belt over, but she did it slowly, a little sheepishly. He spotted a tiny tremble in her hand.

'You okay?' he said quietly.

She blinked. 'Just get me out of this dump.'

'Aye aye.' He flicked the radio on to check the weather but switched it straight back off again when he heard the newsreader mention an 'incident' on Oxford Street. There'd be time to explain about that later.

'So what is it?' Amelia tugged on his car seat. 'What's a *beeeeatch*?'

Lucy leant over and started whispering the answer into Amelia's ear. Her little eyes grew wide.

As they pulled away he caught Wren's eye and sniggered, 'Grow some pubes?'

She shook her head and snorted a laugh. 'I promise I won't say that in Hobbs Hill.'

CHAPTER FIVE

He listened to the drips.

As each of them hit the water the sound echoed off the bathroom tiles.

Bwup.

Bwup.

Bwup.

He closed his eyes, relaxed by the sound, like the ticking of an underwater clock. He was holding himself as still as he possibly could so that there were absolutely no ripples in the bath. Not easy to do, actually. But he'd always been very patient with things. Under the surface he slowly watched his naked body settle as still as he could get it, quaking only now and again.

Funny how water made his legs look so huge. He used to notice that with straws in glass tumblers. The refracted light made them look suddenly bent and bigger underneath. The same thing was happening with his body now. Freaky, but still interesting, physics-wise.

He took in a huge breath, lungs fat and full, then he clamped his lips together and slid under the water. His shoulders squeaked against the back of the bath. He went fully under, ears suddenly closing up with water. The hum of the extractor fan vanished in a dull *zzzzip*.

Sixty seconds. That's how long he usually lasted.

Ten Mississippi, eleven Mississippi, twelve Mississippi.

The water pressed against his eardrums and made him feel a little sick. But it also made a roaring sound like the echo of the falls. So he stayed under.

Thirty-two Mississippi, Thirty-three Mississippi.

Still under he opened his eyes and looked up. They stung a little but he kept them really wide. Crazy wide. Everything was a blur. A beautiful, quiet haze. Being under was the most peaceful place in the world. Just for fun he ran his fingertips along the underside of the water, like it was ice or glass. But the movement made it quake too much for it to work. Worth a try, though.

Forty-nine Mississippi.

It felt like a good moment to start praying. With lips tightly closed he let his thoughts tumble out. Asking God for strength and protection. For angels to shield him from harm so he could carry on his ministry here in Hobbs Hill. Even as he prayed, he could feel his back and legs starting to stiffen and turn numb. Divine fingers were drawing around him. He was being stroked by God.

Sixty-one Mississippi, Sixty-two Mississippi.

Praise the Lord, he thought. *I'm getting better. I grow stronger. Every time I help them I—*

A frantic, gulping bubble shot out through his lips before he even knew it was coming. His lungs contracted into wrinkled bags. Dirty bathwater raced down his throat, and he shot his body up, coughing and wheezing like a calf just born. A huge white globule of saliva sprang from his lips into the bath so he quickly leant across to the toilet. He grabbed the towel he'd left there and rubbed his face with it. Eyes stinging, chest aching, he let out some cold air across his lips, and pulled new life back to fill his lungs.

The water settled again – it took a whole two minutes – then he looked down at his body. Pubic hair wafted softly back and forth like the barbs of a toxic jellyfish, and he decided it might be helpful to shave it all off.

He'd never done that before but he just didn't like the look of how those black strands swayed in the water. Things might get tangled in there, things he didn't want. Who knows, maybe next time one of his short and curlies would drop off and land on the floor and some clever Quincy M.E. forensic-type would trace it back to him. And then he'd be screwed.

Not that he'd got naked with Nicola Knox.

Should he have? Should he be naked next time? Would that be better? More purifying?

He'd pray about it.

For now, something just told him that it would be wise to be more streamlined so he grabbed his razor.

He reached for the plug and pulled it out. The water guzzled and groaned, sounding like the belly of Jonah's whale and he watched the water level sink lower. Gradually the tops of his thighs and his genitals were exposed. His skin sparkled under the light. He guided the plug back over the sucking hole and the force of it dragged it out of his hands like a magnet. The black rubber was quickly sucked in and the gurgling sound bubbled into silence.

He lay there in a few centimetres of water, using his foot to knock the shaving foam from the end of the bath into the space between his feet. It bobbed towards him. He grabbed it and clicked off the lid with one thumb. He felt quite suave, doing that. The sort of thing a cool guy would do with a bottle of beer at a party. Not that he drunk beer. He tipped it on its side, squeezed the plastic button and a spatter of whiteness shot across his legs, like whipped cream. A smooth white teardrop formed on his hand with a low hiss.

He rubbed it on his scrotum, up around his penis where there were a few hairs. Then after taking a breath he grabbed the razor and started to guide it across the skin. There was a serious amount of gunk on the blade, after each stroke. Big old chunks of Hitler moustaches, one after the other. He had to swill it in the bathwater each time. He managed to shave most of it clean without any cuts or nicks. But the shrivelled flesh of his scrotum wasn't so easy to navigate. He lifted his penis back, like a barwoman pulling a pint of Guinness. (The thought of that made him laugh – he could be pretty funny sometimes.) Then he drew the blade across the skin underneath and felt the razor catch.

He sucked in a sharp breath as a drop of blood wisped its way up through the water to the surface, where white foam and black hair bobbed around. Debris from a sinking ship.

Seeing the blood made him feel suddenly afraid because it made him think of her, and how she'd been at the end. He stared at the water between his legs and it was inevitable really. She came back, like she was often doing today. Nicola Knox, with a cracked porcelain forehead slowly reaching up out of the bathwater with her skinny blue hands and white eyes, grabbing his legs to glide herself up. She was still chomping at the air, slowly and in complete silence. Her pottery skin snapping and collapsing as she moved up his body for a kiss.

He snapped his eyes shut. 'She's in heaven.'

She didn't listen. Just kept moving up, sliding her cold sharp skin across his belly. He could feel her razor ribs scratching into his thighs. She was whispering something.

'She's in heaven.'

When he opened his eyes she was gone. Slithered down the plughole for another time. Angry, he flung the shaving foam and razor across the room. They skidded across the floor and rattled against the wooden door. He let the rest of the water out, dried himself. Then he put a little fabric plaster on the cut, dreading when he would eventually have to pull it off. He ran his fingertips across the shaved prickly skin between his legs.

His now bald, freaky crotch looked bizarre in the bathroom mirror. It was like he was looking at someone else's genitals. He ran his hands across the skin again and paused when he felt a pulsing throb down there.

'*Caaaaareful.*' A low voice through the door.

He jumped and snapped his hand back, his foot squeaking a little on the wet tiles. He looked at the door, which he was sure he'd locked. It was open, with a tiny crack in it. Big enough for an eye to be looking through. Then he heard Stephen's heavy boots creak along the landing in his usual slow clumps as he headed downstairs.

He quickly pulled his trousers on before getting himself into any mischief. He looked back at the bathtub where the hair-pocked water bobbed gently and where Nicola Knox was sitting up, laughing at him.

CHAPTER SIX

Hobbs Hill. Home of Cooper's Force: Britain's Loudest
Natural Waterfall!

The ornate arched sign across the top of the road might as well have
been the doorway to another dimension because as soon as the car
passed under it the world suddenly popped with colour. Thatched
cottages appeared by the sides of the road looking pure fairy tale
apart from the expensive-looking front doors in mahogany and oak.
That, and the Porsches and Maseratis in the drives. Rustic wooden
benches made from old wagon wheels sat in rainbow gardens while
white butterflies danced between roses.

They passed a trendy-looking gastro pub called The Petals with
a T.S. Elliot quote written on the sign. Matt could pretty much
guarantee there'd be no kids' ballpool or unlimited coke refills in
that place. He'd bet his life there'd be guinea fowl on the menu. Or
similar stuff he'd never tasted.

Wren leant forward, eagerly taking it all in. Then she laughed
nervously and pulled in a breath. One that she didn't seem to want
to let back out again. Maybe the plan was to keep it locked in her
lungs until her boss Mr Mason said she could keep her job.

Mason – of the architects firm Chase, Penn and Mason – was
the only partner kind enough not to have a life-altering stroke
this year. The other two hadn't been so thoughtful. Chase had his
playing tennis with his son. They say he dropped his racket and

started staring at the net, which was ironically something he did for a joke anyway, when he got bored of losing. So his son just laughed and whacked some tennis ball at him from over the net. Then he collapsed and someone screamed.

Penn, on the other hand, had his stroke right in the middle of a pep talk, three weeks after Chase lost control of his bowels. He was reading out a letter Chase wrote (or rather his wife wrote down, interpreting his grunts). He said how much he loved them all. Wren said people were crying. They figured Penn must be upset too because he stopped midway and hurried to the toilet. He said he felt dizzy and his wife took him home in their Land Rover. Slept all day and never woke up.

Two strokes in one month. The sort of stat that gets bored secretaries talking of a curse. And last-man-standing Mason was sucking on health shakes and vitamins like a maniac.

This was three months back. And since the management side of CPM went tits up, new contracts seemed to be hurtling nose down. Someone told Wren that people were spooked to work with a firm in the grip of a death curse. She knew better. Mason had always been the firm's weakest link anyway. *It's why his name's at the end*, she'd been told. So all in all, Chase, Penn and Mason were sinking. Fast.

She'd been an architect there for three years now, the shortest of all of the team (she tried not to think about that little factoid). And Mason had made it very clear. Three of the five-strong team were 'regretfully, unavoidably and tragically' going to be made redundant at the end of this month.

Everyone was surprised Wren was even put forward as the company rep for this Hobbs Hill pitch. There were others more senior. But for whatever reason she was being sent up for it and this was (she just knew it) her last chance. Land this big church renovation job in Oxfordshire and Mason would keep her on with a bonus, apparently. And that, along with Matt's book, meant that operation 'Get the hell out of Cropsy' would be back on the cards for this year. And not only that, she'd be based *here* for a month.

But if this job slipped through her fingers, then it was pretty much sharia law: come 31st July she'd get a stunning cardboard box, a string of awkward handshakes and a redundancy package that wouldn't be worth pissing on. Still . . . she could always drown her sorrows at the nightclub at the end of her road. And at least they had ten days staying up here for free, courtesy of the client. Cheap holidays weren't to be sniffed at, these days.

'How are you doing?' Matt said, softly.

She set her jaw. 'I'm going to get this contract. Just you watch.'

He wanted to say 'of course you are', but he didn't. Unlike his vicar days, he wasn't so quick to make promises he couldn't guarantee would keep.

Hobbs Hill lay at the bottom of a valley so the road suddenly swooped down in a heart-quivering dip, pulling them on a tilt through a long green corridor of overhanging trees. Wren's face flashed with sunlight, her thick red hair like fire. She had her hands together as if she was praying. She wasn't. But it probably was some sort of cosmic experience reminding her that maybe there really was 'something else'. Something beyond. Something other than 'get your titties out' and kebabs on the path. Maybe there was a higher power and its name was Leafy Village.

She smiled to herself and pulled out her camera, pushing the zoom lens out of the window like a sniper's rifle. *Snap, snap,* giggle, *snap*.

When they eventually left the tree corridor they were in the impossibly pretty village centre. Tudor houses leant into one another like friendly old drunks and cobbled streets ran up the sides of the valley, turning into magical, secret alleys. They passed a busy train station and then rows of tiny shops appeared. He struggled to find a brand name he recognised because they had landed on Planet Bespoke. The further they drove, the closer the pavements – and people – seemed to get to the car.

It was mid afternoon and figures milled about, popping in and out of shops, eating al fresco at wooden chairs and tables. Laughing into their smartphones. It reminded him of the nicer parts of Notting Hill on a summer's afternoon, only surrounded by green not grey. He could smell baked bread from somewhere. Maybe a touch of cinnamon.

But then he noticed something else.

'This is gorgeous,' Wren said.

He drew his eyebrows together. 'Weird.'

'What is?'

'The crosses.'

She frowned at him.

'In the shop windows. Look.' He nodded over to a butcher's shop. A ten-inch wooden cross hung in the window between a row of dead dangling rabbits. They were strung up by their legs, beady open eyes staring at the spread of meat below. 'That's the fourth cross I've seen.'

'Well, isn't that fascinating?' said one-time vegetarian Wren, as if dead animals and crucifixes were suddenly 'quaint'. Evidently Hobbs Hill could do no wrong.

'How can you have a Christian butcher?' Amelia said. 'I thought Jesus was a herbivore.'

'He ate a lot of fish,' Matt said. '*Big* fan of fish.'

'Urgh,' Amelia stuck out her tongue. 'Disgusting Jesus!'

That made him laugh.

'There's another one.' Lucy jabbed her finger at the chemist's. A cross, similar in size, hung on the door.

'Shoe shop's got one!' Amelia was upright now. 'And the bookshop. That's two, which means I win!'

Wren set her camera down for a moment. 'Maybe it's got something to do with Easter?'

'What?' He laughed. 'In July? It'll be vampires. You get a lot of them in Oxfordshire cos the blood here's good. It's like their version of Waitrose.'

'How about this for a theory.' Lucy's tone was droll, with a dash of patronising. 'Maybe they just go to church and hang their crosses because they aren't all screwed up about faith like *you* are.' She started to laugh. 'Aren't you worried you'll burn up in a place like this, Reverend? Being a heretic?'

'I'll get sun cream.'

The crosses weren't everywhere. Every three or four shops, maybe. But there were certainly enough of them to notice. Enough to feel like the place was . . . odd.

With an elbow out of the open window he started tapping out a rhythm on the steering wheel while he glanced around the street, at the crosses and the people milling about beneath them. People must just be big into God here. A few faces looked over at him and seemed to linger their gaze.

He stopped tapping.

For a second, just a split moment in time, it felt like everyone out here in Churchville was about to stare at him. Eyes turning with a squeak. They'd stop talking into their phones, place their knives and forks neatly on their plate. Maybe the butcher would pause with a meat cleaver hovering above a rabbit's fluffy neck so they could all point at Matt Hunter, the ex-reverend, and whisper to each other.

Unbeliever! Backslider!

He sniffed and pulled his elbow back into the car.

The only other odd thing that he spotted was a group of animal protesters in the square. They were holding up banners saying *Stop the Helston Horror!* One of them had a picture of five extremely depressed-looking pigs on it. Suicidal, in fact.

One of the protesters shouted, 'Hobbs Hill is a place of beauty. Don't let it be ugly under the surface! Stop the Helston Horror!'

'Uh-oh,' he said. 'There be trouble in paradise.'

The protesters might as well have been invisible because the locals walked right past them, probably *through* them if they could. No matter, the traffic started moving, and soon they were heading out of the village centre, with the protesters fading in the rear-view mirror.

Wren grabbed the handwritten map she'd printed from her email and guided him up the other side of the hill. They turned right into a new corridor of trees. Then swung into another, skinnier, leafy road lined with huge oaks that blocked out the sun.

'Right,' she said. 'We should be staying along here.'

'How come we can stay for so long?' Lucy said. 'It's just a job interview.'

'Guess they're just generous. They want me to get a feel for the place.'

The road was very long with no tarmac, just packed in dirt. Weeds and nettles grew up from the cracks and brushed the underside of the car. It took a good few minutes to reach the end, the road getting bumpier as they went, their heads jerking from side to side in unison as he navigated the dips. Then a cottage appeared behind a weeping willow.

The cottage.

It was glowing under the sun, sitting for them in a little clearing. The closer they got the nearer Wren's hand got to her mouth, and he almost crashed into a tree.

'Bloody hell,' he said.

'We get to stay there?' Lucy gawped at the thatched roof, the criss-cross windows, the stunning splash of a garden. 'It's Little Red Riding Hood's house.'

Amelia raised both hands and hooked them into claws. 'All the better to eat your brains with, my dear.' She howled and scratched the air.

Lucy clucked her tongue. 'Psycho.'

A Land Rover was parked in the drive. Matt pulled in to park and noticed the stable door of the cottage swing wide open. A guy, who looked like he was in his late teens, stepped out, followed by an older man with a neat white moustache.

'Okay, the older one's Seth Cardle,' Wren said. 'He's my contact.'

Matt turned in his seat and caught everyone's gaze with military precision, 'And we're a wonderful, well-adjusted family, alright?'

'And the other one?' Lucy asked.

'That's Ben, the pastor's son, apparently. Seth said he'd come to welcome us because the main guy can't make it.'

Seth was in his early sixties and wore green wellies and a brown padded body-warmer over a checked short-sleeved shirt. He had most of his hair or at least most of *someone's* hair. He was smiling wide and clapping his hands together with delight. Ben hovered behind him, pushing his trainer in the dirt and making a mark.

Wren apologised for being late as she climbed out of the car, but Seth was standing on the driver's side. 'And *you* must be Matthew,' he said, smiling.

'I am. Magnificent place you have here.' Matt stood and put out his hand. 'Pleasure to meet—'

Seth swatted his hand away with an amused chuckle. 'We'll have none of that round here!' Then he threw both his arms around Matt, squeezing him in a bear hug and sickly sweet-smelling aftershave, saying, 'Welcome, friends. Welcome to the promised land.'

CHAPTER SEVEN

It was without a doubt the most idyllic place Matt had ever seen. Even better than the university dean's uber-house, which was lorded over him every summer at the staff barbecue. But this place, while much smaller, had the edge. He'd call it good feng shui if he actually believed in that stuff.

The roof was topped with the heaviest-looking thatch, and if a fire was ever lit in the hearth he could bet the chimney up there would wisp out the perfect child's-drawing curl into the heavens. Inside, it was classic farmhouse chic but with lots of contemporary touches. The ceilings were low with huge black beams running like veins through the white walls. Every room had halogen spotlights sunk into the ceiling, firing down on solid oak floors. Victorian-style teddy bears sat on the many armchairs, scattered through the place. The only drawback? A big old cross hanging on the door. To keep the evil wood sprites out, presumably. Or the Jehovah's Witnesses.

Here and there Matt saw framed pictures of the family that normally lived here. The pastor's son Ben explained that they were called the Shores – members of the church who were in Hong Kong on business for the summer, hence it being available. There were pictures of the Shores everywhere. Mum, dad, son, daughter. The full set. Impossibly nice-looking, posing in all manner of exotic locales, white teeth bared. The daughter's smiling head was almost constantly resting happily against the dad's shoulder. They were the sort of perfect family who went on rollercoasters, and at the end everyone wanted to buy *their* photo.

Wren audibly yelped when she saw their bedroom. The four-poster bed frame was made from actual tree trunks, a foot thick. And beyond it, an en suite wet room sparkled like a blinged-up spaceship. A white porcelain jug and washbasin sat by the side of the bed, just in case they fancied wiping their arse in the night, Victorian-style.

Seth suggested Ben show Amelia and Lucy the garden. Ben nodded, albeit with an awkward scrawl of fingers through his floppy hipster hair.

'It's this way,' Ben said. 'There's a pretty cool tree house. If you like that sort of thing . . . so er . . . do you?'

'I do,' Lucy said and she and Ben wandered out together, Amelia following quickly behind.

Now, with the kids gone, Seth walked them into the study (in his socks. His green Hunter wellies sat in the sun on the porch outside). The room was lined with old leather books and a wide window overlooked the garden. 'Wren, you can set up your office wherever you like. Even up at the church, if you prefer. But the last company who tried out for this had their man use this room. Seemed to work for him.'

For the first time since walking in here, Wren's smile faltered as she was reminded that, after all, she was only entering a competition. A talent contest. An elongated job interview.

Matt knew Wren would be itching to ask questions. Ones that might initially make her appear neurotic or nosy, so he asked one instead. 'Can you tell us about the other companies that pitched for the job, Seth?'

'Well, we've just had one so far. A single man from Oxford who stayed here last week. Came up with some good plans, we thought. But I think the cottage was rather wasted on him. I'm glad you decided to bring your family.' Seth looked at Matt. 'This is a village for families, don't you think?'

'Rich families,' Matt said, smiling.

Seth chuckled, 'And rich in all the right things.'

Matt ran his fingers across the spines of the books on the shelves.

Wren looked up at Seth. 'Is it cheeky to ask how many more firms you have lined up?'

'Not at all.' Seth leant against the window sill, white moustache curling up over a kind smile. Matt was suddenly reminded of the grandfather from those Werther's Original adverts, who gave the little boy a toffee on his knee. Back in the day when that wasn't the international code for imminent sex abuse. The light from the window picked out his wrinkles more than ever. 'We've only got one other firm lined up after you. Another London fella. Coming up on his own the day after you leave. Once he gets his pitch in we'll have a good old pray and make a choice. So three firms in all. It's rather exciting, really.'

Wren smiled. 'I'm sure you'll make the right choice for your needs.'

'And you've studied the church plans, I take it?'

'Seth. I've lived in every room of your church for the past month and I haven't even seen the place yet.'

'Oooh,' Seth said. 'I *like* that.' His moustache swooped up at the edges, almost a full V. Then he closed his eyes. Kept them closed, actually, for about ten whole seconds. When he finally opened them he just said, 'Splendid.'

They had tea and Battenburg cake on the patio, while Ben and the girls played Frisbee on the lawn. Birds chirped in the trees and swooped over their heads while Seth talked a little about his farming business and about the famous Hobbs Hill waterfall, 'Which you can hear from just about everywhere! You've just *got* to see it.'

Matt pressed his ear to the sky and there it was. A very low, distant hiss.

But Seth's favourite subject was Kingdom Come Church, and the planned renovation.

'Our new pastor's done wonders since he came.' Seth dabbed his napkin at the sugar on his mouth. 'He only joined us four years ago, when we had forty members in the congregation. All of them pensioners. Church had about ten years of life left in it. But wait till you see us now! Congregation's around three hundred, and growing. Young families, students. Lots of children. Which means lots of future.'

'Forty to three hundred?' Matt said. 'That's quite an increase.'

'He's quite a pastor.' Seth reached into his canvas bag and pulled out some leaflets. 'You can meet him tonight at the Purging. He asked if you might come along.'

'We'd love to,' Wren said.

Seth laughed. 'Do you even know what a Purging is?'

'Nope.' Wren glanced at Matt, more for the appearance of consultation than for anything else. 'But we're coming.'

'Ha! I like your enthusiasm, my dear. I like it a lot. The Purging is a party. We have some folks getting baptised next Sunday and Pastor Chris likes to throw them a celebration leading up to it. Give them a good send-off.'

Matt laughed. 'They're getting baptised, not leaving the country.'

'Oh come now, Matthew. Spiritually speaking they're leaving the planet, aren't they? From the Kingdom of Darkness into the Kingdom of Light. The Purging's just a fun night when they get to say farewell to their old selves.'

'Ah,' Matt said, fighting the roll in his eyes. 'Got it.'

'Don't worry if you've never heard of it. It's a Kingdom Come exclusive. Just something we came up with a few years back. Symbolic, you understand. Oh and there'll be Mexican food. It's at 7:30 p.m., at the church.'

'We'll look forward to it,' Wren said.

'Seth. I have to ask,' Matt set his cup on the table, 'why did you pick Wren's firm? Out of all the architects around?'

Seth glanced over at Wren, almost protectively, as if Matt's question was basically: why the hell would anyone want to hire *my* wife? But Wren wasn't offended at all. She'd asked that exact thing out loud back in London, lying in bed, staring at the ceiling, discussing all of this. Why'd they pick us? Especially when word was already out they were crumbling.

Seth paused, pushed his lips in and out. 'It was Chris, our pastor. He's very in tune with God. Prophetic, I'd say. He prayed and fasted for days. Days! And then came up with a shortlist of just three architects. And there was your name. Wren Hunter.'

'You mean, Chase, Penn and Mason,' Wren said. 'He called the firm.'

'No. You misunderstand. He wanted you, Wren. Specifically you.'

She stopped chewing her Battenburg, 'Really?'

'Mr Mason never mentioned that to you?'

She shook her head. 'Maybe Pastor Chris saw my work somewhere. I did help design an office block in Oxford a while back. What's his second name?'

Seth pushed his cup and plate away. 'Kelly. Chris Kelly.'

Matt's eyes flicked up. 'Pardon me?'

'Chris Kelly . . .' Seth opened up a leaflet on the table and prodded a finger at the photograph on it. 'The man himself . . .'

Matt stared at the picture and didn't speak for a moment.

'You look surprised,' Seth said. 'You've heard of him, then?'

'Er . . . yes. I have,' said Matt.

Wren glanced at him, and started slowly chewing again.

'Well, I'm not surprised you've heard of him. He's quite a pastor. And do you know what? When he prayed, Wren, your name just appeared. Ta-da!'

Matt looked down at the photograph, turning the information over in his head. Marzipan lodged in his throat.

'Well.' Wren pulled her gaze from Matt and put a flattered hand on her chest. 'You can't get a better reference than the Almighty can you?'

Seth laughed loudly. It was an odd sound. Everything about him seemed gentle and quiet except that laugh of his, which was sharp and hacking. Wide-mouthed. He went to stand. 'Well how about young Ben and I leave you good people to settle in. Get your feet under the table, so to speak. And eat what you like, the fridge is stocked. Hope you like black pudding!'

Wren stood up too. 'Seth, it's been a pleasure. Really.'

Seth called out a goodbye to the kids and they waved at him, Lucy missing a Frisbee in the process. Ben laughed and headed over too. Matt tried hard not to look too obvious when he was looking over Ben's face, scanning it for familiar lines and features from his dad, Chris Kelly. He found some. The eyes, the high cheekbones. Wow, this was odd.

Then Matt and Wren walked them both to the door. Seth held onto Matt's shoulder as he pulled on his wellies.

'Off to the farm?' Matt said.

'Yes. Sad work today. Got a cow with breast cancer,' he shook his head. 'I mean can you imagine!'

'Oh, how awful.' Wren went to shake Seth's hand but he leant in and planted a soft but hairy-lipped kiss on her cheek.

When he pulled back he took her hand in his but looked over at Matt. Gazing at him, he said, 'And what do you do for a living, Matt? Or are you a kept man?'

'I wish. I'm a university professor.'

Seth gave an impressed whistle. 'And what do you . . . profess?'

'The sociology of religion.'

Seth's eyebrows sprang up.

'It's a mix really. Theology, sociology, philosophy. Dash of psychology. I study why people believe what they do, basically.'

'Sociology of religion . . .' Seth rolled the words around his

59

tongue, like an exotic meal that had bad fish in it. 'What do you make of that, Ben?'

Ben shrugged. 'Sounds clever.'

'Matt's actually on a three-month sabbatical at the moment,' Wren added. 'He's working on a book. Aren't you, Matt? He's going to write while he's here.'

Shit, Wren. Don't tell them the title, Matt thought frantically. *In Our Image: The Gods We Tend to Invent* would probably go down like scurvy here.

'I see,' Seth waited for a moment then looked over at Ben. 'Little favour, ma' boy? Would you mind nipping to my car and getting the engine running? You know how, don't you?'

Ben laughed. 'Seth. I'm twenty-two. I know how to start a car.'

'Sorry. 'Course you do.' He held up an apologetic hand and tossed him the keys with the other. 'The air conditioner takes a while to warm up and it is a rather hot one today. So I'd like to get it going.'

Either Ben was oblivious or just being polite. But he made himself scarce as instructed without complaint. Once he was gone Seth turned back to Matt. 'Just a question, then. An obvious one I suppose. Do you believe in God?' He looked over at Wren. 'Do either of you?'

Matt spotted Wren's discomfort instantly. The shift in her shoulders. The fixed little smile. The glance down at the strange farmer's calloused hand still holding hers. And he could almost hear the gears in her brain clicking. What if this was the only question that truly mattered? The clincher for this contract.

Do you believe in God?

Wren wasn't the lying type. Never really had been. But her pause surprised him and he wondered if the desperation to keep her job might have her flinging her knees to the floor, one hand waving in the air, the other with crossed fingers behind her back: *Hallelujah, Seth Brother, I do. I do, I loves the Lord!*

Matt spoke first. 'Well, *I* don't believe in God.' Some of the birds must have been offended at this because a bunch of them stopped singing completely. 'Sorry, I just don't.'

He wanted to add the words not any more, which would have been more accurate, but he clipped himself. He knew these Christian types. He'd been one of them long enough to know that any info of a past faith would be like a sliver of meat. Juicy enough to release the evangelistic dogs.

'But your job. You teach about religion and the Bible. So how can you not—'

'There are other religions too. And cults and sects. I teach them as well.'

Seth's face fell even further at that. 'You mean you teach people about God but you don't even believe in him? That . . . baffles me.'

'Hey, I've got a colleague who teaches contemporary folklore. I found her in her office last Tuesday in front of a pile of open books, with a roll of measuring tape hanging from her teeth. She was comparing news reports, trying to work out the penis length of the Tokoloshe.'

'The what?'

'The Tokoloshe. Some South Africans are genuinely terrified of a well-endowed, invisible, midget ghost who supposedly rapes villagers. Oh, and some reports say he's made of porridge.'

Seth twisted his mouth and pulled back a little.

'She's writing a paper on it. But it doesn't mean she believes the Tokoloshe actually exists.'

'So why bother . . .'

'Because people are real. And society's real. So if enough people believe Jedi is a real religion, or that the US government are shape-shifting lizards who drink children's blood, then it matters. It just doesn't make the belief itself real, with respect.'

Seth finally slipped his hand out of Wren's.

She seemed to stand up straighter. 'I'm sorry, Seth, but I'm with

Matt on this. I'm not a big believer in God either. I mean I'm *open* to it, I suppose . . .'

A flash in Seth's eyes. A quiver of the nostrils. The sniff of spiritual scalp.

'. . . and I totally admire what you choose to believe but I'm just not wired that way.' She flicked a curl of her red hair out of her eyes. Set her shoulders. 'If you think that might affect my chance of the contract then I'd rather you know that up front. Because I won't pretend to be something I'm not just for a job. Bottom line is we're not the God type. Sorry.'

Seth bit the inside of his mouth and waited for what seemed like an awkward minute.

'Seth. Are you honestly saying that my wife's beliefs are going to affect—'

'Shhhh.' Seth lifted his hand. 'Your spiritual lives . . . such as they are . . . have no bearing on your job prospects. Even if we wanted to, we couldn't hold that against you. Not these days. But thank you, Wren, for your honesty. I'd say that shows character. And potential.'

'Well, honesty's important,' she said. 'Even if you're not religious.'

'Oh, it's everything.' He leant in close. 'Between us, last week's architect said he was a born-again Christian but we found out later he was actually a humanist. Can you believe that . . . a *humanist*?'

So what did you do Seth? Burn the guy at the stake? Cut out his tongue?

'It was the lying that was the issue, you understand. The lying.'

Wren gave a solemn nod and Matt could tell she was trying to resist punching the air at her first little victory. Truthful, upright architect, Wren Hunter. Irreligious but honest. Point number one! Seth reached up to his head and tipped an imaginary hat at them. 'See you at church for the Purging, then. Seven-thirty.' His eyes were a little sad as he wandered off towards his Land Rover, looking more sluggish than before.

Seth and Ben gave a little wave before they drove off and Matt and Wren waved from the doorway of the idyllic cottage as though it had always been theirs. *They* were the Shore family now, only way more heathen and less dentally impressive.

'Well, get me . . .' Wren said, finally. 'I've been headhunted. Actually headhunted.'

Matt smiled, but only one side of his mouth went up.

'So come on, then. Who's this Chris Kelly? He's not a Tokoloshe is he?'

'Not quite.'

She went to speak but then her mobile started to ring. 'Bugger. It's my boss. Probably checking I'm in the right county.' But before she answered she nodded to him to speak. 'Chris Kelly? Quick answer?'

'He's not a Tokoloshe,' he said. 'He just thinks I'm going to hell.'

She looked at him, both confused and sympathetic. 'Oh.'

'You better answer that,' Matt said, nodding at the throbbing phone.

CHAPTER EIGHT

Matt's mum. She was called Elizabeth Jane Hunter. For as long as he could remember she'd been 'religious'. Not in a scary turn or burn way but in a, *wow-isn't-Jesus-great* way. She literally said those words throughout his childhood.

 – How crunchy are these Shreddies? Isn't Jesus great?

 – Look at the thunder, Matt, out on the sea. Isn't Jesus powerful?

 – So your dad was a womanising monster who left us when you were ten, but wow, Matty-boy, isn't Jesus faithful?

They lived in a tiny village called Dunwich on the Suffolk coast, just him, his mum and his big sister, Linda. Mum wanted way more kids than two, but she had what she described as an 'uncooperative womb'. Dunwich was an odd little place to grow up. It used to be a major, bustling seaport but since the fourteenth century the hungry sea had swallowed it up. Most of the old town was drowned and never surfaced again. He sometimes thought of it as the pound-shop version of Atlantis.

All that *was* left above ground was a pub, a beach, a few houses and a wildly expensive fish-and-chip cafe that also sold buckets and spades. It was hardly a thrilling place to grow up. No wonder he became a sci-fi geek, and no wonder mum turned to God.

And boy did she turn. She believed the Bible. All of it. Childlike faith, she said, that's what people need. She threw herself into scripture like it was a swimming pool full of her very best friends.

Such constant spiritual sugar started to make him feel a little sick eventually, but he loved the woman so much that he never felt like questioning her. Maybe he figured she'd been mocked enough for her faith already by that barely remembered letch of a dad who smelt, he recalled, of Fruit Polo Mints and pilchards. Quite the aroma-combo.

Barnabas (what a name!) Hunter walked out on them one morning when Matt was ten and Linda was twelve. The final argument happened in the kitchen in hushed, secretive tones while Matt watched *Ren and Stimpy* on the lounge TV, wondering why it was making him cry. Linda kept telling him to get a grip and grow up – which was a bit rich, since her eyes were brimming too. They took themselves to bed that night and the next morning Mum announced they were a single-parent family and let them both eat cake for breakfast. She tried to make it sound like an adventure the three of them were embarking on. Kept using the word 'team' a lot. But her cheeks were hollow and she kept stopping at the fridge to pause and breathe, before spinning back round all smiles: *Let's all sleep in the lounge tonight!*

Sometimes he liked to think that his dad had just wandered out into the Dunwich sea and joined all the other soulless ghosts. That even now he was wandering in and out of empty, mossy houses, bored and cold and submerged for ever and ever, Amen.

Linda was into church, mainly because she fancied one of the older boys who played drums and wanted to be a missionary. By the time he was thirteen, though, his mother had spotted Matt's 'lack of enthusiasm' (as she so diplomatically put it) for God. She started taking him to a Christian youth group over in Bury St Edmunds.

To his genuine surprise – shock, actually – the place turned out to contain the most fun group of people he'd ever met. There were even a few fellow geeks who suggested they have a marathon of every Planet of the Apes movie ever made. An odd catalyst for life change perhaps, but an undeniable moment. And when he was fourteen that youth group had either worn him down or he'd become convinced that God might actually exist. In all honesty he couldn't decide which, so he assumed it was both.

He went to a youth concert they'd organised at the church with smoke machines and laser lights. Some bizarre Christian rap band called *Boo-Ya* were onstage, changing the lyrics of N.W.A. and Ice-T songs to tell Bible stories instead. It was hideous but sort of fun if you didn't know any better. Which most of them didn't.

At the end the lead rapper invited people to stand by the stage and pray some words that apparently 'made you a Christian'. Matt could hardly even remember getting out of his seat, only that he was suddenly down at the front, digging his nails into the chipped wooden lip of the stage and breathing faster.

Later that night, when they shut the doors and kicked everyone out, he remembered sitting on Dunwich beach, watching the moon over the water. It was hanging behind black clouds, which glowed at the edges, sweeping by faster than he'd ever seen in his life. He pictured the universe ticking like a clock and him ticking in time with it. It felt pretty epic, actually.

A few weeks later the youth group went on a church holiday to Sizewell Hall, a big old manor house by the sea. It sat in the shadow of the nuclear reactor, Sizewell B, which had a huge white golf ball-shaped building in it like something out of *Logan's Run*. That was the weekend that the youth minister baptised Matt in the sea, along with twelve of his friends. Matt's mum stood on the pebble beach shivering in the cold, holding a towel for him, weeping with undiluted joy.

And he'd wept too. There was something so emotionally intense about getting dunked in that water and coming up to rounds of applause.

That's how he liked to remember her.

Clapping her hands together, tears of delight running down her cheeks. Slipping and laughing across the pebbles toward him and swooping the towel around him like a big old eagle's wing. Kissing his forehead and drying his hair.

That was his preferred image. And whenever his mind forced him to remember, as it often tried to do, of the last time he saw her, hair full of blood and sticking to her dining room table, he'd flip a switch in his head and she'd be on that beach again, the fresh wind of the North Sea blowing her hair dry and free.

As he, Lucy and Amelia started to wander through the veiny woods around the cottage, he could vaguely see his mum out there in the forest, tucked between the trees. Still calling to him as they wandered by.

'*Mama neeeeed*,' she said. '*Mama neeeeeed*.'

The sound of his phone went off and fizzled her image into the nothingness, so he gladly went to grab it from his pocket. As usual, Lucy groaned in disgust at his choice in ringtone – *the cave music from Super Mario*. He could hardly blame her for her disdain. Having that was over-the-edge nerdy. Almost as much as the Donkey Kong Jr. arcade cabinet he kept in his office at home.

1 new email.

No subject.

He glanced back at the cottage through the warped ribcage of trees. He could just about see Wren up on the bedroom balcony (yes, it had one) still in the midst of the pep talk from her boss Mason, who had seemingly eluded a stroke for another day. She had her forehead pressed to a wooden beam, phone stuck to her ear. Listening and trying not to groan.

So he shrugged and tapped on the screen.

There wasn't much to the email, just a single blue link. He clicked it and saw a little JPEG picture flick up. A young girl. Fifteen, maybe. It was a head and shoulders shot, face tilted at an awkward angle, smiling but only with the mouth. She was kind of gaunt-looking or just sucking in her cheeks for the cheekbone model effect. Why did girls do that? Her eyes weren't focused on the lens, but at something beyond it.

And at the bottom of the picture a single word in bold white letters.

Where?

He started to chew the inside of his mouth. The message had been automatically forwarded from his public email address at the college.

'What is it?' Amelia said, looking over.

'Dunno. Probably some Internet meme from a student.' They'd often send him links to funny stuff. Dinosaurs pondering the meaning of life. Jesus pointing at an old lady slipping on ice and killing himself laughing. The sort of stuff that shouldn't be funny, but just was. The glum little girl in the photograph looked up and out of the phone at him all forlorn. She was like those kids you'd see in the sad bits of Comic Relief. The ones you fast forward and feel guilty about afterwards.

He showed it to Amelia.

Picture: sad girl's face. Word: where?

'That's lame,' she said. 'What's so funny about that?'

He had no idea.

It was official, then. Oldie Matt Hunter was no longer 'down with the kids' because this went completely over his head. He pointed at the picture, 'Ha ha, hilarious!' Then he dropped the phone back in his pocket. Wren was still on the balcony, stuck to hers.

'So what now?' Amelia said.

He winked at her. 'Now we climb a tree.'

CHAPTER NINE

Nicola Knox's mum gulped back a desperate breath, staring at the kitchen cupboard above the fridge. Glaring at it. It was the one place in the house that she hadn't fully explored yet.

She straightened her shorts, pushed her thick toes down, then reached up to open the doors. It was the cupboard they kept the cereal in. Oh, and biscuits when she bought them, which was now every *other* week since she'd started cutting down. She rummaged around to see if it was in there, even though she knew it wouldn't be.

A cereal box suddenly toppled forward from her scampering hand. She brought up the other but it was too late. Tesco Rice Krispies showered onto the lino, sounding like radio static. Her lips pressed together, very tight. Enough to turn them purple, then flesh-tone. She thumped her forehead against the cold white of the fridge and stared down her cheeks at the floor. Cereal swarmed around her bare feet, like ancient, long dead ants.

'Janet?' her boyfriend Ray called through. 'Have you checked down the sofa yet?'

'Three times.' She tried to keep her tears back.

'What about the garden? Could it have slipped out—'

'I'm not bloody thick. I've checked everywhere in the garden.'

He didn't say anything to that.

Problem was that in actuality she *was* bloody thick. That maybe she'd dropped her phone when she was out shopping or something, probably the other day when she leant over that freezer compartment in Farmfoods to grab the only double pepperoni pizza that was left. She joked with the shelf-stacker that she almost fell in. Maybe the phone had silently slipped out of her pocket and was there right now, trapped, useless and buggered in a block of ice.

Ordinarily she wouldn't be bothered, because she hated mobile phones anyway. She never used it. What was wrong with speaking face-to-face?

But ever since her daughter Nicola hadn't come home, she'd been hunting it down because she had to find out. Maybe, she'd find a message telling her that she had finally done what Janet dreaded.

She trudged across the crunching sea of Krispies, dragging little shards that stuck and dug into the bare skin of her chubby feet. She knew that when she saw Ray she'd sink to her knees and cry like a loon because it was as plain as day that she'd killed her own daughter.

Nicola's anorexia (with generous helpings of bulimia) was the start of it. Janet's constant sniping comments about her daughter's weight had gradually wound themselves around Nicola's brain like a python. Janet had probably known deep down how psychologically dangerous it was to harp on about weight to someone who shared her podgy genes. But her daughter being fat seemed like a worse problem back then. Things had had to be said.

Then the vomiting started, followed by the outright refusal to eat. And running like a constant seam through it all was the self-harming. *The slits*, Nicola called them.

Janet shuddered.

A social worker once spoke to her off the record, when Janet was in despair. In hushed tones in a hospital car park she'd said that simply outlawing the cutting probably wouldn't work. Better to make it safe, at least. So Janet, in a now almost incomprehensible move, had shown her daughter how to disinfect and cauterise a

70

razor with a flame. Just in case Nicola chose the slits again. 'And remember I don't want you to ever actually *do* this, love,' she'd said.

My God, Janet thought as she heaved her heavy, trembling body towards the living room. I taught my own daughter to kill herself. When Nicola left the house the day before yesterday, she'd even *smelt* depressed. Distant.

She'd taken a little bag.

Oh, Jesus.

Ray was on his knees with his huge arse pushing his Primark jeans towards her. His arm was buried deep inside the sofa.

'You deaf bastard,' she said, relishing the chance to direct her self-loathing at someone else. 'I told you I looked in there three times.'

'Shush a minute,' he said, rummaging around.

'You fat, deaf bastard.' She stomped over to him ready to slap her hands across the thin polyester shirt on his back, mainly so he would turn around. Then she would crash her hand against his face again and again so that he might finally stop being so good and patient and understanding and he'd finally bite. Maybe he'd be a real boyfriend for a change and push her to the floor. Crack the back of his hand across her mouth like the terrible, toxic mother she was.

''Ang on,' he said. 'I've got something.'

She blinked some of the tears away.

'There's something in here. Keeps slipping out of my fingers.'

'There can't be, I checked.'

'Did you ever lose a remote in here?'

'No.'

'There's a rip in the fabric. I opened it up a bit and got my hand in the frame. Give me a second.' His face grew steadily more pink the more he strained. There was a minute of wheezing then, 'Got ya!'

He pulled his hand slowly, delicately, out of the sofa's mouth and seemed to grit his teeth with every movement. It could easily slip out of his sweaty fingers again. But then, peeling through the brown grimy fabric lips of the sofa, came the birth of something plastic and black. She spotted the word Nokia at the top and that's when her knees have way a little and she had to steady herself against the worktop.

'Oh, Ray.'

'You've got the charger, haven't you, petal?'

She nodded and smeared away the tears with the palms of her hand. She snatched the phone and raced back to the hallway. The charger sat neatly on the telephone table, next to the perfectly good landline that Nicola seemed incapable of calling her on to say, *Hey Mum. I need you. I'm contemplating the last ever slit of my life.*

She rushed into the kitchen, charger in hand and scrambled across the Krispie-covered floor. She slammed the plug so hard and fast into the wall it made the socket spark. She held the connecting end towards the phone.

'Which hole does it go into? Which one?' she said, panicked, as though this was some rotten game where the phone might simply vanish in her hands if she wasn't quick enough.

Ray crunched over and took it from her, 'Just breathe, okay, love?'

'Don't you bloody drop it,' she said.

'I'm not going to drop it.' He plugged it in. Switched it on.

They waited in the quiet and he put his arm around her as they watched the little lights start. She knew that it was perfectly possible that the phone would have no messages on it at all, and that the front door might suddenly swing open and Nicola's skinny frame would just drift in on the wind like normal.

But somehow they both knew. Sometimes, these things are suddenly obviously. There was a pressure in the air that said that this wouldn't be fruitless at all.

She jumped in fright as the sing-song Nokia tone echoed in the kitchen. They both stared at the screen. She stiffened against him.

'It'll take a minute to collect the messages,' he said. 'Just wait.'

As soon as he said that, the phone chimed.

1 new text message.

She had to pull it close to her face and she read the words slowly, chapped lips mouthing each sound and syllable. Her eyes started to blink, three, four times. She took a shallow breath that quivered in her mouth and then she read it again. Her eyes suddenly bulged.

The phone dropped from her hands, yanking the power cord tight until it swung inches from the floor. Janet fell with it.

'. . . No . . . No . . . No!' With each *no* her voice became a deep wobbling moan as if her throat was suddenly flooding with liquid. 'I've killed her.'

Ray grabbed the phone.

'I've killed her. I've killed her.'

'What are you on about?' He turned the screen to him.

Mum. I jst wnted to let u knw tht I luv u, but I'm going to be with God now. 1 day, I hope u might believe and cm 2. Verecundus Xx Nicola

His mouth fell open a little. Very slowly he set the phone gently on the side and looked at Janet. She saw his face and could tell he didn't want to look at her. Not like this.

She was hunched over herself, saying 'going to be with God . . . going to be with God . . .' If he touched her, she wondered if she might die right there on the kitchen floor. He bit his lip instead, like he did when they watched the gory parts of those animal documentaries she loved so much. *They're educational*, she always said.

'Killed her,' she said. Not crying. Instead she was just scratching her arms over and over with her perfect nails. One of them snapped. She was scratching fast and hard, so that long red streaks pushed themselves deep into the surface of her skin, while somewhere in the street outside, kids were laughing.

CHAPTER TEN

Wren's boss Mason had always been an epic talker, even more so since he thought each day might be the only one left. But now she'd finally got off the phone to him she told Matt that he'd given her a long list of supposed 'contract winning' advice. The most ridiculous and offensive? 'Whatever you do, do not flirt to get the job, Wren. These are *Christian* folk.'

Now she was free they all walked in the forest together. Twigs and branches snapped under their feet as Amelia went up ahead, picking up leaves and tearing them into tiny pieces. She kept flinging them over her shoulder. Matt used to do the exact same ritual when he was a kid. Lucy was wandering behind them, earbuds jammed in, eyes to the floor.

'So, you're sure it's the same Chris Kelly?' Wren said.

'Oh, it's him.' Matt reached into his pocket and pulled out one of Seth's glossy leaflets.

She took it from him. A picture of the church was on the front with a huge arrow pointing from it to the glowing heavens. And in bold white letters: *Kingdom Come Church, This way to THE way!*

'Wow that's corny.' Wren laughed and opened it up. It said *Meet Pastor Chris* under a picture of a trendy-looking guy in his early forties with a dog collar, batting his come-to-church eyes. His expression was pitched somewhere between cool-serious and open-friendly, head on a pre-rehearsed tilt so that three strands of black fringe hung over, just so. He was sitting on the church steps with one elbow propped on one knee. A black leather Bible casually hung from his hand. 'Looks like an album shot, a catalogue man. I bet there's another one where he's looking at his watch and pointing in the distance.'

'Probably.' Matt folded the paper and slipped it back into his jeans. 'I met him in my first year of Bible college. I was nineteen but I reckon he was twenty-seven or so.'

'He was a student?'

'Yeah. Almost all of us lived on-site, but he used to travel home to Hemel Hempstead every night on the bus, because he had a wife and son. Anyway, we were on the same ordination course together.'

Wren gave her usual astonished smile, looking at him as though he was some sort of farmyard exhibit. 'Ah, the righteous years. I wish I could have known you back then.'

'Oh, you'd have hated me.' He stretched his fingers out and started to count them off. 'Firstly, I'd have said you shouldn't drink from a pint glass. That you did too much yoga. I'd have made you stop buying that *More* magazine you used to like.'

She held her hand to her mouth in mock despair. 'No more position of the month?'

'No more position of the century! I'd have gotten twitchy about your hair colour . . . I'd have found a verse to back that up. Oh, and I would have definitely insisted you destroy all your Eminem CDs. Our first date would have been tossing them on a big old righteous bonfire while we listened to Matt Redman.'

'Who?'

'Exactly.'

'So you're saying that you were a tool, basically?'

'We were *all* like that, when we started that course. Obsessed with the Church. Suspicious of the world. But Chris Kelly took it to another level. I mean, nobody liked him. He was loud, obnoxious. He'd bring his guitar into the common room and play really old stuff like Pet Shop Boys songs, but with Christian lyrics. West End Girls became,' Matt paused to remember, then let out a sudden burst of manic laughter as it came to him, 'Best Friend God. That was it. *Best. Friend. God. Da-dum da-dum.*'

She was laughing.

'And he'd stick his foot up on the coffee table like he was playing Wembley.' Matt reached down and grabbed a long stick. Demonstrated on a log. 'But the other guys on the course used to roll their eyes whenever he walked in the room. And they'd actually cheer whenever he left.'

'How Christ-like.'

'I know. It got me angry, the way they treated him. I mean, he was annoying but I felt bad the way everybody ignored him. So I figured I'd get to know him a bit. I started sitting next to him at lunch. Walked with him to lectures. I was a first year, he was in second, but we still shared certain modules together. I obviously ticked the others off because they kept glaring at me. Like my interest was encouraging him to exist.'

She reached for his hand as they walked and smiled softly at him.

'I didn't know what I was letting myself in for. I mean, Wren, he sat with me *everywhere* for the whole first term. Lectures, the bus, the pub. Without fail for the first three months of my course. And he'd just talk and talk. He had all these weird ideas for sermons and impossibly long jokes that weren't even funny. My jaw used to literally ache from all the fake smiling.' He gave her the cheesiest grin he could muster. It quickly faded. 'But after a while we started having disagreements. We'd argue.'

'About?'

'Theology. It was always that. The more time he spent at college the more fundamental he got. Whereas I was getting more liberal as the term went on. Or wet, as he'd say. He got obsessed with hell. It seemed to colour everything for him.' Matt slowed to a stop. 'But there was this icy day. December. I remember because there were decorations up. Chris turned up late for college looking really, I don't know . . . downbeat. And you have to appreciate, Chris Kelly didn't even have a down gear. I

76

went for a pint that night and of course he wandered in. But he didn't sit with me. He sat on his own at the bar, which was unheard of. Just kept sloshing back the pints when his limit had always been one lager shandy.'

'Let's sit.' Wren nodded to a huge tree trunk, resting on its side. She shouted at the girls. 'You two . . . we're parking.'

'I got worried about him and thought something must have happened so I went over. But he . . .' Matt tossed his stick into the wood. The girls went to grab it so they could swordfight. 'He freaked out. He told me I was on dangerous ground. That my beliefs weren't sound any more. And then he just started sobbing. Saying I was the only guy at college to give him the time of day and that he couldn't handle how the only friend he had was going to hell. And he kept pointing at me. The lake of fire, the eternal worm. All of it. He even dropped to his knees and pulled at my jacket. Told me to come back to God and tried to pray for me right there in the pub. Everyone was watching. The locals were pissing themselves laughing.'

'What did you do?'

'I pushed him off. Told him to calm down and he just stood up and cried and told us all that life was short. That hell was real. That we never know when death is coming for us. And then he just sort of ran out.'

Wren blew a breath across her lips. 'Wow. Me and him are going to get on like rabies.'

'It was odd. The week before he was fine, then that day he was just . . . I don't know . . . crushed. I followed him, just in case he tripped in front of a car or something. And it was snowing, I remember. He pretty much slipped the entire way down the hill. Fell into a bush a couple of times. I watched him praying at the bus stop, freaking some old lady out who was just trying to have a smoke.'

Matt looked off into the trees and through the gaps in the trunks he could see faint wisps of snowflakes and the winter street beyond it, Chris rummaging in his pocket for change, the scared old lady pointlessly trying to blend into a bus shelter poster for MacDonald's milkshakes. The hiss of the bus door opening and the belch of white

77

exhaust smoke as the indicator flashed the snow orange.

'I remember thinking then that religion can really screw a person up. It was probably the first time I'd admitted it.' He blinked. 'Seminal moment, that was.'

Wren shifted towards him. The log creaked.

'He just stumbled to the back of the bus and climbed up on the back seats. Started looking out through the back window.' Matt stared off into the wood again. 'And that's when he saw me standing in the snow. Waiting for him to see if he was okay. And he gave me this sad little smile, you know? Like he was going somewhere I couldn't go and that he was really going to miss me. I remember he put his hand on the glass and then he was gone. And I just kept wondering how awkward it was going to be for him when he turned up at college the next day. Plus, I knew the other students were total gits and were bound to grass him up to the principal for getting so drunk.'

'And was it awkward. When he came in?'

'I wouldn't know,' Matt said. 'Because I never saw him again. Nobody did.'

'Until tonight . . .' Wren waited for a moment before speaking. 'You don't think that's why I'm . . .'

He turned to her, 'It's just a coincidence.'

Silence.

'Like both of your bosses having strokes in a month. Life seems patterned, when it's just chaotic,' he reached over and touched her hand. 'We're here for your job and that's it.'

''Course we are!' she said, snapping her gaze from the floor. 'Come on.'

He paused for a while and watched her walk to the girls, so they could all pick up sticks and snap them against the trees.

'Chris Kelly,' he whispered and shook his head. Then he headed over, snapping twigs under his feet to join them.

CHAPTER ELEVEN

He wandered through the kitchen and opened the back door. A breeze ran through his damp hair and made it feel cold, which was very refreshing to him. He took a long sniff, but when he thought he could smell Nicola Knox's fluids on the air he cut it short. He knew that her soul was gone. Happy in heaven. But he wondered if the sinful part of people stick around. Like that's what ghosts are. Like she was deliberately wandering his house, urinating on his floors and bleeding on the door handles. Just so he'd remember her.

He shrugged the smell away and even laughed, because he knew ghosts didn't exist.

But demons do, he remembered.

It made him pause to pray. 'Lord, may Nicola be having the time of her life, right now, at your feet. Because that's where she is. Amen.' Those last words were said louder, as an announcement to any evil that might be eavesdropping.

He could hear the quiet but unmistakeable sound of the falls, rumbling from the other side of the village, across the hills and streets towards him. Always seeking him out, they were. Always saying hello.

Stephen was leaning against the wooden beam of the porch, arms folded. He had his boots on, and a pair of jeans and a tight white t-shirt, as usual.

'I'm looking at the clouds,' Stephen said.

He craned his head up. 'Sun looks big.'

'That's cos it is big, idiot.'

'Don't be like that.'

Stephen unfolded his arms and slipped them into his pockets, barely fitting the fingers into his tight jeans. 'I've been listening to the falls.'

'Oh? And what are they saying?'

'They're saying that God's hungry again. That he wants another.'

'You make it sound like he's a monster.'

'Isn't he? Sometimes?'

'No!' He shook his head fast and a few drops sprang against each side of the door frame. It made him feel like a dog.

Stephen held a calming hand up. 'I just think he might be calling you again.'

The breeze returned, freezing his wet hair, making the trees around his house make a pleasant *shhhhhh* sound.

He stepped out from the doorway, down the steps and leant against the opposite pillar to Stephen. 'I do find it scary, you know,' he said. 'Doing it.'

'I know you do.'

'I'm not as brave as you are.'

'Oh, I know that.'

'But I'll keep going. If that's what he wants. I'll take up my cross.'

'That's exactly what he wants. You know it is.'

They listened to the hiss of the trees for a long time.

He finally turned to Stephen. 'I saw a pig this morning stumbling in the field. I'm pretty sure it's dying.'

'That's a shame. I kind of like pigs.'

'Yeah, me too. That pig reminded me that life is short.'

Stephen smiled. 'Yes, it is. Very short.'

They stood for a few minutes more. There was no pressure to speak or to fill in the gaps.

'I can hold my breath for over one minute now, you know?'

Stephen joined with the trees, clapping his hands together. But his was a slow, laboured applause. 'One minute? I could beat that.'

His eyes fell a little and he felt the sudden urge to scratch his balls. He never realised being shaved down there would be so itchy. But Stephen was watching so he didn't dare do it.

'I'm going inside,' he said. 'You coming?'

Stephen shook his head. 'Nah. Not yet. I like it out here. Good air.'

'Suit yourself.'

'You did get her teeth out? Didn't you?'

'The golden ones?'

'Obviously.'

'They're both in my room.'

'Right. You should bury them or something. Throw them in the lake. Just get them out of the house, at least.'

He looked down at the floor and nodded. 'When my hair's dry.'

'What? Your hair's never dry. You're always washing it.'

For some reason he felt himself shrink at that.

'Just don't forget,' Stephen said, shaking his head. 'Get rid of them.'

'Okay.' He sighed and went inside and read a psalm while the kettle boiled, scrubbing his head with a tea towel. Then he sank into the couch, coffee in hand and flicked the channels of the TV. Seeing if he could make it through a whole advert break without catching his breath.

CHAPTER TWELVE

Kingdom Come Church was a colossal old gargoyle crouching on the top of the hill. Its centuries-old spire crumbled at the edges, threatening to topple over at any point and spike someone in the heart. Its stained-glass eyes, dirty and dull, glared over the iron railings and down the swooping fields to the forest-filled valley below.

'I don't get it.' Wren leant her head out of the car window as they approached, hair quivering in the breeze. 'Why would anyone build a church way up here? It's two miles out of town. Don't tell me they had a decent bus route in the 1700s.'

'Pilgrimage,' Matt said. 'If you get people to make an effort to be somewhere they're far more expectant when they arrive. Sociologists call it the Burning Bush Syndrome . . . Or at least I did once, in a paper.' He nodded down the hill. 'Plus the church is high up over the village. So it looks all-powerful. Back in the day I bet the parson could sit in the bell tower with a telescope and probably make a list of who was deflowering who.'

'And is that what you used to do?' she said. 'Spy on the flock.'

'Only on Thursdays,' he shrugged. 'Those W.I. pensioners used to get pretty kinky in our hall.'

There were maybe thirty other cars parked outside the main

entrance, most of them at odd angles, with their windows down to bring in the cool air. He found a spot near a clump of grass and killed the engine. He buzzed the windows shut.

All four of them noticed the sound as they climbed out of the car. The tinnitus hiss of the waterfall was churning somewhere unseen.

'Where *is* it, though?' Amelia said. 'It's pretty loud.'

'Loud . . . yeah . . .' He wasn't really listening. He was too busy running his eyes across the wrought iron gates and the swaying long grass spurting from the edge of the gravestones, like old man nose hair. A paved, crooked path ran from the gate to the heavy wooden arch of the main church door. It was closed.

Wren was already pushing through the squealing gate when she noticed he wasn't with them. 'Er . . . Matt? Chop-chop.'

He jogged up behind her and they all crunched up the gravel path to the church, Amelia in an exaggerated march because she liked the sound it made. Lucy was trying hard to see the tip of their cottage from here, but it was lost in the fairy-tale forest. When they reached the door, they spotted a strip of tiny wooden crosses up one side of the wall. The low beat of music was coming from somewhere.

Wren straightened her skirt, flicked her fringe.

'You look great, by the way. I'd totally hire you.' He put his arm around her. 'Nervous?'

'Put it this way. I need the toilet . . . *again*,' she whispered to him. 'Are you nervous, Reverend? Ready for Pastor Chris?'

Amelia and Lucy went to push through the heavy door.

It was silly really. All a bit childish, but he *was* nervous. Like a tiny, unexpected feather, flicking back and forth across the ceiling of his stomach. He'd been in a hundred churches since he left his own pastorate.

Left? That was a charitable way of putting it.

Since then he'd visited all sorts of cathedrals and tiny tin-pot chapels, marching his students about to show them how the theology of a social group affects the layout of their buildings. Baptists love the Bible, so it lies there open, front and centre in the Sanctuary. Catholics love the Eucharist, so the altar sits in the spotlight. How you can read a church's beliefs in a two-second glimpse.

But when he wandered those places he was neutral. He'd nod at the vicar and say, *Don't mind me. I'm just a geeky academic from the university. Teaching, that's all.* But he didn't feel neutral at this church, not with *this* pastor. Because he wouldn't be seen that way.

The door creaked open and they stepped inside, nostrils instantly damp with the smell of mouldy carpet. It had a typical stone interior, with huge granite pillars slamming down amongst the pews. His first thought was that they looked like the feet of the fighting machines from *War of the Worlds*. But it also had a large stage at the front. A row of mike stands and a hefty drum kit sat under a huge projector screen.

Wren's gaze swept across the floors, the pillars, the vaulted ceiling. Then over at the far corner, which was earmarked for the main extension. He saw her eyes flicking from corner to corner, brain firing up images of what she wanted to do with the place.

Someone had taped printed A4 sheets to the pillars and walls. *Purging Party: This Way!* It was, Matt noticed, in the world's most satanic font – Comic Sans.

Wren hurried them through the pews and up the centre aisle. As they moved he glanced down at his feet and the iron grille with the heating pipes beneath. The first time Matt ever married a couple he was handed their Argos-bought white gold rings and he placed them on his open Bible. He leant too far forward for an eager nod and one of them rolled clean off and disappeared down the grille with a clatter and a gasp from the congregation. It took the caretaker twenty minutes to prise it up and get it out, dirt, cobwebs, chewed fingernails and all, while the family glared at him throughout, glancing at their watches. Great days.

Wren followed the arrows through a stone arch until they came to an old wooden door lined with cruciform black metal studs. The sun was streaming from under it, lighting up the slabs beneath their feet.

The sign said: *Praise the Lord you found it! Now let's purge! –* Smiley face.

Music was thumping through the wood.

'I really need this job, Matt,' Wren suddenly whispered.

'Just be yourself.' She stood, as stiff as the door. Then out of the corner of his mouth. 'And if you're interested, sociologists call this the shitting-bricks syndrome.'

She hooted out a laugh and he saw her shoulders relax a little.

He squeezed her hand and swung the door wide open.

They stepped outside onto a stone patio, peaking their hands across their foreheads and squinting from the early evening sun. God was deliberately shining his cosmic torch in their eyes. Just to be annoying.

The view though . . . *wow*.

They were faced with a stunning wrap-around sight of green hills rolling down into woodland. Little farms and crops of houses sat in the distance and at the bottom of the steep hill was a sparkling lake with Cooper's Force Waterfall pounding into it.

'Woah,' Wren said.

But Matt's eyes weren't really on the view. They were on the people. Everyone was wearing sunglasses. Everyone. Forty people just standing about on the stones, chatting and nibbling rice and refried beans from dangerously curved paper plates. An iPod sat in the cradle of a massive speaker shaped like a Zeppelin. He didn't recognise the music, but someone was singing about the golden streets of heaven with jangly guitars.

Matt took a step forward and Wren raised her hand in a little wave. Nobody noticed them. Mouths kept chewing and chatting, people lifted their plastic cups for a top-up of what looked like water. Some would cock their necks back as they laughed. But nobody saw them.

Matt was just about to call out a hello when he felt a bony hand landing on his shoulder.

'You *came*!' It was Seth Cardle, looking like a golfer. Pale-pink Fred Perry top on a pair of thin cream trousers. He tapped his sunglasses down his nose (Rayban, Matt noticed). He looked Wren in the eye. 'Tell me you haven't eaten.'

'Nope,' Amelia butted in and slapped two hands on her empty stomach. 'We're empty.'

Seth smiled and pushed his sunglasses back into position. 'There's all the chilli you can handle, little one. But first things first. Wren, I have someone you must meet.'

Seth slipped his hand into Wren's and tugged her away, across the patio, through the crowd of eaters. Matt and the kids shared a shrugging glance and followed behind her.

Clearly Seth had been a validation because people finally started to smile at them. Raising their cups and giving little finger waves, saying 'welcome' and 'hello' through guacamole- and tortilla-stuffed mouths. Seth was heading for a group of about seven people, standing by a low stone wall. All with their backs turned, rocking their shoulders with laughter.

Matt couldn't see who was making them shriek with delight but the sound, tone and rhythms of that voice were riding on the breeze. Instantly recognisable. Like the tune to a novelty single that had lodged itself in the brain through relentless, excessive airplay.

Somewhere in the centre of those people, an unseen Chris Kelly was telling one of his stories. And they were *loving* it.

That feather again, teasing his innards, when there was really no need for it.

Seth raised his fist near his lips and deliberately coughed. Then again, louder. The laughter faltered. A head swivelled back toward Wren. Then another, until all seven sets of sunglasses looked back, eyebrows frowning at first. Looking . . . interrupted.

They were all women, apart from a bald, fat guy in a Hawaiian shirt with a jet-black goatee. He was the only one who smiled and seemed to have a hell of a lot of teeth when he did. His little finger had a streak of chilli sauce that he removed in a quick lizard-lick.

'Helloooo,' Wren said, waving. For some reason she also started bobbing her shoulders left and right, like an eager primary-school teacher greeting her class. And when she spoke, her voice sounded small. 'I'm the architect. I'm Wren.'

Instant smiles leapt from face-to-face.

Wren smiled back, much more at ease and walked towards them. But Matt held back a little; so did the kids.

The smiley faces swung open like a set of doors. And sitting on the low wall, while the others stood, was Chris Kelly in his black shirt and dog collar. He was sat like Jewish Rabbis used to when they taught in the Ancient Middle East. In their system the teacher always sits and the student stands. Chris had one arm across a knee in the exact same stance as the leaflet. Only now he was wasn't holding a Bible, it was a bottle of Evian. Bizarrely, he looked even younger than Matt remembered him being fifteen years ago. Though he had the same pinched little mouth that belied the loudness of his voice.

He hadn't yet spotted Matt.

When Chris saw Wren he sprang to his feet, clawed off his sunglasses and boomed out her name. Singing it like an opera singer: 'Wrennnn Hunnnnnnter!'

People stopped chewing and looked over.

'Everybody. This is her. The one we've been praying about. This is Wren Hunter the architect!' He rushed towards her. 'It's a privilege to meet you. It really is.'

'Oh the pleasure's mine. The village, the cottage are just so—'

'I've got to say it . . .'

'Say what?'

'The hair. I *love* the red hair!'

She gave him an awkward smile.

'In fact . . . may I?' Chris didn't wait for an answer. He leant forward and glided his fingers through her fringe, lifting it to the ladies behind him like it was a wig on a stand they all might buy. A few smiled with eager nods, nudging each other. One or two seemed gutted and looked to the floor.

'You're a lot prettier than the last architect we had!' Chris said.

Seth barked into his hands with that loud, tuberculosis laugh of his.

Nobody seemed to notice Wren gently cock her head to the side, so her hair slipped from his fingers. 'Chris. I'd like you to meet my family.'

'Yes, of course! Bring them on!'

'And funnily enough,' she turned her head back to Matt, 'I believe you know my husband.'

'I do? Point the rascal out and I'll . . .' his words fizzed into silence.

Eye contact.

'Chris . . .' Matt took a step forward. 'It's been a million years.'

It was odd. Because at first Chris did absolutely nothing. He just stared. Tilted his head like an only child studying a fly in a jar. And as irrational as it seemed, Matt could swear the rest of them did that exact same movement too – the hive mind telling all eyes to narrow behind the black lenses and . . . *1, 2, 3 . . . Tilt!*

'You might not remember me,' Matt took another step forward. 'We trained at Bible college together.'

Chris closed his eyes, and just said, 'Halleh-bloomin-lujah!'

Lucy sniggered.

Chris's eyelids shot open and he stomped over. 'Matty Boy!' He hugged Matt hard, adding three sharp pats on the back, the way some men do to signal that they might be hugging another guy but dammit . . . *I'm. Not. Gay.*

'Everyone. This is unbelievable. It's my old study buddy!' Chris hooked a thumb at the living coincidence that was Matt Hunter, a look of wonder on his face. 'I mean, really! What are the chances?'

Someone shouted, 'It's the Lord.'

Chris said, 'Amen to that.'

'And this is Lucy, and Amelia.' Wren shuffled them forward to display them. Probably because Mr Mason had just instructed her on the phone that *'reasonably well-adjusted kids were part of any good CV.'*

'Wow, lovely. Pretty and lovely.' Chris shook the kids' hands vigorously. 'And of course you've already met my Ben.' He leant over and waved a little group apart. Ben came stumbling out.

'Hey guys,' Ben nodded politely at Lucy and Amelia. 'I brought my Frisbee again. If you want a game, we're all going to play later.'

Chris spoke before the girls could answer, in a voice that was suddenly whiny and bizarre, and aimed point-blank at Matt. 'Of all the architects . . .' His mouth was moving at odd angles and he pushed out his hands like Tommy Cooper. It took Matt ten seconds of utter bafflement before he realised that Chris was attempting a Humphrey Bogart impression. The kids were unsurprisingly oblivious. They'd barely even heard of Elvis Presley. 'Of all the architects in all the world, you happen to be married to the one who walked into mine.' Chris laughed hard, everyone did the same. Then as the chuckling died down he quietly said. 'But seriously. The Lord's brought you to me. That is a *rare* treat, Matt.'

'Good old Matt Hunter,' Chris said, throwing an arm around his shoulders, pushing his knuckles playfully into the top of Matt's head like they were both in an 80s Mafia movie. 'At a Purging party, in my church! What are the chances?'

The chances? Matt thought, as he pulled his ruffled head out and smiled politely. The chances were slim.

CHAPTER THIRTEEN

Matt and Chris sat on the stone wall, facing out from the church. From that angle they could look out across the valley, legs dangling over the side, Huck Finn style. The waterfall looked petite as waterfalls go, but it was surprisingly loud, and wild enough to look worthy of a postcard. Or a tea towel at least. The sun was going down.

He could hear Wren and the kids being fussed over behind him in amongst the ants-march munching of taco shells on the patio. The overweight youth worker with the Hawaiian shirt and toothy smile – 'Call me Billy, everybody does' – was inviting the kids to a video games tournament at the church on Saturday.

'How great is this?' Chris said, rubbing a hand on Matt's shoulder and making Matt almost shake the food off his plate. 'Meeting up again.'

'Yeah, it's a small world, isn't it?'

'Yep,' Chris said. 'But I wouldn't like to paint it!'

The oddness of the joke and the sheer pet dog eagerness in his eyes made Matt laugh out loud. This delighted Chris no end.

'How old are you these days?' Matt asked.

'Forty-two and counting.'

He gave an impressed nod. 'So how come you look younger? Are you drinking virgin's blood out here? You have a painting locked away in an attic?'

'Funnily enough, no. You'll be oooo . . . thirty-four now, right?'

Matt nodded.

'Then how come you look older than I do, eh?' Chris slapped him on the back, hard enough to make Matt cough into his fist. 'Kidding. Kidding! You're quite the Dapper Dan these days, aren't you? You were always . . .' he looked into the air and grabbed at a word, 'Suave.'

Matt burped.

'So . . .' Chris eyed him. 'How's The Hunter been all these years?'

'The Hunter . . . Wow. No one's called me that in a looooong time.'

Chris sloshed some water into Matt's plastic cup and spilt a bunch of it across his thumb. He was, of course, oblivious to it.

'I've been really good, thanks.' Matt shook the water from his hand. 'Great, actually.'

'Well, I can see that. We all can. Wonderful family. Lovely kids.'

'Your son, Ben. Seems like a decent human being. How on earth did you manage that?'

Chris gave a mock wag of his finger. 'Perhaps I'm just premium stock.'

'Clearly,' Matt said. 'People circle the day in their calendar when they first meet Chris Kelly.'

It was supposed to be a joke but the flash in his eyes made it clear he took it as a compliment. 'Speaking of premium,' Chris's eyeballs darted left and right then he put a hand over his mouth, 'can a minister say this? . . . You have a . . .' he coughed the words out, 'a very foxy wife. Walks with a little Christian swagger.'

Matt laughed, more in disbelief than anything else. 'You really haven't changed at all, have you?'

'Hope that's a compliment. You remember how we used to laugh?'

How tempting it was to say no, not really. But he found himself nodding, half from politeness, and the other because actually it was quite fun seeing the guy again. Weird, but still . . . amusing. And as Matt pondered it, he wondered if Chris might be even *more* manic than he used to be. Unless it was nerves, of course. Running into an old friend like this . . . with their last moment in the snow being so monumentally awkward.

You'll burn, Matt, he'd said that night. And the fire will never go out.

Matt held up his cup and toasted him. 'Well here's to you, Chris. Your church is growing. The congregation seem "into" you. You've got a big building project on the way. Principal Wilder would be proud.'

Chris's eyes softened, a gentle smile changing his face. 'Thank you for saying that. Really . . . but what about you? I hear you're a professor.'

'How come you know that?'

'Seth.'

'Ah. Of course. Well, yes, I'm a professor.'

'Of?'

'The sociology of religion.'

'Ooof. You always were more intellectual than me.' He flicked a hand straight over the top of his head. 'I guess I'm more . . . practical. But you like teaching it?'

'It's not just teaching. I do a fair amount of research, some writing. A bit of consultancy work. I prefer that sort of thing to the lecturing to be honest. Actually I'm on sabbatical at the moment.'

Matt waited for the usual polite response to the mention of the word sabbatical. Something along the lines of, 'Oh . . . and what are you doing in that time, hmmm?' And he'd reply cheerfully, oh just a book about how belief in God is a psychological construct, not an external reality. More sour cream? Instead, when Chris made no response Matt added, 'I guess Seth told you that I'm not with the church any more.'

Chris winced. 'What on earth happened? Why'd you leave?'

Matt flicked a piece of rice from his plate through the air. 'You must *really* think I'm going to hell, now.'

Chris said nothing.

'I don't mind, by the way, if you do. It's your opinion.' Matt was feeling lighter and more himself now that his vicar aura was established dead. It always felt easier, once that was sorted.

Chris ran his tongue around the inside of his mouth. It made his top lip bulge out. 'Maybe you will go to hell. Maybe you won't. I guess only God knows that.'

'That's if God exists, of course.' Matt took a loud chomp of a tortilla chip.

The look on Chris's face was nothing less than depressed astonishment, like when a man comes home to find his house has been burgled. He looked like that. That his old 'study buddy' would even entertain such a notion. 'Oh, but Matt, God does exist. Believe me, he does.'

'Yeah, well, let's just get this clear. I respect your beliefs.' *Hmmm, do I?* 'But I'm just not there any more, okay? I hope you can respect that.'

Matt spotted a flock of birds swooping across the sky. Rising and falling, rising and falling. It really was beautiful out here.

'You know,' Chris said, 'you were the most Christ-like person in that place. You looked out for me, Matt, and I've never forgotten that. Ever.' Chris reached over and put a tentative finger on Matt's knee. 'Which makes it very difficult to see you this way. To hear about you turning . . .'

'You make me sound like milk.'

'Turning away from him. Seeing it. Hearing it. It's painful. Gets me right here.' He pounded his fist into his chest. Quite hard.

Matt tipped his drink in Chris's direction. 'Don't you go worrying about me. I'm chugging along just fine.'

Chris closed his eyes, lips moving in silent prayer. Matt just shrugged and took in the view. That's the thing about believers. They spend half their life with their eyes shut.

A subject change was in order.

'Anyway, Chris. Moving on. Am I finally going to get to meet your wife?' Matt turned his head to look through the crowd. 'Or is it how I always suspected and you just made her up to—'

'Lydia's dead.' Chris pulled his hand back from Matt's knee.

Sometimes people say things in a conversation that are so deep or intense, that it's easy to miss their importance first time round. Matt heard the word dead echo in his ears and yet he still went to grab another handful of tortilla chips. But then his hands slowed, and his eyebrows slowly moved together. 'Oh shit, Chris. When?'

'Christmas, my second year of college. You know the night when I drank too much?'

'What?' Matt just stared at him.

'I'm not even sure why I came into college that day. Lonely, I guess. Lydia died the night before.'

Silence. Long seconds of silence.

'Oh, man. I'm so sorry . . .'

'So I had to leave college, didn't I? I had a seven-year-old son to look after.' He ran his index finger around the lip of his plastic cup, one entire revolution. 'She died and I had new responsibilities. She died in our flat.'

'That was Hemel?'

Chris's eyes suddenly flickered as though Matt had just said something electric.

'Chris?'

'I don't like to talk about that place. I think it's got a bad spirit or something.' He stared off at the horizon. 'Sometimes I think demons must have a hold over certain cities and towns. Certain postcodes. Don't you?'

Matt sighed and put his plate on the wall. 'Why didn't you just tell me that night in the pub?'

Chris blinked, and his mouth creaked into an odd-looking grin. 'God's shown me how to deal with grief and *all* my deep wounds. And I'm helping others do the same. You see that building down there, opposite side of the lake from the waterfall?'

He nodded.

It was a modern-looking building, reminded him of a council office. Two floors and a car park, near the edge of the lake. It had a heck of a lot of windows, on the lakeside.

'We call that Bethesda. It's where people come for deep healing. We're doing miracles down there. And you know, God keeps bringing me wounded hearts to heal.'

'Well I'm happy for you,' Matt said, although he wasn't sure if he really meant it. Wasn't it disingenuous to be pleased when people were deluding themselves? Who cheers with approval when a dementia patient shouts, 'I'm fifteen again'? Isn't that supposed to be the part where everybody cries at the utter loss of rationality?

'You know what, Matt? I honestly don't know how you can live a single day without God.' He put his hand to his dog collar and pulled out a silver chain with a chunky-looking cross on it. He gripped the base and pushed it towards Matt.

Eager to lighten the mood, Matt pulled a look of fake shock and held up his hands. 'Ah! You keep that away! It burns, it burns!'

Chris frowned for a second then let out a breath. 'Well aren't you the witty one.' He pulled the cross close to his chest. '*Et teneo, et teneor.* You ever heard that?'

''Course. It's Latin,' Matt said. 'It means I hold and I am held.'

'Exactly. I hold this and it holds me.' Chris gave a case-closed smile and slipped the cross back behind his collar. 'So come on. What happened? Why'd you turn your back on church ministry?'

'I didn't.'

'Huh?'

'I was suspended.'

Matt turned just so he could watch his reaction. The confusion, the shock. Then a sort of eye-twinkling curiosity.

'Suspended?'

'The denomination kicked me out for twelve months. Which was plenty of time to decide I didn't believe in God any more. So I never went back.'

'Suspended? What did you do?'

Matt had the impression that people round here would suddenly drop at Chris's feet and tell them their darkest little secrets, but he didn't feel like joining that swooning clan. 'It's personal.'

Chris arched his fingers into a steeple, which came to rest on his chin like he was some wise old Kung-Fu Master. It was an oddly patronising gesture. 'I don't believe in personal.'

And there she was, back again.

It was strange because Matt could usually shake that life-changing image from his mind. The image of his dying, murdered mother. Over the years he'd learnt to switch it off as efficiently as a TV, or a radio. But it lingered on that patio like the flicker of an old film, projected on top of everything else so that blinking it away only zoomed it in. Made it more vibrant.

Et teneo, et teneor.

I hold and I am held?

Shame you dropped the ball on that day, though, isn't it, God? You useless bloody fumbler.

Matt looked up at the slowly darkening sky and noticed sharp little lights starting to float a few metres over his head. 'What's this?' Matt said. He turned and saw Seth and the fat guy, Billy, helping people light Chinese lanterns. They laughed and lifted them high. Matt noticed a few of them were crying.

Chris swung his legs around and stood up. 'They're Purging.'

'Purging what?'

'The old self. Eighteen of these beautiful people are going to be baptised next Sunday morning. They've become new creations. The old has gone and there it goes.' He pointed up at the lanterns gliding silently up and drifting off into the evening sky. 'And the new has come. Come on, let's join them.'

They left their plates of food on the wall and headed over to the others, Matt grabbing a chicken goujon to take with him. All around him he could hear the striking of matches so they could fling the last of their old selves free. A golf-clap rippled out as more lights slowly lifted into the air.

Amelia ran up with ice cream on her lips and slipped her hand into his. 'Aren't they pretty, Daddy?'

Wren appeared and slipped her arm around his waist, head resting on his shoulder. She was smiling a lot. And Lucy was over by the wall chatting to Ben and some other boys, watching the lights and filming it on her camera-phone.

While everyone cooed over the metaphysical power of cheap pound-shop lanterns Matt wondered if he was the only sane person left in the world. Which seemed like a good cue for them all to start singing some old negro spiritual: *My shackles are gone, My spirit is free* . . .

It was just as they started clapping (on beats one and three . . . because white Christians *never* clap on two and four) that the arched studded door Matt had used before suddenly clattered open noisily. Loud enough to make people turn their heads.

People saw who it was and started to nudge each other. Some, interestingly, slipped their sunglasses back on.

A young-looking policeman with rimless glasses and an almost complete lack of chin appeared. He strode across the patio with a pile of white papers in his hand. 'Pastor Chris? Is he here?'

Chris was shielding the flame on somebody's lantern. He turned, announcing him like they were in a kids TV show. 'Hey everyone . . . it's PC Taylor. Grab yourself a burrito.'

Something was up because PC Taylor didn't grab anything, he just leant in and started whispering in Chris's ear.

Lucy slipped her phone into her pocket and walked quickly over to Matt. She looked nervous. It was the way she always looked when a policeman turned up, as if the entire force in Britain was only ever working on one single case – the possibility of her dad, Eddie Pullen, breaking out of prison and tracking his wife and daughter down. 'Why are *they* here? What's happened?'

Matt shrugged, 'It'll just be a local thing, I guess.'

They all waited, eyes moving from the whispering policeman to the floating lanterns of rejected sin, then back to the policeman again. Eventually Taylor handed the pile of papers to Chris. Then he turned and glanced over at Matt, wriggling his nose and holding Matt's gaze longer than necessary.

Matt wasn't a master at lip-reading, but it wasn't rocket science to see the policeman lean into Chris and ask 'who's that?' Then after getting his answer he turned and raised a hand. 'I'm sorry if I interrupted your party, folks. I'll see you all next Sunday.' He turned to leave, raising a hand to wave.

'Chris?' Matt said. 'Is everything okay?'

Chris just looked up at the pink sky and the lights fading into it and started to shake his head. 'Sorry, everyone, but gather round. I've got some news here.'

People swept in quickly, taking off their glasses.

'Disturbing development I'm afraid. A fourteen-year-old girl from the village has been reported missing. She hasn't been home for two nights now. Her mum suspects she might have' – he looked in pain when he said it – 'hurt herself.'

Seth screwed up his face. There was an ominous sucking in of breath from the others.

'Taylor's asked us to pray, and I think under the circumstances we ought to do that straight away.'

Billy the youth worker shouted out, 'Who, Chris? What's her name?'

'She's called Nicola. Nicola Knox.'

A few gasps. Hands to chests. Eyes closing.

'I'm afraid I don't know her, but some of you might,' Chris said. 'Taylor has copies of her photograph here. How about we all hold one and we can pray for her safe return. Okay with everyone?'

A murmur of enthusiastic agreement.

Matt glanced at Lucy, who was holding her mum's hand.

'Hunters?' Chris thrust one of the sheets into Wren's hand, 'I hope you can muster some of that old faith for a girl in trouble?'

She turned the sheet over and spoke to Matt. 'Oh, look at her. She looks . . . lonely . . .'

Matt looked down and suddenly snatched the paper from Wren's hand. Seth noticed the grab, and frowned.

'Matt?' Wren whispered, flushing a little red. 'What are you doing?'

The others were slowly starting to kneel, heads bowed, hands together.

Matt stood, paper in hand and whispered back. 'I've seen this girl before'.

'When we drove through the village?'

'No,' he whispered again so the others couldn't hear. Then he took her by the elbow a few steps back. He noticed Lucy looking over, frowning.

'What's with the cloak and dagger—'

'Wren, I have her picture on my phone. Someone emailed it to me this afternoon.'

Her face dropped.

'It's a different picture, but I'm telling you. It's the same girl.'

CHAPTER FOURTEEN

Matt slowed the car and shifted into second gear as he spotted the police station up ahead. It had one of those old-school wrought iron lanterns above the door, with blue glass. The sort you might see in old Jack the Ripper films with a flat-capped cockney kid yelling *murdah! murdah!* Now that the sun had truly sunk on Hobbs Hill, the bulb in the lantern was glowing, and flickering. He pulled the car in and parked, patting his pocket just to make sure his phone hadn't slipped out.

Other than the distant hiss of the falls at the other end of the valley, the village centre was weirdly quiet. Okay, it was 9:30 p.m. on a Sunday night, but he at least expected people to be wandering between the pubs or couples heading home after a meal out.

Matt and the girls had left the Purging Party just before the prayers started in earnest. The kids' Frisbee game was cancelled. He made polite excuses, saying it was past Amelia's bedtime, they'd had a long day, blah, blah. But really, he just wanted to get down here and show the police the email. He'd dropped the girls at the cottage and headed straight out, promising he wouldn't be long.

He stepped beneath the blue glow of the lantern and spotted a wooden plaque on the wall. Apparently the chief sergeant here was called Sergeant Miller. He pushed on the heavy wooden door. It creaked as it opened.

The reception had a high ceiling but was small, and alongside each wall ran what looked like church pews. A heavy iron radiator (painted the same ill-advised green as the walls) pushed out a little heat. There was a purple stain on it where some jokey kid had probably dumped a crayon. And he thought he could smell burnt toast in the air. He stepped up to the glass partition, with the desk behind it.

Matt went to tap on the glass but snapped his hand back instantly. Police Constable Taylor, the chinless policeman who had dished out Nicola's photo at the Purging was in the back room. He'd left the door ajar just enough so that Matt could see he was on his knees, leaning over the picture of the missing girl. One hand hovered over her face, his fingers were outstretched.

What the hell is he—

Praying. He's not masturbating, he's praying. Must be.

Matt waited for a moment, then gently tapped on the glass.

Taylor's body jerked and he pushed his heel back against the door, which slammed it shut. A few seconds later he emerged, pulling his uniform straight, pushing his glasses into place. 'Oh. You.'

'Yes. Hi, I'm Matt Hunter.'

'I know that. You're the architect's husband.'

'That's right.'

'Is the Purging over?'

'Almost fully purged. Now they're praying for the missing girl.'

'Well good. Cos, that's vital, that is.' Taylor started to nod, slow and serious. 'I hear you don't go in for God?'

'News travels fast round here.'

'Yup.'

'Well the news is true. So . . . Sergeant Miller . . . is he here? I'd like a word with him.'

Taylor's eyebrows crept together and he tilted his head. 'And why would you want to see Sergeant Miller at this hour? Something wrong?'

'Is he here?'

'Nope. He's over the road in The Chequers pub. He heads over there after his shift.'

'Great, I'll nip over.'

'Er . . .' he raised a hand. 'He's off duty. So you'll just need to talk to me.'

'Nah, I don't want to disturb you. Besides,' Matt nodded over to the back room, 'looks like you're hard at work.'

Taylor pushed himself up onto the balls of his feet, jutted his chin out a bit.

'Besides, I fancy a pint myself,' Matt raised a hand. 'Thanks, Constable Taylor.'

'Not a drinking man, myself,' he called after him. 'I prefer spirits of a different kind. You should try that sometime.'

'Tried it, didn't like it.' Matt smiled. 'I couldn't handle the hangovers.'

He stepped out before Taylor could speak. He looked up the road, each way. There was nobody else. In the distance, over the treetops, he thought he saw an aeroplane hovering. He squinted again and realised it wasn't and for one thrilling moment his inner geek thought he was finally seeing a UFO. But as he took a few steps forward he realised it was just one more Chinese lantern. One more purge. Somebody's old self floating silently over the village, through the gathering dark. He thought all the lanterns would have gone out by now.

He shrugged, headed across the street and pushed his way through the doors of the Chequers, starting to realise how tired he was.

There was a grand total of four people in there, including himself. A barmaid sat at one of the tables, eyes fixed hard on a book of Sudoku. Over in the corner sat a tiny old man with a bulging hunchback, which genuinely threatened to tear the back of his tweed jacket open in a full-on Hulk-split. He was leaning zimmer-frame-style on an Abba-themed fruit machine, his squinting face flashing in the lights as he pondered which buttons to nudge and which ones to hold.

A TV on the wall was showing the final scenes of *Smokey and the Bandit 2*. The one with the elephant. It was on an obscure high-number Freeview channel; the sound was muted. And in the other corner, sitting in a wooden booth below a dangling art deco-style lamp was a man who was clearly Sergeant Miller, still in uniform, one hand clasped around a pint glass and another poring over a small pile of papers.

Matt wandered up. 'Can I get you a refill?'

Miller stuck a finger on the papers to keep his place and looked up. A swoop of brown hair flecked with grey hung over one eyebrow. He looked mid fifties. There was a flash of recognition in his eyes. 'Are you chatting me up?'

'I'm afraid not,' Matt said. 'And I imagine if I was, I'd probably be castrated round here.'

Miller paused for a moment and then smirked. 'Ain't that the truth.' He lifted his pint glass. 'Bombardier.'

'Coming up.' Matt headed to the bar and had to cough loudly for the barmaid to pull her attention from her puzzles. She kept looking at him as she pulled both pints, eyes up and down him. Smiling and tugging at her lower lip with crooked teeth. He ordered two bags of overpriced hand-cooked crisps and headed over to the table. 'Do you mind if I sit with you for a moment?'

'Actually, I'm quite busy. Thanks for the—'

'I need to talk to you about something. My name's Matt Hunter.'

Miller waited, assessing him. Then he suddenly bundled his papers together and turned them upside down. He placed them on the seat beside him and motioned for Matt to sit. 'So you're the ex-vicar.'

Matt laughed and sat down, dragging a beer mat over and leaning back in the booth. 'And I reckon everybody knows that I had Pop Tarts for breakfast too.'

'I saw you on telly tonight.'

'Really?'

'That possession thing in London this morning.'

'Ah, that.' God, that felt like a month ago. 'I thought it'd just be on the local news.'

'Oh no . . . you're national. Looks like you've had a pretty hectic day.' He paused then tapped a finger to his temple. 'Possession, eh? Some people are just nuts, don't you think?'

'Absolutely.' Matt took a long swig of his beer. Cold fizz buzzed down his throat, making him sigh.

'Nice to see you helping out the coppers, though. We need a few friends. Anyway, I know all about your wife vying for the church renovation. Big news round here.'

'I heard about the missing girl.'

His face fell a little. He ran his hand across the tabletop.

'Sergeant Miller—'

'Terry.'

He nodded, 'Terry. Let me get straight to the point. Something rather odd is going on.'

He leant back in his chair, taking a drink.

'Your missing girl, Nicola Knox.' Matt started to rummage in his pocket. 'I saw the photographs your colleague is handing out.'

'So?'

'Well this is going to sound weird, but I'm sure I was sent a picture of the same girl today. By email.'

Terry stopped sipping.

'This afternoon. Just as we arrived in Hobbs Hill. My family are staying for ten days in—'

Terry waved his hand. 'Yeah, I know that. Show me the email . . .'

Matt set the Blackberry on the table and tapped it into life. 'I thought it was some random picture from one of my students. They sometimes send me Internet—'

Another hand wave: get to the point.

'Just take a look.' Matt held the phone at an angle so Terry could see and started scrolling up through his emails. He quickly found the one from this morning. 'Here we go. Tell me if this isn't her.'

He clicked the link and pushed the screen toward Miller.

A picture flicked up on the screen.

Terry sighed. 'Are you taking the piss?'

Matt edged forward on his seat and turned the phone back to him. He frowned hard, clicked back and then onto the link again, but the same picture came back. Not a fourteen-year-old girl. No sign of the word *Where?* In its place was a little piece of clipart: a rainbow. And next to it, an animated Smiley Face, winking, with its thumb up.

Terry clucked his tongue. 'I've got stuff I need to get on with. Grab yourself a table over there, eh?'

'Hang on, this isn't right.' Matt clicked on it again, just to make sure. Rainbow. *Click*. Rainbow. *Click*. Rainbow. 'I opened this link this afternoon and it was a picture of a young girl, early teens. And it had the word *Where* written under her, with a question mark.'

'And now it's a rainbow.'

'Yes . . .' Matt looked down at the table for a moment, then fixed his eyes on Miller. 'I'm telling you, I saw her face on here today. I have no reason to make this up. I showed it to my daughter.'

Miller set his pint down and wiped the froth from his top lip. 'Okay. So maybe it was a picture of another girl. Some sort of joke.'

'No, I really think it was her.'

'Is it possible you might be mistaken?'

Matt sighed. 'Well it's possible, yeah.'

'And who sent you this email?'

'It came to my university inbox, which is public. But it looks like the message source was anonymous.'

'I thought there wasn't any such thing as anonymous on the Internet.'

Matt shrugged. 'There are sites that you can send untraceable emails from. Links that'll sort of self-destruct. Change into something else.'

'Use those a lot, do you?'

'No,' he said, defensive. 'But I work with students. They prank and bully each other with this sort of thing all the time. The staff have to be aware of the techniques. You send a link to someone that says "I hope you get crabs soon" and then it changes to some random image before the staff can see it.'

Miller glanced over at the old man as the fruit machine suddenly belched out a pile of coins. He called out, 'Good work, Fred,' then turned his eyes back to Matt. 'Well, if it happens again, take a screenshot or something. But for now I've got bigger fish to fry.'

Matt stared at the rainbow on the little screen. At the mocking little smiley face, which was no doubt laughing at what an idiot Mr Professor now looked. 'Up at the church, PC Taylor said Nicola might want to harm herself. You think this might be suicide?'

'That's the mother's theory and she might well be right. Nicola was anorexic . . . troubled. That's common knowledge.' He let out a long breath and looked at the wall. Through it. 'But she could have just run away.'

'Let's hope so.'

Miller nodded, turned back and grabbed his pint. 'Incidentally . . . how are you finding Hobbs Hill? You been converted yet?'

Matt leant over and whispered across the drinks, 'I notice the police station doesn't have a cross on it.'

'Damn right it doesn't. I worked here long before the bloody Holy Ghost descended on the place. That church on the hill, it's taking over this village. Won't be long till this pub closes down, just like the others. I can see that happening with crystal clarity. I have dreams about it. That they'll turn The Chequers into some sort of poncey gastro joint. Bloody tragic is what it is. And I'll be next.' He took a final swig of his pint. 'Well listen, thanks for the drink but I'm heading home. Got an early start tomorrow.'

'Oh?'

'Me and a bunch of the villagers are starting the search for Nicola in the morning. Not much use doing it in the dark.'

Matt thought for a moment. 'I could help with that, if you need an extra pair of hands.'

Miller looked at him for a moment, and there was an unmistakeable flash of suspicion in his eyes. A tightening of the lip. After all, who was this crazy academic ranting about emails and rainbows and offering to help with the search of a girl he barely knew?

'What makes you so eager?'

'I've got daughters myself.' Matt pushed his pint glass away. 'I'm just saying if you need help, then—'

'Seven a.m. sharp,' Miller said finally. 'At the station. Wear decent boots.' He pushed himself up from the table and gathered up his papers. Matt glanced at them and spotted Nicola's face staring out. She really did have sad eyes. Her face reminded him of those ghostly old photographs you see hanging in stately homes, only she wasn't wearing a Victorian night dress. She was wearing a leopard skin onesie.

Miller caught him looking.

'I really do think it was her, you know. In the email,' Matt said, trying his level best not to sound psychotic. 'And it did say *Where?* underneath.'

'Well, if it did, you need to find out who the hell thought to let you know she was gone, before the yokels here even knew she was missing.' He grabbed his jacket and said his goodbyes to the old man and the barmaid. He threw Matt a glance before heading out the door.

Matt slumped back in the seat and tried the link one more time. That cheeky little smiley was winking at him again. 'Oh piss off, rainbow,' he said and flung the phone back in his pocket. He headed out to the deserted streets and noticed the lights were still on in the police station. He headed to the car park, which now had only one vehicle in it. His.

And no matter how much he looked to the skies, he saw no more Chinese lanterns. It appeared that all the 'old selves' of the Hobbs Hill faithful had finally been extinguished. Ready to become new creations at the baptism next Sunday. He thought of Nicola, out in the cold woods maybe, somewhere in the dark, shivering. Or not shivering at all, because corpses don't. He tutted at his morbid mind and headed to the car. To take his mind off it all he tallied up the crosses he saw as he drove home, but quickly lost count.

CHAPTER FIFTEEN

The car climbed the lonely track to her house, twigs and branches fingering the windows with eager squeaks. Gradually he saw the tip of the crooked chimney, glowing under the moon. One loose brick seemed eager to tumble. He pulled up outside her place, crunching into ridges of dried mud.

Tabitha Clarke lived about four miles up a winding little dirt track out of Hobbs Hill. Out of sight. Exactly how she liked it.

It was an ancient farmhouse made of crumbling, leaning stone, with no phone line or decent plumbing. It was a place where she could paint her pictures in relative solitude. He'd seen some of her pieces in a local shop. Apparently she used to have swanky shows in London, which didn't surprise him. That was a twisted city. Personally he didn't care for her work. Not one bit.

His car radio was playing 'You've Got a Friend' by James Taylor. But the melody clicked off as he killed the engine and turned off the headlights. He sat for a moment, feeling the darkness wrapping itself around the car. Pictured Nicola Knox crawling on all fours through the hard, cracked soil to greet him.

Another tremble crept through his hand so he glared at it, willing the shivers to stop. Somehow his body obeyed. He opened up the glovebox, which contained, of all things, gloves. Black waterproof

Thinsulate things he'd bought from Millets in a sale. Thick, like astronaut mitts. He yanked them on.

'Won't be long,' he whispered as he stepped out of the car.

Once again, he was shocked by the silence here. When you lived in Hobbs Hill long enough you expected the constant sound of the waterfall to be literally everywhere in the world. But up here, out of its range, the world was strangely bare and dry. Boring, in other words.

She had a wooden porch with steps that groaned and creaked when he stood on them. He glanced back at the car for reassurance. *Get on with it.*

Breath whistled in his nose. He leant forward, then knocked three times. He always did three knocks on doors, for as long as he could remember. Two never seemed enough and four was one too many.

It took her ages to get to the door, but then he expected that. When it finally opened and light flooded onto him she just sighed and hovered in the doorway. She had a blue silk headscarf wrapped tight against the curve of her head, and he could see that round the back she was just as she said she'd be. Completely bald. How weird she looked. How alien.

'Hi, Tabby.'

'It's Tabitha,' she said, eyes blue and piercing.

'Sorry.'

'You do know this is difficult for me. Don't you?'

'Of course. I'm sure it's very odd.'

'Odd . . . yes.'

'So are you going to let me in?'

She nodded, closing her eyes as if it hurt to move her head. Then she stepped back from the door.

When he went inside, the place smelt of some fancy incense, the type that stinks out those weirdo New Age shops he'd seen with the candles and the crystals and the idiots. The smell was strong enough to sting his nose.

The hallway was lined with her paintings. Her usual style: naked women wrapped around trees. They weren't even attractive women, either, just fat old heifers with folds and bulges and hidden rivers of body sweat. The pictures made his flesh crawl because fat people annoyed him almost as much as anorexics.

She led him to the kitchen and they sat down at the heavy oak table.

'Why are you wearing gloves?' she said. 'It's summer, for crying out loud.'

He said, 'I've got a skin condition. The doctor told me to keep them covered.'

She laughed at that. 'Drink?'

'No thanks.'

'Well, I will.' She'd already set two glasses out in the centre of the table. She grabbed one of them with a disappointed grunt and pretty much threw it back into the cupboard, slamming the door shut to stop it from tumbling back out. With her thumb she flicked the top off a half-bottle of vodka. The red metal cap spun, lifted and fell off onto the floor. A nifty little move.

'You learn that in London?' he said.

She looked at him as if he was a moron. She didn't pick the bottle cap up, just ignored it and sloshed a few measures out for herself.

'So how are you feeling, Tabitha?'

She raised her glass. 'I feel like someone shoved a rat down my mouth when I was sleeping and now it's eating me from the inside out. That's how I feel.' She threw the vodka back down her throat and her face seemed to spasm as it went down. She poured another straight away but hung onto it for now.

'How's the chemo going?'

'Smashing, thanks. They say I might have another year in me. Doctor Raglan says I might even reach the big five-oh.' She held up her drink like it was a toast.

He said nothing.

'If this were the sixteenth century I'd be the very image of longevity.' She followed that with a bitter chuckle then swallowed half of the vodka in one wincing gulp.

'Tabitha. You asked me to come. Do you want me here or not?'

Her tense shoulders seemed to shrivel and her voice turned softer. 'I wouldn't have asked you if I didn't want you to come.'

'Then how would you like to proceed?'

'You talk like a solicitor.'

He sat more upright and smiled. 'Do I?'

She tossed the rest of the liquid down her throat. He was about to tell her to slow down, but he stopped himself. If she was drunk she'd be easier to handle. Easier to catch if she somehow wriggled away.

'If you want God to heal you of your cancer, you're going to have to accept something first.'

'And what's that?'

'Well, you need to become a Christian, don't you? Do that and then I'm sure he'll consider making you better.'

He saw a tear bulge out of her eye and roll down her cheek. 'Christ,' she said. 'I've been reduced to this.'

'You know God can use the worst of circumstances to finally get our attention.'

'Oh, he's got my attention, I'll give him that.' She wiped the tear away then spat dark brown phlegm into a handkerchief. She folded it neatly and slipped it into her cardigan pocket.

'Do you repent of your sin?'

She looked at him, pursing her lips. A sort of quiet desperation ticking through her features.

'Do you repent of being a lesbian?'

Another tear rolled down her cheek followed by a long silence. Somewhere in the house a clock was ticking.

'Yes.' The word finally came out in a single sob, which she stopped dead before it had fully formed. She composed herself. 'If it takes the pain away.'

'Do you mean that?'

She closed her eyes and nodded. Another tear left a glistening trail.

'Will you burn your paintings, Tabitha?'

Her eyes flicked open. 'Why? Why would that be necessary?'

'Because they're flesh. They're the old you.'

She stared at him with such distaste that he thought she might lunge for him at any second, she might even try to rub her cancer all over him. But she didn't. Her face settled. 'If my doctor says I'm clear I swear to you that I'll burn the lot of them. But not before, do you understand?'

'Fair enough.'

'Not before.' She swallowed another vodka and slammed the empty glass on the table in what must have been defiance. That was at least five measures she'd had, just since he'd arrived. He could see her eyes were getting glassy and the lids hung over a little more.

'Then I think we're ready,' he said.

'So do we just pray or something? Should I kneel?'

'Not quite. First we fill the bath.' He pushed his chair back and it scraped along the wooden floor.

'Pardon me?'

'Your bathroom. Where is it?'

A slurred giggle rippled through her lips. 'And why the hell are we filling the bath?'

'So I can baptise you, Tabby.'

She let out a shriek of hollow laughter. Her eyes glistened with tears. 'You're serious?'

'Always,' he nodded. 'Take my hand.'

She looked at his outstretched glove for a few seconds, then after taking a breath she slipped hers into his and stood up. He didn't like touching a lesbian hand, not one bit. It looked slimy. He wondered what seedy little things these fingers had done but it pleased him that they'd be clean soon.

She put the lid of the toilet down and sat on it as he knelt by the bath. Her knees pulled together, body resigned and folded in on itself. 'I'm not getting undressed.'

'That won't be necessary.'

They sat in silence while the bath filled.

Steam from the hot tap started to wisp around them like ghosts, fogging the mirrors. While she waited she leant forward on the toilet and started to draw something in the mirror over the sink. A perfectly formed tree, the start of a naked fat lady. She smirked when she saw him looking and rubbed it away with the back of her hand. 'All gone,' she said.

'Good.'

'Just so you know, this is the weirdest moment of my life. And believe me, I went to Art School so that's saying something.'

He twisted the taps closed. 'Okay. I'm ready.'

When he looked at her, the smirk was gone. She just stared at the water as it quaked against the sides of the bath.

'Do you really think this will cure me?'

'Trust me.'

'Then look away for a second.'

'What?'

'Look away.'

'Why?'

'Just do it. Please.'

He frowned and didn't like it, but then he realised he could turn and still catch her outline reflected in the curve of the taps.

He shifted completely away from her but he was still watching.

She sat upright on the toilet, her shape twisted in the chrome like a circus freak. Then she put her hands gently together. Bowed her head. He heard faint whispering from over his shoulder. She was praying. *My God. Praying on her own!* The sudden glimmer of her faith set him on fire.

'It's going to be okay, Tabby. I promise.' He spun back round, excited. She stood up straight, stepped toward him. He moved to the side as she climbed in. 'I've made it nice and warm. It's cosy.'

Her green argyle sock turned instantly black in the water. She winced a little.

'Too hot?'

'It's fine. It's fine. Let's just get this over with. So you want me to sit?'

'Yeah.'

She sunk her body into the water. Slowly. He could see her biting her lip as she did it, moving like it was obviously painful for her. She pushed a trembling hand to the headscarf and had to claw it off her head. A smooth bald scalp appeared as the headscarf slipped off. A few single hairs sprang out like wires. Yuk! The full reveal of her hairless head made her nose and top lip appear suddenly huge, as though they were jutting out with an overbite. Her eyes instantly looked more sunken.

She's a gargoyle, he thought, almost wanting to laugh.

'Shouldn't you take your gloves off?' she said, throat suddenly rattling with phlegm. 'Believe me, catching your skin infection's the least of my worries.'

'Shhhh.' He pulled out his Bible. 'Do you confess Jesus Christ as your Lord and Saviour?'

'Yes.'

'And do you repent of your sin and trust in him for eternal life?'

She waited for a moment before answering.

'Tabby?'

'Yes. I repent.'

'Then Tabitha Tansy Clarke,' he slipped his gloved hand over her head and put the other on her shoulder, 'I baptise you in the name of the Father.'

He immediately pushed her down and she slid quickly, squinting her eyes closed. She was fully under in about a second. Her knees came up out of the water. That wasn't ideal because she should really be fully immersed but he figured God would understand. It felt irregular, but valid.

She came back up with a gasp.

'And the Son—'

Down again before she'd even grabbed a breath. She came back up with a heaving, aching sound of pain. 'Give me a second to breathe—'

'And the Holy Spirit.'

He pushed her down one more time.

When she came up out of the water he couldn't tell if she was smiling or just wheezing in agony.

She winced then spluttered out the words, 'Is that it?'

He should have kept her under then, but he figured she needed a little reassurance before it happened. That felt like the gracious thing to do. So he leant in and spoke directly into her ear. 'Tabitha. Trust me. Heaven is healing.' Water from her hair touched the bridge of his nose. It made his spine shiver from top to bottom. She may have been pretty when she was younger, with hair. 'Do you understand? Heaven is healing.'

'But I don't feel anything. Shouldn't I be feeling—'

'Heaven is healing,' he whispered and pushed as hard as he could. She went under a fourth time, her words swamped in the water, her open mouth filled up. He felt her body jolt against him, hard and panicked. Because she knew. She knew that this time she wasn't coming back up.

Her chest, stomach and hips suddenly surged up out of the water and her legs started to kick out, but he kept the head down. One of her fists pounded into the side of the bath banging, banging, BANGING, while the other scrambled up like a mad spider, fingers scraping across his arms, tugging at his shirt.

A huge bubble of air peeled her lips back and shot out of her mouth, popping on the surface.

She was kicking at the taps with her feet but her sock slipped off the chrome. It sent her heel smashing into one of the white tiles. Three sudden cracks shot across it. He thought she was going to kick both taps clean off until he realised what she was doing.

She was trying to hook her foot behind the chain of the plug.

The end of her toes suddenly swooped under the chain. His mouth dropped open.

She's pulling it.

He gasped out in panic, and craned his head over his shoulder. 'Help!' he shouted.

Her knee rose up, the chain became taut.

'*Help!*'

Then the gurgling sound. That hideous, terrifying gurgling sound of the bath emptying. She lifted her foot and the plug came springing out of the water, dripping and dangling.

'*Stephen, for God's sake! Help me!*'

He kept pushing her down and could tell she was getting weaker. But if he reached for the plug to stick it back in he'd need to take his hands off her shoulders and head. She might rise up and sink her queer teeth into his throat. He didn't know what else to do.

He moved both of his gloved hands from her head and shoulder and quickly slipped them round her neck. He pressed both thumbs into her throat, keeping her under as the water went down slowly.

'Stephen! *Please!*'

She made a hideous muffled roar from under the water, and tiny bubbles filled with her screams, popped on the surface. Her gargoyle eyes glared at him from beneath the surface.

The water was going down . . . down . . . down . . .

Any minute and the tip of her nose would be out. He pressed his thumbs in much harder and suddenly felt something in her throat click and collapse under the pressure. The feeling sent a jolt of nausea through his body.

'Stephen!'

The bathroom door finally slammed open and Stephen raced into the room. 'The plug's out, you dick.'

'Put it back in. Please.'

'*You* do it.'

'I can't, she'll get up.'

'She's half dead. Put the bloody plug back in and I'll keep an eye out.'

He took a deep breath and pulled his hands from her throat. The skin seemed to grow dark purple by the second so he must have burst something. There was one other detail that disturbed him no end – her left eye had almost swollen out of its socket and he could barely look away from it. He grabbed the plug and pushed it back into its hole. It took a few attempts because of the chunky gloves. When it finally sunk into place he span the hot and cold taps on full pelt.

Then he screamed.

Her hand shot suddenly out from the water, flinging drops everywhere. She grabbed the side of the bath.

'Push her down!' Stephen said. 'Sit on the bitch, if you have to.'

He slammed his hands back on her shoulders, but this time it wasn't hard to keep her under.

The glugging of the emptying bath stopped as the taps hammered in. Finally the water began to rise.

He just kept her there. The kicking, the grabbing, grew laboured and spasmodic. Still holding her, he leant against the bathtub; after what seemed like a long time bubbles stopped coming from Tabitha's mouth, and she was still. Peaceful. That single evil eye, misting into a glass marble as her soul shook off its skin.

He went to pull his aching hands away, thumbs hot with pain. But Stephen shook his head. 'Wait,' he said. 'Just wait.'

He did as he was told and waited, trying hard not to cry but he couldn't stop it. He wept, willing her to be completely dead this time. Arms stinging with the effort of it all. He tried not to look at Stephen but he could feel those eyes digging into his back, monitoring his weakness.

He went to vomit.

'Don't you dare,' Stephen said. 'Now come on. Let's get her in the car.'

CHAPTER SIXTEEN

It was a pretty quirky way to start a holiday, searching through the woods for the body of a dead anorexic girl. They'd given him a tool, too. Or more specifically a broom shank to slap the branches and tall grass back. At times he felt like Indiana Jones only in a much more grim, depressing instalment of the franchise.

He'd seen dead bodies before. Lots of them in fact. But he still found that his heart froze in his chest when the stick whacked against something soft in the brush. It was usually a moist mound of earth or in one case an abandoned black bin bag full of porn mags, sticky with sperm and insects. Seems like he'd discovered Hobbs Hill's under-the-radar sex scene, hidden near the hollow of a tree.

He called PC Taylor over to check it out. When Taylor saw what was in the bag he audibly gulped then shook his head in disgust. But he still gazed at the covers, adjusting his glasses. They were bagged as evidence and the search resumed.

They were sweeping the fields and woods in a single line, edging across with almost synchronised steps. Every now and again Sergeant Miller would wander over to see what Matt was up to. Matt certainly felt . . . surveilled, if that was even a word. Maybe Miller thought that the strange and eager professor from London might come across a body and hide it up his jumper. Replace it with a stupid picture of a rainbow.

They finished the search at two in the afternoon and, like the others, Matt was shattered. He sat against a tree and held a cold bottle of coke to his forehead as Miller announced that the team at the lake hadn't come up with anything either. Though, Miller admitted, it wasn't a full drag through the water. That'd come later if, 'God forbid', they still needed it.

A few people looked positively disappointed that they hadn't come up with a corpse, as though they'd gone on a specialist safari and hadn't got to photograph the rarest animal. But the trudge in most of their feet wasn't disappointment. It was depression. A sense of collective foreboding that could freeze facial muscles on a hot day. Because these were friends and family. Their kids went to the same school as Nicola. At one point a few of them swooped around a large lady who was bent over the bonnet of a car. He guessed it was Nicola's mother. He could hear her sobbing as he slipped back into his car and heard that wailing on repeat in his short-term memory long after he'd driven away and headed up the leafy roads to the cottage.

He was halfway down their dirt track when he saw Chris's son Ben Kelly rumbling along the road on a white mountain bike, away from the cottage. No helmet. Matt slowed the car so he wouldn't wipe the lad out and he gave a gentle toot of the horn. Ben looked over and nodded with a smile. Both hands locked on the handlebars. He slowed the car to talk, but Ben was already bombing through the gravel.

When Matt got back he asked what Ben had wanted. He'd just dropped off an SD card for Lucy, packed with Christian albums that he was recommending. The surprising part? She was so keen to hear them. She slipped awkwardly past Matt with the card clutched to her chest, hiding it from him. Like it was some sort of contraband propaganda that he would stamp on if he saw it.

They were all going out for the afternoon but there was still an hour before they headed off. So he took his laptop into the garden and flipped it open. He clicked to the desktop and spotted the Word file for his book, batting its sad little eyes like a neglected toddler. '*In Our Image: The Gods We Tend To Invent*'.

He opened it up. Stared at the flashing cursor, ticking on and off like the countdown on a thermonuclear bomb. He clicked it off and decided it was a cue for more coffee.

In Our Image was turning out to be the proverbial 'difficult second album'. The most annoying part was that it actually was his first.

How eagerly he'd pitched his grand vision on the 'psychology of religious invention' and the 'nature of reality denial inherent in all religious belief'. The proposal had slid out of him easily, like butter across plastic. On a warm day. And so had writing the actual book. At least at first. Until it suddenly felt like passing gravel. It scared him that he might be one of those chumps that gets a publishing deal and suddenly finds he can't work out 'how to say stuff'.

He came back with his coffee and jabbed at the cursor, and spoke in a low Vader tone. 'Right, you little twerp. I have you now.' But he needn't have bothered.

Every time the keys clicked, unpleasant little mind-shots flashed into his head. Of him whacking down his stick and hitting Nicola Knox on the head. And when he tried to ignore it the clicks became Wren, Amelia or Lucy in the grass, with blue skin and dry, chapped lips.

Ten minutes of this and he'd had enough. He called Amelia over and they had one of their YouTube sessions. She sat on his knee as they watched clips of people falling over, cats chasing laser beams. *You've Been Framed* stuff. Anything to shake the grim things away.

The plan was for him and Wren to work in the mornings, and then go out in the afternoons. So over the next few days, from one in the afternoon, they ended up devouring everything fun, relaxing or touristy they could find. It was with a certain delicious irony that Hobbs Hill turned out to be named after Hobbs, the old English word for devil. He'd suspected as much, but it was fun to find out he was right. And he wasn't surprised, either, to find that the church had started a campaign to change the village name to something more heavenly. Their first choice . . . ye Gads! . . . *High Hopes*. Sounded like a 90s American sitcom. He preferred Hobbs Hill. It sounded folksy and English and odd.

They visited the so-called Devil's Den (reason number two for the name change campaign) which was a decent-sized cave *behind* the waterfall itself. They had built a little viewing platform in there. Just some stone steps and a metal rail overlooking a large hole in the rock. But with the waterfall gushing down at the mouth of it all, it was actually pretty decent. A guy sat in a wooden booth at the top of the stone staircase, selling tickets. He said the cave was where old Hobbs himself washed his toes when the moon was right. But, Matt noticed, that wasn't mentioned in the floppy yellow pamphlet. It was all about the wonders of the natural world, and he spotted the word 'creation' twice.

Then they had a barbecue up on the top of the ridge, where you could follow the river as it toppled over the edge and became Cooper's Force Waterfall. Keeping with family tradition they bought a magnet to add to their fridge collection. This one said, '*I Fell for the Falls*' on it.

All in all, the days were good here. And he got a bunch of time to laze in the bath, reading H. G. Wells. That was always welcome. But there were a few odd things too.

For a start, the cottage didn't have any curtains whatsoever. No blinds either. Nobody had realised this when they first arrived, until the night started falling. The owners, the Shores, must have figured the place was too deep in the woods to warrant them. Or perhaps they were so perfect-looking they were more than happy to swing their dicks for the woodland sprites. But Matt wasn't so keen. In their bedroom, he had to drape a bed sheet across two unlit floor lamps to give them at least some privacy. Maybe he'd lived in the city too long but he didn't fancy some pervy local jogger climbing a tree and salivating while he and his wife were making love on that massive, fairy-tale bed. Matt was old-fashioned that way.

The other slightly weird thing was Nicola Knox's face. It started to stare out from shop windows and telegraph poles on 'Missing' posters, yet no matter how much he clicked the email link on his phone or computer screen he got nothing but a rainbow. It made him wonder if who he'd seen there might have been someone else, after all. The searches went on and he joined them a few more times, though he could tell by the way people were whacking their sticks that hope was fading.

All things considered, it had been a surprisingly good holiday up till then. But the next day was a Saturday. And that's when things began to change.

CHAPTER SEVENTEEN

Seven-thirty in the morning and Matt was brushing his teeth over the sink. The bathroom window was wide open in front of him. His chest was bared to the trees. He felt earthy. Tarzan's monkey, Cheetah, might suddenly swing in, slink a hairy arm around his shoulder and kiss him on the cheek. The thought made him look down, stop brushing and suck his gut in.

When it didn't contract as much as he expected he knew it was time for a run.

He was hurrying up the scrubbing while he listened to the birds when he spotted Chris Kelly's silver Audi creeping through the tree trunks and up the dirt road. Matt swilled some water, spat it out and quickly stepped into his running shorts. By the time he'd pulled his last sock on, there was a rattling knock at the door.

Chris stood on the doorstep clutching a paper bag splitting at the seams with croissants. 'Well aren't you looking aerobic.'

'Morning, Chris.' Matt yawned and stepped back to let him in. The smell from the bag wafted under his nose.

He lifted it and theatrically licked his lips. 'Kids up? Is Wren?'

'Not yet. Just me. I thought I might go for an early run. You want to come?'

'Pah! Forget that. You're on holiday. Besides . . . you need some carbs first and *then* you can burn them off.'

Matt took another sniff, deep and long. 'Okay, I'm convinced. I'll call the others down.'

'No.' Chris quickly shook his head. 'Don't do that. How about we talk? Just you and me. Seems like we haven't had a decent chance for a catch up yet. In fact, anyone'd think you were avoiding me.'

Matt frowned. 'Oh. Sorry. Just a bit busy. It was nice to see Ben here the other day.'

'Ah, yes. Dropped off a bit of muzak, I hear? Always willing to help, that lad.'

Chris padded into the kitchen and Matt followed. He poured out a couple of coffees while Chris grabbed plates and knives. He seemed to know where everything was.

They headed outside onto the patio and Matt sat at the table, carved from teak wood. It was small and rectangular. Social etiquette would normally dictate that Chris would grab a seat on the opposite side. But he didn't. He scraped up a chair next to Matt, fairly close, so that the two of them were looking out across the garden and the deep woods beyond.

For a minute or two they didn't speak. They just ate the food. There was just birdsong in the air along with the tongue slaps and swallows, knives clinking the plates. Silence wasn't a problem for Matt but Chris was the type who'd fill gaps in conversation like they were holes in a boat. Yet it was Matt who finally spoke first.

'What's with all the crosses,' he said, 'in the shop windows?'

'Ah, you noticed them?'

'They're everywhere. I feel like I'm in Transylvania.'

'The crosses are just us raising our profile. It's part of the vision to grow the church. Anyone with a cross in their window is a member of our congregation . . . and you've heard how many people we get on a Sunday, haven't you?'

'Yes,' but he'll tell me anyway.

'Three hundred. But then you'll see it all for yourself tomorrow.' He paused. 'You *are* still coming in the morning, aren't you?'

'Yes.'

'All of you?'

'Yes.'

'And you'll stay for the whole thing?'

'Yes, chef.'

'And the videogames tournament today . . . Billy the youthworker says your girls are coming?'

'Yes, yes, yes, yes,' Matt nodded.

'Perfect.' Chris sat back and popped his lips. 'Bottom line is the crosses are there because we're proud of Jesus and refuse to hide him. We want him . . . everywhere.' He ran his palm across the air like a magician's assistant. 'Everywhere!'

'There're so many of them I half expect to see Jesus creeping through the woods at night.'

Chris screwed up his face. 'Jesus doesn't need to creep.'

'No?' Matt cleared his throat. 'What rough beast, its hour come round at last, slouches toward Bethlehem to be born?'

'What a horrible thing to say.'

'Relax, it's a poem. And it's by Yeats, not me.'

They were quiet for a moment.

'Funny you should say that though . . .' Chris flicked his eyes to the woods and back. 'I reckon things do creep around here. Despite the prettiness and the waterfall, this place has . . . a dark heart. Like there's something under the surface. Something demonic. There's lots of places like that. My last place was definitely like that. And here too. There's still a lot of unsaved people in this village. Lots of shadows.'

'And it's the non-believers that are automatically in darkness, is it?'

'Of course.'

'You ever think it might be the other way around? That maybe you're wrong and everyone else is in the light?'

He shook his head slowly. 'Never. The kingdom of darkness is for people who haven't got time for God or who've turned their backs on him.'

'Like me?'

Chris didn't hesitate. 'Yes. Just like you. But now you're here, who knows? Maybe the church might rub—'

Matt pushed back his seat, looked at him straight, glad that the time had come for him to finally ask his next question. 'Is that why you got Wren up here? Did you Google me or something and find I was married to an architect? Did you get me here just to save me from hell? To save her?'

Chris bit his lip, almost smirking. 'And if I did? What if God told me he wants you back?'

Matt blew out an uneasy breath, suddenly feeling deflated on Wren's behalf. He looked back at the house where she was still sleeping, and whispered, 'Look, if that's the case then I suggest you save your renovation money for some other backsliders . . . or on second thoughts, give her the job and pay her extra.'

'You are incredibly jumpy about God.' Chris sniffed. 'I mean, do you even believe in him any more?'

'Nope.'

'But your kids. You still had them baptised, right? Even if you don't—'

'Wrong.'

Chris actually gasped and clattered his knife loudly on the plate. 'Very funny. Ha, ha.'

'They aren't baptised. Neither of them. So what?'

Chris shook his head slowly. 'Then you're playing with fire. I mean they're your *kids*.'

'Exactly. They're people, not Tamagotchis I have to program. If they want to be baptised one day then fine. But I'm not going to force it on them. I think they call that brainwashing. Which is only one step away from drinking the Kool-Aid, as they say.'

'And if they get hit by a bus tomorrow? Or have a heart attack? They could wind up dead like poor little Nicola Knox.'

Matt shot him a look. 'Who hasn't been found. Who might have just run away.'

'You *believe* that?' Chris actually laughed. 'Seriously, though, how would you feel if your unbaptised daughters died without—'

'Alright, Chris,' Matt slammed his empty coffee cup down on the table, 'number one. Talking about my daughters' possible deaths is not my idea of croissant-worthy chit-chat. And second, would splashing them with water really make any difference anyway? I mean, since when did baptism become the be-all and end-all? They didn't teach us that at college. It's a symbol. Nothing more.'

'I'm finding that there's a lot of things they didn't teach us.' Chris brought his elbow on the table and rested his chin on his fist. 'Something must have happened to make you like this. Come on, you can tell me.'

'Let's just say I got a chance to stare long and deep into that dark heart you keep talking about.'

'And what did you see?'

Matt paused for a moment, and then thought, oh what the hell. At least telling Chris the story would get him off his back. Make him understand. And besides, some stupid delusional cell of his brain was making him see his mum over by the roses with her hands clasped together, nodding eagerly for him to tell.

CHAPTER EIGHTEEN

Just shifting his focus onto the subject seemed to make the forest grow quiet.

'So after college I got ordained . . . and I started working for a church in Luton. An Independent Evangelical Church. Not linked to any denomination. Thought I could do some good work there.'

'And did you?'

'Well, I prayed for a lot of people, preached a lot of sermons. Buried or cremated about two minibuses-worth of pensioners. A few younger ones as well. And a baby called Shenoa.'

'Ouch.' Chris twisted his mouth into a grimace. 'I've done a few of those. Small coffins.'

An image of the little box with a pink tulip on it scuttled across his brain like a persistent spider he could never get rid of.

'So did you like it? Being the minister I mean?'

'I liked it less and less because everyone kept wanting me to be black and white all the time. They wanted absolute truths, constantly. God *absolutely* exists. Jesus is *absolutely* the only way to heaven. Homosexuals are *absolutely* raging perverts.'

'And you struggled with that?'

'Yes! Because doctrine gets more . . . well . . . it gets more grey the older you get.'

'Interesting. I find it's the opposite. The older I get, the more clear it all is.'

Matt looked at him for a moment, studying his face and eyes.

'But,' Chris said, 'you can be grey in the Church, surely? You can be honest about your doubts in a pulpit, don't you think?'

'No, you can't. People don't want that. They don't want to hear someone preach a sermon about God and then admit he's not even sure if the guy exists. They want absolutes, more and more these days they want that.'

'So that's why you jacked it in?'

'It's half of the reason, yes.'

'Your suspension . . .' Chris poured them both another coffee while he waited for the answer. Classic pastoral gambit, that was. Grease the wheels of sorrow with caffeine. He heard his mother whispering in his ear.

Go ahead, son. It's okay.

'I'd been a minister for about five years and my mum still lived in the house I grew up in. Up in Dunwich, overlooking the sea.'

Chris audibly moaned. 'Oh, I'd love a pastorate by the sea.'

'Yeah, well the church she went to started this hosting programme. The congregation took homeless people into their houses until government accommodation came up.'

'What a wonderful idea.'

'It was a bloody stupid idea. Stupid. Totally irresponsible. This little church had no idea what they were doing. They were trying to be good Samaritans to some seriously messed up people. It was completely naïve.'

Chris sat quietly.

'She was assigned one of these "lodgers". A guy in his late twenties called Ian Douglas Pendle. From Glasgow. As far as the church knew, he was just some young bloke down on his luck. Said he needed a place to stay for a few days until his sister could take him in. But of course he had no sister. The church had no idea what they were doing. They did no research on him.' Matt turned to Chris. 'Turns out he was a paranoid schizophrenic and they asked my mum to take him into her home. Her *home*.'

Chris seemed to know enough to keep quiet, and Matt realised that for the first time that he could remember Chris Kelly had given somebody else the centre stage.

'She told me about this Pendle guy on the phone. I said I wasn't keen on her taking him in but she said to stop being so selfish, and that she was only doing what Jesus would have done. The church were behind it. She got upset on the phone. Said she was "worried for my soul". So I decided to drive up there.'

'And something happened?'

'I turned up late on a Sunday afternoon. I would have got there earlier but I had a church service. Harvest festival . . . I mean, what a joke. Sixty minutes of wasted time praising God for local farmers, even though every one of us bought imported apples from the nearest Tesco. By the time I finished and drove up to Dunwich . . . it was already too late.'

Matt took a breath and was surprised at how fast his heart was beating. It wasn't like this was the first time he'd told this story but as he sat under these trees, in this strange little village, it almost felt like the place itself was dragging the tale out of him whether he liked it or not.

'The radio was on. Elvis was singing "Love Me Tender". I could hear it coming from the kitchen diner but straight away I knew something wasn't right.'

'Go on.'

'I pushed the door open and there she was. My mum. Two plates of food sat on the table untouched. She'd cooked Pendle a Sunday roast. A little pile of presents sat on the table for him. A woolly hat, a pair of gloves. Some deodorant. The salt shaker was knocked over and had spilt against her hand. It must have happened just as they were starting to eat.' Matt lifted both hands and placed them flat on the table. He wasn't sure why. 'For whatever reason Pendle opened up her kitchen scissors and attacked her with them.'

Chris pulled in a quick breath.

'There were three wounds. In the front of her throat.' Matt reached up, pointing a finger an inch to the right of his windpipe. 'Pendle reached over the table and just shoved it in her. Just like that. She fell forward and he stabbed her two more times. One in her left shoulder, the other in the top of her scalp. She bled to death. Never even moved from her chair.'

'And Pendle. Did they catch him?'

'Oh, he was still there. I could hear him breathing heavily in the lounge. I went in and he was sitting on her chair, stark-naked with a raging hard on. He was talking and pointing at the TV when it wasn't even switched on. He spotted me come in and he saw my dog collar. I'd left it on because I knew my mum loved to see me in it—' Matt suddenly paused and saw her face. The tilt of the head, the chin out with pride. The look she had on Sizewell beach, as she held out the towel after he was baptised. The first time he'd told Wren this tale, this was the point he'd cried. But he wasn't about to do that now. He moved on. 'Pendle saw the dog collar and he just . . . well he just stopped talking and he laughed at me.'

The memory of it slipped its fingers around Matt and tugged him backwards. Pendle sitting there on that high-backed chair with his balls resting on the lip of the same seat his mum had sat on through weekly phone calls to him. Where she'd watch old episodes of *Dallas* and *Columbo*.

He couldn't see it, but the unmistakeable smell of faeces was mixing with the blood-metal reek from the kitchen. He remembered how he'd jumped when the kitchen scissors slipped off the arm of the chair and bounced on the carpet. Pendle creaked his eyes up to meet his and started singing that damn, disgusting, presumptive little hymn. Laughing in the gaps.

Amazing Grace, how sweet the sound.
That saved (not 'will save' but saved – past tense) *a wretch like me.*
I once was lost but now I'm found.
Was blind, but now I see.

'Pendle opened up his hand and showed me what he was holding,' Matt said, quietly. 'It was my mum's bottom lip. He'd cut them both off. He'd eaten the top one already.'

'Dear God.'

'I grabbed the bastard's throat. Yanked him out of the chair and I beat the living crap out of him. I mean, I went for it. At one point I even got the scissors from the floor and pushed them up under his chin. And I would have done it, you know? Shoved it right up there. But someone from her church turned up at the house and saw me doing it. Dragged me off and checked if *he* was alright. Then they reported me. Despite the circumstances, the church suspended me for what they called my lack of forgiveness and restraint.'

'Man, that's harsh.'

'Yeah, weird isn't it? That I struggled to forgive the guy who cut my mum's lips off.' He looked down at his lap and slowly brushed the food crumbs away.

'And Pendle?'

'He was charged. Put in a secure psychiatric ward. He asked some chaplain to pray with him to become a Christian, which apparently I was supposed to be pleased about. Then another inmate strangled him one afternoon and killed him. When I heard that it was the only time I thought that maybe God might be real after all.' Matt leant back. 'But that thought didn't last long. Anyway, after a while I just thought screw them and I never went back. Bummed around for a bit. Then got into teaching instead. And that's that.'

Chris paused. 'Listen, can I ask you a question?'

'Go ahead.'

'You say that you don't believe in God any more.'

'Yeah. Funny, that.'

'Then let me ask you this. Do you *want* to believe in him? Despite what you've been through. Despite your doubts. Do you still want to believe that there's . . . something else?'

Matt waited. 'That's an irrelevant question.'

'No, it's not. Maybe that's why he brought us back together. So I could show you he still—'

'It's *irrelevant*,' Matt said with a snap. 'He either exists or he doesn't, regardless of whether I want him to, or anyone else. And when you see your mother for the last time and you lift her head and there's a ragged little hole where her mouth used to be, you start being more logical about life, Chris. Because a world where that happens makes more sense when there isn't a God in it.'

The back stable-style door of the cottage suddenly rattled on its hinge and Wren stepped out in a dressing gown, holding an empty plate and cup. 'I smell calories!' she said, but then she slowed, and her smile faltered. She'd walked into the tension as if it were a tangible fog.

She looked at Matt for a long moment and saw something in his face that she hadn't expected.

She silently mouthed, *you okay?*

Before he could answer Chris reached over and took Matt's hand and covered it with both of his. 'Well, all I can say is thank you, Matt. I really feel privileged that you could tell me all that. I bet you've barely told anyone.'

Matt stared back at him and a realisation started to blossom in his mind, like a toxic flower. This is about him. He's making this about him. This is another notch on his pastoral headboard.

Matt snapped his hand back and for an uneasy second he felt like swinging his fist into Chris's jaw and splaying him out across the roses. But he saw Wren and the hopes of a job in her eyes, so instead he got up from the table and grabbed another croissant, feeling kind of embarrassed for being so . . . bothered. He munched it in big chunks and looked off into the woods. The taste filled his head.

'So how are you liking Wren's designs?' Matt said in a monotone. 'She's good, isn't she?'

It turned out to be the right question because it sparked Chris off on a new tangent. He and Wren started talking enthusiastically about load-bearing struts and graveyard relocation. Eventually, after a string of polite nods, Matt made his excuses. 'I'll leave you to it.' He nodded a thanks to Wren for helping him escape.

He headed back inside and the cottage felt surprisingly dark to his sun-scorched eyes. It almost made him dizzy as he headed to his laptop and flicked it open at the kitchen table. He checked his watch.

Okay, forget the run. He could get showered and dressed and be able to get a few writing hours in this morning. And right now he was in the mood to write it. Today's target: fifteen hundred words on personality type and its effects on religious suckerdom. When that was done and his breakfast went down, he'd definitely go for a run before lunch. Pound out some of that tension on the forest floor.

He was yanking his pile of jotters and notebooks from his other bag when he heard the email chime through. He creaked onto the kitchen stool and clicked on the new mail. No subject. Just another link like the last one. Blue underlined letters floating on a blank white page.

He felt his heart twitch, hurrying a little behind his ribs. He glanced behind him to make sure Chris or the girls weren't lurking. He clicked the link, with little thought to viruses or Trojan horses, and a picture flashed up on screen wth those same white bold capital letters along the bottom.

WHERE?

But this time he wasn't looking at a fourteen-year-old girl. This was a much older woman, probably forties or fifties, a bandana stretched across her smooth-looking head. Ears sticking out, pressed slightly down by the material. There was a snarl on her mouth, a generally pissed-off demeanour.

Before even thinking about it he grabbed his phone and accidentally knocked a pot of pens onto the floor. The phone also chimed the same email's arrival. Then he snapped some pictures of it, which was just as well because when he went to right-click on the picture to Save As, the woman's face had vanished. In its place – zooming from behind – came the rainbow. And the winking little git of a smiley face.

'Ha! Got you,' Matt said and quickly checked the picture on the phone. Still there. He saved it, emailed the photo back to his laptop and held the phone up in front of him, eye to eye with the miserable-looking woman, like some bizarre one-sided Skype call. 'So who on earth are you?'

'You calling your fancy woman?'

Matt spun round to see Chris carrying the plates and cups back into the kitchen followed by Wren. Matt plunged the phone into his bag. 'It's work.'

'Mmmmm,' Chris said.

'Wren, I just need to get changed, then I'll be popping into town for a bit. I want to get a newspaper.'

'I thought you were writing?' she said. That familiar smell of an excuse in the air.

Chris set the plates into the sink, 'Well hey, I'm heading off. Like, right now. I can give you a lift.'

'Nah. I'm fine thanks.'

'Come on, it'll be fun.'

'No, I'm sure you've got lots to do.'

Chris went to speak then just nodded instead, eyes switching to serious. Weighted with a self-imposed authority. 'Actually I do have some major things today. Got a healing session in the afternoon, which is kind of a big deal. Plus this morning I'm off to see Nicola Knox's mum, would you believe. Ever since the little one went missing she's been having me over every day for prayer and counsel. How great is that?'

'Well I'm sure it's rather shitty for her. Her daughter's missing.'

'Ah, but my point is that she doesn't even come to the church! But *this* . . . it's making her think about God. I mean, isn't it amazing how he can bring great things from the bad? Every cloud as they say . . .'

The bubble of anger, quivering in Matt's gut, finally popped. 'You're unbelievable.'

'Excuse me?'

'Basically, as long as you or God or whoever gets a cross over her door, then that girl's death is going to be worth it. Is that right?' He turned to his laptop bag and yanked the zip shut. 'Unbelievable.'

Wren's mouth dropped at him. 'Matt. What's got into you?'

'Hey, Wren,' Chris said, 'it's all okay. Be gentle with old Matty Boy.'

Wow. Chris was a master at inspiring punches.

But Wren ignored Chris and just glared. 'Matt, he's only trying to help.'

'Whatever,' Matt sighed and grabbed his bag. He caught Chris's eye, wondering if the guy would be upset. But he wasn't. In fact he didn't look offended or put out by the comment at all. No look of annoyance, no expectation of an apology. On the contrary, Chris just looked at him. Silent. Lips rising at the edges, in an odd satisfied smile.

CHAPTER NINETEEN

At the police station, Miller's eyes were half closed and he was drumming his fingers on his office desk while Matt rummaged in his bag for his phone.

'You do realise,' Miller said, 'if this is another rainbow then I'm pushing you over our famous waterfall.'

'Just wait.' Matt pulled his phone out and started clicking into his photo gallery. Scrolling through. The mystery woman popped into view, looking as grumpy as ever. He felt a quick beat of relief that the picture hadn't magically evaporated into the SIM card and come back as a rainbow or some cute rabbit hopping over a flower. '*See.*'

He thrust the phone at Miller who had to tap his reading glasses down his nose to see it. He squinted once, then his eyebrows came together. 'When did you get this?'

'About thirty minutes ago.'

'Email it to me.'

'What . . . you mean, right now?'

'Right now. Address is on here.' He pushed his business card across the top of the desk, and they sat in silence while Matt jabbed the address into his phone. They looked at each other until a computer in the corner pinged.

Miller stood up, checked the screen and nodded. 'Thank you.'

Matt shut down the photo gallery on his phone and went to the original email message. He spun the screen round so that Miller could see. 'Look. It's got the same little self-destruct thing going on. I clicked on her picture once. Just once and then—'

'Rainbow.'

Matt nodded. 'So who is she? Do you know her?'

Miller pushed his seat back, reaching over to the wooden coat rack for his uniform jacket.

'Terry, do you know her?'

He pulled on his jacket and paused halfway. 'She's a local.'

'And does she have a name?'

'Why are you getting these emails?'

'I have no clue. Literally.'

Miller pulled the rest of his jacket on and jangled his pockets to check he had his car keys.

'So is this woman missing as well?' Matt said.

'Not that I know of.'

'Then you're going to see her? Right now.'

'Seems wise, don't you think?'

'Then I'll come with you.'

Miller whistled. 'Well aren't you the eager beaver? Is this your idea of adding a little spice to your holiday?'

Matt stood up, looked him in the eye. 'Now just a minute. I'm not role-playing here. I've seen neither of these women before those emails appeared in my inbox. But someone is sending me this stuff and frankly it's getting kind of creepy now.' He paused before speaking again. 'Besides . . . maybe I can help. I told you, I do a little work with the Met. I'll happily give you Larry Forbes's number if you want to—'

'No need.' Terry held up his hand. 'I rang him the day after I met you.'

Matt pulled his head back, surprised but then not surprised all in the same moment. 'And?'

'He reckons you're one of the good guys. His exact words. Says you have a decent eye for detail.'

'Meaning?'

'Meaning grab your stuff. We're going for a drive.'

CHAPTER TWENTY

'Her name's Tabitha Clarke.' Miller turned the police car up the hill and crunched into a lower gear. 'She's a forty-nine-year-old artist living up at the old Spencer farmhouse, a few miles out of Hobbs Hill.'

Police Constable Jim-*Prayer Warrior*-Taylor twisted in his seat so he could speak to Matt in the back. His face looked even more bizarre in profile. 'She moved up here from London. She's got some weird ideas about art.'

'Weird how?'

'She likes to paint pictures of tits and tree trunks,' Miller called back. 'Seems to be her thang.'

Taylor shook his head. 'It's *weeeird*. And not very wholesome if you ask me. It's certainly not art.'

Miller snorted a laugh. 'Thus speaks Brian Sewell here.'

'Who?' Taylor said.

'Tabitha's not well. She's got stomach cancer.'

'Aaaaand . . . ?' Taylor threw a look at Miller. 'Go on. Tell him.'

'Oh, and she's a lesbian, which my colleague doesn't approve of.'

Taylor widened his eyes at Matt. A sort of *can you imagine!* face.

'Life really is vintage out here, Terry,' Matt said.

Miller went on, 'She moved up here with her long-haired lover from Liverpool. And I mean literally. She had a lover, from Liverpool. With long hair. But that woman moved to Zimbabwe last year.'

'To paint pots and pans or something.' Taylor shook his head and laughed. 'I mean, how easy is that?'

'How bad is the cancer?' Matt asked.

'Bad. Last I saw her they were prolonging her life with chemo. Notice I said prolonging, not improving.' Miller went silent and the car started to slow. 'Here we go.'

He turned the car left up a skinny, potholed dirt track, surrounded on each side by nettles and thorns.

'I'll never understand why anyone would want to live up here and not in the village,' Taylor said.

Matt popped his seatbelt free. 'Maybe you guys are too cosmopolitan for her.'

Taylor frowned but Miller let out a low, gravelly laugh.

The car pulled into a small clearing with a crooked-looking farmhouse. A rusty barbed wire fence ran behind it, and beyond that was a wide treeless field, wild grass swaying in the breeze.

They all stepped out.

Matt's mind kept replaying a question, which was difficult to shake. Why was Miller letting him tag along like this? Answer a) because he thought Matt could actually help. Answer b) because he wanted to keep the strange professor in his sights because he was a suspect in this. He decided not to ask which one was right.

The sun was fierce in the sky, more like its nuclear-furnace self than usual. But despite the blaze, the racing breeze made it somehow cold on the hill.

'Tabitha?' Miller called out as they walked towards the house, one hand cupping his mouth like a yodeller. 'Tabitha, it's Sergeant Miller from the village . . . just a courtesy call to see if you're okay.'

No answer.

He stepped up onto the groaning wooden porch and tapped his knuckle on the door. 'Hello? Tabitha? Miss . . . Clarke?'

While they waited, Matt scanned the dirt on the floor, looking for traces of car tracks or footprints. But the muddy floor was dry and cracked. Even Miller's police car hadn't left a trail.

'Let me.' Taylor stepped up next to Miller and pushed on the door gently with an outstretched hand. Matt noticed his fingernails were really long. Creepy banjo-player long. He gave the tiniest tap of those nails on the door; it must have not been shut because it swung wide open, creaking like a Bela Lugosi coffin.

'Miss Clarke?' Taylor called out. 'Hellooooo in there.'

Nothing.

Miller tugged at his nose with his finger and thumb, gave a sniff, 'Let's go in.'

'Don't you need a warrant or something?' Matt said from behind.

The two officers just turned and looked at him with a *you're still here?* expression. 'She might be at risk. Maybe she needs medical attention. And the door was open so we can enter. Is that okay with you, Rebus?'

They didn't give him time to answer. Miller stepped inside first, then the three of them stood in the hallway, taking the place in with all its moth-eaten splendour. It was a jumble sale nightmare of a house. Water-damaged paperback books sat in teetering piles of varying sizes along one side of the wall. The opposite floor was lined with pot plants in various stages of death. One was tipped to the side, dry soil spewing across the dirty paisley carpet.

'Wait here with Matt,' Miller said to Taylor, as he headed off down the corridor, dipping his head into each room. Thirty seconds later he came back. 'There's nobody here.'

'Maybe she's at the hospital?' Matt said.

'Possibly, but I don't think so. She's got a calendar in the kitchen. There's a few blocks next week that say "Chemo". She's drawn skulls across those days. But today's blank.'

'So she's out shopping or something,' Taylor said. 'We should just go.'

Matt closed his eyes and took in a long, deep sniff.

Taylor looked puzzled. 'Er . . . there's nothing cooking in here.'

Matt walked a few steps and dipped his head into the living room. Sniffed again.

'What are you smelling for?' Taylor asked.

'A corpse.'

'*What?*'

'You spend enough time around corpses, you get to recognise the scent. Sticks up your nose for hours.'

Taylor shot a confused glance at Miller. 'What did you say his job was again?'

'University professor,' Miller said.

'I used to be a vicar and I got called into a fair few rooms where old people had died.' He sniffed again, drawing in the memories like a screwed-up Bisto-Kid. Ah, the other side of church ministry. Being called to pray over old ladies who'd been rotting in their beds for weeks, melting into the cushions. All the heart-warming stuff. 'I can't smell much, here.'

'Me either,' Miller said.

Taylor looked at them both, hands on his hips and shaking his head. 'So she's out for a walk or something.'

'Shhhhh,' Miller said.

They moved through each room trying not to touch anything but still sniffing deeply, from bedroom to backroom to dining room. Like visitors in the most depressing stately home on the planet. A wide utility room at the back looked across the field and down towards the valley of Hobbs Hill. It must have been her studio because the floor in that room was smeared in various shades of paint. There were hand marks on the back of a sofa. A few easels leant against the wall and buckets of paintbrushes were strewn across the floor.

In the kitchen they spotted a bottle of vodka in the centre of a wooden table. A single glass tumbler sat alongside it, empty and upturned. They checked the bathroom last and were just about to

144

leave when Matt raised his hand. 'Wait. That's weird.'

'What is?' Miller said.

'Those.' Matt pointed to the end of the deep bath, which had a grimy, queasy ring of body dirt around it. Behind the limescale-encrusted taps was a pile of cheap toilet rolls stacked neatly on top of each other.

'Whoah, hold the phone. Toilet paper in a bathroom,' Taylor said. 'Somebody call Sky News.'

Matt shot him a glance. 'But look *where* they are. Since when do people keep their toilet rolls right under a shower head where they'll get wet?'

'Especially when they have room for them up there.' Miller nodded over at the window where the other rolls were stacked. There was a definite gap where those extras could easily fit. 'They've been moved from up there to the bath.'

'So she's eccentric with her bath habits.' Taylor blew out a breath. 'You know, I'm not being funny but maybe we should just leave. I mean she's liable to turn up any second. If she finds us lurking around her house without a decent reason it'll probably give her a heart attack.'

He was making a perfectly reasonable point and if Miller was the one saying it, Matt would probably have agreed they left. But Miller wasn't budging. Ever since they'd got to this place he'd been scanning the rooms, his jaw clenched with a depth of tone when he spoke. Maybe some police had a little spider sense. Whatever it was, there was a hardness in his eyes that told Matt that he wasn't the only one who felt something was wrong.

Miller leant toward the toilet rolls. He pulled out a pair of white plastic gloves and slapped them on.

'What?' Taylor said. 'Are we in CSI Oxford now, Terry? I never even knew we had those.'

'For God's sake, Taylor, will you just shut up? For one second?'

Taylor pouted and swung his head out of the bathroom. He

looked nervously down the corridor at the wide-open front door, waiting for his worst fear to turn up: an angry, militant lesbian.

Miller only had to pull a few rolls away before he saw a damaged tile. Three cracks. 'So why is this covered up?'

'Cos it's easier than fixing it,' Taylor called through.

'Have you seen this place?' Miller said. 'It's falling apart. There's peeling paint, cracked tiles, dodgy skirting everywhere. So why cover *this* particular bit of damage?'

Taylor swung his head back in, 'I don't know, maybe she needed toilet roll handy when she was in the bath. Chemo does stuff to you. Apparently.'

'The crack in that tile is clearly from an impact,' Matt said.

Taylor came over and put his hands on his knees, bending over. 'So she accidently knocked it with something.'

Matt turned, 'You think? When was the last time you took something big and heavy in the bath?'

He smiled, 'You mean apart from my wife?'

Matt spluttered out a laugh, but it was a nervous-sounding one. The smile that framed it quickly disappeared.

'You two finished?'

'Sorry,' Matt said.

'Taylor. How tall would you say Tabitha was?' Miller asked.

'Er . . . pretty small. About five-four maybe.'

'Yeah, that sounds about right.' Miller, still kneeling, leant towards the tile. 'So if she made that with her foot, then she'd have to be lying down.'

Matt's eyebrows slowly moved up as he started to nod. He leant over the bath, eyes scanning it. 'She'd have been flat on her back to smack that wall.'

Miller quickly stood up, knees creaking like a loud twist of rope. He quickly set the toilet rolls back into position. 'I need to make some calls. Find out if anyone's seen her.'

'You should ask Pastor Chris. He knows pretty much everybody round here,' Taylor said. 'Though I'd bet my youngest kid that Tabitha was an atheist. I mean that much is obvious, what with her sexual choices.'

Matt stared at Taylor. 'Can you hear yourself when you talk?'

'I don't understand what you mean.'

Miller cleared his throat and motioned for them to leave. They headed out of the bathroom and back down the corridor. By now Taylor was out on the porch, soaked in sun and greedily breathing in the now-warm breeze that raced across the fields. He seemed to need a quick lesbo detox. Miller went to step outside too, but he paused on the front step when he noticed Matt still hovering in the middle of the corridor, his feet in a sharp rectangle of sun from the door. He was leaning into rooms and scanning them. 'You lost something?'

'You said Clarke was an artist?'

Miller turned a little more, 'Correct.'

'Well . . . haven't you noticed something?'

Miller stepped back inside while Taylor let out an exasperated breath. 'Gentleman . . . I'll be in the car.'

'We've looked in every room in this house,' Matt said. 'And I've seen a lot of paintbrushes and a couple of easels.'

'So?'

'Well, where are the *paintings*?'

Miller followed Matt's gaze to the bare walls of the corridor. A few picture hooks stood proudly from the peeling wallpaper. Nothing was hanging from them. Nothing except a subtle line of dust marking the dim outline of a frame.

'Were they worth much?' Matt asked.

'Hardly. The shop sells them for like twenty quid a pop. I hardly think this is an art heist.'

'So where are they?'

Still wearing the latex gloves, Miller laid a fingertip on the wall. 'And where's *she*?' He said it quietly, almost a whisper, and Matt

147

noticed an unexpected sound in it. A tremor of stress. Then he snatched his hands back and pulled off his gloves with a rubber snap.

'Better hurry up you two,' Taylor called from the car. 'The heavens are opening.'

As soon as Taylor said it, Matt heard a low rumble of drops hitting the corrugated roof of Tabitha Clarke's creaking, lonely house, and the rectangle of sun he'd been standing in was gone. In its place, he saw a family of woodlice scuttling toward his foot. It felt like as good a cue as any to leave.

CHAPTER TWENTY-ONE

Wren, Lucy and Amelia did that giggle/squeal/giggle sound as they rushed down the path from the cottage. Jackets were pulled over their heads as the rain pounded into them. Matt flung the car doors open and they all bundled inside, gasping and laughing.

'Oh my word.' Wren dragged her fingers through her wet hair. The bright red was now a dark, copper brown. She held up her soaked hand. 'Look at that. That's ten seconds' worth.'

He turned the ignition and the wipers squeaked into life, clearing the windscreen. They watched the cottage for a moment. It pulsed in and out of focus as the heavy drops filled the screen, quicker than the wipers could manage. Around the cottage, around the car, *everywhere* in fact, the shaggy clumps of tree branches were swaying and quaking madly to a long, low hiss of water, like they'd all been flung to the base of that waterfall.

He flicked the lights on, reversed and swung the car round. Then he headed off down the long dirt track, their heads bobbing on the uneven road. The trees on each side grew dense and far-reaching. The rain on the roof made it sound like they were in a helicopter, not a car.

They were halfway down the track when Amelia jerked upright in her seat. 'Whoah.'

'What?' he said.

'*That*. What's that?'

'What's what?'

'Over there. Running in the woods.'

All four of them swung their heads to the left.

'What are we looking for, exactly?' Lucy groaned.

The rain on the windows was making it hard to figure out, but then Wren tapped her finger on the glass. 'Oh. I see it. Over there.'

'Congratulations,' Lucy said. 'You just found a tree in a forest.'

'No *there* . . . the foxes.'

He looked over and saw them straight away. They were running at full pelt to keep up with the car. Two of them. Weaving in and out of the tree trunks, hopping over fallen logs, springing through the forest.

'Daddy?' Amelia tugged at Matt's shoulder. 'Why do they keep looking over at us?'

She was right, they were. Running and flicking their heads toward them. 'I guess they're partial to a decent Mondeo—'

Thud.

A huge, loud and sudden bump pounded through the car.

Amelia screamed and Matt automatically slammed his foot onto the brake. The car skidded on the dirt track, back wheels locked into a drift a couple of feet to the right. Ah crud . . . there was a ditch on the side of the road, racing toward them.

'Brake! Brake!' Wren shouted, like it was a helpful suggestion he may not have considered yet.

'*I am!*' he shouted back, annoyed, as the wheels slowly crunched to a stop and the grinding ended. The car was still upright, just short of the ditch. Two seconds' worth of trauma, at the most, but enough to plunge them all into a gaunt, sudden silence.

The entire car was still, but the rain rumbled on. The wipers scraped and squeaked, over and over and over again.

'Crap,' Matt whispered. 'We hit something.'

All eyes flitted to the windscreen and out across the bonnet. Every couple of seconds the wipers cleared a view but all they could see was rain bouncing off the car in hundreds of tiny fountains.

'What'd you hit?' Lucy slipped her seat belt off so she could lean through the two front seats.

'Is everyone alright?'

'I said, what did you hit?'

'Look,' Amelia said. 'The foxes have stopped running too.'

He looked over at them, now distorted brown smudges. They were panting and milling around a tree stump, looking over.

'Pass me my jacket,' Matt unbuckled himself.

Lucy grabbed it from the back seat and bundled it through. He swung it around his shoulders, clicked the door open a crack. The once muffled rain sounded suddenly sharp and crisp.

Wren was popping her belt to join him but he put up a hand. 'You might as well stay in the car and keep dry.' Then he gave a silent nod toward Amelia. She looked pale.

'You okay?' Wren nodded and reached over, grabbing her hand. 'Be careful, Matt.'

The tremble in her voice made him look back at her.

'Probably just a log in the road,' he said, as much for his own benefit as theirs.

He winced as the rain hit his face then he glanced over at the foxes. They were suddenly much nearer to the car. Maybe it was due to the rain but all of their ears seemed to be down, flat and folded back. He didn't like that look at all.

Fat drops seeped into the back of his collar and ran down between his shoulder blades, making him shiver. So he swung the jacket over the top of his head like a makeshift tent and moved round to the front of the car.

They hadn't hit a log, because logs don't bleed.

A bright red splash covered the first three letters of his registration plate and spattered up into the radiator grille. His first thought:

151

after all that searching he'd finally found Nicola Knox wandering in the woods, only now she was dead and buckled under their car.

He looked up to see all three girls staring out of the windscreen from behind the frantic wipers.

He went round the back of the car to check and found a dark furry lump. He let out a sigh, which was part sadness and part relief. Running a kid over would have been a definite holiday downer.

He knocked on the boot and Wren wound her window down a touch, squinting as the rain came in, 'What is it?'

'It's just another fox. Keep the girls in the car for a bit.'

The little mound of coppery fur had tried to curl itself up into a ball. It was so still he thought it was dead but as Matt leant down it suddenly jerked in a freaky little spasm. Enough to make Matt jump. It flipped itself onto its other side, and for a moment looked like a furry little fish flopping on the bottom of a boat, gasping for air.

'Aw shit, little man. I'm sorry.' Matt cringed at the long, gaping slit in the fur, running in a jagged line from its chest down to its groin. Wet leaves were stuck to its bloodied belly and the smell reminded him of uncooked steak.

As the fox flopped slowly back and forth, darker blood quickly pulsed out onto the dirt. The dying fox's ears were folded back exactly like the others at the tree stump. The fox would be dead pretty soon. A few minutes maybe. Ten?

He was suddenly startled by a knock on the rear window. He looked up to see the two girls trying to pull on their jackets while Wren was obviously telling them to stay still.

Oh great. They were coming to see it.

You can't let it die like this.

For a second he considered just kicking the fox to the side of the road so it might drop into a ditch, out of sight. Flashing his hands and saying nothing to see here, kids! But the thought of the poor little guy twisting in pain down there caused Matt to move his foot towards its throat. He put one hand on the car's boot to steady himself and pushed the toe of his shoe forward. Keeping it poised, he looked away.

Is this really necessary, Professor?

The girls' doors clicked open.

'Stay in the car.' He pretty much barked the words. Then holding his breath he pushed the toe of his shoe in, the other foxes observing his every move.

He pushed harder.

Harder still. Quickly, so nobody else would see.

Matt's eyes closed when he heard a tiny snap, muffled like a twig in jelly. Part of him didn't want to open them again, because he had no wish to see what he'd just done.

But he did open them. And when he did, Lucy was standing there, one hand over her mouth. She'd moved quicker than he expected. The hood of her jacket was sparkling with little stars of rain, her other wet hand touching the edge of the boot. Her face was a paper-white mask of shock and disgust.

He quickly moved his foot back, away from the fox.

'Lucy,' he whispered. 'It was in agony . . .'

'Oh, my God.' Her eyebrows had drawn together as they so often did with him. But this time they were drawing up in the middle, a sort of organic expression of a brain unable to compute. And when she spoke it was in tiny, frightened gasps. 'You killed him.'

'Lucy.' He reached out towards his stepdaughter, which was a bad idea. She stumbled back.

'Don't you even touch me.'

The heels of her white Stussy trainers sank into a ridge of mud.

'Oh, just calm down. It was dying—'

She spun on her feet and threw herself back into the car.

Oh, great. Just bloody perfect.

He checked to see if any of the blood was on the tip of his shoe. There wasn't any, just a few wisps of fur. So he shook his foot, wiping the tip in the dirt. The animal was dead, one eye open, one eye closed in a sort of unamusing death wink that said, *Thanks . . . but I'd rather you had posted me to Dignitas, you brutalist!*

'Urgh.' Now it was Wren, standing there with her hood up.

Lucy wound her window down and shouted, 'You better be going to bury it. You can't just lob it in the woods.'

Matt looked over at Wren, who shrugged.

To be honest he had no clue what to do with it. Tossing it into the woods sounded like a pretty good plan. Wouldn't that be the most natural thing to do? File it somewhere in the food chain. But then, maybe burying it would be a good thing for the kids. They'd never had any pets. Too many allergies. Maybe doing this would teach them about death or something.

Hey, Matt. What's next on this holiday adventure? Take them to the airport to teach them about plane crashes?

'Let's bag it up,' he said.

Wren quickly grabbed a plastic bin bag that they had in a cubbyhole of the boot and held it open. With a curved thick branch he managed to peel the animal from the track and flip him into the bag. It was like the most bizarre game of golf he'd ever played, and it took him four attempts to eventually flick him inside. All the while, rain pounded onto them both.

He gazed a little too long at the pool of dirty blood on the track, but at least the rain was diluting it. Wren grabbed a handful of leaves and started to rub the blood from the registration plate.

The toes on his euthanasia foot felt suddenly warm and tingly.

'So, are we cooking this bad boy or not?' she said, catching his eye. 'Road kill's got a lot of nutrients.'

He smiled softly at her and wiped some rain from his brow. Then he tied up the end of the bag and lifted it, sickened by the weight, picturing the blood and dirt pooling in the bottom of the black plastic. After a quick, whispered discussion with Wren he set the bag neatly at the side of the road and climbed back into the car, shivering as the seat pushed the cold wet shirt into his back. He braced himself for Lucy's town crier announcement that good old Matthew here had just broken a fox's neck.

'That's it, then?' Lucy said. 'You're just going to leave him there?'

'We need to get to the church,' Matt said.

Lucy screwed up her face. 'For videogames? Don't you think that can wait.'

He checked his watch. 'I promise we'll come back and bury the fox later.'

'No way, we're doing it now,' Lucy said.

'Er . . . no we're not. It's pouring down, and I'm not bringing him in the car.'

'He'll have diseases,' Wren added.

'So we bury him now, then.'

'With what? Your phone?' Matt said, getting annoyed. 'We haven't got a shovel.'

'Then we'll use our hands. We're not leaving him.' She went to open her door again.

'Lucy,' he caught her eyes in the rear-view mirror, 'do *not* open that door.'

'Why? Is this how you used to bury people when you were a vicar? Leave them on the side of the motorway to rot in a bag?' He heard her door click open, the sudden hiss of the rain filling the car.

Wren shot her a glare, mouthed the word's, *Don't*.

'Do *not* go back out there,' he said.

'Oh, get lost, Matthew—'

'Dammit Lucy, get in the fucking car!' The words came out of him with such a hard deliberate snap that both Amelia and Wren jumped. 'For once will you do as you're told?'

He turned the ignition and the engine came to life.

Wren stared at him, jaw open a little. 'Close it, Lucy.'

A few seconds passed. It clicked shut.

The hiss of the rain may have vanished but the car was now filled with the low buzz of stress and tension. He straightened and glanced out of his window as rain pelted the bin bag, holding the first non-insect he'd ever killed.

It was Amelia who broke the silence. 'You think that fox was the daddy?' She was staring out at the other two foxes who were still looking over at the car, blinking slowly and watching. 'I think it was the mum.'

'I'm sorry,' Matt suddenly said. 'I shouldn't have sworn at you but—'

'Oh, don't bother,' Lucy said.

He glanced down at his right foot, pressing the accelerator, feeling pretty miserable. Wisps of fur, invisible against the dirt track, now clearly stood out against the black carpet of the footwell.

They drove the rest of the way in silence.

CHAPTER TWENTY-TWO

They left the kids in the Sunday school hall. It was a 60s holiday-camp building that had been bolted onto the seventeenth-century church with plenty of thought to practicality, though zero to aesthetics. A common crime amongst Protestant types.

The youth leaders had filled the room (pig-pink walls with orange carpet) with a circle of LCD screens, all facing in. A bunch of teenagers sat gazing at them, their pupils flashing with white squares as they jabbed at controller buttons. A stiff-looking woman with her shoulders back marched from one child to the other, recording their scores silently on a clipboard. It was all quiet and serious and positively Orwellian. Matt was tempted to join them for a quick game but he was a few decades short of the entry requirements. Shame.

Lucy and Amelia settled themselves in front of a PS4. But just as Lucy picked up a controller she gave him a look. A sort of eyebrows-up flash of defiance, which said loud and clear: *I know what you did to that little mummy fox.*

He was amazed she hadn't told his crime to Wren or Amelia yet. But that look told him she felt like keeping this knowledge in for a while. It was probably more strategic that way. Gave her a power chip. She was mistaken. He'd beat her to it and tell all when he got the chance. There was no shame in what he'd done, was there? He'd have to convince his feelings of that too.

The harsh woman with the clipboard stepped into his view, snapping him out of his fox thoughts. 'We don't bite,' she said. Then flashed a smile ironically lined with sharp, jagged teeth. 'Your children are safe with us, so please stop leering.'

'I'm not *leering*,' Matt said, looking for the bald guy with the goatee that they met the other night at the Purging. 'Where's Billy, the youth worker? Isn't this video game thing his idea?'

'It is. I'm not sure where he is, but he might be upstairs, praying with the others.' She nodded to a tiny window to some upper room. 'They're asking for the kids to sense God here today. That he'll speak to them.'

'What . . . through Angry Birds?' Matt glanced over at a kid, feverishly sweeping an iPad.

'God'll speak through everything . . . *anything*. You just have to listen.' She smiled again. 'Now if you'll excuse me.' She strode off, plunging the point of her high heels onto the thick carpet.

He wandered over to Wren. She had one hand on her hip, staring up at an arch in the ceiling. He took her elbow. 'Come on. I think we're cramping the kids' style.'

They headed back out of the Sunday school hall and back up into the church foyer. Carpeted floor turned back to stone.

She had a stack of yellow notepads under her arm and a pencil shoved behind her ear; she'd dried most of her hair with the toilet hand-blower moments earlier, so it looked like it was moving toward 80s power rock video. She didn't seem to mind. Today's task was sketching out the new lobby. *Lots of glass*, Chris had insisted. *We want to be transparent!*

'Well, I'd better leave you to it.' Matt went to kiss her but her lips felt stiff and cold against his. He pulled his face back, waited for the appropriate seconds to pass. 'Look. I'm sorry for swearing back then.'

'Good.'

'I know you don't like—'

'Since when were you . . . such a nob?'

'Please . . .' he put his palms up. 'Don't hold back.'

'Matt . . .' Her face softened. 'Is something wrong?'

'Well . . . apart from just ripping a fox in two, I'm pretty chipper.'

'No,' she shook her head. 'Since we got to Hobbs Hill you seem . . . distracted. I know you're worried about the book. You've hardly done any work on—'

He wafted the comment away with his hand, like an annoying wasp. 'I've been busy. The police stuff.'

'Yeah, about that,' she groaned. 'You're supposed to be at home writing your chapter, not searching for this Nicola . . . Nixon girl.'

'*Knox*.' He frowned at her. 'She's called Nicola Knox.' He had a sudden image of Tabitha Clarke for a second and Arima Adakay too. Both of them writhing on the floor, one in the bath, the other in the noodle bar. In his mind, they were flickering into the same person. He wondered why he hadn't really told Wren about either woman yet. 'The police needed help and I was happy to offer.'

'I know you do,' she reached for him. 'You *always* do . . . it's just . . .'

He looked up at the ceiling, blew some air up at it. 'Go on.'

'Since we've been here . . . in Hobbs Hill. You seem a bit down.'

'I'm fine.'

Her fingertips landed on his shoulder. 'I think you should maybe talk to Chris about—'

'*What?*' He shrunk away from her.

'He's a really good listener.'

He looked at her, and said something he instantly regretted. 'You're not on the payroll yet, Wren.'

She pulled her hand away. 'Well excuse me, Mr Menstrual.'

Crap.

'Wren . . .'

'Bye. Some people have work to do.' She marched off in the other direction, stopping only once to catch a yellow notepad that was sliding down onto her hip.

'Wren.' He stepped after her but quickly thought better of it. He just leant wearily against a cold, stone pillar and watched her disappear through a door, feeling like a complete cretin and wondering why she always had this knack of figuring his feelings out before he did.

Was it the book? Was it Hobbs Hill? Was it the fact he'd crunched the neck of a dying fox? Or was it just being in the same orbit as Chris Kelly again? Whatever it was, he had felt distracted and a little on edge ever since he'd driven into this village. With its blank-eyed smiley people, and its constantly hissing waterfall.

Maybe it was all those crosses.

He dropped his eyes to his feet and spotted a rogue thread of fox fur stuck to his shoe. He wiped it on the edge of a pew and made a snap decision.

He'd head off to find Chris.

The church was a warren of low ceilings and tilted corridors. Most of the odd, fun-house shape of the walls was caused by a mixture of subsidence, odd architectural choices and frankly psychotic paint jobs. He trotted down some stone steps with a strip of old carpet bolted down the middle and followed the signs to Chris's office. A thick, shiny gold-coloured nameplate said *SENIOR Pastor: Rev. Christopher Kelly*. That first word wasn't only in bold, it was slightly bigger than the rest.

The door was closed.

He waited, looked around, then pushed his ear towards it, just in case Chris might already be in there with someone. Didn't he say earlier that he'd be chatting to Nicola Knox's mum today? Was he in there doing that, right now, dishing out Bible verses and cups of peppermint tea, insisting that the worst of times and the best of times can occasionally come at the same moment?

He was about to rap his knuckle on the door when a voice came from behind him.

'He's not there.'

Matt jumped a little and quickly pulled his ear from the door. He turned around, cheeks on fire.

Chris's son, Ben, was coming out of what looked like a cellar. He was carrying a crate of Diet Coke with a transparent tub of lollipops on top, holding them down with his chin so they wouldn't slip off.

Matt's startled brain made him say, 'Wahey, lollipops!' As if that was how young people spoke, these days. He felt like an instant dick.

'They're for the youth group. For the tournament. I'm helping out.'

'Cool. Do *you* play?'

'Huh?'

'Video games. Do you play? I'm a fan.'

'Some. I like driving games . . . sports stuff.' He lifted his chin to ask, 'What do you play?' but it made him almost drop everything.

Matt nodded and stepped forward. 'Hey, let me give you a hand.'

Chin still in place, he shook his head. 'I'm fine, thanks,' he nodded towards the office door. 'My dad's down at Bethesda.'

'That's the healing centre, just down the hill?'

'That's right. So you won't be able to see him till later in the day. Sorry.'

'I just need to ask him a really quick question. I'll pop down.'

'No.' Ben shifted the crate in his hands. 'They won't let you.'

'Who won't?'

'Look, I've got to run. The kids'll freak if they don't get their sugar. You know how it is.' He turned and headed off in the opposite direction, calling back, 'You can catch my dad later. He said he'll be done at around four. You could come to the house.'

And then he was up the stairs and gone.

Matt turned back to the office door. He gazed down at the

handle then back at the corridor to make sure it was empty. Before he was even aware of it, his hand was on the brass, creaking it down, waiting for the click—

Locked.

He pulled his hand back quickly and looked back up the corridor, half expecting Ben's eyes to be hovering in the dark.

Watcha doin', Noseybonk?

Matt rushed up the steps and back outside into the car park.

The clouds were wringing out the final dregs of the rain while the sun crept slowly across the lush, hilly field towards him. He thought of Nicola Knox and Tabitha Clarke, out there somewhere, and he felt a pulse of worry for them both. He pictured those two faces on his laptop and started to realise that it was, of course, *them* who were causing him to feel so edgy. A depressed teenager who supposedly had anorexia and possible suicidal tendencies, and a cancer-ridden artist, no doubt hounded for her sexuality by chumps like Taylor.

These two women felt like anomalies in the otherwise perfect, crucifix world of Hobbs Hill. Just as he felt like one. So he slipped into his car and pulled away, heading down the short, steep road that led to the Healing Centre.

It had that nondescript modernish look. Like an out-in-the-sticks wing of the county council. Or a Job Centre from the late 1980s. Orangey bricks, lots of glass, green spiky plants you never had to tend. Over the doorway was a strip of black stone slate saying *Bethesda*. This, he knew full well, was the name of the pool of healing waters in the Gospels where disabled people were thrown in and supposedly came out well again. At the bottom of the slate was a Bible verse from John with white mock handwriting: 'Only if you are born of water and the Spirit, can you enter the kingdom of God.'

He stepped out of the car and quietly closed the door, looking across at the waterfall pounding into the lake. From here he could have wandered right around the shoreline, and thought up some angles for his book.

But he thought he could hear music so he tilted his ear towards the Healing Centre. Which is when his heart stopped for one single beat. Because a sound swept from one of the upper windows and raced out towards him, across the gravel.

A single, long scream.

Muffled but unmistakeable.

He had to blink to let the sound compute and then the scream came again. Louder this time, and more manic.

'Holy shit,' he said, and sprang towards the building, pounding his feet to the main door and finding it locked.

Another scream ripped through the air. This one pitiful and full of bitter tears. Someone turned the music up louder.

He grabbed a rock and barely even thought about it. He slammed it through the glass strip in the door and reached through, fiddling with the lock on the inside. The *Do NOT Disturb!!!* sign fell from the handle and wafted into the gravel. The door popped open.

The music grew far, far louder as he stepped inside, crunching his shoes on the glass shards. Then as he scrambled to the top of the stairs it sounded like someone was still turning it up, to cover the screams. The booming sound devoured the air like it was a nightclub.

He recognised it, too.

'*I can't live* . . .' Mariah Carey warbled as 90s power drums punched holes into the space–time continuum. '. . . *if living is without you.*'

'You're kidding,' he said.

In answer, another blood-thinning scream tore through the corridor, followed by a crashing sound. Something breaking. Everything was coming from behind a door at the far end of the corridor. The etched plastic sign said: *The Reality Room.*

'Hey!' a voice boomed from downstairs.

Matt stopped for a second and leant over the balcony. The fat guy Billy, the youth worker, from church. He was looking up, carrying a Bible in one hand and cardboard coffee holder in the other, about to spill.

Their eyes met.

'Hey. Get out of here!' Billy called up, coffee sloshing onto the carpet. 'Right now.'

There wasn't time to speak. Matt bolted towards the door and the screams behind it. From below he could hear Billy thumping his humongous Yeti feet up the stairs behind him. Shouting over and over in his horrible, gravelly voice as the screams went on, 'Leave her alone. She wants it. She *wants* it!'

CHAPTER TWENTY-THREE

Matt heaved his weight against the door and the music swelled to ear-splitting volume. Then his jaw literally, un-metaphorically, dropped.

Everything: the floor, the walls, the windows were covered in a blue plastic tarpaulin kept in place with silver gaffer tape. And tables were set up against the walls, each one filled with white dinner plates, propped up against wooden blocks. There were at least a hundred bits of crockery lining every wall with hundreds more shark-fin shards lying shattered on the floor.

Wedged in the far corner, Chris Kelly was perched boyband-style on a high chrome bar stool. Black shirt tucked, clerical collar tight . . . and a yellow hard hat. A pair of safety goggles were strapped across his eyes while a baseball bat hung from both hands. His head was bowed, eyes tight in prayer. And in the middle of it all there was a woman in a wedding dress, cheeks streaked with eyeliner. Like Chris, she held a baseball bat. But she was swinging it wildly, obliterating pots and plates with squeals and yelps.

Matt called out, 'What's going on here?' But the music was too loud. He shouted it again, straining his throat. '*What's going on?*'

The woman slowed the swings to a confused stop. The bat trembled in mid-air. Then she turned her Alice Cooper face fully around. When she saw Matt she retched, dropped the bat and ran sobbing from the room. She almost floored Billy who by now had appeared in the doorway, panting and gripping the door frame.

'How dare . . . you come . . . in . . . here,' Billy said, between gasps.

'*I can't live* . . .' Mariah's car alarm trilling went on.

Matt turned and shouted at Billy. 'Turn that damn thing off!'

Billy groaned, grabbed a remote from his pocket and, seemingly pointing it into thin air, jabbed at a button. Mariah vanished. When Matt turned back, he saw Chris slipping off the stool, tossing the hard hat and goggles to the floor. His hands were gripping the bat.

'Chris. Put that down.' Matt's voice sounded suddenly huge in the silence.

Chris looked at the bat and one eyebrow sprang up. 'What. You think I'm going to hit you?'

'Drop it. Now.'

'You think I'd *actually* hit you with this?' He gave a flabbergasted, bitter little laugh then flung the bat to the floor. It clattered against the shards of plates.

'You need to explain this. Right now.' Matt stepped forward and kicked both bats to the side.

Chris opened his arms theatrically. 'Oh, here he comes everybody. Here he comes, to the rescue. Religion Professor who doesn't even believe in anything!'

Matt narrowed his eyes. 'How about you just calm the fuck down.'

The swear word was a deliberate, if childish, choice. A sort of manifesto statement to distance himself from the weird Christian faithful in front of him. It worked too. It brought a hiss of shocked breath from Chris.

Billy manoeuvred his hefty body between them, his Welsh lilt raspy and dry. 'You should go, right now. This is *none* of your business.'

'I'm not going anywhere till you tell me what's going on here.'

Billy took a single step forward, and drew in a breath to puff out his chest. Cavemen probably did that when they challenged a wild boar. 'Please don't make me carry you out of here, Professor.'

'I'm not moving,' Matt said. 'I'm checking on that woman too. And if one of you doesn't tell me what all this crazy stuff is, then I swear to God I'll call the police.'

'To God?' Chris said. '*To God?*' He looked like he might fling his head back in some manic cackle, but the sarcastic smile soon faded and slowly his shoulders sank in defeat. 'You ruined it for her.'

'Ruined what?'

'The session. The healing. She was close.'

'What's the matter with her?'

Chris and Billy shared a glance. A flicker of the eyebrows and a twitch of the lips. Some unspoken conferring. Then Chris sighed. 'Her name's Isabel Dawson. She's a physics teacher from Oxford.'

'*And?*'

'Six weeks ago she was due to get married in London. Horse-drawn carriage, gospel choir, doves getting released. Except her fiancé of sixteen months didn't turn up. Completely jilted her in front of two hundred guests.'

Matt shrugged. 'And what's that got to do with all of this?'

Billy set his shoulders coat-hanger straight. 'Izzy's been part of our deep-wounds programme. Pastor Chris's counselled her for a few weeks now. And today's the penultimate part of her therapy.'

'This is *therapy?*'

'What did you think it was?' Chris said, then he instantly lifted his hand. 'Actually, don't answer that. I'd rather not know.'

Just as he did that, Isabel appeared at the door, cheeks wet, sweaty hair pressed to her forehead like tentacles.

'Izzy,' Chris said. 'How about we get you that cup of coffee?'

She said nothing.

'Izzy, it's going to be fine, love. Mr Hunter here's just leaving, and then we can get back on with it.'

Nothing.

'Isabel?' To Chris's clear disapproval, Matt took a step towards her. 'My name's Matthew Hunter. I apologise if I've interrupted something here but I just need to know if you're okay and happy with all of this. Is this what you want?'

'Of course she's happy with—'

'Chris!' Matt glared at him. 'Let her speak.'

They waited. A full minute. Maybe more. Chris put his hands on his hips and puffed out a few frustrated breaths.

Matt smiled gently at her, 'You have to admit that this looks kind of unusual. So I just want to make sure you're okay. Okay?'

Finally, she spoke. Whispering to the floor. 'Entropy.'

Matt frowned. 'Pardon?'

'Entropy.'

'You're harassing her.' Chris stepped closer. 'Come on, Izzy. Let's get you in the car.'

'I was teaching entropy, the week before my wedding.' Her eyes stayed locked straight down. 'A-level physics.'

Matt nodded, voice calm. 'I see.'

'Entropy means,' her voice grew louder, 'that everything in the universe naturally wears down. That everything dies. Which it does, doesn't it?'

'Get her in the car, Billy . . . and Matt, give her some space.'

She ignored everybody. Just looked up at Matt, never seeming to blink. 'Dogs die. Fingernails die. Stars even.'

He nodded, 'You're absolutely right.'

That prompted her to give a sad smile.

'And faith dies too, you know?' she said, then finally turned her gaze toward Chris. Her eyes narrowed. 'And I can feel my faith right now. It's pouring out of my shoes.'

Chris screwed up his face. 'Izzy, don't you even say that. We'll get you back on—'

'On track? On track? There *is* no track! That's what I keep telling

168

you people.' After a long tense silence Isabel turned from Chris back to Matt. 'I'm okay.'

Matt gave her an encouraging nod, 'Would you like me to take you home?'

'I said I'm okay, shithead!' She turned and marched for the stairs. They all went out to the landing and watched her descend one slow step at a time, her thin lace-covered hands shaking as they slid down the golden bannister. Billy went down to open up the front doors for her, glaring back up at Matt at the shards of glass on the floor.

Matt and Chris just stood on the landing in silence, the tension between them crackling like an electrical hum.

'I won't lie to you, Matt. I'm furious with you right now.'

'I picked that up. But what did you expect . . . I heard screaming.'

'Look . . . I'm the *senior* pastor here.'

'You're the only pastor here.'

'Exactly. And maybe you've forgotten it but pastors help people.'

'Yes, but you're not qualified in mental health, are you?'

'*Aren't I?* I've used this programme for rape victims, child-abuse survivors. Name it. And it works and it's mine.'

'And what if you do more damage? I mean look at her.'

She was hobbling to the door, bent over and groaning like a Disney witch.

'*Excuse me?*' Chris said. 'I let people externalise their emotions so they can get it out of their system. Before they do something stupid. That's the *real* purging by the way. And you think that's . . . amateur?' He sounded more sad than angry now. 'Have you ever considered that if you got all that bitterness out after your mother was murdered, in a controlled way, you'd never have been suspended? Maybe I could have helped you back then.'

Matt felt like scooping Chris by the legs and chucking him over the top of the bannister. He could have done it in one fluid movement. But instead he spoke in calm, measured tones. 'Smashing plates wouldn't have brought her back, would it?'

169

'Not her. But you . . . it could have brought *you* back.' Chris turned his head and leant over the balcony. Looking through the broken window onto the car park. He was watching Isabel stuffing herself into her Mini, still in her wedding dress. Billy was pleading for her to let him drive.

'You said this was the penultimate part of the programme,' Matt said. 'So what's left?'

'The best part. The entire point of it all.' He kept watching Izzy, his eyes fixed and intense. 'Though I assume that these days it'll mean very little to you.'

'Try me.'

'That's when we baptise them. Tomorrow morning, on the lake. Right after the service. It's what all this leads up to. The Purging, the healing sessions . . . all roads lead to water. You'll see it at church tomorrow, providing you don't dive in and save them. And maybe God will speak to you and tell you how insanely narrow-minded you're being.'

The sound of Isabel's Mini fired up outside. Chris moved onto his tiptoes to watch it buzzing out of the car park, and up the hill. His hands were gripping the railing, tight enough to turn the knuckles white.

'I'll pay for the window,' Matt said, then turned to Chris. 'Are you going to be alright?'

'Of course I'm not. I'm going to be incredibly sad for her.' He wasn't just sad. The gaunt look in his eye was more like devastation. 'She was *so* close. If she'd just reached a little further. Touched Jesus's fingers. Maybe . . .'

Through the second-floor window they watched her car hit the top of the hill and she vanished behind the stone monolith of the church.

'Maybe there's still time.' Chris started heading for the stairs. Then stopped mid step. 'Hang on a minute.'

'What?'

170

'Why were you here, Matt?' He still didn't turn. 'Why did you come down here today?'

Matt swallowed. Then asked his question to the back of Chris's head. 'There's a concern that a lady called Tabitha Clarke might be unwell. She lives just out of Hobbs Hill and I was wondering if you knew her. I heard you know everyone. Maybe she'd come to you for help?'

'The artist?'

'Yes.'

'The *lesbian* artist?'

'Yes.'

'Well, we all have our cross to bear, don't we?'

'And hers is that she's dying of cancer.'

Chris started to walk down the steps. He didn't appear curious as to why Matt might be asking these things. 'Well, I've heard of her, but I've never had the pleasure.'

'Where are you going?'

'I need to pray now. See if I can salvage what you ruined.' He headed for the door. 'And I'm sorry, but I can't guarantee I won't pray for you.'

'You say it like a threat.'

He stopped walking and he finally turned, shaking his head in sadness. 'A *threat*? You see prayer as a threat? That's how you feel, these days?'

Matt said nothing.

'Do you *really* want a threat? As much as it breaks my heart? Then how about this . . .' His eyes held the shimmer of tears. 'You have no faith. And neither does your family. Your beautiful wife, your wonderful children. Which means that when their hearts stop beating, the flames are going to start. And they will never, ever stop burning. Shoot me if I don't want that for you, Matt.' He sniffed and a tear suddenly ran down his cheek. He announced his next word like a promise or a prophesy. Like a curse, lifting a trembling finger to point. '. . . *Entropy.*'

171

Chris moaned, turned to the door and left.

Matt stood there for a whole minute, watching Chris leave. Then for a moment he thought he could smell that fox again, dead and mangled. Its metallic, meaty stench floating on the air. He wondered why he hadn't noticed it before: how much that slit fox had smelled like his mother, in the kitchen that day.

And he knew then that she was behind him, in the doorway with her ragged mouth opening. So he left.

CHAPTER TWENTY-FOUR

Wren tilted the second bottle of Shiraz towards him and he thrust his glass under it like a man parched in the desert. He checked his watch as she sloshed some into each glass: midnight. The rain today seemed to have sucked a little heat from Hobbs Hill, so the night was the coolest so far. But it wasn't exactly chilly. Still, this hadn't stopped them from setting a fire going. They had a house-sized pile of logs in the garden after all, which he'd been itching to use all week. And they had this old stone fireplace, straight from a Grimm's Fairytale, with a row of old clocks lined up on the crooked mantel. The swaying flames in the hearth were worth the effort.

'You do realise,' he said, 'that we're going to wake up tipsy for church.'

She held up her glass and wiggled it. 'Might make it more fun.'

It had always been the plan to go to an actual church service here. Wren wanted to see the building in full swing so she could get a feel for what people wanted from the place. Matt was curious too, especially since the church website described the services here as 'lively, unconventional and contemporary'. He wondered how true that was. Some churches claimed that simply because they had flushing toilets.

Her face suddenly cringed into worry. 'They won't put us into holy huddles, will they? Make us pray out loud?'

'Of course. Plus there's a goat sacrifice . . . and some interpretive dance. And the live crucifixion of fornicators—'

'Fornicators. What a *great* word!'

'Isn't it!' he nodded. 'And copulators.'

She laughed and threw back a mouthful. 'Seriously, though, you'll have to talk me through all the church-speak. Translate it for me.' She took another swig of her wine then paused, looking genuinely nervous. 'They won't do that speaking in tongues thing, will they? That would seriously freak the girls out.'

'Agreed. Pingu is the only life form who should ever talk like that.' He laughed into the wine glass and some of it splashed onto his top lip. He wiped it with his hand. 'I can't believe Lucy's actually coming. I thought she said church was for . . .' he did air quotes, '"paedos and losers".'

'Oh, she's changing her tune on the whole church thing. It's ever since she met the boys at this church and realised Bible-bashers could be good-looking.'

He dropped his mouth in mock surprise and pointed to himself with both thumbs. 'Er . . . see figure one. I used to bash the Bible like it was going out of fashion. And I'm crazy-hot.'

'Mr Inferno!' She leant over, kissing him with salted breath and laughed against his lips. She sank back into the couch. 'Who knows, by the time we go back to London we might have a couple of converts.'

He sniffed a little laugh but the thought of it made him stare off into the fire. Wren saw the shift in his face.

'Which wouldn't be the biggest deal, if it happened . . . *would* it?' The flames gave her eyes an odd shimmer.

'Oh, great. The Hobbs Hill whirlpool's sucking you in too.'

'It *is* not!' She closed her eyes, put her hands together in prayer and spoke in a long monotone voice. 'Dear Lord, please get my husbandeth to chilleth out about ye. And have him poureth me another glass of wineth. Cos I'm in it for the whole botteleth. Amen.'

By the time she opened her eyes, he was topping up her glass. He waved a mystical jazz hand in the air. 'Praise de Lord. He provides!'

She snorted a laugh. 'Well, don't fret. I'm not joining the church anytime soon. I think you're supposed to believe in the big guy for a start. So you needn't worry yourself.'

'I'm not worried.'

She shorted again. 'Of course you are. You're freaking out being here.'

He stopped looking at the fire. 'What are you talking about?'

'Every time someone talks religious round here there's this flicker in your face. Like you just sat on a syringe.' She paused, eyes fixed on the ceiling for a moment. They widened as an epiphany struck. 'Bloody hell, that's it!'

'That's what?'

'I've got it.'

'Got *what*?'

'You! You see God the way other people see heroin.'

'Huh?'

She patted her knee excitedly. 'No, that's it. God's like this drug you got hooked on for a while. But he let you down and screwed you up. And now you're paranoid your kids are going to want a sniff and get let down too.' She hiccupped, and her words started to slur. 'Maybe sometimes . . . *you* even feel like a sniff too. For old time's sake?'

He slapped one of the cushions across her legs. 'Stick to blueprints, Wren. Your psyche assessments are way off.'

'Yeah. Way off.' She raised her eyebrows and smiled smugly. They were silent for a while, until she cleared her throat and said, 'Right . . . I'm about to mention Chris Kelly. Don't vomit in protest.'

He looked sheepish. 'Chris is alright, really. Just lives on a different Earth than I do.'

'*All* I was going to say is that maybe seeing Chris is bringing it back. You know. What you used to believe. It was a big part of your life, so maybe you do miss it a bit.'

'Like people miss the mind-altering, life-destroying drug heroin?'

'Exactly.' She slapped an I-rest-my-case hand on her lap. But her smile sank a little when he said nothing back. She put her hand over his. 'There's no shame in it, you know. To at least . . . *want* it to be true. Everyone wants a bit of . . . I don't know . . . enchantment.'

'Which is another word for bewitchment . . .' He looked at her. 'But the main point is that it just isn't true. There's nothing in the sky but stars . . . which are nothing more than big balls of gas. Which I just reckon is very beautiful in its own way.'

'Hang on,' she said, making a mental note. 'You just said balls were beautiful.'

They laughed again, but then they sat in silence for a while gazing over at the flames that were dancing and crackling in the fireplace. Eventually she asked him for a glass of water so he padded through to the kitchen in his socks and poured her one. By the time he got back to the lounge she had that vibe about her that he'd seen many times before. She was sitting upright, chewing her lip, drawing spirals on the arm of the sofa with her index finger. It was her signal that she had something important to say but Wren was the type who needed to brew up to such things.

Just before she'd first said she loved him, they'd sat in an Italian restaurant in a similar gaunt quiet. She was gawping at her olives, prodding them with a breadstick for four minutes of silence which, in date terms, is the Grand Canyon. He thought it was turning into the worst night of his life. But by the time she spoke it ended up being the best.

I've fallen in love with you, Matthew, she'd said, then she finally popped an olive into her mouth and said, *How about that?*

So he knew the procedure. He just waited, watched the fire, smiled at her every now and again.

She sipped her wine then water in sequence, then finally spoke. 'About the fox. And the way you spoke to Lucy.'

'Look, I'm sorry about that—'

'Don't be. I've given it some thought and she might not share your genes but she *can't* expect to walk all over you. I didn't like you swearing at her, but you were right to tell her off. She's really giving you a hard time lately.'

He gave her a thankful nod. 'I guess the bottom line is that she just . . . well, she just doesn't like me very—'

Wren pretty much slammed her finger against his lips and shushed him. 'Don't *say* that. She loves you, Matt.'

He said nothing.

'She's just testing you again. You know, like when we first met?'

In a flash he saw all those moments back at the beginning of their relationship. When Lucy was eight. The naughtiness, the arched-back screaming she would do when he tried to get her out of the car to go swimming. The food thrown, the toys he bought – broken, even the screen of his TV cracked with a toffee hammer. This was in the days before Amelia was born. When he felt that there could be nothing worse than being a father. He'd started reading up on the Internet about vasectomies, like they were the very epitome of liberation.

'I think it's cos she's getting older,' she said. 'She's going to end up going to university and leave home in the next few years, so she's testing you.'

'To see what limits I might cross . . . make sure you're safe with me?' He tried to hide his frustration. 'Did she tell you about the fox?' He grabbed his drink, and looked at it. 'That I—'

'Killed it with your foot? Yes.'

'Bet she thinks I'm Norman Bates, now. I was going to tell you.'

'I'd have been more worried if you'd left it to die in the rain. And I think deep down, she would too.' She squeezed his hand again. 'She just saw a lot of crappy things growing up so she's protective.'

If Wren was talking about some other family, he'd nod his head sagely and say things like, ah yes, childhood wounds cut deep. You can't expect them to just vanish. But this wasn't anyone else, damn it. It was him. And after ten years of things getting better and better, of actually being called Dad for a while, the thought of Lucy testing

177

him again, of having even a little distrust, was as deflating as it was understandable.

An image of the photographs taken of Wren (after Eddie Pullen's final beating) flickered in his mind. The attack had almost killed her but at least it finally put Pullen behind bars. Matt had broken all policy last year and managed to get Larry Forbes to dig up the old file with the pictures. Call it morbid curiosity, call it wanting to confront the truth of what she'd been through, but when he'd sat looking at those photographs in Larry Forbes's office he remembered how the wind had rattled the windows inwards, so much he thought they might crack. He'd been horrified. And then, as the horror had sunk deeper, he'd wiped a tear from his cheek. Right in front of Larry.

Because he saw his amazing wife, younger yet somehow much, much older, with swollen slits for eyes and skin that looked like she'd been rolled in purple and red paint. Eddie Pullen's art.

Which meant that Lucy had trust issues. Wasn't that, like, the norm? Matt looked back at the fire and didn't say anything for a long moment. They hadn't discussed this for a while. Hadn't needed to.

'So what do I do?'

'Just be patient.' She reached over and held his hand. 'And for God's sake, Matt, keep being you.'

'I'll always be me. And I'll never be him.'

It felt strange, assuring her of his lack of violence, while at the same time relishing the thought of slamming Eddie's forehead into the corner of a wall.

A peanut suddenly slipped from her hand and bounced on the floor. They stared at it. Then, eager to climb out of the intensity of the last few moments they both lunged to get it, toppling off the sofa and onto the rug. The wrestling became laughs, became kisses, became something else.

They made love in front of the fire, giggling into each other's necks like a couple of babysitters, clothes strewn across the floor.

As Wren kissed his shoulder, he happened to look over at the curtainless window above the dining table. Outside, the jet-black woods hung like a dark sheet against the criss-crossed pane, up-lit branches swayed from the glow of the cottage.

For a second he couldn't take his eyes off it. Couldn't peel them away from that dark rectangle in the wall.

He even heard what sounded like the crack of twigs out there.

'Matt?' she said in a breath. 'You're slowing down.'

Just branches, probably, rolling in the night wind. Either that or all the people of Hobbs Hill were marching through the trees towards the cottage, with pitchforks and burning torches shouting Fornicators! Copulators!

'Sorry.' He turned his eyes from the window and kissed her hard on the lips. Then moved to her shoulder and the cruel streak of scars that crept across it and up to the back of her neck. Shiny whip marks from a length of electrical flex Pullen had used on her. Like they were his signature, a sort of tribal mark to say he'd *always* own her. That she'd never truly be Matt's.

She crushed her lips into his and all dumb thoughts were instantly blown away.

When it was over they lay for a while listening to each other breathe.

She stumbled a lot when they climbed the stairs to bed and shushed herself with a finger across her laughing lips. As they lay in bed, staring at the ceiling, she spoke, clearly slurring now. 'If you ever . . . you know . . . *did* decide you believed in God again. I . . . I could handle it, you know.'

'It's not going to happen, so there's nothing to handle.'

'And all this stuff with Lucy,' she hiccupped, 'you do know that . . . we really, really love you. All three of us.'

'I know.'

'That *I* love you. Very much. And you helping look for this girl . . .' she put her head on his shoulder. 'I'm *so* glad you're *that* guy. That type.'

He kissed her forehead.

'So I love you. Like every day and every night.'

He laughed. 'Wren, go to sleep.'

'Mmmmm.' She turned over.

He lay awake long enough to hear her breathing sink into waves of heavy sleep. And just long enough for him to turn on his side, hand under his pillow, eyes closed like the shutters were down, brain in recharge mode. Face muscles relaxing, limbs sinking into the mattress.

He heard the crackle of twigs outside again.

It was like feet walking through the forest, underneath their window. Lazily he slid out of bed and shuffled to the curtainless window to look. He saw only shadows out there, and trunks and layers of black around the cottage. He considered heading down to check it out, but he was drunk enough to leave it. Forests made noises. That was the country way.

So he waited, head pressed against the window frame. Pretty much fell asleep against it.

The ghost of his mum tugged at his ear, speaking in the days when she had a normal mouth. *Church in the morning, boyo, and don't you forget it!* He sighed, rubbed his eyes and found himself sinking back into bed again, and very quickly into sleep.

His first and only dream told him exactly what was snapping the twigs out there tonight. He dreamt of two huge foxes, almost shadows, walking like men on their hind legs. They padded around the cottage and pushed the door quietly open, striding in. Then they slowly climbed the stairs, with their paws sliding up the bannister, noses sniffing at the air, so they might find the room where the human was. The one who had killed mother.

CHAPTER TWENTY-FIVE

To call it creepy was a masterclass in understatement.

A crowd of six-year-olds was up on the church stage in front of a three hundred-strong congregation. They were pretending to hammer one of their friend's wrists against a mini wooden cross, as the kid cried out in Aramaic. The *Mini-Me Jesus* even spat out some red across his lips as he chomped down on a stage-blood capsule. Wren screwed up her face at that part. 'Well, that's unnecessary.'

Amelia just said, 'Cool.'

Then a pipsqueak of a voice cried out from the little Christ, 'It is finished!' And he dropped his little head.

Perfectly on cue a bass line started from the band, instantly recognisable as people stood to sing the words on the huge karaoke screen thing. A middle-aged white woman with a South African accent trotted up to the microphone, raising her hands as the kids onstage started to dance. Her t-shirt genuinely said *Does My Faith Look Big in This?* She started talking about marriage and how beautiful it was between a man and a woman. Then she closed her eyes and prayed against modern society. She mentioned the so called 'tragedy' of same sex marriage, twice. Both prayers prompted hearty 'Amens' from the crowd. He'd need to unravel that with the kids, later.

Then she started to sing while an undeniably badass bassline started funking up the room. Three hundred people sang along with her. Hips were moving.

'I *know* this,' Wren said, screwing up her face as she tried to place the melody.

He leant over and whispered, "Course you do. It's "Ain't Nobody" by Chaka Khan. You know, the famous hymn-writer.'

As the music played he saw Lucy and Amelia looking through the crowd. They were checking out the youth group, who were crammed into the front pews. Of course Ben was there, bobbing his head to the music. Fringe a-flopping: while the younger kids were either clapping or doing over-literal dance moves to each lyric. Some of them were crumbling into fits of giggles, others holding hands in the air with eyes closed in devotion.

Big old Billy was standing at the side of the church. Not singing. Just watching the kids, smiling, and looking smug. Scratching at his goatee, like there were things in it.

He noticed that Lucy had an intrigued little frown on her face as she watched these teenagers. The corner of her mouth moved up in a smile. Maybe if she were on her own, she'd wander down to that group and join in.

And so it begins, Matt thought with a shiver.

When the speaking in tongues kicked in Wren looked like she'd got instant indigestion. Amelia just stuffed her fist in her mouth to stop herself from laughing. The disturbing racket went on for a few minutes then finally died down into a weird, alien murmur.

Church . . . he thought . . . *is literally another planet.*

The worship leader grabbed the microphone. 'Ladies and gentlemen, let me hand you over to our pastor. God's man for our church and our community. The Reverend Chris Kelly.' It was like the intro to *The Price Is Right*.

Applause rippled into a crescendo as Chris emerged through a side door and onto the stage. There was no dog collar this time. Now he wore a white shirt and a skinny black tie, hanging a little loose at the neck as if he was fronting some 40s swing band. It felt like it would only be a matter of minutes before he shot finger pistols at the crowd and said, 'Ayyyyyyyyyyyyyyy! Wha's happenin'?'

Matt suddenly pictured Chris back at Bible college, playing his guitar in front of a seething, unappreciative crowd of fellow ministers. For the first time he wondered if the reason why people didn't like him back then was because they were jealous. That like it or not, he had something that they didn't. A little stardust, a little charisma. Wasn't that what everybody wanted in their leaders, religious, political or otherwise?

'I do hope . . .' Chris held up his arms and the applause died down, 'I do hope you're clapping for him and not for me.' He pointed one finger up to the white plastic cross hanging over the stage.

Oh, please.

The crowd clapped even harder, painfully loud, like a huge bank of water was gushing in from behind to drown them all.

Chris wandered the stage as he spoke, one hand wrapped around a cordless microphone, cocked close to his lips. His voice seemed to take on an American lilt. 'It's great to have you here as we unpack God's word and we lift him up in prayer and song and thanksgiving, saving souls from hell and the grave.'

Someone whooped at that.

'Especially this morning, because we're doing two extra, *extra* special things.' Chris nodded to the band and they started playing some background music. It sounded like the wallpaper jazz you hear in coffee shops and waiting rooms. 'Question!' he said, as a tenor sax slinked out a backing melody. 'Does anyone know what a dominical ordinance is?'

The crowd murmured. A few people raised their hands to answer. Chris ignored them.

'I'll tell you, shall I? A dominical ordinance refers to any ritual that Jesus himself introduced. Not some church leader, not some pope. Not some committee trying to be . . .' he made finger quotes, '*relevant to the age*. But something Jesus himself told us to do. And you know what? Despite what you might think, he didn't introduce many. There are only two. Do you want to know what they are?'

'Yes!' One voice, hundreds-strong.

'Holy Communion and baptism. Jesus's greatest hits, I like to call them!'

Laughter from the crowd.

'And this morning, we'll be doing both. We'll take bread and wine and remember Jesus's death. But then after the service . . . we're gonna see some . . .' He shot that finger of his to the band. A drum roll started. An actual, prerehearsed drum roll, '. . . we'll see some resurrections!'

The loud crackle of applause made Amelia cover her ears.

'We'll be heading down to the lake for our baptisms. We've got eighteen people showing their commitment to the Lord today. Eighteen people who've beaten hell! They've purged their old selves and watched them drift away and die in the sky. Give us a wave, you lot!'

Suddenly various people from the Purging Party stood up, scattered through the crowd. They held up towels in the air and waved them like flags. Every one of them was dressed in a white flowing shirt. It was supposed to symbolise purity, but frankly they looked more like extras from *One Flew Over the Cuckoo's Nest*. Bat-shit crazy people dancing in the rec-room. Matt wondered how many of them had gone through those special 'sessions' at the Healing Centre that Isabel had been going through.

Isabel.

Who Matt kept scanning the crowd for, but couldn't see. Didn't Chris say she was getting baptised too?

'Prepare to get wet!' Chris shouted, and the people cheered and clapped for at least half a minute. 'But that's later. This morning's also important because God's brought some very special people into our midst. As you know, we're rebuilding this place into a state-of-the-art house of worship.'

Matt felt Wren's body stiffen against him.

'And I'm pleased to say that God's rustled up a fantastic young architect to help us. Wren Hunter, can you come on up here, so we can pray for you?'

'Oh, shite,' she said, just as the crowd turned to see where Chris was looking.

'I know you weren't expecting this, Wren, but it just came to me,' Chris said. 'I'd like to pray that God will help us make the right decision about who to hire here. How about you come up for a second?' He flicked his eyes to Matt. Spoke a little lower. 'And bring your family.'

The people in front turned in their seats and started nodding towards the stage, hurrying them up. One of them, a hard-eyed woman wearing inexplicable dungarees said, 'Go on. He said get up there.' A sort of *do-not-defy-the-master* look in her eye. She hurried them with open palms. 'Mush, mush.' Her voice was so whiny, it sounded like kittens being strangled.

'Come on,' Matt stood up. 'Let's just do it.'

Amelia was eager and beaming at everyone. She grabbed Matt's hand and sprang up. Then as the congregation started to clap and applaud, Wren and Lucy stood up too. He saw Lucy glance across the crowd, head lowered. She smiled politely at the nodding heads.

As they made their way up, the band started to play an impromptu song. The musicians giggled at each other at their apparent ingenuity. It was probably the only architect-sounding song they could think of.

The theme of Bob the Builder filled the room and a hundred guffaws followed. It was strange, the feeling of three hundred pairs of eyes watching him as he went up the steps onto a stage where he didn't belong. As the crazy music died down, Chris lined them up like action figures facing the crowd. The spotlights felt hot on his forehead. Matt looked out at the smiling faces and realised that when he was a minister he'd never spoken to a crowd anywhere near this big or this responsive. Not ever. He'd done it plenty in lectures, but the people there weren't looking at him as a demi-God. Or rather, a God-conduit. But these guys were doing just that. You could see it all in those sparkling eyeballs.

He could understand how vicars could get a power buzz from this.

Then Chris waved his hand over each of their heads as he went down the line, like a clapometer in an old game show.

Which one of the Hunter family do you think disappoints God the most? Clap your answers . . . NOW!

But instead he just ran through their names. 'This is Wren, Amelia, Lucy and Matt. Matt's an old, old friend of mine. And Wren's the very talented architect who may well help build something special here in Hobbs Hill . . . or should I say High Hopes.' More applause. 'Wren, have you got anything you think we should pray for, specifically?'

How irritating it was, Chris putting her on the spot like this. The guy knew full well that she wouldn't be used to this sort of thing. But as Matt glanced up at her she seemed strangely at ease. Smiling wide. Performing for her employers, he assumed.

Chris pushed the microphone close enough so it pressed against her bottom lip. Matt saw it crush against it as Chris pressed it there. Her flame-red hair blazed under the lights. She ran her hand through it and scooped it back from her face. 'I guess you should pray that whoever you choose, the renovation will be on time, on budget and safe.'

'Anything else?'

She shrugged, with a cheeky glint in her eye. 'How about world peace, Chris?'

He squeezed her arm. 'Now *that's* a prayer.' He stepped down the line towards Matt, placed a hand on his shoulder and pushed the mic in his direction. He quickly tried to think what he might say. Maybe he could go all buzz-kill and ask them to pray for Nicola Knox and Tabitha Clarke but he needn't have bothered. Chris didn't ask him anything. He just hung his head low. 'Let us pray.'

Every head swung down and the crowd began to murmur.

'Please, reach out your hands toward this family so that they might feel blessed and touched by the hand of the living God.'

He didn't like this, being forced into being prayed for. Annoying, presumptive and not a little bit freaky. He'd met an ex-churchgoer who once described unprompted prayer as 'spiritual rape!' Which was a bit much. But then if God didn't actually exist, what difference did it make?

It still came as a shock, though. To feel his heart quickening under his chest, the nervous quiver in his skin as the prayers started buzzing toward him in swarms. From a bunch of odd, but still human people so caught up in strange fantasy. He felt a sudden beautiful urge to write his book like his life depended on it. To write about the manipulative chemistry of our brains where the left hemisphere senses the existence of the right and interprets it as some 'other' presence out there. When it was actually, and quite literally, all in the head.

For a moment, he pitied them all. Not the patronising type of pity. This was genuine, heartfelt concern. He thought of Tabitha. Statistically speaking, there'd be a sizeable portion who would be struggling with their own sexual identity. But unlike her, they'd be rejecting that part of themselves because of the evangelical party line. Trying to bury it, as if that were possible. He looked at the teenagers, growing up in a place that made it very clear what was right and wrong. Stats flickered across his brain, of young Christians deciding suicide was preferable to disappointing their religious communities, their families, their God. He thought of old spinster ladies saying they'd 'been called to singlehood', when actually they had simply fallen in love with the same sex, and assumed it to be abhorrent. He sighed as he looked at them. Wanted to grab the mike and tell them there were alternatives out there.

But by then the arms had started to rise and outstretched palms opened in the crowd. All eyes closed, deep in devotion.

Except, Matt noticed, one person.

Billy was standing at the side again, leaning against a radiator. His eyes were open in a blank-looking stare. But his lips were moving.

Matt always thought kissing without closing your eyes looked sort of wrong. Praying with your eyes open appeared just as demented.

Billy stared hard at Matt and then at Wren and Lucy. And finally at Amelia. His gaze stayed there, lingering on her for longer than seemed right. Then finally Billy closed his eyes again, chewing on his bottom lip like a famished man.

The entire building pulsed with their murmuring.

Churchy types get used to it. Average people don't.

He listened to hundreds of people whispering at the same time, making a sound that slithered through the room like there were snakes under the chairs.

He looked down the line and saw that the rest of his family had their eyes closed. He was the only one who didn't, so he just looked down at the carpet.

A little x-mark of yellow insulation tape was under his foot. He saw three more in front of his wife and children. Four marks, the sort that stage managers put in studios so that they know where to put the guests for the best camera angles. This little moment wasn't off the cuff, despite what Chris just said.

Then Chris began to pray. He moved down the line and placed a hand on Wren's shoulder first, then on Lucy and finally Amelia.

'Lord, you are so patient and understanding with us. Please, let this family know your presence. Not in their mind, but in their heart. Their soul. And may they meet you here in Hobbs Hill. May they know your patience with them. And the depth and intensity of your fierce and faithful love for them. May they turn . . . may they turn to you. In Jesus's glorious name, Amen.'

Three hundred voices said '*Amen.*'

Chris opened his hand towards the steps, giving them permission to leave the stage. The girls headed down first, then just as Matt went to go Chris leant in and whispered something into his ear, out of range of the microphones: 'Matt. I forgive you. For interrupting us with Izzy. I forgive you.'

He gave a presumptive, but hard, little squeeze of the shoulder that was supposed to signify closure. And then Chris sprang off toward the lectern and started leafing through the Bible.

Matt stood there for a moment, looking like an idiot. And so he hurried down the stairs and back to the seat, wishing he could be heading straight for the door where he might be able to catch his breath. It felt like Mars in here, the air was so thin. Back in their chairs hands were patting Wren on the shoulder, reassuringly. Like people do on the brow of an obedient pet dog.

'We are *so* rock stars,' Amelia said, as they settled back down.

Chris started to read from the New Testament so Matt went to grab a Bible from the back of the seat in front of him, when he felt a silent buzz from the phone in his pocket. He saw the words Sergeant Miller flashing on the screen.

'Sorry,' he said to Wren. 'I have to take this.'

She nodded, unphased by the people who kept looking back, tutting under their breath at the commotion.

'Hello?' Matt whispered.

'Matt, it's Terry. What are you whispering for?'

'I'm in church.'

'You're kidding.'

'No. What do you want?' Chris was speaking louder now, so Matt pressed a finger into one of his ears. The Bible grew muffled.

'Look, I had my officers do a wider sweep of the land around Tabitha's place.'

'And?'

'Matt, we found the paintings. I think you need to come and see this.'

'Now?'

'Yeah. Well, if that's—'

'That's perfect.'

'Good. I'd be interested in your thoughts. Come on up to Tabitha's farmhouse. I'll send someone to meet you there and bring you down to the woods.'

Matt checked his watch. 'Give me fifteen minutes.' He tapped the phone to hang up and slid it back into the pocket of his jeans.

'What's wrong?' Wren said.

'I have to go.' Then in a quiet whisper. 'Local police need me.'

She nodded, but she did it very slowly. 'Just don't forget to—'

'*Do you mind?*' A hissing voice from dungarees woman in front of them.

Wren leant closer to him and whispered directly into his ear. 'Don't forget to come and pick us up after, or I'll have to ask Seth. And quite frankly I don't fancy being with this lot on my own for too long.'

'Understood.'

She smiled and shooed him away. 'Go on then. Have fun.'

He smirked. 'And you.'

'Shhhhhh!' Another voice, from behind this time.

Wren held up her hand in apology.

Amelia looked over at him, frowning. He mouthed sorry then headed off.

By the time he reached the end of the row the Bible reading had come to an end. Chris must have been about to start his sermon but seemed to deliberately wait before speaking. So for about ten seconds the only thing that echoed in the church was the sound of Matt's footsteps as he hurried up the aisle. A tiny piece of gravel was stuck in the grips (or was it a little neck bone from the fox?) Whatever it was, an echoing clatter came from his heel so that every eye was fixed on him as he made his way through the glass doors.

Some frowned, some whispered, some curled their lips. But every eye said the same thing.

Why would anyone in their right mind look so relieved to be leaving a church as wonderful as this?

CHAPTER TWENTY-SIX

'Not long now, Professor,' the special constable said, as they clambered through bushes and over hills. She looked about fifty years old and regularly puffed air in and out of her cheeks. Mostly as she used her hands to lift her own hefty legs over logs. Her dyed black hair was thick with toilet roll-sized curls. They bounced as she walked. She was taking him across the sloping fields from Tabitha Clarke's farmhouse down towards the edge of a thick forest.

'What's your name?' he asked.

'Marion Fellowes.'

'Matt Hunter. There's no need to call me professor.'

They shook hands as they walked.

'Actually,' she said, 'I already know your name because I saw you on telly, didn't I?'

'Uh-oh.'

'No, no, it was good. I was impressed, you saving a possessed lady like that.'

'Nah . . . she wasn't possessed.'

'No?'

'It was psychological.'

'Aww, are you sure?'

'Hundred per cent.'

'Well isn't that a crying bloody shame,' she said. 'Where's all the mystery going these days?'

He could already see the other officers in amongst the trees. Their jackets hung on branches and they'd rolled up their shirtsleeves in the heat. Most of them were kneeling down and sifting through things on the floor, kneecaps crushing twigs and bugs.

Miller was in the middle of it all in full uniform. He had that tight-lipped, strutting thing going on. The move that stressed people do. Matt sympathised. The guy was used to a fairly sedate life here in Hobbs Hill. The more they uncovered about these missing person cases (or 'mis-pers' as Miller called them) the more challenging it was becoming.

For some officers who ran stations in small villages, the sudden appearance of a crime on the scale of murder was an opportunity to put their police work into practice. A time to test their training and, dare he say it, get some excitement.

For others, though, it was the mark of failure. That somehow good old village bobby Terry Miller had let two women vanish while he was supposed to be watching over them. Like when a shepherd finds one of his sheep dead and covered in wolf bites.

'There you go,' Marion said, struggling to catch her breath. 'Nice chatting.'

He thanked her with a nod.

Miller lifted his hand to greet Matt. 'You get any more weird emails?'

'Nope.'

'Well that's a relief. Good time at church?'

'If by nice you mean bizarre and uncomfortable, then yeah. It was extremely nice.'

'Well. I reckon this'll be more your style.'

A pile of canvas frames, charred and burnt, lay in a messy black pyramid in the centre of a small clearing. The floor was scorched with white ash and black soot. It filled his nostrils with the smell of old smoke. Like that hideous Lapsang Souchong tea Wren insisted on drinking.

'How many paintings are there?'

'We're laying out the debris and rebuilding the frames. We've got about fourteen so far.'

Matt ducked under a hanging branch to get closer. 'I don't get it. Why burn them them? Did any of them survive the fire?'

'Three.' Miller nodded towards a huge spray of nettles. Three canvases were leaning against three separate trees, all in a neat row. Fire had eaten into a third of one of them and half of the other two were charred.

Matt wandered closer and heard his knees pop as he crouched in front of each.

Because of the fire damage large areas of detail were missing, but there was enough to get the idea. All three pictures were variations on the same theme – a large naked woman sitting by, on or near trees. The curves and marks on the canvas were clearly made by someone who knew what they were doing. Tabitha Clarke actually had talent.

Which made the rest of it so odd.

Each of the three paintings had a thick crucifix daubed across it. In bright and vivid red paint, peeling only where the fire had tried to eat it away.

'I told you we had a lot of crosses around here,' Miller said, nervously.

'They look splashed on, done quickly. I take it she didn't normally have these slapped on her work?'

'Er, no, she didn't,' Miller said. 'I suppose she could have turned against her own pictures. Defaced and burnt them down here.'

'Or someone else did this. Did you find anything else?'

A voice called over from a distance. 'Sergeant Miller?' All heads spun in the direction of a tall woman in a black jacket, crouching between two trees about fifty feet away.

Miller leant in, 'That's Benson. Brought her in from up the road.'

Up the road, Matt was learning, was local speak for the City of Oxford.

'I think you'd better see this,' she said, and held up the edge of a clear plastic bag between the tips of her blue rubber gloves. Inside it, nestled in the corner, was a mobile phone. Switched off. 'I just found this under a bush. It wasn't hidden that well.'

Miller squinted at the bag and curled his lip. 'You put it in a Tesco's sandwich bag? I thought you guys had proper evidence bags for—'

'Calm . . .' she pressed the air between them. 'This is how I found it.'

'Oh.'

She smirked at that. 'It was sealed pretty tight. Whoever left it wanted to keep it protected from the rain and dew. Maybe they planned on picking it up later.'

'Or they wanted someone else to find it,' Matt said.

'Quite possibly. Give me a second to clear it.' Benson popped her black briefcase open as she set it onto a flat-looking tree stump. She pulled out brushes and tweezers then she popped up a little mini box thing made of blue plastic, big enough to put her hands in. She shimmied out a rugged-looking laptop and got to work examining the bag and phone.

Matt spotted a twisted log nearby. 'Can I sit on this?'

She nodded. 'Be my guest.'

He was just about to sit when he felt a buzz in his pocket. He pulled out his phone.

A text message from Wren:

They're singing 'It's a Wonderful World'. I kid you not, everyone's singing in a Louis Armstrong voice while two pensioners do an interpretive dance. Just thought you should know what you're missing xxw

He sent her a quick response.

Get up on stage and do some body-popping. God commands it xxm

194

He slipped the phone back in his pocket and watched Benson. Taking photographs of the phone and swishing her brushes as it lay in the bottom of the blue pop-up box. She did this with such delicate precision, it was like she was cleaning up the precious, hidden bones of a T-Rex. He glanced back at the crosses on the canvases and around the woods, as officers lifted bushes and kicked dirt around. Maybe there were houses or farms nearby and they'd seen the smoke from the fire. He'd ask.

'Done.' Benson handed the phone back to Harris, then she packed her dusters and tweezers away. She spun her laptop around so they could see.

'Anything on the phone?' Miller asked. 'Or the bag?'

'A couple of fibres. I'll have to check them out at the office. Other than that, there's nothing, except the prints. I ran them through the optical reader and checked against the prints from Clarke's farmhouse.'

'And?'

'She definitely touched this phone, a lot, so I assume it's hers. Found her prints, mainly on the side and back. Not so much on the buttons. But I couldn't find any other prints. Feel free to switch it on, by the way.'

Everyone's eyes flitted down to the mobile.

Miller hit the 'on' button. They waited for what seemed like a minute but was probably closer to twenty seconds. Then a sudden Samsung chime echoed through the wood. A bird must have thought it was the four-minute warning because it squeaked in panic and fluttered off in the opposite direction.

Miller started working his way through the phone menus. Impatient, Matt stepped behind to peer over his shoulder.

Texts received: 0
Texts sent: 0
Calls received: 0
Calls sent: 0

'Check her address book,' Matt said. 'Maybe there's a friend in there you don't know about.'

Miller clicked a few buttons then shook his head.

Phone numbers: 0

'Someone's blanked this,' Miller said. 'There's sod all on here.'

Matt was itching to grab the phone himself and rummage through the files. 'Give it some time. It takes a bit for phones to pick up messages from the network. Have you tried her notes or diary?'

Miller flicked to the call log screen and, like everywhere else, it was empty. But as he moved back, he spotted something else. 'Haaaang on a sec.'

Personal notes: 1

Miller clicked it open and read it to himself, first. He started to frown, then his face seemed to plunge. 'Oh shit.'

'What is it?' Matt said.

'Quote,' Miller cleared his throat, '*I've repented and I'm with God now. Maybe one day you could come too xx Tabitha Tansy Clarke.*' Miller narrowed his eyes and read the final word. '*Verecundus.*'

'How odd,' Matt leant in, intrigued, all but snatching the phone and looking at it himself. 'That sounds like Latin.'

'Is that what it is?' Miller's voice was almost a whisper. There was something weird about the way he was staring at the floor.

'Miller? What's going on?'

He looked up. 'Do you speak Latin?'

'A bit. I can't remember what that word means, offhand but . . . it sounds familiar.'

'Well, it sounds very familiar to me.'

Matt lowered his voice a little. 'You've seen this before?'

Miller didn't answer at first. He seemed to be turning thoughts over in his head. Finally he looked back at Taylor and Benson, standing there and listening. 'Oh, what the hell. Maybe you can help with it. Nicola Knox's mum found her daughter's phone. She assumed it was a suicide note. It had a very similar message to this one.' Miller rubbed his temple for a second, leaving a little white scratch. 'That *verecundus* thing was on it, too.'

'So that's two missing women with the same message on their phone . . .' Matt waited for a second. 'This doesn't sound good . . .'

Miller stared at the phone screen, tugging at his lip.

Police Constable Taylor, who hadn't said a word so far suddenly piped up. 'Suicide theory still stands.'

'What?' Miller said. 'For *both* of them?'

'Yeah. Why not? Maybe these two ladies got to know each other. Maybe they were even . . .' he could hardly even bring himself to say it. '. . . you know . . . lovers. Like a suicide pact or something. Haven't you seen *Thelma and Louise*?'

Matt skipped the detail that Thelma and Louis were actually Brad Pitt-level straight, and got to the point. 'Putting Nicola and Tabitha in a relationship would make for a forty year age gap. That seems speculative at best and—'

Taylor shrugged, 'I've read these older gays can be pretty darn predatory.'

Matt gasped and threw up his hands, 'You can't *say* that.' He looked around at the others. 'He can't just say stuff like that. Not without any evidence.'

'Watch your phrasing, Taylor,' Miller said, quietly.

'Look . . .' Taylor went on. 'Tabitha was dying, right? And maybe it got too much and so she euthanized herself . . . but she burned all this sinful stuff down here before she met her maker. I would have done the same thing if I was like her. I'd have repented.'

Miller blinked slowly, not saying a word.

'So you have two ladies, at least one of which is suicidal, possibly

197

both. And they have the exact same note? Obviously they must have been talking to each other.'

'Or,' Matt said, 'someone killed them both and wrote these texts to confuse us. Doing it on the phone means the killer didn't have to fake her handwriting.'

'*Or,*' Taylor held up a finger, alive now, 'Tabitha wound up killing Nicola and she wrote these texts as a deco—'

'Enough,' Miller shouted, and a squirrel froze halfway up a tree. He took a long breath. 'We don't even have a single body yet. You can't have a killer without a—'

'Mrs Benson?' Matt asked.

She looked up from the paintings, seemingly transfixed by them.

'Shouldn't a phone have strong prints on the number keys?'

'Pardon?'

'The phone. You said Tabitha's prints are on the sides and back, but not much on the keys.' He nodded down at the phone in Miller's hand. 'Isn't that odd?'

She shrugged. 'Potentially. But then she'd have used the same keys over and over. She could have rubbed away some of her own prints.' A slight breeze rattled the leaves above them. 'Unless . . . and I take it this is what you're getting at . . . someone wearing gloves typed this message and smudged hers away.'

Matt took a step and a twig snapped loudly under his shoe. 'Look, maybe Tabitha Clarke's just run off, that's entirely possible. Maybe even with Nicola Knox. But how far is a cancer victim going to get without seeing a doctor and getting her pills? You think she could clamber down here, burn her own stuff and still be able to stand up? I mean, me and Marion were out of breath just getting down the hill.'

Marion was obviously listening in, because she raised her hand. 'He's right. I nearly split a gizzard.'

Miller listened, quietly.

'So unless one of them suddenly sends you a postcard saying

they're all happy and out on a field trip then clearly murder is a *very* real possibility here.'

'That makes a lot of sense, Terry,' said Marion. 'A hell of a lot.'

'I think you're wrong,' Taylor screwed up his face, like he'd just eaten a burnt cornflake. 'I think the first thing we do is check the lake properly. Get some divers in. You may not be aware, Professor, but Cooper's Force is quite the hot spot for jumpers. It's like that forest in Japan. People from up the road come down here all the time and do themselves in. We get a lot of stressed academics flinging themselves off too . . .' He tilted his head when he said that, to make some sort of point. 'Besides . . . you're from London. So you need to understand that we just don't tend to get things like murder out—'

Miller suddenly yelped like a little dog, cutting Taylor off. His body jerked spasmodically and everyone saw the phone drop straight through his fingers to the ground, chiming as it fell.

'Terry?' Matt said.

'Bloody little thing. It just moved in my hand.'

'Just like "The Monkey's Paw",' Marion said ominously. 'You ever read—'

'Christ, Marion, will you just zip it?' Miller bent over, plucked the phone out of the dry leaves and turned the screen towards him. It was finally gathering a signal and was starting to collect voicemails and texts.

Two more chimes came through, one quickly after the other.

One text and three voicemail messages. Nothing more.

Miller pulled the phone close to his face, so that the others couldn't see. 'Okay . . . the text message is . . . some competition offer. Irrelevant.' He held the phone to his head and listened to the voice messages. Matt could hear the odd electronic warble coming from the phone, but not enough to work out what the voices were saying.

'Can't you put it on speaker phone?' Matt said.

Miller pushed out his lips. 'Shush.' Then his eyes suddenly

widened. 'I don't believe this . . .' Finally, he pressed a button then pulled the phone from his ear. 'Right. The last two messages are from her doctor, asking why she didn't turn up for her appointment.'

'And the first?'

With a sort of twisted, satisfied smile, Miller held the phone up and replayed the message on speaker phone. A tinny, computerised voice gave the details: 'Message. Sent. Tuesday. July. 12th. 12:24. AM.'

'Just after midnight, which is a weird time to call anybody,' Miller said. 'Which was also a week or so before Tabitha was noticed missing.'

The message began. Matt could feel his heart pounding harder with each beat of the sentences.

Hi, Tabby. Got your message on our machine. Thanks for getting in touch. I'm happy to come and see you on Sunday night. About eight o'clock, alright? Oh and Tabby, I'm only going to come if you're serious about this. Okay? God bless you . . . and bye.

Miller tilted his head. 'Didn't you tell me that Chris Kelly said he'd never met Tabitha Clarke?'

Matt was surprised to find himself pushing his tongue against the inside of his cheek, as if some schoolboy loyalty was preventing him from dobbing in a friend, however loose that label hung. He quickly ignored it and started to nod. 'He said he'd never had the pleasure. Those exact words.'

'Which means Pastor Chris is a bloody, barefaced liar.' Miller checked his watch. 'Come on. I suddenly feel like going to church.'

CHAPTER TWENTY-SEVEN

Matt quickly cranked the gears of his car. He had to floor the pedal just to keep up with the police car he was following, weaving fast through the country roads. They hadn't put the siren on, but he could just about see Sergeant Miller in the driver's seat, head bobbing up and down like a crash test dummy on the bumps as PC Taylor held on in the passenger seat. They'd left the rest of the team behind, crawling through the dry leaves looking for clues. Who knows, maybe they'd find a big old footprint with the backwards imprint of Chris Kelly's name on it.

He pictured himself standing with Chris at the healing centre, asking him about Tabitha Clarke.

I've heard of her . . . but I've never had the pleasure.

What the hell did that *mean*? Was it a lie? An actual bona-fide untruth? And if Chris was lying (and this was the part that prickled the skin) what the hell had he done? That was about as far as Matt was permitting himself to think at this stage. Just questions. Miller's reaction since, on the other hand, was far less subtle. He was monumentally pissed at a 'full-on lie'. His tight-lipped shake of the head and clucks of the tongue (he did this at least three times before leaping into his police car) made that obvious.

The two cars raced their way back up the hill, very fast and towards the church. And despite the unsettling throb in Matt's stomach, there was an undeniable thrill to bombing through the roads of Hobbs Hill, screeching tyres on the bends. His window was down, hair frantic and flapping. At one point he actually had to grip the roof and steer with one hand on a super tight bend. A rare thrill. He didn't get to do *this* stuff at uni – another tick in the box of police involvement.

When they reached the church car park they found that it was still full, rammed in fact. And they came to a gravel-crunching stop outside the main entrance. When they stepped out of the cars all three of them could hear the sound of cheering. The roar filled the air around them, but it wasn't coming from inside the church and they couldn't see its source.

'It's coming from down by the lake,' Miller said and started to climb back into the car.

'Then they must have started the baptisms already.'

'Yep,' Miller clunked the car door shut and spoke through the open window. 'Come on, Professor. Bet you've never seen anything like this.'

Miller spun some gravel as he headed off and Matt quickly followed to the top of the track. He jerked over the ridge like a rollercoaster tipping over the biggest dip. The bonnet plunged downwards and he saw the Healing Centre, the lake and Cooper's Force in all its roaring glory at the bottom.

A few hundred people were gathered on the natural slope of the hill, cheering, singing. The nutty acoustics from the rock-walled lake made it sound more like a gladiatorial arena than a church outing. All were turned towards the water where a long row of white figures stood in single file along the shoreline. It reminded him of an old Hammer movie. Robed devil worshippers, lining up for sacrifice.

They reached the car park at the bottom and parked, blocking people in because it was so packed. They stepped out. Matt glanced at the entrance of the Healing Centre and at the glass in the door he'd smashed yesterday during his confused attempt at heroism. It was boarded up now.

'Are you coming, or what?' Miller said, then marched towards the edge of the crowd with Taylor behind him (who looked pale and slack-jawed at the thought of striding up to his own beloved pastor and calling him out for a sin). Some punters were starting to look over, wondering what on earth was going on.

Matt caught up to hear Taylor in deep debate. 'I take it you're not just going to call Chris out, right in the middle of this? There might be an explanation . . . and it's not like he's going anywhere.'

'Don't panic. I'll wait till he's done.'

Matt frowned, 'Should we just talk to him right away? Find out what he—'

'No. I want to give him some time to stew. I want him to see us here.'

Matt noticed a tiny crucifix badge, glinting in the sun, on Taylor's lapel. Was he wearing that before? Or had he just pinned it there, on the way over here?

'Besides,' Miller said. 'I hardly want to make this lot unhappy with me, do I? Probably wake up with a dead chicken nailed to my door.'

'That's voodoo, Terry,' Taylor said in disgust. 'That is *not* Christianity.'

'Bloody hell, it was a joke.' He stomped deep into the crowd.

There were hundreds out here. And the summer heat meant that most were wearing t-shirts or short-sleeved blouses. As the crowd grew more dense, Matt could feel his own arms smearing against hot bare skin as he squeezed his way through. The stink of perfume, fried onions and summer's day body odour swept by him in nauseating waves, but that wasn't what was making him feel so uncomfortable.

No.

What made him so uncomfortable were the narrowed eyes, the whisperings, which were not in his head but were real and external and happening right then. The collective crowd consciousness turned in his direction as he slid himself through their clammy bodies. Two policemen were nudging through the crowd, clearly on a mission and yet everyone was looking, *kept* looking, at him.

Isn't that the architect's husband? Didn't we pray for him this morning and then he ran off? Allergic to the truth, this one. Can't you smell it on him? He isn't here to worship, he's here to destroy.

They battled through the quicksand of the crowd and finally the three of them stumbled out from the front line, near the shore. A few volunteer stewards were there in dayglo vests keeping a busy eye on the people, making sure nobody got trampled to death since that would put a downer on the whole proceedings.

A lovely, sudden breeze swam past Matt's skin and he took a breath of the crisp air coming off the lake. His hair quivered a little as it passed through him.

And there was Chris, hands clasped together. He was kneeling under a green and white gazebo, just next to where the band had set up on the grass. He stayed kneeling like that for another minute, a very public picture of holiness. Someone handed him a handheld radio mike and he sprang to his feet. He tapped the end of it before speaking.

He didn't say much. But it was enough to get the whole crowd cheering with delight. 'How about we start . . . dunkin' some disciples!'

Like a talk show house band the musicians surged into life as Chris slipped off his shoes and walked towards the water. They were playing some sort of country hoedown version of 'Abide With Me' – insane but bizarrely catchy. Chris was wading into the lake, the water lapping at his shins, his knees, then his thighs. Then finally it reached his waist. The ever-present Billy waded out too, fat and bald and quickly becoming Igor to Chris's Dr Frankenstein. By the time they both turned back round, the first candidate had already started to step into the water.

It was a skinny lady in jeans and a long, white, flowing shirt. She was being helped along by a blonde woman from the congregation while people in the crowd cheered them all on.

Finally the lady sloshed her way through, all the way to Chris and he tried to grab her hand. She planted her fingers on Chris's chest and started to rub it. Quite sensually.

'Eh up,' Miller said, throwing Matt an uncomfortable glance.

Then the lady ran her hand up Chris's chest and tapped her fingertips across his face, feeling his forehead, the bridge of his nose, his lips and chin. Chris gently turned the blind woman to face the crowd.

He moved her hands up to her chest then crossed them over as though he was preparing her for the grave. Little hands clasped together. Then he and Billy grabbed a forearm each. Their other hands were supporting her back.

There were no microphones because of the water, so Matt couldn't hear them as they spoke to her. But he could tell what was being said. Matt had used those words a fair few times himself, in his minister days. He tried not to whisper along with them.

– *Do you confess Jesus Christ as your Lord and Saviour?*

– *I do.*

– *Then I baptise you in the name of the Father . . .*

Boom . . .

. . . down she went. The water quaked out beneath her as her volume displaced the lake. Instantly it flooded back over her hair, into her eyes, up her nostrils, through her open mouth, which she hadn't managed to close in time.

The crowd roared as they pulled her back to the surface, coughing.

Chris's mouth moved, making silent words.

And of the Son . . .

Down again . . .

Under . . .

Under . . .

She crashed far beneath now, looking on the way down like a drowned corpse, soaked to the skin, then back up again, hair gooey and matted against her head. No longer a corpse, she was now a baby calf, freshly born and sticky with amniotic fluid.

And then the third and final time.

And of the Holy Spirit . . .

Slam . . .

Under.

Deeper than ever. Almost as if she might smack her head on the sharp rocks at the bottom of the lake. There was an oddly stretched second when it wasn't clear if Chris was even going to bring her back—

—up again now, with a panting, undignified gasp as the bedraggled woman sprayed water, spit, snot and tears everywhere. And then, after she knew it was done, the blind woman crumbled against Chris. She shuddered with loud, orgasmic-sounding tears and sobs. Then Billy did something bizarre. He snapped his head back and howled like a wolf.

And for a moment Matt could hear her.

Not the blind woman. Not her.

He could hear his own mother, weeping with joy from somewhere in the crowd, behind him, saying *Hallelujah* . . . *isn't Jesus great?* Holding her towel out to Matt on the pebbly shore of Sizewell beach as he was baptised, fourteen years old, in the shadow of the nuclear power station.

He blinked, and the millisecond his eyes were shut was enough time to see something else, flickering the neurons of his brain. His mother. Out there, on the lake. And she was weeping while a naked schizophrenic grabbed her wrists and slammed her into the water three times. Each time a thousand blades rose like Excalibur to meet her. And he sliced and sliced until his mother was no more than slivers of skin, floating on a lake made of blood.

Then for a second, he looked at the hand, forcing his mother onto the blades. But it wasn't Ian Pendle's.

It was his own.

Matt's eyelids flickered and he felt a dangerous urge inside him, the type he had when he was a kid in school exams, where he'd have a burning notion to stand up on the table and shout something loud and inappropriate in the quiet exam hall just to let out his tension.

Now, by the lake, the real man inside him, the true honest man who he rarely let come to the surface in front of anyone but Wren, and sometimes not even to her, *that* man wanted to climb out of his skin and march over to the band, tear the microphone out of the smarmy bitch's hand who was singing like a maniac and shout down into those speakers and across the field,

Just you wait . . . just you wait till God turns off the happy taps and lets you drown under there . . . just you wait till he pushes you under and doesn't let you come back up . . . and some schizo stabs your mum in the throat, or beats your wife till she can't part her lips to say her own name. Hallelujah, praise the psychotic, useless Lord.

A wave of dizziness hit him and he was shocked at the intensity of it. Somehow furious with Chris Kelly whose very presence seemed to pull Matt back into that first term Bible college world, a place where God was real and loving and had some sort of purpose for Matt's life. The blissful, easy land where possessed black women didn't writhe and call for him. Where his mum still walked her neighbour's dog and still had a heartbeat.

And lips. Don't forget she had them once.

A pre-fall world that told him life made sense.

But from this side of the glass, in the company of all these believers, he knew how he felt. He was gutted. Gutted that it turned out that the old world of belief proved to be an utterly false one, made of paper and bread and cheap red wine without any alcohol in it.

And most of all . . . he felt deceived. Yes! That was it. That was the exact word that now crackled in his head like it was written in the bulbs of the Blackpool illuminations, flashing on and off for eternity so he would never, ever forget it. He felt deceived by all of God's finger-crossed promises of grace and mercy. Promises that wound up drowning in so much (*so* much) blood on his mother's kitchen table.

And all those tricked people in churches across the globe, stretching both forwards and backwards through time, deceived, by heroin that utterly screws you up.

And whenever Matt felt deceit, anger was sure to follow.

'Matt?' Miller whispered. 'You okay?'

'Erm . . .'

'Well?'

He grabbed the first excuse he could think of. 'I'm just wondering why nobody helped the blind lady pick a white bra.'

Miller looked over as the blind woman was helped back to the shore. Her jet-black bra glared out vividly and clearly under the white of her shirt. 'Wow,' Miller said.

Then Matt noticed something else. Chris wasn't looking for the next baptism candidate any more. Instead, those sharp eyes of his were falling on Matt and the other two police officers standing beside him, who were as welcome here as undertakers at a baby's first birthday party.

There was no doubt about it. The wide, beaming grin on Chris's face completely slipped away.

'You see that?' Miller said. 'You see his face drop?'

Chris held Matt's gaze. What was that look in Chris's eyes? Guilt? Disappointment? Fear? Pity?

Ah, crap. Don't let it be pity. I'm supposed to be pitying you, not the other way around.

But before Matt could figure it out, the smile flashed back, almost as quickly as it went.

Miller leant over, his lips close to Matt's ear. 'You can't tell me that isn't the face of a man who just pissed his pants. He's worried that we're here.'

CHAPTER TWENTY-EIGHT

The row of baptismal candidates moved along a notch, hitching their white gowns as a nervous-looking elderly man walked slowly out into the lake. He dragged his cream chino's through the water and shivered with the cold of it.

Matt looked over his shoulder to see if Wren and the kids might be somewhere in sight but no matter how much he craned his neck, he couldn't find them. All he saw was a couple of burger vans the church had hired. God, he was famished.

The rest of the baptisms seemed to take forever to finish but as soon as they did the crowd began to dissipate, quicker than he expected. He watched them all gather up their things and head off. He could tell this was a church group because they all took their rubbish with them. The grass looked spotless once they'd moved off. And Matt watched the mass of them trekking up the dirt track back to their cars.

They were laughing and smiling, arms round each other. They munched on the remnants of hot dogs and ice creams and looked . . . happy. Content with life. Even the ones in wheelchairs, or that blind lady with the black bra. They all seemed completely at ease with the world.

Some of them would visit the doctor over the coming months

and the doctor would say something like, 'I'm sorry, but I have some good news and some bad news. The good news is you have twenty-four hours to live and the bad news is I was supposed to tell you that yesterday.' And even so, they would *still* stumble out of that office shocked and devastated but not crushed.

If he wasn't such a stickler for old-fashioned concepts like 'Is it true?' he might even envy them. But their hope was based on a mirage, the shifting ghost of a folk tale.

He turned back to Miller. 'I think we should get on with this.'

He nodded quickly and they walked towards the shore while Chris and howling Billy waded out of the water. Chris was rubbing his arms and the back of his head vigorously with a bright-yellow towel, like he was putting out a fire. He nodded towards them as they approached. 'I thought you came to Hobbs Hill to relax, Matt? Are you working here now? You one of those PI types?'

Miller spoke much more gently than Matt had expected him to. 'He's helping us out with a few things, Padre.'

'Terry, I keep telling you, you have to call me Chris.'

Some of the band members were packing up their equipment. They coiled jack leads around their arms while trying not to look over at the drama. They were failing spectacularly.

'Just a few quick words.' Miller took Chris by the elbow and led him out of everyone's earshot. Matt and Taylor went with them.

'Why the long faces?'

'We need your help with something,' Miller said.

'Fire away.'

'It's about Tabitha Clarke.'

'Ah, the missing lady?' His tone swooped up at the end of the sentence. It sounded hopeful. 'You've found her?'

'Not yet, because between us . . .' Miller leant in, '. . . there's a possibility that she's been murdered.'

Chris blinked once. 'I'm sorry?'

'I said there's a chance she might have been murdered.'

There was a pause, then a strange twitch of the mouth. Shock? A nervous tick? A millisecond smile? When Chris spoke next it was nothing more than a whisper. 'Then may God rest her troubled soul.'

'I said there's a *chance* she's been murdered. We don't know for sure,' Miller said.

'Oh. I see.'

'There's something else,' Matt added. Feeling incredibly awkward about this entire situation. 'The police have found her phone.'

The blood in Chris's face seemed to drain away. Matt could tell both Miller and Taylor saw it too.

'You okay, Padre?' Miller said. 'You look upset.'

'Of course I'm upset. What a shock. To think this poor lady might have been killed . . . possibly.' He asked no questions about the phone, Matt noticed.

'Then you won't mind coming with us? Just to help us with our enquiries.'

The smile he gave was utterly devoid of humour. 'Isn't that what you say just before you arrest someone?'

'It means what it means,' Miller said. 'We need you to clarify a few things for us. Are you dry yet?'

'I suppose I am.' He folded the towel neatly (and slowly), then set it on the grass. 'I'll need a few minutes. My car's up top in the church car park so you'll have to wait till I get it.'

Miller shook his head. 'You'll come in my car.'

'Seriously, my car's just up there.'

Most of the crowd had gone but there was still a bunch of people heading up the dirt track. Clearly, Chris didn't want the crowds to see their minister riding past them in the back of a police car. What sort of gossip might that cause?

And to be fair to Chris he was hardly under arrest, so there wasn't any need to risk the guy's reputation.

'How about you come up in my car,' Matt suggested. 'Would that work better?'

'Yes,' Chris breathed deeply. 'That'd be much better.'

Miller shrugged. 'Fine. Then let's go.'

As they walked, Matt hung back a bit and grabbed his phone to call Wren.

She answered after one ring. 'Oh, it's you,' she said. 'Where *are* you?'

'I'm down at the baptism.'

'We didn't see you.'

'I was down the front. Listen, I'm sorry for being a pain but can you get Seth to give you a lift back to the cottage? Is that possible?'

Silence.

'Wren, are you there? Is it possible you can get Seth—'

'It's already happening. Seth saw us mooching around like little lost sheep and offered us a lift home. I'm sitting in his passenger seat right now.'

'Hiya, Matt,' Seth's voice crackled in the background. 'It's all under control, so you take your time. Lovely to see you in church today.'

'Wren, I'm sorry. I said I'd be back in time.'

'And you weren't.'

'Hi, Daddy,' Amelia suddenly called out from the back seat. 'Lucy's having pizza. She's gonna be a fatty!'

'Amelia. Shush . . .' Wren said, then spoke back into the phone. 'The older kids at the youth group. They're having pizza at the church. Lucy's joining them.'

'Right.'

'But we've got to go,' Wren said. Then in a hissing little whisper she added, 'Hey, here's an idea. Maybe you could write a book about police stations instead.'

'Wren, be reason—'

Click.

Gone.

* * *

He slipped the phone back in his pocket and jogged after the others who were hovering at the cars. Matt held up his hand to a waiting family he'd blocked in, 'Sorry, guys.'

The dad gripped a picnic basket to his chest, frowning at what was happening.

'Just doing my bit for law and order,' Chris said.

When he and Chris finally sank into the car seats and closed the doors, Chris turned to him. 'I'm not a murderer. Obviously you know that.'

'They're not saying you are.'

'Then why's Miller looking at me like I'm Lucifer?'

'Maybe you shouldn't talk until the station, okay?' Matt turned the key in the ignition. 'But listen, Chris, don't get all panicky. I know this is weird for you but you're not under arrest, do you understand? Don't let Miller freak you out. Just tell the truth and it'll be fine.'

Chris went to say something but then closed his mouth. He looked out of the window at the field and dips in the dirt road as they rose up it. At the tips of swaying grass running up the ridge, his eyes like a sad old Labrador who'd memorised the route to the vets and dreaded it.

As they drove up the track and approached the dregs of the crowd trudging up the hill, Chris suddenly smiled and buzzed his window down. He leant his head out. 'See you next Sunday, everybody,' he grinned with a full blast of the *how you doin'* sparkle he'd shown on the church stage today.

They all looked back, genuinely delighted to see him. A few of them even high-fived him through the car window as they slowly headed up the track. Matt had to concentrate like hell not to knock any of the congregation over.

I've maimed foxes with this thing, you know!

When they reached the top of the hill, Chris finally shut his window and sank back into his seat, looking exhausted. The sad dog look returned and despite Matt telling him not to speak, he said, 'I was angry yesterday at the Healing Centre, I said some harsh things to you. I'm sorry.'

'That's okay.' Then he couldn't resist it. 'I forgive you.'

Chris smiled gently. 'I'm glad of that. We ought not keep a record of wrongs, should we?'

That rather depends on how wrong those wrongs are, Matt thought, but he didn't say it.

'You shouldn't hold what I was doing with Isabel against me.'

'Chris, let's just wait till—'

'No!' he slapped his hand hard on the dashboard. 'Just give me a second. What we do up here is some specialist therapy. I am helping people.'

'I know that, you told me.'

'And yes it's a little unorthodox. But all that stuff with Izzy hardly means I had something to do with Tabitha Clarke's disappearance. Or Nicola Knox.'

'I know.'

'Or any others.'

Matt's ears pricked up. 'Others?'

'I'm just pre-empting your questions, aren't I?'

Matt could feel his foot easing off the accelerator. Wren always said he did that when he was distracted by something on the radio or when a sweet sports car whizzed by. To be honest, sometimes it was just a funny-looking cow in a field.

Chris had his focus now.

'So who else has disappeared?' Matt asked.

'Don't tell me you're not wondering where Isabel Dawson is? Why she wasn't at the baptism today?'

'Well I noticed she didn't get dunked, if that's what you mean. But I'm not surprised she wasn't there. She didn't sound that keen, if you ask—'

'Obviously you upset her with your heroics. Because she drove off yesterday after . . . the incident. And nobody's heard from her since. So I suppose I'll be guilty of that too. You probably think I bashed her little brains in with my bat.'

Matt shifted in his seat. 'Did you phone her?'

'Billy did. Last night and early this morning. We were going to let her come and finish off the therapy so she'd be ready for the baptism. Or at least watch it.'

'And?'

'Her phone said it wasn't in service.'

'Let's just wait till we get to the station, alright?'

Chris clasped his hands together like he was praying and locked his knuckles against his chin, staring into the footwell as if God himself might suddenly pop his head up like a mechanic on a trolley, rolling under the car and listening in. 'Our crime,' he suddenly said into his hands, 'is that we want people to meet Jesus and avoid a hideous, eternal death in hell. Is that really so bad? It's what we all want up here. That's just what this church does. Good work. Specialist work. God's kingdom come on earth.'

Matt shifted gears. Stayed silent.

'We're a *good* church. And we do what needs to be done.' Chris turned those old dog eyes back out of the window and watched the trees whizz by. A minute passed and he spoke again, voice quiet. 'We're still old friends, aren't we, Matt?'

'Yes.'

'And that still counts for something?'

'Of course.' He meant it.

'Because you always were so charitable to me. You saw me different to the rest of them. Didn't you?'

'Yeah, I guess I did.'

'Then you'll tell Miller . . . that I mean well. Won't you? That my intentions . . . they've always been good.'

'Just leave it until the station, okay?'

Chris nodded. A tiny, timid gesture.

'Unless,' Matt said, unsure of the wisdom in asking this when there was nobody else around to hear it, 'is there something you want to tell me before we get there?' He waited. 'Is there anything you want to get off your chest?'

Chris pressed his lips hard together, then shook his head, locking his fingers in place and folding up his hands. It seemed like the only way he could stop them from trembling. And for the first time ever in the history of the cosmos, Chris Kelly sat in a car with another human being and for the entire journey didn't say a word.

CHAPTER TWENTY-NINE

Matt and Miller closed the door and it clicked shut, leaving Chris Kelly inside the 'holding room', though up until today it had mainly been used as a storeroom for two old printers and a pile of old sandbags in case the lake, and the river that fed it, ever spewed forth. Evidently, there wasn't a lot of holding required in Hobbs Hill.

Matt glanced back through the little square window. Now that the questioning was over Chris was sitting on a plastic chair, elbows wedged on the wooden table, head in his hands, praying.

Police Constable Taylor stood outside the room, shifting his weight from one foot to the next. Miller caught a glimpse of his constant tense two-step. 'Matt, give me a second with Taylor. I'll meet you in my office.'

Matt nodded and headed off, but he lingered a little when he turned the corridor, just so he could listen.

Miller whispered, 'If you need a piss, then go and have a piss. I'll watch the door till you get back.'

'I don't need the toilet,' he whispered back. 'I'm fine.'

'Yeah, well you don't look fine.'

'Well it's not very nice, is it? Dragging your own vicar in.'

'He's just a man, so don't stress about it. And don't you let

217

this guy just walk out of here, just because he's your guru.'

Taylor's voice snapped louder. 'I wouldn't *do* that.'

Matt heard Miller's footsteps clicking on the stone floor so he hurried along the corridor to the office. Miller seemed none the wiser when he caught up and just pushed the office door open. They went inside.

'So what do you think?' Miller creaked into his high-backed seat. 'You reckon Chris had something to do with Tabitha's disappearance? Maybe Nicola?'

'The evidence. It's . . .' Matt sat in the chair opposite, 'flimsy.'

'What about the voicemail? You asked a man of the cloth straight out if he'd seen her, and he told you no.'

'Because he hadn't actually seen her.'

'Oh, you're playing semantics now. Just like he was.'

'No. Think about what he said. Tabitha calls the healing centre out of the blue. Leaves an answering machine message for him. Says the pain of the cancer is making her desperate.'

'*That* I can believe.'

'So Chris calls her mobile back and leaves the message that we heard today. Says he'll visit her, nothing more.'

'Yeah, and he blatantly told you he'd never met her.'

'Because he *hadn't* met her. Hadn't even spoken to her on the phone. Just returned her message with another message. He says he turned up at her house and she'd already gone. He didn't mention Tabitha's phone message to me because she'd sworn him to secrecy. Pastor confidentiality.'

'And you believe him?'

'I believe that she'd want to keep something like that quiet, yes. A known atheist asking for help from the church? It's embarrassing for her. Makes her look . . . weak.'

Miller grabbed a paper clip from the desk and started to pull it apart. He moulded it into something approaching a straight line. 'So you think he's legit?'

218

'Look, *all* I'm saying is that his story's plausible and that you have no evidence to say otherwise.'

'And the wedding woman? That stuff with the smashing plates.'

'Specialist therapy. Radical counselling. On the whole I'd say Isabel seemed complicit.'

'Yeah. But where the hell is *she* now?'

Matt waited. 'I don't know.'

Miller flicked the mutilated paper clip into the bin in the corner. He missed. Matt noticed fifty others lying there on the carpet.

'I've been thinking,' Miller said suddenly. 'What if it's something else, that therapy thing?'

'Like what?'

'I don't know. Some sort of sex game.'

'What?'

'A sex game. You know. You get those in London, don't you?'

'Legend has it. Yes.'

'Well, you saw that blind woman today, feeling him up. You know how weird some people get. And think about it. Chris is single, isn't he? A widower? Bound to be frustrated in the trouser department. Maybe that's how some of those church folk get their rocks off. Dress up in wedding dresses, smash things up. Did you notice if his flies were down when you walked in on them?'

'Well it's usually the first thing I look for but sorry, I missed that this time.'

'Maybe you should have. And I'll tell you for why . . . because you can get some premium-grade perverts in churches.' Miller put his elbows on the desk. 'You know there were some child porn issues up at the church a few years back.'

'Really?'

'Yes, there were pictures printed from the internet. Found them stuffed in a drain outside the church. I saw them and let me tell you that it was off the scale of normal sexual behaviour. Made me sick to my stomach. Couldn't sleep for a month during that. Even put me off shagging my wife.'

The projector in Matt's mind suddenly rattled into life, and images he'd tried to forget began to flash past him. Most of them were from some research he did for an academic paper he gave one Christmas at the university on the cheery, festive subject of ritualistic sex abuse. A long sigh rolled up through his throat but never seemed to leave his mouth.

Yeah thanks, Miller. Thanks for pulling those out of the files, just when I'd managed to bury them.

'What I'm saying, Matt, is that Christians can be some of the sickest buggers out there. And I grew up in Catholic Ireland in a church school for boys. So I'm an authority on this stuff.' The sudden slip at the edge of Miller's mouth made Matt pause before speaking. Miller just sat there, staring at him, chewing at the inside of his mouth.

The silence was growing too intense. 'But you said the church abuse cases happened before Chris came here.'

He nodded. 'About a year before.'

'And the people responsible were arrested?'

'Well it could have been anybody.'

'Was Billy here, when all that happened?'

Miller's eyebrows went up. 'Yeah, why do you ask?'

'I was just curious how he handled it. Must have been pretty intense having that happen under his nose, being the youth worker.'

'He handled it pretty well. The guy's alright, actually.'

'Right.'

Miller sighed deeply, then swung round in his chair for one entire revolution. 'So what we're saying is we don't have anything on Chris Kelly.'

'Nothing substantial.'

Miller seemed to gaze into the air, hoping for ideas to suddenly drop from the ceiling. 'You told me he got jumpy when he talked about Hemel Hempstead.'

'It's where his wife died. Makes sense that it's not his favourite place.'

'How did she die?'

'He didn't say,' Matt stared at his fingers for a moment. Then he put a palm on the desk. 'Anyway, the bottom line is we've got a couple of emails sent to me, and some text messages and the paintings. But we don't have any bodies.'

'Not yet.'

Matt stood up. 'I've been thinking about those text messages.' He walked over to the noticeboard. A yellow Post-it note was stuck amongst the photographs of Tabitha and Nicola. He peeled it off and read it aloud, giving a voice to their sad, lonely-looking faces. *'I've repented and I'm with God now. Maybe one day you could come too. Kiss kiss. Tabitha Tansy Clarke.* Verecundus.'

Then he grabbed the green Post-it note alongside it and did the same, *'Mum. I just wanted to let you know that I love you all, but I'm going to be with God now. One day, I hope you might believe and come too.* Verecundus. *Kiss kiss. Nicola.'*

'You remembered what that Latin bit means yet?' Miller said.

'I looked it up on my phone.'

'You have a Latin dictionary on your phone?'

'I have Google on my phone.'

Miller looked suddenly sheepish. 'So enlighten me.'

'Verecundus. It's a Latin adjective. It means to feel shame. To be shy or modest. And it also means something that's worthy of reverence.'

'Well.' Miller clapped his hands together. 'That just about cracks this case wide open, doesn't it?'

'Okay, it's pretty obscure. Interesting, though. So either Tabitha and Nicola are saying they're with God, and they feel shame, which might explain the burnt paintings. Or they feel reverence. Not sure why they'd choose Latin, though. That's bugging me.'

'Taylor still thinks it's a suicide pact. That they were lovers. I supposed *I'm with God now* sounds as suicide-y as it gets.'

'Maybe the first bit sounds . . . suicide-y. I agree. But it's the second part I don't get. *I've gone home to be with God now, maybe one day you might believe and come too.*'

Miller shrugged.

'It sounds like she's talking about heaven, and *that's* what's doing my head in. Here we have a known atheist and a young girl who apparently never went to church. They're talking in Latin, with confidence that they're with God. And they're encouraging others to go there too. Sounds almost . . . evangelical, wouldn't you say?'

Miller nodded slowly.

'So what I want to know is if she really did write this, then what happened to make an atheist suddenly believe so strongly in God? Because statistically speaking people converting to religion *on their own* is extremely uncommon. Almost everyone does it through a contact at a church or a place of worship.'

'So who was their contact?'

'Exactly. *That's* the question. Who made them trust in God? Who made Tabitha so turned on to faith that she burns her own paintings? Assuming she wrote that message herself, of course.' He put the notes back on the wall, pressing the glued strip so it stuck. 'You met Tabitha before, right?'

'A few times.'

'What was she like?'

'A little aloof. Had that big-city London sneer, you know? You've got it a bit. No offence.'

'None taken, peasant.'

Miller tapped his hand on the desk. 'I just think she used to look down at us locals. Like we'd only just learnt how to piss in a bucket and not on the floor.'

'And was she the type to write kiss, kiss on a text message?'

Miller thought about it. 'Not really.'

Matt ran his finger along the top of the Post-it notes, pressing them in place. 'Either someone helped convert her. Or she didn't even write this message, and she didn't destroy her own paintings. If that's what's happened here, then I want to know why someone would go to all this trouble to make us think these two women died happy and content and at peace with God.'

'You want to know what's bugging *me*?' Miller said.

Matt nodded.

'Why you happen to have had two emails with these poor girls' faces on them when you don't even come from round here.'

'Well, you heard Chris. He says *he* didn't send them.'

Miller gave an odd little nod. 'I heard him.'

'But you're saying you don't believe him?'

Miller waited for a moment before speaking. And when he finally did it was quiet and low. 'I'm saying I'm not sure what to believe right now.' Miller held Matt's gaze for a beat too long, then pushed his seat back. 'I'll go and tell him he can go home.'

CHAPTER THIRTY

Matt didn't expect to see any cars when he got back to the cottage but sitting there, catching the falling blossom of the trees, was a red Honda Civic. The windscreen was peppered with the exploded bodies of motorway insects.

Frowning, he swung his car to a sharp stop.

Halfway up the path, he could already hear the muffled laughter from inside, big old booming peals of sound that felt way too harsh and deep for this setting. It grew louder and more irritating when he swung the front door wide open and headed into the lounge.

'Daddy?' Amelia said with a quick jerk of her head, clearly shocked to see him.

'Hiya, Prof.' It was Billy, sitting on the couch with one hand resting on the curve of his gut, the other waving hello.

Matt ducked under the long wooden beam in the ceiling and scooped Amelia into his arms. Once she was settled into him, Matt nodded a reluctant greeting. 'Billy.'

He didn't stand but creaked forward a little from the sofa and reached his huge brick of a mitt out to shake. He may have been a paid-up member of the Happy Jesus Gang but he squeezed like he could break fingers.

Just letting you know I could mess you up, Prof. Just putting that out there.

Matt slid his hand free, clammy with Billy juice.

'Amelia, where's Mummy?' Matt asked.

'Here!' Wren hollered then appeared from the kitchen holding a flowery, plastic tray. It had a pile of cupcakes on it. She blew a little breath from her pursed lips, clearly relieved to see him.

'So we have a guest?' Matt said.

She smiled and shrugged at the same time, setting the tray on the coffee table.

'Actually,' Billy said. 'I'm here for little Amelia.'

Oh, are you now?

'She was at the baptisms this morning and she asked a few questions about it. Since I'm the youth worker I thought I'd pop down to fill her in.'

Matt sat down, perching Amelia on his lap. She grabbed a cake from the table and started chewing it far more slowly than normal, as though she wanted something constantly in her mouth, so she wouldn't have to speak.

Matt shifted her a little on his knee and spoke gently. 'You asked about baptism?'

Her eyes flashed something that he didn't often see in her. Guilt. Palpable, pulsing guilt. 'I was just curious. That's all. No big deal.'

'Hey, now come on, little one.' Billy slowly peeled the paper case from his cake. Sucking each finger with a horrible sounding *pop*. 'You don't have to be scared of your dad.'

Matt glared at him. 'She's *not* scared.'

Billy raised his eyebrows and prodded his cake towards Amelia. 'Oh, I dunno. Maybe she thinks you'll be angry. That she's interested in this, I mean.'

What is this? Matt thought. 'Well, that's fine if she's interested. Not a problem.' He smiled at her, and squeezed her towards him like he often did, when they sat watching astronomy shows on National

Geographic. But this time, she didn't squeeze back. 'If you want to learn more about it, then it's okay. I don't mind.'

'Great,' Billy said, slapping his hand on his knee. 'Then fire away, Amelia.'

She chewed a little more, unable to look at Matt. Then she visibly gulped. And for one sharp buzzing moment Matt knew that Billy was right. Amelia was terrified of saying this in front of him, as though her asking about baptism was tantamount to him finding her with an eighth of cannabis in her room. Matt felt a sudden comprehensive awareness about himself. That when all was said and done, his protectiveness of his family might simply be signs that he was a selfish prick with metaphysical hang-ups.

'It's okay, Amelia,' Matt said. 'Ask your questions.'

She bit her lip. 'Why did you push them under three times?'

'Aha! Great question! One for each member of the Trinity. Father, Son and Holy Ghost. And you always push them under the water. Total immersion.' He lifted his hand and swooped it down. 'That's how you baptise someone. The original Greek word for baptism is Baptizo.'

'Sounds like a super hero.'

'It *does*, you're right. It means to dip or immerse. That's exactly how Jesus was baptised too. And everybody else in the New Testament. And do you want to know something fascinating?'

She nodded.

'It's done that way because it's supposed to symbolise going into the grave. Of us dying to our old selves. We purge the old and when we come up we're born again. So those people who just sprinkle water on the forehead are chumps.' Billy winked at her. 'You don't look like a chump to me. No, you're very intelligent for your age. A bright little button, you are.'

'Thanks.' She looked delighted at the interest he was taking in her.

Wren had sunk into the sofa opposite. Matt could see her cheekbones were more prominent than usual, which meant she was clenching her jaw.

Just then Matt heard another car pulling up outside. He leant his head back to look out of the window to see a Land Rover with some teenagers from the church youth group in it.

Wren got up. 'Lucy's home,' she said.

For some reason everyone stopped speaking, waiting for the door to open. Billy sat patiently, eyes on the door, then back to the buttercream he was licking from his fingernails. The door rattled and in walked Lucy, with a lollipop in her mouth and a book under her arm. She stopped sucking when everyone turned in her direction.

'Ooo, cake.' She reached over and grabbed one.

'Did you have a good time at church?' Billy said.

'Yeah. Thanks for organising it. Pizzas were amazing.'

'Pleasure,' Billy laughed.

'Mum,' she said, heading for the stairs, 'I just need to charge my phone. Is that okay?'

Wren nodded, probably wondering why she was even asking permission. Lucy never normally did that. She hurried up the stairs and they all listened to the bedroom door close.

Billy gave Matt a smile and was, he noticed, not just sitting in the chair, but lazing into it, so utterly at home that he might scratch his balls at any moment and switch on the TV.

'So why not babies?' Amelia asked. 'Why don't you baptise them?'

'Because they wouldn't know what's going on. Heck, a baby doesn't even know how to ask for a Farley's rusk, never mind salvation from the Lord.' He giggled for a long time after that. 'We wait till people are old enough to choose God for themselves, which is *way* more sensible. You saw today how meaningful it is to people. It can change a person.'

Wren was sitting up now, leaning forward. 'Change how?'

'It gives them a fresh start. It fills them with the Holy Spirit. Baptism plucks you from the kingdom of darkness and plants you in the city of light. And I mean, literally.'

Amelia's eyes were widening a little. 'Wow.'

Billy nodded quickly, his triple chin expanding with each flick of the head.

'I'm confused.' Matt rolled his tongue across the inside of his lips. 'Most Protestants see baptism as just a symbol. That the new creation stuff starts at conversion, and the baptism just shows it off to the world.'

Amelia looked confused.

'Like a wedding ring, Amelia,' Matt went on. 'A wedding ring doesn't make you married, does it? It's a symbol that you just *got* married. And baptism's a symbol that someone's become a Christian. Is that not what you believe, Billy?'

Billy pulled in a long breath and let it out slowly. 'Maybe you should give the dominical ordinances of Jesus more credit, Professor.'

Matt gave a sarcastic laugh. 'So you're saying it's baptism that makes someone a Christian?'

He shrugged. 'I'm saying Jesus commanded us to baptise. Matthew 28, verse 19. The great commission. It's there in black and white. It's not optional and never has been.'

Wren stayed quiet, listening and sipping her tea.

'So am I too young to be baptised?' Amelia almost whispered the words. Her eyes were fixed on Billy, avoiding Matt's eye.

'Oh, you're old enough, alright. Mature little thing like you.' He spoke with half-shut eyes. 'Makes sense to get baptised as quick as you can though, Amelia. You want to go to heaven when you die, don't you?'

'Yes.'

'And who wants to go to hell, right?'

Her face dropped a little. 'I don't want to go there.'

'Er . . . right,' Matt said, lifting Amelia off and standing up. 'I reckon we'll have to wrap this little pow-wow up.'

Amelia raised her eyebrows. 'What? Are we going somewhere?'

'Yes we are,' Matt said. 'We're going to the Monster Trucks.'

Amelia's head spun in Wren's direction. 'Mummy? Are we?'

It would have been the first Wren had heard of it, but she nodded like she'd planned it all week. 'Yep. Monster Trucks. Go and grab your stuff.'

'I guess that's my cue to leave is it?' Billy said.

'Yes it is,' Matt nodded.

Billy pushed himself to his feet then reached down towards Amelia. She wasn't always that confident with other adults. For whatever reason she'd often turn into a timid little rabbit around grown-ups she didn't know. But she slapped her free hand into Billy's like they were old pals.

'If you ever want to talk more about this,' he said, 'then here's my card. My door's always open. And remember. Don't sit on the fence with baptism. You should go for it before it's too late. You never know what might happen. Life is so, *so* short.'

Amelia went to lift the card from his hand and Billy held it just out of her reach, making her stand on her tiptoes. She laughed and so did he. Wren leant in and plucked the card from his fingers, 'I'll look after that, thank you very much. Now go on, Amelia. Tell your sister we're leaving in five minutes.'

'Yay,' she said and headed up the stairs.

Billy walked towards the door, which Matt was already holding open. 'Well, I'm sorry we didn't have more time to talk.' He slapped his bouncer hand against Matt's back, hard enough to bring up a lung. Then Billy stepped out into the sun. 'Glorious day, isn't it?'

To Matt's surprise, Wren followed Billy outside, so he went out too.

'Can I have a quick word, please Billy?' she said.

''Course,' his eyes flashed. 'Are you interested in baptism too?'

'No.' She shook her head. 'How about you just back off a bit.'

Her tone was matter-of-fact, but it still seemed to shock him. 'I beg your pardon?'

'I don't think it's appropriate for you to come in here and start telling my daughter where she might go when she dies.'

'Are you kidding?'

'I'm serious. This church stuff's new to her and I don't want her being press-ganged into some religious ritual.'

Billy dropped his mouth and shook his head. '*Ritual?* You think

229

I'm talking about a ritual? I'm talking about saving her soul.'

'You heard her, Billy,' Matt said. 'Do *not* threaten my daughter with hell again.'

'Threaten? But she's almost at the age of accountability.'

Wren frowned. 'The what?'

Matt whistled, half in amusement and half in shock. 'Some people think that kids automatically go to heaven when they die. Until they reach a certain age and they become—'

'Accountable,' Billy finished his sentence. 'Amelia's what . . . seven? She's getting old enough. She'll be a woman soon enough—'

'Excuse me?' Wren glared at him.

'—and she'll have to account for her sins when she dies.'

Wren shook her head. 'You're telling me kids go to heaven when they die, unless they reach a certain age? Then they go to hell?'

'Of course . . . unless they're baptised. It's not rocket science.'

She threw up her hands. 'Then why don't you just kill every kid before they reach seven and be done with it? Surely that's the most humane thing to do.'

Billy said nothing, just held her gaze for a while, like what she had said was perfectly reasonable. 'All I'm saying is that your daughter *must* be baptised one day. She has to be. And so has Lucy.'

Both Wren and Matt spoke the same words at pretty much the same time. 'No they don't.'

Billy took a step back, looking like he'd just bumped into Fred and Rose West. 'This is like neglect, you know? You're depriving your child of living for ever.'

'Listen to yourself,' Wren said.

'But keeping them from it. That's like . . . abuse.'

'Oh, don't be so bloody ridiculous,' Matt snapped.

Billy's mouth dropped a little. 'Well, if little Amelia wants to come to my house to talk about God then you can't stop her. My door's always open for girls like her.'

'Oh, I bet it is,' Wren said.

'What on earth is that supposed to mean?'

'Alright,' Matt said. 'Just go home, Billy. Right now.'

Billy didn't speak. He just looked up at the second-floor windows, then down at both of them. 'You're just a couple of sad lonely people aren't you? Kings of your own little world. What's wrong? Hasn't life been kind to you? Oh and Mrs. Hunter? You know this won't go well for your getting the building contra—'

'Oh, fuck off,' Wren said. 'And stay away from my daughter.'

The two of them turned back to the cottage and when they got inside, Matt kicked the door shut with the back of his heel. Matt went to the window to watch Billy squeeze into his Civic and drive off. Though he kept looking back at the house, driving slowly.

Matt turned round slowly and caught Wren's eye. 'Well, that went well.'

The girls were already bounding down the stairs. From the looks of it they were oblivious to what had just happened outside. Amelia had her camera slung round her neck along with a little pair of binoculars she used for stargazing.

'Monster trucks!' Amelia said. 'Cars. Will. Explode!'

The girls ran on ahead and started to climb into the car while Wren and Matt held back for a second on the path. Both of them a little breathless.

'Can you believe that?' Wren said. There was an undeniable trembling in her voice. 'How he pushed that on her? She's nine years old, for crying out loud.'

'Well, I think he got the message.'

'Are all Christians like this? Were *you* like that?' she said, then before he could say anything she hurried to the car and opened up the driver's side, eyes not seeming to blink. She didn't let him answer her question. In all likelihood, she just didn't want to know.

231

CHAPTER THIRTY-ONE

Matt rolled over in the bed and pulled the pillow around his skull for a minute, as if it would help. But his ears kept on ringing. The last time they'd buzzed like this was when he'd been to a Metallica concert in his late twenties. The chest-quivering roar of the Monster Trucks had climbed deep into his head and twanged away at every cord and sinew in there. They sold ear defenders up there, but when he got to the counter the bored teen at the till told him there were only three pairs left. So he dished them out to the girls and took a hit for the team.

So Wren had filtered out the high-pitched whine legacy and had already fallen asleep. But not him. Yet. It wasn't just the ringing that kept him awake. The more time he spent in this cottage, this village, the less he was sleeping.

The red digits of the clock flashed, telling him it was 1 a.m. Ears buzzed as he sank back into the pillow. He stared up at the ceiling. It was bathed in moonlight and the shadow of branches that scraped at the white plaster above him.

He tried to filter out the voices that rode the hum in his ear. Relentless ones that asked him questions incessantly, demanding an answer now. Right now.

– *Where are Tabitha and Nicola and Isabel?*

All three-syllable names he noticed. Irrelevant perhaps, but of major intrigue at this time of night.

– Is there a killer out there, lurking?

Weirdly, the answer that kept coming back was in one single word that kept relentlessly tugging at him, like a kid who spotted the chocolates at the checkouts and wanted his dad to buy them.

Verecundus.

He whispered the word a few times to accentuate the different syllables and sounds. Then ran through the definition in his mind. To feel shame, bashful, shy or modest. Or for something to be worthy of reverence.

He shook his head and turned onto his side, distracted by the loudest question of all.

– And why's that fat bugger from the church looking at my daughter like that?

They had three more days to go in Hobbs Hill, land of the wooden crosses, then they'd all return to London to wait for the answer of whether Wren got this job or not. And all he could think was that he hoped she didn't.

I don't want her here. I don't want my family here.

He stared up, watching the black fingers caressing the cottage. Eventually they moved softly enough to stroke him into a deep, haunted sleep.

'Daddy?'

Amelia's voice came from somewhere under the water. He looked down and she was gazing up through the darkness of the lake, skin blue with the night moon. Her face was shrivelling.

'Daddy?' Her voice, trapped in a bubble. 'I can hear them. Can *you* hear them?'

He reached down and put his hands in the lake. Ice-cold water spiked up into his fingertips, deep like needles and all he could do was snap his hand back and suck his fingers as she drifted down, down and down again.

Her mouth was moving and though he couldn't hear it he could see the shape of '*verecundus*' on her lips. Over and over. She sang it like a nursery rhyme as she went down. Her tiny blue eyes, the last things he saw, shimmered in the dull light before the black reeds slowly – horribly slowly – wriggled themselves around her face and body, covering her cheeks, her chin, one of her eyes. And with a sharp, hard yank, dragged her into obliv—

'Daddy!'

His eyes fluttered open.

'Daddy, you've got to wake up.'

Little fingers pushed at his shoulder. He sucked in a long chest-filling breath. Amelia was standing at the side of the bed in her favourite nightie. The one with the cartoon moon on it with its winking eye and its two thumbs up. *All aboard for Dreamland* it said. It looked frankly psychotic in the light.

'What's wrong?' He pushed himself up on his elbow and clocked that Wren was still snoring softly beside him.

He tapped the backlight on his watch.

3.01 a.m.

Amelia's chin was trembling. 'Daddy, I can hear children.'

'Huh?'

'Little children. I think they're near my window.'

He sighed and swung his legs over the side, feet touching the cold wooden floorboards. Then he knelt down and wrapped his arms all the way around her. 'It's a bad dream, okay. I'm here.'

'I'm seven. Don't talk to me like I'm an idiot. You should check.' She pursed her lips. 'They're crying.'

When he stood he heard the creak of the floorboards before realising that actually the sound came from his knees. She led him by the hand to the door in nothing but his boxer shorts. The day had been hot, but the night had a bite of cold about it. So he grabbed his dressing gown from the hook on the wall and he stepped into his Yoda slippers.

He glanced across the lump of Wren in the bed to the curtainless bedroom window above her. It showed the same relentless channel it always did. Forest by day, forest by night. He squinted. The trees had shuffled themselves closer to the house. They seemed to do that at night, as though the entire wood contracted in the cold.

His trusty little torch (a stocking filler from his mum, years back) sat on the dressing table. He grabbed it but didn't switch it on.

He put a finger across his mouth, *shhhhhhh*, as they slowly pushed open the bedroom door. He and Amelia crept along the landing to the other side of the cottage where her room was. Boards creaking beneath them, like they were living in a huge wicker basket of a house.

The landing was a surprisingly long and lonely walk in the dark. Old paintings of hunting dogs and wild-eyed, red-jacketed men on horseback glared out: pub wall images that were bland and innocuous in the daylight but looked mad and deranged at night. Even the normally enigmatic Shore family photos looked a little unhinged in the dark.

Two stuffed weasels sat on the side table along the wall, looking like they might suddenly wiggle their backsides like a cat and pounce, despite being dead.

So this was the walk Amelia had to do each night when she went to the toilet? Across this wooden floor, past those eager little weasels and the black gaping mouth of the staircase. All because she was the only one without an en suite in her room?

It made him want to scoop her up and let her sleep in their bedroom for the rest of the holiday.

They passed Lucy's room where the floorboards creaked louder than at any other part. He winced, pulled up his foot and took a double step over them. He lifted Amelia over like it was a ravine.

Her bedroom door was next. Half open. Lights off inside. He closed it softly behind them and stepped over the teddies that lay on the floor and past her telescope that stood on its tripod, aimed up at Orion's Belt.

They both knelt at her window, which, like all the others, had no curtains. Their arms and faces quickly glowed bright in a sharp block of moonlight falling into the room.

'I'm going to push the window open, alright?' he whispered.

Her body tensed. 'Don't fall out.'

'Not planning to.'

The hinges on these windows were wide enough to push each window all the way open, fully flush with the external white walls of the cottage. Suddenly there was a rectangular hole in the wall. No glass at all between them and the forest.

He heard the low hum of a breeze running through the trees.

'Why would children even be in the woods?' she whispered. 'At this time of night?'

'It'll be owls or something.' He ruffled her hair. 'You're safe, okay? I'm here.'

Calming words that did absolutely nothing to change the look of dread on her face.

For a few minutes they just watched the dark garden and listened to the crackling trees. The torch wasn't much use, due to its limited range, but he still swung his little beam about and swept it along the hedge. He stood up. Leant out.

'Daddy, careful!'

Lucy's room was on this side of the cottage too. As he leant out he noticed that her window was open halfway. Thick vines crawled like a beanstalk up from the ground and gathered round the glass and the—

Crack.

Amelia jumped.

'What was that?' She tugged at him to come back inside.

It was the faintest sound coming from somewhere in the garden. Or just beyond it. A twig snapping? He flicked the torch over. Nothing. He slowly moved the torch to shine out into the woods. Beyond the nearest trees the feeble beam of light faded into nothingness.

It happened again.

Crack.

Quieter this time.

Blood pulsed loudly through his head. Instinctively he went to push Amelia back. 'Get down,' he said to her. 'Go on.'

She started to crouch on the floor, and it was just as she put her head on the carpet that the other sound came. Not a crack this time, but a sound so terrible that Amelia threw her hands over her ears, crying into the floor. 'I told you. I told you.'

A cold shiver shot through his chest as a child screamed, deep in the woods.

'*Jesus.*' He locked his legs against the window sill then leant further out, as far as he could without falling.

'Daddy, don't.' Her voice was muffled, because her hand was clamped over it. 'You'll fall.'

'I just want a closer look.' He clamped the torch between his teeth, moving his head so the beam crept along the hedge. Which was when he saw it.

The tip of a brown hood, dropping from sight behind their hedge.

Then the unmistakeable cracking of twigs as someone ran off.

'*Hey!*' When he shouted the torch dropped clean from his mouth and bounced silently on the grass below. The beam lit a jagged path across the garden. 'Who's out there?'

Amelia burst into louder tears and grabbed his legs, hugging them, heaving him back in so that he started to lose his balance.

He clamped both hands on the sill. 'Stop pulling me!'

Heartbeat, clicking fast now.

The hedge was long and thick enough so that whoever was there could have easily run around the entire perimeter of the cottage and stayed unseen. They could have run straight off into the woods if they'd wanted.

He pushed himself back inside and Amelia finally let go.

'I told you,' she whimpered, shaking against him.

He picked her up and she gripped him painfully tight as he rushed back onto the landing, his breath shallow in his chest. Wren and Lucy were already emerging from their bedroom doors, bleary-eyed.

'What's with the shouting?' Lucy rubbed her eyes.

'Wren, get the girls into our bedroom. Go!'

The sharpness in his tone shocked them fully awake and Wren rushed over. 'What's happening?'

Amelia was sobbing, but she managed to speak. 'There's someone out there. Watching the house. They're killing little kids.'

Lucy's hand flew to her mouth.

'No, they're not.' Matt handed Amelia over. 'Just calm down, Amelia. Stay with your mum and sister. And Lucy?'

She looked over at him, eyes wide. He could tell exactly what she was thinking. That her dad had finally got himself out of prison and had tracked her and Wren down. Climbing up the vines as they spoke.

'Don't worry, okay? Don't worry.' As soon as he said it he thought, *how the hell do you know it's not him?*

The two girls raced towards the bedroom but Wren told them to wait. Instead she ran to grab Matt's arm, halfway down the stairs. 'Where are *you* going?'

'To have a look.' He cleared the last few steps in one stride, then grabbed his keys from the little basket by the phone. He picked up one of the iron pokers from the fire, holding it up like a light sabre.

'Don't,' she called after him.

'I can catch him,' his keys were in the door now, 'if I'm quick.'

'Daddy, no!' Amelia yelped desperately. It was a heartbreaking sound. Lucy stayed silent.

'Let's just call the police,' Wren said.

'He'll be long gone by the time they get here. Now please, Wren. Go back upstairs.'

When he pushed the front door open a cold breeze slammed into him like it had raced through the woods all in one moment. The entire dark forest seemed to swing in his direction.

So, we've got your attention now? You're finally coming out to play? He saw the shadows between the trees. Thought of those two foxes striding out.

'Just don't,' Wren said, more pleading than a command. 'You're being stupid.'

He hovered for a moment.

'Matt, please. What are you doing?'

He sighed, frustrated. Unsure how to answer. Then slowly, he closed the door and locked it tight. When he turned back she was already jabbing at the 9's on the phone.

He reached out. 'I'd better do it. I'll tell them what I saw.'

She passed him the phone.

'Hello,' came the police voice. She had a buzz for a voice, a pissed off robot. 'Which emergency service would you like?'

'Police.'

He talked as he walked through every room on the downstairs floor, shocked at how vulnerable he felt having no curtains anywhere. He wandered past each dark window, heart bracing itself to see a hooded figure there, scratching its fingernails on the glass. But there was nothing apart from the dull silhouette of him in a dressing gown. Then after what seemed like a million questions the woman on the phone said they'd send someone out. Wren had already gone back upstairs and after hanging up the phone he rushed up too. He found all three of them huddled on the bed. Wren with her arms wrapped round her young like a seagull in the storm.

When he ran to them, Lucy was the one he hugged first and, although it could have been his imagination, he thought he felt her muscles relax a little as he did it.

'Don't worry, the police are on their way.'

But he knew.

He knew full well that the second he closed that front door he'd missed his chance. And whoever it was that had been lurking under Amelia's bedroom was gone.

CHAPTER THIRTY-TWO

They ran together.

Leaping over loose logs and crooked tree stumps because God had given them eyes that could see in the dark. For the most part they moved fast. But every now and again they'd have to slow down. Out here at this time of night, it was easy to lose your way home.

Soon there'd be street lights. If they were moving in the right direction, they should emerge at the far edge of the wood. And the harder they ran the more the tree trunks seemed to glow.

Gradually, the eyes of civilisation blinked themselves into view. Seeing those lights told them that they'd been clever and fast. That they'd run far enough away to breathe again.

It was as they were pushing through the wall of trees and out onto the long empty road that he started to struggle. Maybe it was the relief of having an entire forest between them and the cottage. But now he could actually feel his body. The creaking pain of it. His heart pounded against the inside of his ribcage like a rabid dog fighting to get out of him, so he pressed a hand up there to keep it from splitting the skin.

Then, as the silent moonlit road took a hefty curve upwards, he slowed to a stop. He leant over and grabbed his knees for support. Stephen kept on running.

'I can't, Stephen,' he gasped, trying to call out. 'Just stop a second.' He grabbed the edge of his hoodie, finally confident it was safe to pull it back from his head. His chest pulled his breath in and pushed his body up and down, up and down. It made him feel dizzy, like he wasn't just standing on the road but falling through it.

Stephen was fifty feet ahead now, on the brink of the hill. From this angle it looked like his silhouette was standing flush with the star-covered sky. Like it was all some big black stage curtain, and he might slip between the folds of it at any second. But then Stephen finally turned. His cheek shone blue and he sighed as he headed back down.

'What you stopping for, dingbat?' Stephen said. 'We're almost home.'

'I can't. I need a rest. Just sixty seconds.'

Stephen's eyes moved towards the forest, just to make sure that Professor Hunter hadn't followed them. 'Okay. Sixty. But for God's sake, let's get out of sight.'

This part of the road was lined with cornfields. Perfect to hide in. So Stephen pulled some of it back like a door. Once they stepped through he let go and the corn sprang back, letting the field swallow them up. They found a section where they could sit and both dropped to their knees, crunching the corn beneath them. They felt the sheer beauty of rapidly filling lungs.

Sixty seconds passed and he was about to stand up when Stephen turned his head and said, 'Just haaaaaang on a minute.'

'What?'

'We need to talk.'

'About what?'

'What do you think? We need to talk about you. And your issues.'

'What issues?'

'About her.'

'I just wanted to pray for her.'

'Oh, really?' Stephen's smile looked crooked in the moonlight. 'That's all? That's all you wanted?'

'Yes.'

'That's why we came all this way tonight? To pray?'

'Yes.'

'Bollocks. I saw the bulge in your pants when you were under her window.'

'Shut up.'

'Quite a package you've got—'

'Shut up! It's not like that. I just want to get her ready.'

'Can't help but notice . . .' Stephen giggled as he looked down, 'the bulge is still there. You should sort that out. Make it go away.'

'Stop it, please.' He didn't like it when their conversation turned this way.

'Go on. Just get unzipped and sort it out. I bet it'll make you run faster.'

'I don't want to. It's not right.'

Stephen groaned. 'Oh and you think keeping all that tension in is the right thing? You need to get it out of your system. You know how it works. Externalise what you want to do with her. It's quicker that way, especially now you're getting on a bit. Then it's out of you and we can forget it and get on with the real stuff.'

A breeze ran through the corn and all of it swayed to the left at the same time. 'I don't know, it just feels wrong. God doesn't like it.'

'You think tossing yourself off is wrong but you can strangle Tabby Clarke? Just like that?'

'That's different.'

'Is it?' Stephen started edging a little closer. 'Listen . . . if you don't want to do it then . . . let me do it for you.'

The shock of what Stephen said made him spring to his feet. 'Don't *ever* say that. That's disgusting.'

Stephen lay flat on his back, laughing. 'I'm kidding you, gay-boy. Wow, you are so uptight.'

'I want to go home.'

'Don't we all.'

'No, I mean we need to get home. Maybe he followed us all this way.'

'Nah, he's still at the cottage. I saw him open the door and shut it again. He chickened out.' Stephen snorted a laugh. 'He's a wuss.'

'Then come on. Let's go.'

'You know, you're going to have to do it sooner or later. Or I swear to God your penis is going to explode. *Boom!*' Stephen sat back up and reached up his hand. 'Help me up.'

He waited for a moment, not sure if he wanted to touch him. Then before he knew it Stephen's hand was in his and he was already on his feet.

Suddenly, Stephen wouldn't let go of his hand. 'What's this?'

'What?'

'Your fingernails. Why are they so dirty? There's soil under them.'

'We're in the forest. I must have slipped.'

Stephen frowned and held up his own fingers. 'Mine are clean.'

'Well, hooray for you,' he said. Then he smiled. 'At least I got to pray for her. That's what matters. It's good to prepare the ground, Stephen.'

'Yeah, yeah. I know,' he said, still looking at his outstretched hand.

'I think she'll be good soil. For the seed, I mean.'

'The seed?' Stephen guffawed. 'There you go again.'

'You know I mean the Gospel.' For the first time tonight he laughed too. 'I think heaven's calling her.'

Stephen smiled softly. 'So do I.'

'Then come on, let's go home. We could pray some more.'

They pushed through the corn and ran again, back to the dark silent road and then up the hill toward the vast night sky where the fat moon hung and space was black and the stars seemed pleased with all they could see.

CHAPTER THIRTY-THREE

Twenty minutes later, at almost 4 a.m. Wren spotted the flash of blue lights in the trees outside, pulsing the branches like a weird folksy disco. By now Matt was dressed so he creaked down the stairs and peeked out of the lounge window, just to make sure it was definitely a policeman walking up the path and not some monk in a hood with a flashing blue light in one hand, butcher's knife in the other.

It was PC Taylor, in fact. The Chris Kelly fan. There was no one else.

Matt opened the door before Taylor got to it.

'Hi, Professor Hunter.'

'Look, just call me Matt.'

'Uh-huh. So . . . the drama continues . . . you've had a disturbance here tonight?'

'That's right.'

'A prowler?'

'Seems to be, yes.'

'And have you had a good look around? Seen anything out of the ordinary?'

'I haven't had a proper look yet. I wanted to wait for you.' Some macho quadrant in his brain made him feel like a six-year-old, saying that. Adding *my wife would have been angry if I'd gone outside* probably wouldn't have helped.

The tiniest hint of a smirk flashed on Taylor's face. 'I suppose it *is* pretty creepy out here, this time of night. Especially if you're used to the city. Are you ready to brave it now, sir?'

'Yep.' Matt grabbed his jacket from the peg and locked the door behind him.

The woods were chilly, no doubt about it. But it was nowhere near as icy as before, when he stood alone in the doorway earlier. The breeze still fizzed in the branches, swelling into subtle crescendos.

Taylor switched on the heftiest torch on the planet and Matt led them round to the back of the cottage. He spotted his own meagre Maglite, still shining on the grass. He quickly picked it up and shone it towards the hedge where he'd spotted the hood earlier.

Taylor's torch was amazingly bright, like a spotlight from an old warship. He heard voices from behind him and quickly shone the brilliant beam up the side of the cottage. A perfect circle of harsh light fixed the three girls in a full moon, as they gathered up at Amelia's open window.

Amelia looked more relaxed now. She squinted, covered her eyes and waved. Both Matt and Taylor waved back.

'I'll show you where I spotted him.' Matt opened up the back garden gate that led through the hedge and into the forest itself. They swung their torch beams from left to right and he half expected to suddenly see some guy in a hood, glaring at him with bloodshot Dracula eyes. But there was, of course, nothing.

'So do have you any idea who it was?' Taylor flipped open a notebook and pulled out a little pencil with IKEA written on it. He licked its lead point, which was something Matt had never seen anyone actually do in real life, and started scribbling.

'It was too dark to tell for sure. But he was wearing some sort of hood. It was brown. All I saw was the tip of it.'

'You saw the tip?'

'Yes.'

'Of something brown?'

'That's right.'

'You saw the tip of something brown. In the woods.'

'Yes.'

'Not much to go on now, is it, Professor—'

'Listen,' Matt locked his eyes on Taylor's, 'it wasn't a tree or a leaf or the ear of an owl. I saw the tip of a brown hood. Just over an inch of it. Made of soft material. It dropped out of sight when the light fell on it and whoever it was ran off. My daughter and I clearly heard the branches snapping.'

Taylor was starting to yawn so he twisted his face in an attempt to stifle it. It looked like he was having a mild stroke. 'So . . . brown hood . . . got it. You mean like a monk would wear?'

'Yeah. I guess. Or it could have just been a hoodie.'

'And did you see anything else? Hair colour, face?'

'No, just the tip.'

'Just the tip.' He gave the lead another lick before writing that down. 'And you say he was standing right here?' Taylor swung his torch onto the floor. Twigs, dirt and leaves were scattered everywhere. It was too dry for anybody to have left footprints.

'I know it doesn't look like much but,' he said, 'but . . . I really—'

Matt froze.

That sound again.

Crying from somewhere deep in the woods. One quick moan and then it stopped, leaving silence again.

'Daddy,' Amelia shouted down from the window. 'They're back. The children.'

Taylor gave him a confused look, 'The what?'

'I was going to get to this. My daughter said she heard children, crying in the woods.'

Taylor's eyebrows shot straight up at that. 'Really?'

'Yeah. Didn't you just hear—'

Another long and distant scream of what sounded like a little child, a girl maybe, flung itself through the wood. But the little chuckle coming from Taylor's face did something to the sound. That distant wailing became less and less like a child and more and more like something else.

A sudden sense of idiocy started to fill Matt's body, from the feet up. *Oh, dear.*

'You haven't lived in the country much, have you, Matt?'

He shook his head, as the mocking little cry went on. 'It's an animal, isn't it?'

'Indeed it is,' he actually tittered, then shouted up to Amelia. 'It's alright, princess. It's just a fox.' He turned back to Matt. 'They always make that sound at certain times of the night. And don't be embarrassed. They sound like little kids screaming. Freaks a *lot* of people out who don't know any better.'

'Daddy?' Amelia shouted down. 'Do you think it could be the fox that we killed?'

Even from here, he could spot Wren had nudged the kid to shut up.

Taylor looked suddenly wide awake. 'You killed a fox?'

'Well . . . yes.'

'You know that's illegal, don't you?'

'Well obviously I didn't do it on purpose. I didn't hunt it. We hit it with the car.' He saw no need to go into the extra detail.

Taylor started to shake his head.

'You know . . . an accident. We accidentally hit a fox with a car. It happens. We buried it out in the woods.'

'Who did?'

'Us . . . the family.'

Taylor looked rather disturbed by that. Killing and burying animals probably wasn't how he spent *his* family time. 'You know what? Round here, killing a fox means bad luck. Unless you're hunting it, of course. Then it's good luck. But then you can't do that any more because that's illegal. So killing a fox with a car? Bad luck, that.'

'I thought Christians didn't believe in bad luck.'

247

'Well, maybe they don't. But put it this way. I'm bloody glad *I* didn't kill it.'

The animal moan grew a little louder, more desperate and shrill and Matt thought of that Edgar Allen Poe story, 'The Tell-Tale Heart'. Only this time, it wasn't a heart under the floorboards. It was a fox in a bin bag that was crying out from under the soil, *Officer, that man didn't just hit me with a car. He stamped his fake Italian shoe into my adorable little throat!*

'Well, let's have a little look around to see if there's anything amiss, shall we?' Taylor said, clearly enjoying this.

The reconnaissance mission did little to help because they found no evidence whatsoever. Nothing to say that someone had been lurking about. Matt pressed the bridge of his nose hard and asked himself some perfectly legitimate questions.

Did he imagine it? Was the tip of the hood a leaf dropping from a tree that just happened to catch the light? The crack of twigs just a fox scampering across the floor when they saw the torch?

He felt suddenly weary beyond anything he expected.

'Well, I'd better call it a night,' Taylor said.

'Thanks for coming out. I do appreciate it. I'm surprised you're working so late.'

'Actually, I need the overtime . . . I'm saving for a big trip.' He took his hat off and held it across his belly, pushing up on the balls of his feet to prompt the logical follow-up question.

Matt smiled, 'So where are you going to?'

He ran his hand across the air. 'Israel. The Holy Land. Me and my wife are going to walk where Jesus walked. Every single step. I'm going to do everything he did.'

'Apart from get crucified, I take it.'

Taylor was looking up at the stars, flickering over the forest. 'It's going to be amazing. Life-changing, I reckon.'

Matt watched the officer, at a guess in his mid twenties, bouncing at the prospect of going to the Middle East (a trait disproportionately common among evangelicals). Watching the flash of his eyes made Matt wonder if Taylor might be a prime candidate for Jerusalem Syndrome. He ran a seminar on it at the university. Where religious devotees build the Holy Land up to be so significant that they suffer a sort of mental breakdown when they actually get there. Their brains are unable to cope with Jesus's land being more like *Jesusland*, a theological amusement park with a tourist soul, political rumblings and multiple birth sites of Christ.

'Well, try not to build it up so much,' Matt said softly. 'Then you won't be disappointed.'

'You wha'?' Taylor looked baffled. 'How could any true believer be disappointed with that? His home?'

'Well, I hope you and your wife have a wonderful time,' Matt pushed his hand out. 'Listen, thanks again for coming out.'

Taylor had to blink hard to snap himself back into England. 'No worries. I'll log the incident and we'll see if anything else comes up.'

Which really meant that unless the hooded guy turned up at the house again and stabbed Matt directly in the chest, this was where this investigation ended.

'Oh,' Taylor said, 'and how about I forget about the fox that you killed.'

Matt fought the urge to go and grab the dictionary off the shelf, look up the word accident and press it directly into Taylor's face.

Instead he stood on the doorstep, watching the young officer climb back into the car. The headlights flicked on. No flashing blue this time. He watched the car move off and the white beam creep down the dirt road, lighting the underside of the branches like a ball of light drifting down a tunnel. Then the lights flicked off and the forest was as it wanted to be. Its preferred state. Bedded in shadows.

He wished like hell that he'd run out of that door when he'd had the chance to see who it was.

Because he was almost certain it was someone watching their

house at midnight, picking (he couldn't fail to notice) the side of the cottage with the kids on it. And the more he played it over in his mind the more he remembered how loud those cracking twigs were. Whoever ran off was a decent size.

The thought of someone watching Amelia's window would normally make him angry. Furious, in fact. But that wasn't the emotion he was feeling. Not right now. Not here in the deepest ditch of the night as the wind whistled and the dry leaves scattered. As the ice crept back into the air and the distant, unseen waterfall rumbled somewhere in his ears.

As he stood there, rubbing his arms with the cold he wasn't angry. Instead he felt unsafe. Feeling how tiny the Hunter family was in a cottage that was little more than a fragile glass bauble dangling amongst the branches of a million ancient trees.

He clicked his torch one more time and shone it across the drive.

His body jerked with fright.

A mean little pair of green eyes had punctured the darkness, in the light of his beam. And they were staring at him.

Who is *that?* he thought, before good sense corrected him. *What* is that?

Then after a few, creeping seconds, he figured out the obvious. He whispered over in the fox's direction, way over by the oak tree, 'Yeah, get lost, you little shit. Thanks for making me look like a moron.'

The cretin was defiant. Didn't even blink.

He reached down and grabbed a handful of gravel and tossed it in the animal's direction. 'I said, get lost!'

The two green fluorescent circles, swamped in black shadow, remained utterly still.

He frowned, felt his heart starting to pulse.

He checked behind him to make sure the front door was still closed and grabbed the poker he'd left propped up by the wood store. Hoping he could just scare this one off, rather than make a habit of killing them. He squinted, pushing his insipid little torch beam toward the lights and walked on. *Crunch, crunch*, under his feet. Sounding horribly loud in the night. The cottage shrinking behind him. His eyes kept flicking to the right and the left looking out for someone in a hood racing between the trunks.

Gradually, as he got closer, the beam finally picked up the autumn-orange brown of the fox's fur. Its eyes constantly open. A few more steps and it lay in full view, by the side of the dirt road.

'*My God,*' he whispered, quite involuntarily. Then his arms rippled instantly with gooseflesh. It took all of his willpower not to run straight back into the cottage and bolt the door.

The dead fox lay on its side. Head propped towards the cottage like it was slyly looking at it. Folded ears, peeled gums, misshapen neck. The unmistakeable, long gash down its belly was now thick with hard, brown blood. And snagged around its ankle and strewn across the dirt track – like it had dragged itself all the way here – was the ragged torn bin bag he and Wren had buried it in.

CHAPTER THIRTY-FOUR

Now that it was morning and the lights of the forest were switched on, the kids seemed surprisingly upbeat.

What once were murdered children hidden in the woods were now just vocal, grumpy foxes. And even the scary house-watcher was a possible (to chill people out Matt and Wren were suggesting probable) trick on the eyes. But of course neither of them had dared mention to the kids the one little detail that would have sent them squealing back to London. That their beloved dead fox was back.

Taylor was less than impressed when Matt had called him straight back out in the middle of the night. And even when he turned up – yawning and rubbing at his eyes – he still shrugged when he actually saw the fox's body, suggesting there could be a natural explanation.

'How do you know it's your bin bag? How do you know it's your fox?'

Your fox. Matt had bristled at that. 'And how come you didn't spot it, when you drove off?'

Taylor had shrugged and simply reminded Matt how early in the morning it was.

When Matt suggested that he and Taylor go out and check the grave to see if it was empty Taylor just shook his head. 'Not at this time, you don't. You're liable to break your neck walking in these woods at night. Someone'll come up to you in the morning. And if it makes you feel better, I'll stick around up here for the rest of my shift. It'll be like a stakeout. Like in that film . . . what was it called again . . .'

'*Stakeout?*'

'Yeah. That.'

Now that the morning had come, Matt was up and leaning out of the bathroom window. He noticed that Taylor's police car had already gone. What puzzled him, though, was that the fox was missing too. They'd left it there, exactly where he'd found it, on the side of the dirt road. But now the road was empty. He might have wondered whether it had all just been a dream but he knew it wasn't. He'd shown Wren the body just after Taylor left.

Taylor must have taken it. Evidence, he supposed.

So despite the sun and the laughing kids, the sense of tension was ticking in the background like his granny's old clock. Whenever he visited her as a kid that noise was always there, behind every conversation, every TV show, every tray of tea and pink wafer biscuits.

Matt had breakfast, rinsed his Weetabix bowl in the kitchen sink and set it to the side. It wasn't fully clean but as long as he got the big bits off he'd thank himself later. That stuff dried like concrete. He yawned as he checked his watch, 8.12 a.m., and wondered what time the police would come, so they could check on the empty grave.

He popped his head into the study to see if Wren was there, but she wasn't at her desk like he thought she'd be. There was a half-finished sketch of the church foyer lying flat and the pencil she'd used to draw it was lying next to a steaming, half-filled cup of coffee.

He was about to turn so he could see where she'd gone when he saw a movement through the French doors.

Her red hair suddenly popped up from behind the hedge. He walked across the room and pushed both doors open.

'What are you doing?'

'Hang on.' She came back through the gate still in her pyjamas. She was wearing her Kermit the Frog slippers. Each bare foot was thrust deep into Kermit's gaping mouth, who stared, goggle-eyed, up each leg. Odd that such a design looked cute rather than barbaric. 'I thought maybe in the daylight, there might be footprints. Or some sort of trail.'

'And?'

'I couldn't find anything.'

'Me neither. I checked before breakfast.'

She sighed and leant against the cottage wall, splaying her hand on the rough painted stone. 'Do you really think it might have been Billy coming back? Maybe he was angry with how I spoke to him.'

'It's possible.'

'But how would he know we buried the fox?' She bent over to pick the leaves and twigs from Kermit's cheeks.

'Well somebody found it and dragged it here. Unless, of course, that fox crawled out of the grave on its own.'

She visibly shivered at the thought. And after one glance back at the woods, she said, 'It is kind of spooky here. Isn't it?' Then she blinked her eyes in a snap, like a quick re-programme. 'Anyway. Got to get these plans finished.'

'Okay. I'll be upstairs. I've got a call to make.'

He headed up as the two girls passed him on their way down.

'It's still okay for us to make cookies, isn't it?' Lucy said.

He nodded. 'Just give me a shout when it's bowl-licking time.'

'Hosay, no way!' Amelia said, then hurried down the stairs. Lucy followed, hastily correcting her phraseology. They vanished behind the click of the kitchen door and both girls became muffled sounds.

He passed those two stuffed animals on the landing and for some reason he tipped his imaginary hat to them. 'Morning, you little oiks.' Then with his phone in hand he closed his bedroom door and sank into the white quilt of the creaking bed.

Larry answered after the first ring. 'Detective Inspector Forbes.'

'Larry, hi. It's Matt Hunter.'

'Well, well, well . . .' There was a ruffled sound of movement on the other end. 'So how's the old sabbatical thing going? Is it sunny? Is your book published yet?'

'I think you're supposed to finish writing it first, and yes, it's sunny. Mostly.'

'Ah, right. Well it's pissing down here. Everything stinks of wet concrete.'

'I'm very sad for you.' Matt switched ears. 'Look, I wanted to know how the Adakays were doing?'

'Arima's been psych assessed.'

'And?'

'She's completely normal, apparently.'

'They did actually meet her, didn't they?'

'Yes, and they said there were no red flags. She acted weird in the noodle bar because of shock. Which is fair enough, considering the husband-knife thing.'

Matt shook his head into the phone. 'How *is* Kwame?'

'You shattered his kneecap when you kicked him.'

'Crap.'

'Yep. The guy's in agony.'

'I feel bad about that.'

'Don't. Nobody died. Kwame's going to prison for a bit, their son's being assessed by the Social. But all in all, it's turned out okay. He'll be back with his mum soon enough.' There was a pause. A long silence on the phone. 'You think that's the wrong decision?'

'Frankly?' An image flicked up, of Arima in a kitchen eating salad with her trembling, wide-eyed son. Glaring at him while she sucked lettuce slowly through her lips. 'That makes me feel edgy but then what do I know? I'm not a psychiatrist.'

Larry sniffed. 'So is that why you called?'

'There's something else. I'm helping out the police here. With a case.'

Low laughter came from the other end of the phone. 'So I

hear. Do you find university life boring or something?'

Matt ignored the comment. 'They've got two, maybe three missing people.'

'Yeah, I heard that too. Tell me the bits I don't know.'

Matt told him all of it. The missing women, the prowler last night, the emails, the zombie fox. Even the part about the Bridezilla with a baseball bat. Larry laughed hard at that. Eventually, Matt got round to his requests. 'So can you free up some of your staff to do a bit of digging for me? I just need a few checks doing.'

'I'm not sending them up, if that's what you mean. I need them all down—'

'They can do it all from the office. They never even have to leave London. Maybe get Worthington or Ribchester on it. They owe me a favour.'

'Worthy owes everybody favours,' Larry said. 'I take it the officer in charge knows you're doing this?'

'Yeah, I called him. He figured you might be able to speed things along a bit. Plus he's not really used to using Holmes 2.'

Holmes 2 was a massive computer database which Larry's team used a lot. It was filled with searchable records on murders, frauds and missing persons. Throwing a few names at it might cross-reference some interesting results.

'Email me the details,' Larry said. 'And the search terms. I'll get Worthy on it. Ribby's mine, though. He's busy helping me with a rapist.'

'Tell Worthy I appreciate—'

'Sorry, Matt, but I've got to go.' Voices suddenly filled the background of Larry's office, but Larry said one more thing before ringing off. 'Finish the book, mate.'

Click.

Matt ran a hand through his hair and let himself crash back onto the bed, head plunging in the pillow. Then he lifted his phone and flicked it on, to write the email for Larry. At the same time he pulled out a folded piece of A4 paper from his back pocket and set it on his knee. He'd written down all the case details earlier and started to jab them into the phone with both thumbs. *Tabitha Tansy Clarke, Isabel Dawson, Nicola Knox, Chris Kelly.* And why not check out *Billy Stephenson* while they were at it?

Then finally he typed in the *Verecundus* messages they'd found on Tabitha's and Nicola's phones. He didn't need the notes for that because by now he knew them by heart.

I'm at home with God now. Maybe someday you could believe and come too. Kiss Kiss, Verecundus.

He clicked send and dropped the phone on the bed. He had to wiggle his thumbs to get some feeling back into them.

There was a tiny knock on the bedroom door.

He quickly gathered up the paper and stuffed it into his pocket. 'Yes?' He swung his legs off the bed as Lucy walked in. She was holding a big pink plastic bowl with a wooden spoon sticking out of it. 'We saved you some of the sugary bits, if you still want them.'

'Wow. Thanks.'

She waited, holding onto the bowl.

'Everything okay?' he asked.

'Mm-hmm.'

More silence. She was just looking around the room, at the ceiling, the carpet. Anywhere but him.

'Lucy?'

'Thanks for staying with us last night. For not chasing after him, whoever it was.' She started to look into the bowl as she spoke. 'Amelia was pretty scared. You being there and not running off. It helped.'

'That's okay.'

She hovered in the doorway. 'You know I did think it was him, for a bit. Thought he might have hopped the prison wall and tracked us down.'

He caught her eye and held it, his voice gentle. 'He won't get out for a very long time.'

She nodded, but her smile was crooked.

'Lucy, are you sure you're alright? Is this stuff with your dad getting you—'

She shook her head, and her eyes flickered. Like her brain was gearing up for something. 'It's not that.'

'Is it the fox thing?' he said. 'We should probably talk about it. I'm sorry you had to see me killing—'

'No,' she raised her hand and quickly shook her head. 'It was dying. You set it free.'

Matt could hear Amelia downstairs, cackling loudly about something.

Lucy waited for the laughing to stop, then softly said, 'Can I ask you a question?'

'You can ask me anything.'

'Well, I know you hate God and everything. But . . . I'm just confused. If a person hates God, does that mean God is going to hate them back? Like, is that how an eye for an eye works?'

Matt frowned. 'I don't hate God.'

''Course you do. You dropped him. You ran away.'

'I just stopped believing in him. I can't hate something I don't believe in.'

She looked back down at her bowl, like there was something at the bottom of it, looking up. '*I've* hated God for a very long time.'

Her words hung so heavy in the air that he found himself pausing for a long time before speaking. 'I don't blame you for that at all. You've been through a lot.'

'But, the thing is. I'm pretty sure he hated *me* first.'

'Why do you say that?'

'He must do. Otherwise he would have stopped . . .' her voice trailed off. 'You know. My dad, and everything.'

They hadn't talked like this in such a long time.

All he really wanted to do, in that moment, was to slip off the bed, rush over and hug her. One of those proper dad hugs with one arm around the back, and another cradling her head into his chest.

Chin in her hair. But it had been ages since they had done anything approaching that. He had no idea if it would be right to do it now. Lately with Lucy, he felt like a bomb disposal expert trying to pick the right wire to cut. Only it was always more complicated when you happened to love the bomb.

'And now?' he said. 'Do you still think God hates you?'

'I hope not . . . because . . . because I really don't want to go down to hell. And I'd rather you didn't either, to be honest.' She turned the bowl a full 360 degrees in her hands, caught his eye and shrugged. 'Anyway, here's the goo.' She handed the bowl to him quickly and then headed back down the stairs.

He called after her but she either didn't hear him or she ignored it. So he just sat in the room for a moment, stunned at her sudden vulnerability, wondering how hard Chris must have preached on hell and damnation at the service the other morning.

He was getting very sick of this church, this place.

He headed down to be with them, taking the bowl with him. Perhaps today they'd head up the road into Oxford. Catch an industrial-sized pizza and a film. Something funny and stupid and normal.

It was just as he was leaning against the butcher's block kitchen counter, licking the edge of the spoon, that the front door of the cottage suddenly hammered under four hard knocks. Lucy jumped and spilt some shards of white chocolate across the black-tiled kitchen floor.

Amelia rolled her eyes. 'You're a Scooby Doofus.'

Lucy looked at Matt, shoulders tense. 'Who's that?'

Wren suddenly appeared in the kitchen doorway, staring at the door.

'It's okay. It'll be the police.' Matt set the bowl down and headed for the door. 'They're just following up from last night.'

Another four hard bangs rocked the door as he headed to answer it. Like that ticking clock of tension had suddenly demanded centre stage.

'Alright,' he called out. 'Just a second.'

He checked through the spyhole before opening it.

It was Marion Fellowes, the mystery-loving special constable from the other day. Who helped him find his way from Tabitha's farmhouse to the pile of torched paintings. When he opened the door, the first thing he spotted was a tiny sliver of fingernail resting on her bottom lip. She looked pale.

'Hi, Marion.' He stepped out and closed the door behind him. 'So you've come to find a fox?'

Her face crinkled with puzzlement, but it quickly turned gaunt again. 'Morning, sir . . . I mean Professor.'

'Matt's fine.'

'Okay . . . erm . . . Sergeant Miller wonders if you might be able to join him up at Cooper's Force.'

'When, now?'

'Yes, right now.'

'Why, what's going on? What about the fox?'

'I don't know anything about that.' She shifted her stance. 'We've found a body, sir. A woman.'

A tingle, like tiny drops of ice, rippled down the back of his neck. 'Who?'

'It's not Tabitha. Or Nicola, thank God.'

'Isabel Dawson, then?'

'We're not sure.'

He frowned at her. Miller had already dished out pictures of Isabel to the other officers. They knew what she looked like. 'What do you mean you're not sure? Doesn't anyone recognise her face?'

'That's just it.' The curls in her hair quivered in the breeze. 'She doesn't have one.'

CHAPTER THIRTY-FIVE

A policeman with long fingers lifted the plastic cordon tape. 'Mind your step, it's slippy down there.'

Matt and Marion ducked under the tape and headed up to a slimy-looking metal gate, welded into the arch of the rock. It felt wet and cold as he pushed it. The old iron groaned and squealed, like a warning telling them to keep away. But they pushed through and stepped into darkness, down a few damp steps and along through the corridor cut from rock. Electric lights in shielded plastic buzzed along the side of the rough wall. Like a bomb shelter.

The waterfall, unseen, echoed furiously.

The ceiling pushed itself down in places, so they had to hunch over now and again to avoid slitting their scalps on the jagged rock above. Huge drops of water fell to the floor, making black puddles under their feet.

Marion said, 'Blood and hatred down here.'

'What?' he shouted over the gushing water, pointing at his ears. 'I can't hear you!'

'I said I bloody hate it down here.' She held the wall on each side so that she wouldn't fall. When Matt felt his trainers squeak and slip, he did the same.

Weird how this very same corridor had been filled with the

laughter of his wife and kids just a few days ago when they came to view the falls from inside the rock. He'd pretended he was Bruce Wayne strolling through the Batcave as Amelia tried her best impression of the Joker.

There wasn't much giggling now.

They turned the curve of the corridor and stepped into the arched room of rock that history, like it or not, had called the Devil's Den. It was, to be fair, pretty magnificent. He could see the waterfall gushing down at the mouth of the cave, morning sunlight trying its best to push itself through. It cast the most unnatural natural light he'd ever seen.

Ever since they'd found Tabitha's torched paintings, Miller had brought officers in from other forces to help out. One of them, a policewoman, had Matt sign into a logbook. Then Marion handed him a white paper face mask. Matt slipped it over his head and breathed in the plastic smell. Insipid but infinitely preferable to dead flesh.

He turned to Marion but she wasn't following. 'Aren't you coming?'

'I'd almost break my neck to get down there, but sadly this is as far as I'm allowed.' She gazed over his shoulder trying to see the body but it was out of sight. She gave a disappointed little shrug. 'Have fun.' She headed back up to the corridor and the darkness swallowed her instantly.

'Matt.' Sergeant Miller's barking voice echoed into the cave.

There was a gap on either side of the waterfall, where the cave opened up to the outside. Miller's voice was coming from the far left edge, well beyond the safety barriers. 'Come on out. Use the ledge, it's plenty wide.'

He climbed over, hoping his shoes had enough grip, then made his way toward the light. When he got out there he found Miller standing half outside, half inside the cave. A shaft of sunlight cut his body in two. His hair was already slicked back from the spray from the falls, gradually soaking into his uniform. He made no attempt to step out of it, as if he didn't even notice he was slowly getting drenched. Instead, his eyes were fixed on the body at his feet. His normally ruddy forehead was the colour of meat left in the heat too long and it looked filled with new lines.

'Would you look at that,' he said, shaking his head and holding his mask.

The police had covered the almost naked woman in a transparent plastic tarpaulin, to keep the water out and the evidence in. The falls weren't actually hitting it, but the spray spattered hard against it, like a tiny machine gun sound.

Matt quickly pushed the mask against his face to seal a slight seam in it and crouched down to look. He'd seen his share of dead bodies, in all manner of bizarre and undignified positions. But as he stared at this one, his body was generously and instantly splashing about whatever acids were required to produce nausea.

She'd fallen from the top of the falls. That much was obvious. And she was lying face down on her stomach in her underwear, white bra clasped tight on her spine. The faded label of her knickers stuck up and out, pressing against the wet skin. And though her body looked distorted under the wet plastic, it was still possible, unfortunately, to make out the details.

It started with a long brown streak just under her buttocks that splashed upwards, thick through her knickers and into the small of her back, then carried on in a long coffee-coloured stretch up her spine, jutting off at an angle.

She'd lost control of her bowels in the fall.

Oddly enough, other than being a hideous final robber of dignity, the forensic guys would be very happy to see a decent streak like this (probably the only job in the world when that statement was true) because they'd probably work out what angle she fell at.

It also said something even more important. That when she fell from the top she was fully capable of crapping herself in abject terror. Alive while she fell. It was strange, the language the body chooses to speak in, once the mouth can no longer do it.

The rocks here were massively uneven and a cluster of what looked like stalagmites (-tites down, -mites up, he reminded himself) shot up to hip height all around them, like the surface of an alien planet.

And there, exactly where she'd fallen, was a huge, thick stalagmite. The daddy. An unforgiving bastard of a rock around the size of a Land Rover tyre at its base, but honed to a screwdriver-sized point at the top, groomed by nature for billions of years, eroding itself into the perfect little spike. All, apparently, for this.

She'd hit that stalagmite with her face.

A forty-foot drop would have generated frightening levels of momentum for the human body. So when her head hit the spike it had sent her spine snapping right back like a hinge. It was the yoga move from hell.

She'd obviously tried to look away in those final seconds as the ground hurtled toward her because her face (could you even call it that any more?) had hit the spike side on. The tip had entered her left cheek and pushed straight out the other, snapping the end of the stone with the force of it. With the skull shattered, most of her features had collapsed in on themselves. Flaps of skin hung like folds of bacon and the blood looked black under the plastic. He saw fragments of bone, lots of them, scattered on the wet rock. Identical, he thought, to the flakes of white chocolate he'd seen Lucy spill on the kitchen floor earlier.

A twisted voice in his subconscious said, *Oh, Isabel, you Scooby Doofus*. He quickly grabbed at the humour of it.

Because while he'd seen various bodies, this one was so extreme and grotesque, so Grand Guignol, that the real solution wasn't nausea or a rush to throw up, but just to think of something else quickly. Scooby Doofus, the waterfall, the fact that he'd run out of dental floss this morning and he needed to pick up a new pack. Anything else in the back of his mind.

It was a danger to the psyche to look at that plastic ghoul on the rocks without anything else in his mind to balance it out. The mad gallows voice in his head tried to keep him sane: *She really 'fell for the falls', didn't she, Matt? Give that lassie a fridge magnet.* Then he really did want to throw up.

He wrenched his gaze from her, stood back up and breathed again.

'So you saw her in the flesh the other day,' Miller said, his eyes flickering on his choice of words. 'Is that your wedding dress girl?'

Matt had to shout through the mask. 'I think so. Same sort of build and hair. It's certainly not Tabitha Clarke. She's got hair.'

'And she's way too plump for Nicola Knox.'

They waited for a moment in silence. Matt pushed the mask against his face again, convinced he could smell fluids. Then slapping his damp fringe back he said, 'How many suicides *do* you get at this spot?'

'Maybe four a year. Sometimes more, sometimes less. Just before the millennium there were twelve but then you know how people were, back then. Come out here a sec.' He motioned for Matt to follow him and they stepped out of the mouth of the cave, grabbing onto the rock wall for balance. They came out fully into the sunlight where the waterfall churned loudly to their right. Miller was ignoring the signs that said *Danger: Risk of Death*. He winced from the sound of the falls and glanced across the lake, at the field swooping up the hill to the church. At the Healing Centre tucked at the bottom of the hill. The shore where the faithful were baptised. All of it now dream-like through a mist of white spray.

They stopped on a flat section of rock which ran about four feet from the edge of the lake, which lapped hard against the stone. Then they turned back and looked up. Miller tugged his mask off and let it dangle from his neck. Matt did the same.

'Thing is,' Miller shouted, 'they *never* fall from this side.'

Matt followed Miller's pointing finger as they both craned backwards, looking up the rock face. They had to squint as drops of the falls splashed into their eyes and mouths.

'You see that ridge over on the left side of the waterfall?' Miller's voice seemed to croak at this angle. 'At the top? That's flat up there and it's easy to get to.'

'Yeah, we had a picnic up there. There's no railing.'

'Exactly. No railing. Plus that side's a sheer drop into the lake. You jump from there and you know you're going to hit the water. Quick death.' He flicked his finger to the right side. Directly above them was a tree, curled like a giant witch's finger hanging over the edge. 'But on this side, there's a barbed wire fence blocking that entire ridge, so you'd have to clamber over that. Then there's the old tree up there, and the little rocky slope before you'd fling yourself off. And it's obvious that the rock comes out a bit down here with all these spikes, which is a bad place to land. I tell you, nobody ever jumps from this side.'

'Unless . . .' Matt pondered it.

'Unless what?'

'Unless she wanted to avoid the water for some reason,' Matt said.

Miller nodded down to the spikes coming up from the floor. 'Well she'd need a bloody good reason for this side to be preferable. Unless of course she didn't jump.'

They waited again, silent. And after a pause, Miller quite unexpectedly pushed both hands against his face, like he might scream with frustration.

'You okay?'

A sudden movement came from back inside the cave. An officer was cupping his hands and shouting, his outline flickering like static through the falling water. Neither of them could hear what he was saying.

Miller looked up and wearily started to trudge back into the cave, passing the entropy monster that most likely *was* Isabel Dawson. Matt spotted one of her hands, warped under the plastic. It was flat against the rock with the palm up. He pictured her standing in a comprehensive school somewhere, teaching kids the power of momentum and velocity and gravity. He shivered and had to look away.

He slipped a couple of times on the metal walkway before finally getting back behind the barrier where the visitors normally stood.

'We've been up top,' the other officer said. His badge said PC Boyd. He was fighting to keep his eyes from clocking the body, like a teenager trying not to check out his teacher's cleavage.

Miller jabbed a finger towards the main entrance. 'I can't hear myself think inside here. Let's get out in the open.' He marched off and they all followed him back through the stone corridor, up the damp stone steps and into the sun.

'So what did you find up top?' Miller said, as the metal door clanged shut.

'It's the strangest thing. There's a wedding dress. An actual wedding—'

Miller clicked his fingers. 'Good.'

Boyd frowned.

'That narrows things down a bit. Where was it?'

'Tangled up on the barbed wire fence. Looks like she clambered over it and got the thing caught. I guess that's why she wriggled out of it. Explains why she was hardly dressed.'

'Anything else?'

'There was something lying in the grass, on the other side of the fence. Me and the SOCO had to climb over to secure it. Almost ripped my danglers off doing it.' He opened his leg to the side and pulled back a flap of his trousers, torn in a perfect corner.

'For God's sake, Boyd. Get to the point.'

The officer, shocked at Miller's sudden shout, closed his legs quickly. 'It was a white strip of material.'

'A what?' Miller said.

Matt's eyebrows flicked up. 'You mean like a dog collar? Like what a vicar would wear?'

'Yeah. Could be. The SOCO's got it bagged up. You said you were questioning a priest guy, didn't you?'

A tiny flush of satisfaction came to Miller's face. He turned to

Matt. 'Chris wasn't wearing the dog collar yesterday, was he? At the baptism. He had a tie on, but no collar. Maybe he lost it up top.'

'I'm sure he has more than one.'

'There's more.' Boyd leant over a little, like this was a campfire story. 'It looked crunched up. And . . . there was a little bit of blood on it. Looked to me like it could have been ripped off in a struggle.'

'Right,' Miller grabbed his car keys, 'I'm heading up there to check this out. And you, Boyd, you find out where Chris Kelly is this morning. I bet you he's the last person who saw Isabel Dawson alive. Radio me straight away and we'll chat with him.'

Matt tugged at his elbow, 'Can I have a minute?'

Miller looked up at the ridge and blew out a breath. 'Make it quick.'

The two of them walked to the other side of the entrance, by a row of seats carved out of the rock. Miller swung his foot on top of one of them and rested his elbow on his knee. He looked like a hunter with his foot on a moose's head, posing for the camera.

'I told you this guy was dodgy,' Miller said. 'I bloody told you.'

'You're right. This is important but . . . think about it. Anyone could have gone up there with a dog collar on. Isn't there another vicar in the village? The one at the little Anglican church?'

'Who, Dave Walden? He never wears one of those. He says it puts people off. Besides, he's pushing ninety. He can't even get up his own staircase without a Stannah, never mind up this rock.' He glanced at the ground for a second. 'To be frank with you, Matt, the only other person I can think of round here who has a dog collar . . . is you.'

His eyebrow went up. Just the one.

'I saw you on TV, remember? You had one then.'

'Which just proves my point. You could buy one of those in any joke shop. Chris may well have nothing to do with this, Terry. You get me? Nothing.'

Miller looked unconvinced. 'Well, we can see that once the

thing's tested, can't we? In the meantime, I still need to talk to him.'

'Before you do,' Matt paused, 'maybe I should speak to him first.'

'Why?'

'Because I know him. He's the type of guy who's going to clam up if you go in all guns blazing. Maybe if I speak to him first and tell him a body's been found, I could even mention it might be Isabel. I don't know, it just might be interesting to see how he reacts when it's just me.'

Miller started to bite the inside of his mouth, weighing up the suggestion.

'Well?'

'You're not trying to protect him, are you?'

Matt narrowed his eyes. 'Of course I'm not. It's just . . .'

'Just what?'

'Well . . . Chris and I have our differences but . . . I really think he trusts me.'

Miller waited for a long moment, then popped his lips. 'Do it, then. See what he thinks. But no mention of the collar until we've tested it.'

'Understood.'

Miller went to head off.

'Hang on a sec,' Matt said. 'There's something else.'

He stopped walking. 'What now?'

'Last night we had a prowler. Around the house.'

'I know. I know. Taylor told me it was foxes.'

'Yeah, but did he tell you about the dead one on my drive? Did he tell you about that?'

'Tell me? He brought the bugger into the office. It's sitting in a plastic crate in our backyard, just so I can have a look at it.'

'It's there? Good. Then what did you find?'

'Well I haven't properly looked at it yet, have I? Diary's kind of chocka today.'

'Listen to me,' Matt flung up his hands. 'I really think the prowler put the fox there. And I saw a hood. And my daughter and I heard someone running off. So this is important—'

'For Christ's sake, Matt!' Miller shouted. 'Can't you see I'm fucking drowning here?'

Matt was startled into silence.

Miller's chin seemed to contract for a second, and he looked utterly lost. Then he seemed to quickly lock his spine in. Probably a stress management technique. And when he spoke he barely opened his teeth. 'I am going to drive up to the top of that ridge right now to see that collar. And I'm going to hope to high heaven that Tabitha Clarke or little Nicola isn't lying somewhere round here with their faces ripped off as well. So if you don't mind, Professor, we can discuss your animal issues another time.'

Miller stomped towards his car, running his hand through his hair and smearing a palm on his trousers. Maybe it was spray from the falls, maybe it was sweat. But when Miller got in the car Matt noticed he didn't move off straight away. He waited in the front seat for a very long moment, like he was trying to catch his breath. Then the engine kicked into life and the car headed up the high track that led to the top of the falls.

Matt heard a soft footstep press into the ground behind him. When he turned he saw Marion, the keys of her patrol car dangling from her fingers. She looked at Matt for a few silent seconds. 'I'll take you home,' she said.

CHAPTER THIRTY-SIX

For some reason the air conditioning in Matt's car wasn't working so the car was surface-of-the-sun stuffy. Even having the windows down and the driver's door open did little to bring in any extra air.

He wanted to get out but he'd be spotted if he did. So he wiped his palm across his brow again, smeared it on his jeans and waited.

He was watching the entrance to Meadow Lane Crematorium from the far side of the sun-drenched car park. The building was small and wooden with an Austrian vibe to it. He'd spoken in Innsbruck a few years back at a *Star Trek* convention – perhaps the pinnacle of his nerdiness. He'd lectured on Buddhist themes of karma in *Star Trek 2: The Wrath of Khan*. (The lawyer in the plane seat next to him had laughed for almost the entire journey.) But it paid well and he'd stayed in a gorgeous chocolate-box chalet with hanging baskets and the smell of ham.

This crematorium reminded him of that. It was the sort of place you'd whizz past on skis, not somewhere you'd be incinerated in. It sat in the very centre of landscaped memorial gardens lined with neatly paved paths and flowers.

Dense oak trees packed with legions of birds hung over the garden's memorial stones. Somehow they looked pretty clean. Quite an achievement. He wondered which poor sod had to clean the bird crap off them in between burying the dead. What a job. He'd stick with *Wrath of Khan* any day.

Against all this nature, an industrial stone chimney thrust itself up from the wooden cottage and up into the sky, ready to spurt out the last gasps of the locals as they withered in the ovens below.

A couple of text messages had already come through from Wren. They'd both decided that she and the girls should go into Oxford for the whole day and planned to stay till late evening. Apparently, right now they were having the dead skin of their feet bitten off by tiny Japanese fish. How quaint.

Still, it was better than hanging around the cottage today, which felt weird and vulnerable after last night.

He smiled and winced at a picture she'd texted. Three pairs of bare female feet, lolling in water, filled with tiny mouths.

It started to feel like forever so he drummed out a rhythm on the top of the dashboard, and waited. Then he started to count the hanging baskets, and waited. Turned on the radio and listened to the news. Kids were being burnt alive by gangs in Nigeria. He cringed and switched it off.

Then finally . . .

Movement.

He sat bolt upright in the clammy leather seat, surprised at how much he'd slouched. A hearse came on a slo-mo creep through the iron gates and moved towards the entrance, hugging the kerb. Following it was one single funeral car, no more.

They pulled to a stop silently. There was no other sound except the birds in the trees until the door of the second car clicked open, and out stepped the man himself, Chris Kelly. He was wearing a black suit. His white dog collar shone fluorescent in the sun. Matt made a mental note of its presence, though like he'd said to Miller, the guy could have an entire bullet belt stocked with these things. He also held a Bible across his stomach. Then he squinted into the sun and reached into his pocket for something. He pulled out a pair of Aviators and slipped them on.

From the other side of the car a young woman stepped out. She was quite small, with a bob of blonde hair that she kept tucking behind her ear constantly. She and Chris both stood silent and morose as the undertakers spilt out of the hearse. Three men and one woman. They looked a bit like gangsters.

The undertaker popped the boot and eventually a group of them heaved the coffin out, lurching it up on their shoulders. That move they did, the hoist, was a vivid pull back to the various funerals Matt had performed in his brief time in the church. Most of the undertakers he worked with did the job as well as could be done. But there were some who fully relaxed when there wasn't any family to notice. They'd fling those coffins up like they were baggage handlers at Heathrow. It was just as well hardly anyone had open caskets these days or families could easily find their loved ones looking like they'd just fallen out of the top bunk.

What was it the old undertaker from the Co-Op used to say, sometimes even in earshot of the grieving families and friends? *If they aren't already dead then the ride to the crem'll finish them off.* Yeah, it wasn't a shock when he was fired.

The four figures got themselves steady, settled their chins into professional mourner mode and then Chris moved in front of them and opened his Bible. He gave them 'the nod', that powerful little jerk of the head that said, let's do this thing. Let's pin down the devastating metaphysical mystery of death with songs and fire and tuna sandwiches after.

The woman gave a proper hinged-at-the-hips bow towards the coffin, like you'd do to the Queen or Darth Vader.

Chris waited for a few dramatic seconds, then he turned and led the coffin quietly inside.

Matt buzzed the windows up, pushed the car door open and sprang out, breathing in the air as though he'd just stepped out of a submarine. He jogged along a neat path, sweat on his back, and hopped over a row of white roses, clipping one with his foot. The petals fell to the floor.

The plan was to tell Chris about the body at the bottom of Cooper's Force but he had no intention of doing that just yet. He'd wait till the end of the service, partly out of respect for the deceased (whoever that was) but also because he just wanted to observe and see how Chris might behave as he led this funeral. Would he act like a man serving his local community in their hour of need or a twitchy psycho who had pushed a woman to her death the previous night?

Did it feel odd thinking of Chris in these terms? They may not have been great friends, but Chris certainly wasn't a stranger. Yes, it felt very odd indeed.

'Hi,' Matt acknowledged the undertakers with a nod as they filed back out. They jerked their bodies into a more solemn, upright mode.

The front doors were designed to be silent as they opened and shut so Matt slipped in without making a sound. He was in a foyer section surrounded by wood-panelled walls with no windows whatsoever. The double doors led into the chapel itself where families could grieve, unseen, in private.

The sanctuary doors were closed now so Matt could wait in the lobby out of sight. The service had already begun and he could hear the sound of Chris's voice seeping through a tiny speaker on the wall.

From the number of mourners that had turned up (i.e. one, the blonde lady) Matt was positive this must have been an elderly death. When he first started working at churches he was shocked to find how many old people die with no family either alive – or willing – to come and say goodbye. In those cases the care homes usually sent one of the staff along so that the place wasn't completely empty. One of the carers, perhaps, or maybe a cleaner or the cook if the rest were busy. Most took it seriously, though he'd seen one or two slip out their phone to update their Twitter feed, as the coffin rolled away.

How sad is this? LOL Only person at a funeral. #YOLO

Funerals reminded him of a simple, shitty fact: that when it comes down to it, we all die alone. Every one of us. No hand to guide us. No soft whisper in our ear to say you're home, little one, you're home. All those relationships we grow and nurture over a lifetime are just hurtling daily towards this.

Cold, quiet, in a box. On our own.

He was starting to bum himself out so he shook his head and checked that his phone was still on silent. There were no messages from Larry Forbes, but he hoped that by the end of the day Worthington might have come up with something from the Holmes 2 computer search. He slipped the phone back in his pocket, then sat on an old wooden chair near the entrance. Like a kid waiting to see the head teacher.

The strains of 'All Things Bright and Beautiful' moved through the wood and then Chris started to preach a sermon. Usually at these things (when there was no family present) the undertakers and care staff just wanted things over with quickly. Shove 'em in, hit the switch, go pick up the next box. A sort of fast-food, Ronald MacDonald version of death. He'd seen vicars follow suit and sing one verse of a hymn, pray the Lord's Prayer as quick as the terms and conditions on a cinema ad, and that was it.

It turned out that Chris was different. He took his time, even to an audience of one. Two if you counted the guy in the box.

He started to speak.

'One of the most positive-thinking songs in the world' – he spoke loudly, with confidence – 'has got to be "Pack Up Your Troubles". We all know how it goes. "Pack up your troubles in your old kit bag and smile, smile, smile". In both world wars and beyond, it's been the anthem for hopefulness and looking on the bright side. I bet our deceased friend, Reginald Arthur Keech, sang it many times in his life, growing up in Basildon, through his years at the Boys' Brigade, and especially through his times fighting in the Royal Navy. All those years at sea. And maybe he sang that song recently, as he battled the toughest enemy of his life, bowel cancer . . . and lost. But still, that song would have given him comfort, as it did for millions. What's the use of worrying? It says, it's really not worthwhile.

'And how true that is. Jesus said it himself: worrying and stressing in life won't add a single hour to it. In fact it will take life away. Yes, stress will literally shave the days off us. We keep heartache in and it chews us up. Unreleased, unexternalised, it becomes the cancer of the soul. But let me ask you. Is it really so easy to grab our tragedies, our sadness, and pack them up in that old kit bag? I'm afraid it isn't.

'You see, it's a little known fact that the man who wrote the music to "Pack up Your Troubles" was called Felix Lloyd Powell. And in 1942, he dressed himself in the uniform of the Peacehaven Home Guard, took his rifle and shot himself through the heart.

'For him he found that his old kit bag simply wasn't big enough to hold all the sorrows of this world. And no amount of singing or whistling that ditty was going to make that bag any bigger.

'Felix Lloyd Powell took his own life, and let me tell you . . . I shudder to think where he whistles that tune now. Because it's not just suicides that go to hell. The truth breaks the heart . . . it's anyone who doesn't have faith. Who's never felt the loving touch of Christ's forgiveness. Making them new. God forbid that we end up in that position.'

Chris stopped speaking and there was a long pause. So long that Matt wanted to push open the door just to see if everyone hadn't run off. But then it started again.

'But, you know, Jesus Christ has a kit bag big enough to hold every sorrow. Cos he *is* a man of sorrows. He said if we are born of water and the spirit we will inherit the kingdom of God. And we'll live with him *for ever*.

'So it's my ardent prayer that Reginald Arthur Keech will have thrown his soul deep into the arms of Christ. And perhaps he did. Who knows which angel might have come to him in those final moments. When his heart stopped, did his new home begin? Was he transported from this decaying ball of rock to the glorious beyond?

Because, after all, heaven *is* healing. The only healing that matters, in the end. If he took God's hand and let the Almighty wash him clean, then we know that as we mourn Reginald on this dark, lonely earth he now sits by the Lord's right hand, charting new waters, new seas. And he smiles, smiles, smiles.

'But if he didn't turn to Christ then perhaps he appears to us today as a warning from the Lord. The proverbial head on a stick, like warriors used to display on the old roads. But not from a God of hate or malice: from one who longs for his people to renounce their sins and escape the lake of fire.

'So where will you pack up your troubles?' He paused and cleared his throat. 'I guess I'm speaking to you, Penny, since you're the only one here. Will *you* pack up your troubles in a flimsy bag that only has room for one catchy little song? A happy little tune, which came from the pen of a fatally depressed man who ended his own life in despair? Or will you give your troubles to the creator and saviour of the universe, who can hold every song, both happy and tragic?

'Choose him. Always, choose him. For with him, death is not the end. Merely the end of the beginning. But without him, it is the beginning of something else. An eternal storm. It's not popular to talk about, these days. But, by God, it's the sad, sad truth.

'And so may the blessing of the Father, Son and Holy Spirit be with us all, ever more. Amen.'

There was a moment of silence, and Matt listened to the words of Chris's sermon echoing in his head, the hell-obsessed rhetoric that kept springing from this church, not to mention the insistence of heaven being some place 'out there', some celestial cloud world where believers were shipped after their hearts stopped. Didn't these guys even read their Bibles? Didn't the texts tend to say that heaven wouldn't be elsewhere, but would be this very earth? Renewed. Weren't they aware that much of the fiery chasms and pitchfork-prodding images of hell came more from Hollywood and Dante and Milton than the Bible?

But at exactly the same moment as his theological posturing his mind was flashing up a depressing image of Lucy and Amelia and Wren and him, trousers rolled up to their ankles, skeleton feet lolling in the lake of fire.

Wow, he thought, *crematoriums make me Gothic.*

The strains of the organ began. And exhausted from last night, he found himself standing again, tilting his head towards the melody.

He recognised the tune as Chris's tinny voice hummed out of the speaker like a wasp.

A shiver ran through his skin.

The song of Arima Adakay, reaching for him from the noodle-covered floor. And the song of the schizophrenic Ian Pendle, singing as he sat there stark naked in Matt's mother's armchair, fingers painted in the crusty brown-red of her life, chewing the ragged slug of her top lip.

Amazing Grace, how sweet the sound
That saved a wretch like me.
I once was lost but now I'm found,
Was blind but now I see.

Matt closed his eyes and felt the tiredness from last night plunge his feet through the carpet. It was impossible not to drop into the memory of that day. *Impossible.* And the echo of Pendle's mocking voice started to sing into his head as he went down, as sure as if the man's bloodied lips were pressed against Matt's ear with that same tone of smug entitlement.

The Lord has promised good to me,
My hope he will secure.
He will my shield and portion be,
As long as life endures.

Pendle waving at him with a happy face (happy because he saw himself as forgiven), waving from somewhere up above Matt as he fell down some bottomless pit in the floor. And as Matt breathed in he was amazed and disgusted at how much the black metal studs that ran through the wooden panels in here smelt like his mother's blood.

The music surged.

You've never dealt with this.

He pushed his fingers into the bridge of his nose, and squeezed. And there he was.

Is.

Landing with an ankle-snapping bump into Dunwich Village Hall, at his mother's funeral. Standing up and finding he's twenty-five and everyone's wincing and putting down their teacups to see the spectacle of it. As his mum's friend from church, Sylvia, is distraught, losing it in fact, she's leaning across a serving plate filled with sausage rolls, jabbing her fingernail at him, saying, 'You know the real reason, don't you? The real reason why your mum took Ian Pendle in?'

Her husband, tugging at her to stop. 'Sylvia . . . leave the lad alone.'

'I will not, Barry. He should know.'

Matt's own voice, uneven, watery. Little more than a whisper, 'Know what?'

'Matt, she took Pendle in for you. For *you*! Cos you'd been ranting on the phone to her, hadn't you?'

He pressed the bridge of his nose harder, the skin turned white. The hymn, the memory, was seeping through the wall of the crematorium and crawling up his legs.

'You told her that church was a waste of time, didn't you? That it never did anything practical for people. Too much praying, not enough *doing* . . . that's what you told her. Wasn't it?'

'For God's sake, Sylvia, the lad's just buried his—'

'*She took him in for you, Matt.* Don't you get that? She didn't want to, because she was terrified, but she did it for you. To show Christians could care, that she was as brave as you. She thought you

279

might stick with church because you'd see your old mum trying to make an actual difference. And look where it got her.'

'Sylvia!'

'See what you did, Matt?' Sylvia sobbing now. 'To the best friend I ever had? But you'll run from this, little Matthew Hunter. You'll run. Because that's what you do. Like your dad, you always run.'

A sudden tap on Matt's shoulder shot a charge through his body. Chris Kelly swam into his vision.

'You look pale.' Chris said.

'We need to talk.'

'Are you ill? Would you like some water?'

'We need to talk, Chris.'

The blonde woman came wandering out of the chapel area, her face gaunt, and Matt spotted a damp line where a tear had fallen down her cheek. She reached over to Chris and shook his hand.

'Are you okay, Penny?' Chris said.

She hesitated before touching his hand. 'I suppose you tell it like it is, Pastor.'

'Somebody has to. See you in church on Sunday?'

She clearly had no idea how to answer that because she seemed to nod and shake her head at the same time so that it just moved in an awkward circle. Then she hurried out. Raced out in fact. They watched her leave and it was only when the door was fully closed that Chris spoke. 'Did you listen to the service?' He motioned towards the chapel. 'You were here the whole time?'

'Yes.'

'And the sermon, did you hear that?'

'Every cheery word.'

'That's good. You should hear those things, and from the white of your cheeks it looks like it made you think. Maybe the Holy Spirit got you a little, ey?' Chris smiled softly and started to gaze around the chapel foyer. 'It's a pretty little place this, isn't it? I own it, by the way. Well, the church does. I often come down here and sit. It's a great place to pray and ref—'

'A body's been found. This morning.'

The smile that had been plastered on Chris's face since he'd spoken to Penny slowly started to sink. Matt counted the seconds until he said something.

Six.

'Is it Tabitha Clarke?'

'We aren't sure yet. But we think it might . . .' Just then Matt paused. Deliberately. To leave it hanging. He felt like a game show host, *We'll tell you the identity of this week's cadaver, right after this break.* 'We think it might be Isabel Dawson. I'm sorry to have to tell you this, Chris. But it looks like she threw herself from the falls last night.'

Chris's expression didn't change. He waited for a long moment then he started to do something odd.

He walked backwards.

One step, then two, then three. A pause, then four. Distancing himself until he was a few feet away.

'Chris?'

He said nothing.

'Chris? Did you hear what I said?'

Chris's lips were so dry that when they finally went to open they peeled apart, as if they might make a sound like Sellotape. But what came out of the emerging hole wasn't speech. Instead, he sang. His voice was tuneful, but tiny and weak.

'Pack up your troubles . . . in your old . . . kit bag . . .'

'Chris?'

'. . . and smile . . . smile . . . smile.' His eyes were grey, staring through Matt like he was made of water, then he said the words, rather than singing them: 'What's the use of worrying? It never was worthwhile.'

'Chris, how about we sit down.'

He started to shake his head and then pulled a trembling hand to his mouth. He bit the nail of his little finger, peeling the white tip completely off, tearing a little into the skin. Then he let his arm drop down again. 'It wasn't me.'

'I never said it was.'

Silence.

'Chris?'

'It wasn't me.'

'I told you. I didn't say—'

'But do you want to know something?'

'Yes.'

'I know who did do it. I know who dragged Izzy up there and pushed her off.'

Matt took a step toward him. 'You've got to tell me, Chris.'

Chris lifted the little finger again, now holding a bead of blood where he'd torn the skin. Then he curled the other fingers back so the bloody one pointed towards Matt. 'It was you.'

'What?'

'You did it.' Chris moved closer, little finger prodding forward. 'You did it. And maybe people should know.'

'What are you talking about?'

'The *second* you burst through that door the other day, you sealed her fate. Not me.' His eyes flicked to the floor then back up, shimmering with tears. 'She wasn't even baptised.' Another bite of the fingernail. Pulling off a full line of skin. 'My God, what have you done?'

'Chris, this isn't my—'

The sudden shout that sprang from Chris's lips made Matt's eyes flicker. 'Suicides go to hell! They all do!' Then Chris just wiped away a tear, turned on his feet and headed to the door.

'Where are you going?'

'To call her mother. And to pray for Izzy's soul. Though I know it's too late.'

'I told you, we don't even know if it's definitely her yet.'

'Oh, it's her. *I know it is.*' He turned back and actually smiled.

'And you know it too, don't you? So I'll pray for her unbaptised soul. And I'll pray for you too, Matt. You're my friend but . . . but maybe you shouldn't have come to Hobbs Hill. Maybe it was a mistake bringing you here. Because you're running too far from him and you're letting the demons in.'

'What demons?'

'I can see one. It stands with you.'

'*What* demon?'

'Since I saw you at the Purging, and ever since. I saw a shape with you. A figure. I hoped I was wrong.' His eyes flicked across Matt's shoulder and he seemed to shiver. 'Matt, it's with you right now.'

'You're crazy.'

'I think the dark has its eye on you, Matt. But I pray that God can wash your hands of . . .'

'Of what?' Matt was the one shouting now. 'Wash my hands of what?'

'Of the blood.' And then, quietly, with tears in his eyes. 'Of all that blood.'

It came quick, the lunge towards Chris, the grabbing of his shirt and pushing him against the door, with a slam of wood. The hissing, breathy words, directed straight into his face. 'You don't know me,' Matt barked at him. '*You don't know me!*'

All that blood. Pooling in plates of lamb and carrots.

His fingers scurrying up Pendle's chest, just so he might reach his throat. Where he could grab and press and kill. Press his boot in till he heard the pop.

Matt gasped at himself, and uncurled his fingers from Chris's shirt. But Chris had already pulled himself free and had flung the door open. It cracked against the wall and the sound shocked Matt out of . . . it. Whatever it was.

Chris marched over to his car, a new-looking Insignia, which was parked in the designated minister's space. And Matt watched it jerk back hard in reverse. The driver's window came down and when

Chris's head appeared, there were tears running down his cheeks. 'Don't you realise, Matt . . . that God gets angry? He gets *very, very angry*.' And his face was identical to how it had been in the back of that bus, all those years ago on the night of frost and soft, falling snow. There was fear in his eyes, but he could tell it wasn't for himself.

It was for Matt.

Chris looked back at the road and surged the car forward, racing off up the lane. The engine screamed as it rushed through the heavy iron gates of the crematorium.

Matt just looked at the tips of the trees swaying in the breeze, and felt his own shallow breath drawing in an unexpected smell. The rotten food and vinegar stench of Arima Adakay.

He blinked a few times. Confused. Assuming this was all just exhaustion.

It's not like he blamed himself for Isabel's death. If anything, Chris Kelly's specialist therapy had pushed a psychologically vulnerable woman to the edge. Literally. But that sickly echo of 'Amazing Grace' mocked him; it pushed its accusing fingers deep into the tapioca mush of his brain. Bringing everything down to the only sentence that mattered. In all of it.

She took him in for you, Matt. To please you.

He looked down at the carpet and for a moment he thought if he were to turn around, he might see something was with him after all. Something that had crawled out of Arima Adakay and followed him home.

But when he turned there was nothing.

And he laughed into the empty space like a stressed out, mad person, and put his hands in his pockets to stop them from shaking.

CHAPTER THIRTY-SEVEN

Matt trudged back through the foyer and into the now-empty chapel, feeling embarrassed at how much he'd let Chris get to him. His head throbbed, hard enough to hear the rhythmic pulse of blood through his ears. A lady, probably in her seventies, suddenly creaked out from behind the organ holding a foot-thick music book under her arm. She flipped her other hand outwards and a telescopic walking stick clicked itself into place like an oversized flick knife.

'You're too late,' she said, thinking he was a mourner. 'Mr Keech is already in the oven. But you could pray, I suppose.'

She turned up the aisle and headed slowly for the door.

Matt sat on one of the pews for a minute. It was quiet here and it felt like a good place to calm down and get himself together.

Assessing Chris's bizarre reaction to the news about Isabel was a helpful distraction from his own hang-ups. But as soon as he started to mentally walk back through Chris's words, his phone buzzed in his pocket. He grabbed it, eagerly.

'Hi, Matt. You got a minute?' It was Larry.

'Tell me you have something on those names.'

'Nothing major.'

'What about Chris Kelly? He's acting seriously weird about all of this. I think he's hiding something—'

'Are you alone?'

Matt sat up a little in the pew and looked around. 'Yes. Why?'

'Do you want some advice?'

Matt waited. 'Go on.'

'You need to watch yourself.'

'What's that supposed to mean?'

'It's Miller. My grapevine says he's asking questions about you.'

'What sort of questions?'

'If you're trustworthy. What sort of work you do for me. If you have any prior police record.'

Matt turned to look at the chapel door. It was closed and silent. 'What are you saying to me?'

'I have a DS friend of mine up there. Works in Oxford. I mentioned your missing women situation.'

'And?'

'Are you sitting down?'

'Bloody hell, Larry, just tell me.'

'Miller's thinking you might have something to do with the missing women.'

'*What?* Because of a couple of emails? That's ridiculous. I get a couple of—'

'Look, I've known you for years and I know you're not the type. That's why I'm giving you the heads-up. But there's more. My Oxford guy says that in the last hour Miller's asked for forensics on a fox they found outside your house.'

'What about it?'

'Nicola Knox had anorexia and bulimia.'

'I know that. So?'

'She vomited so many times that the acids apparently rotted her teeth. So she got gold ones put in on the NHS. Two of them, apparently.'

'You're losing me here. What's this got to do—'

'They found one of them stuffed down that fox's throat.'

The room tilted.

'My guy says they've got plier marks on them. Probably ripped out of her head. They haven't found the other one,' he sighed. 'So listen, mate. I hate to say it but if someone really did put that fox on your doorstep then someone is setting you up.'

Matt hunched forward, eyes closed and sank his head on the pew. 'This is completely insane.'

'I'll drive up tomorrow morning, alright? It's the first I can get there. But I have to let these guys do their thing for now.'

'Holy crap, it must be Chris. It *must* be him. He got me here through Wren, sent me those emails. Dumped the fox. And you think he might have actually pulled her teeth out, just to plant evidence on me?'

'Well, what other reason would he have to pull them? It obviously wasn't to sell them.'

Matt said nothing because he was, for the moment, incapable. His mind was a rally car racing around the facts, skidding past them in the hope they might suddenly make sense.

'I thought you said he liked you,' Larry said. 'Why would he frame you?'

Matt laughed bitterly. 'I thought he liked me, too.'

'For what it's worth, up until this I really think Miller trusted you. But now the fox thing's spooked him. So for now I suggest you find out all you can about Chris at your end. I'll look up what I can from here. And don't panic, alright? The truth has a way of coming out.'

They both stayed silent for a moment, neither of them daring to state the simple fact that there were plenty of cases when the truth stayed permanently and thoroughly buried.

'Just hang in there, mate,' Larry said, then he was gone.

Matt sprang to his feet, unsure of what to do, or where to go. And after pacing for a few seconds he found himself, perhaps through old instinct, standing behind the little pulpit with its hymn books and control buttons for the curtains and the coffin rollers.

He looked up and gazed out desperately at the empty chapel, visualising Nicola, Tabitha and Isabel sitting there, drumming dead fingers on the pews, waiting for him to figure this out.

Nicola was opening her jaw and pointing a skinny finger into her mouth and the gaps there, where there once was gold.

And when he looked Tabitha and Nicola in the eyes, he heard his own whisper, 'How does anyone just disappear?'

He blinked and the three women faded into nothing.

He ran his hand through his hair and headed for the chapel door, which led back out to the foyer. It was just as he reached for the handle that he heard a low rumble coming from somewhere. His hand hovered on the metal and he looked back down to the pulpit and to the curtains beyond, to the buttons that Chris Kelly would have pressed only moments ago, to send Reginald Arthur Keech on his final little trip.

The rumbling started again and he knew if he was to walk to the pavement outside, right now, there'd be white smoke belching out of that chimney. Essence of Keech would be wisping its way, literally fading . . .

. . . into thin air.

It was as if the three girls had suddenly tapped him on the forehead with a glowing finger and planted a thought there. But in reality he wondered if it had been lurking in his subconscious ever since he'd parked the car here and stared for so long at this building. It was an idea that made him quicken his step.

Surely not. Can't be.

He headed back down the aisle, towards the curtains and tried to work out which door led to the furnace room.

CHAPTER THIRTY-EIGHT

Deep green curtains hung across the back wall of the sanctuary but as he lifted them back he didn't find some creepy old Wizard of Oz, cranking levers and burning bodies. Just a closed white door that said No Entry. He glanced back over his shoulder. The chapel was still and empty. He held back the heavy material and pushed the handle down. It made a pleasant-sounding click and, rather randomly, made him think of a cassette cover on a very old stereo he used to have. It had opened its mouth for audio tapes with an almost identical klunk-hiss.

The door swung open to a steep staircase made of old wood. It looked like it might crack apart with each footstep but it didn't even creak as he hurried down it. This place was built on solid stone. A fire precaution? he wondered. He reached the bottom and noticed that the natural light had faded as he moved under the floor of the chapel. The corridor down here was lit with bare electric bulbs, hanging on chains.

It was impossibly clammy down here as if the concrete itself was sweating. The rumble of the furnace had become a steady roar. A grimy metal door stood at the end of the short corridor and he noticed that it wasn't fully shut. Light sparkled in a line around the edge of it.

He paused, wondered what on earth he was doing, then pushed it open.

It was a room lined with pipes with a thin layer of dust, all leading to a huge furnace in the centre like any other heating or boiler room, apart from the corpse lurking in the middle of it. Matt could see a flicker of flames coming through the small circular viewing window at the front.

Sitting on a high stool and staring through the glass at the burning body was a young man in his early twenties with an industrial mop's worth of straggly hair: ginger, and wet with sweat. He was wearing dark-blue overalls and had his back to the door. He hadn't noticed Matt come in.

'Hello,' Matt called out. Then again, louder. 'Hello?'

The man turned and almost slipped off his chair.

'Can we talk?' Matt asked, nodding at the furnace.

'You can't come in here.'

Matt ignored him, moved closer.

'Listen, you can't be in here. So get out. Like, right now.'

'I'm helping Sergeant Miller with a few things. And I've got some questions. What's your name?'

The man slowly wiped the back of his hand across his lips with a long streak. The ball of his thumb glistened instantly with sweat. 'James Talbot.'

'And you run this place?'

'I just work here. Look, can't this wait? I'm burning someone. He's almost finished.'

'May I?' Matt leant over and looked through the reinforced glass. The heat pulsed out from it and flushed his cheeks. Inside was a single roar of flame coming from the ceiling of the furnace. It looked like a huge Bunsen burner, only firing down.

The flame was scorching into a white heat at the centre, while orange flames roared across the grille. Squinting through the fire he could see the coffin had already completely burnt up. A black skinny lump of bones sat in the centre. Arms and legs had collapsed. He could make out the cranium of the skull, the home of Keech's personality and his memory. His favourite songs, his secret dreams, his memories of moonlit nights out with the women he loved or hurt or both, the films that made him cry. The totality of the man was in that head shell. But now there were cracks in his skull and each of them was glowing bright orange as the hot flames hollowed it out.

Some of the bones in the deformed torso were rocking back and forth with the sheer force of the flames, as if Keech's soul was holding on to it. An angry tenant refusing an eviction notice.

'How much ash is left after a body?' Matt grabbed another stool. He plonked himself next to James so they were like tennis umpires.

James said nothing.

'Listen. These questions aren't optional. I want you to answer them, alright?'

'Sorry. I'm just a bit weirded out hearing a voice out loud down here. These guys aren't exactly in the mood to chat.'

As he said that, the arch of Keech's ribcage, now just a black set of sticks, collapsed in on itself.

'About three and a half litres. You've seen the urns they get put in.' James pushed out his hands to demonstrate the top, bottom and sides of an urn. It looked like he was doing a dance move. 'Obviously the amount of ash depends on the size of the deceased. You should see a baby in there. That really is something. Barely over a litre of ash left. Sometimes with the premature ones there's nothing at all, so you've got to give the parents an empty urn. You're not allowed to fill it with anything else, though, so you have to tell them that there's nothing left. You should see the look on their faces when they hear their kid is *all* gone.'

'Could someone burn a body in here without your knowledge?'

Talbot turned in a pivot on his stool. 'Why on earth would anyone want to do that?'

'Answer the question.'

'Of course they couldn't. Besides, I'm the only one who can operate the machinery.'

'I see . . . does anyone else work down here?'

'No. Just me. The actual funeral service part happens upstairs. The undertakers and vicar sort that out. They get organists in. I just lurk around down here and make sure the bodies are fully cremated. I put the ashes in the right tub, then the undertaker puts them in the urn.'

'Do you record how many times the cremator gets used?'

'Yes.'

'Would it be possible to tell if it was used more than was recorded?'

'What's this about?'

Matt paused. 'I'm investigating the disappearance of Tabitha Tansy Clarke and Nicola Knox.'

'Oh, them.' His eyes flashed with a sort of tabloid glee. 'I heard they'd run off together. Sailed to the Isle of Lesbos as they say.'

'That's unlikely.'

'So what . . . you think it's *more* likely that they ended up in here? Because I'm telling you that they didn't. I'd know.'

'You didn't answer my question. Would it be possible to tell if the cremator was used more than was recorded in your logs?'

'Yes. The gas metre would have a different number. I record those figures religiously. If someone used it when they shouldn't, the records wouldn't match.'

'Where are these records?'

'But they do match. They always do.'

'Where are they?'

'They aren't kept down here any more. They're upstairs in the office.'

'Then let's go and have a look—'

'Sorry.' He slipped off his stool and stood up straight. He looked a hell of a lot bigger on his feet. 'Are you even a policeman?'

'I work with them. I'm a consultant.'

He laughed at that. 'Yeah, well you can't just waltz into a legitimate business and see private records like that. I watch TV. I know you need a warrant or something.'

'Then I've another question.' Matt paused. 'What else is left from a body after the cremation?'

'Ash, obviously.'

'Obviously. I mean is there anything else?'

'Only the stuff that makes it through the cremulator.'

'The what?'

'The cremulator. I've always thought that'd make a good American wrestler name. It's a machine. I sweep up the ashes and put them in the cremulator. It's got two big stone balls that smash the leftovers up.' He pointed his fists towards each other and started to hammer them together, making crushing noises with his mouth like a morbid version of that old coffee advert, where people pretend they had a fancy coffee-maker when really it was just instant. He stopped crunching. 'The cremulator pulverises them. Helps make sure all the bits are ground down. But before I put them in I get the metal bits out with a magnet.'

Talbot wandered to a shelf and grabbed a blue metal container. It was an old tin of Roses chocolates.

'Check this out.' He opened it, now excited for some reason.

The tin was filled with chunks of metal, the melted remnants of rings, hips, even an old pacemaker.

'I throw the bits in here,' he said. 'Probably two hundred people in this tin. Fathers, daughters, wives and sons.'

Matt gave an eager look inside, eyes scanning for something resembling a golden tooth. James must have noticed his sudden staring too. He curled his lip a little in disgust, 'Er . . . there aren't actually any chocolates left in here, if that's what you're thinking.'

'I'd like to sort through this. With you watching me do it.'

'Why? What are you looking for?'

'I can't tell you that. Not yet.'

Talbot looked down as he pressed the lid back on. 'I don't think so.'

'Why? What do you do with this stuff?'

'I sell it.'

293

Matt just looked at him.

'There's a precious metal refiner who buys the stuff off me, once a year. It's a little bit of pocket money.'

'And that's legal?'

''Course it is. Post cremation this stuff doesn't legally belong to anyone. It's fine. So you needn't look at me like that.'

'Sorry,' Matt sighed and watched Talbot place the Roses tin back on the shelf. When he turned back round, Matt asked the question he'd been brewing up to for the entire time he was down here. 'Who else has access to this part of the building, and to the furnace specifically?'

'Well, we have a few keyholders, but—'

'Who?'

'Me. Phyliss Bainbridge, the organist. But she'd never come down here. Chris Kelly, obviously.'

'Come to the crematorium often, does he?'

'When people die, he does.'

'And does he ever come down here? Has he ever asked you questions about all of this?'

'Not that I recall. Only a proper weirdo would creep down here and do that . . .' Talbot's eyes started to narrow. 'What did you say your name was again? Why are you so interested in cremation?'

A bead of sweat wriggled itself down Matt's face and he wiped it with his fingertip. 'But Chris would have access to this place, yes?'

Talbot gave a weak nod, but his frown was growing. A little glance to the door.

Matt slipped off the stool. 'Well, thank you for your help. I'll go now.' Before heading for the door Matt scanned the room one last time. There was a row of fire extinguishers and an old metal table with a kettle, a tea-stained cup on it and an open copy of *Auto Trader* on it. A packed toolbox sat on the floor with a dirty blue rag hanging out of it.

As Matt was leaving he noticed something above the door, leading out. A wooden cross. Skinny and low-tech. Pretty much just two strips of balsa wood hammered together with a nail in the join.

The lights smeared their ominous shadows up towards the ceiling.

'So you're a churchgoer, James?'

'Of course I am. Aren't you?'

'And you go to Kingdom Come, I take it?'

'Where else?'

Suddenly, the rumble of the cremator started to dissipate and the room fell into an unsettling hush. Matt glanced into the viewing window again and saw that there was hardly anything left now. He shook his head, amazed at the efficiency of it.

'Pretty much everyone gets cremated these days,' James muttered. He turned some levers on the side of the cremator to help cool it down. 'It's cos all the green places are shrinking. No more room to plant full-sized folk in the ground. But not me. I'm getting buried.'

'And why's that?'

'Because when Jesus comes back he's going to raise the dead. I know Pastor Chris says Jesus made us from dust and he reckons he can easily resurrect a body from scattered ash. But I'm not risking that. I'm getting buried, me. Intact. Arms on, head on, spine in a straight line. I want to be myself when I get to heaven.' He sniffed then flicked a switch on the machine. A row of lights on the wall went off. 'Besides, it'll save Jesus the hassle of gathering up all those tiny grains.'

Before he turned, Matt looked over at the Roses tin. Stared at it. His inconvenient lack of x-ray vision made him tempted to just march on up to it, fling the lid off and tip it all out on the floor. Sift through it until he found the other golden tooth of Nicola Knox and call Miller there and then. Tell him that he'd found the shiny Wonka Bar that might be his ticket out of suspicion.

But James was staring at him again and he realised he'd paused for long enough and asked enough odd questions to appear comprehensively psychotic. So he just turned and closed the door, rushed up the steps and didn't look back. Desperately he tried to figure out his next move.

CHAPTER THIRTY-NINE

Matt was still in the crematorium car park but he'd shifted the car so that it was parked around the back of a couple of oversized wheelie bins. He was hiding out like the fugitive he might well become. Putting that label on himself made him feel physically ill and forced him to rifle his brains for an idea.

After a minute of drumming on the steering wheel (his preferred method of inspiration) he quickly grabbed his phone from his pocket. He called Directory Enquiries and asked them to put him through to his old Bible college. It rang three times, then there was a tiny click at the other end.

'Hello. Kimble Theological College.' It was a woman's voice. She sounded happy and young. His mind pictured a teenager, swinging her legs and chewing a pencil. He ditched the image, knowing full well that phone voices usually turned out to be the very opposite of first impressions.

'Hi . . . my name's Professor Matthew Hunter. Can I ask if David Wilder's still the principal of the college?'

There was a moment of breath and silence. 'Can I ask what this is about please?'

'I can't say on the phone. I just need to ask him a question about a former student.'

'Well, I'm sorry but he's about to give a lecture. Can this wait, Professor?'

'Frankly, no, it can't. It's an emergency. I only need a few minutes of his time.'

A sigh. 'Just a moment, please.'

Click.

At first he thought she'd hung up on him because there was utter silence. Then he realised he was on hold, only without the muzak. He sat there, listening to the gaunt quiet. It was probably the first time in his life he'd actually desired the sound of pan pipes or a tenor saxophone.

Click.

'What did you say your name was again?'

'Matthew Hunter. Profess—'

Click. A pause.

'Okay. Putting you through.'

Click.

The phone crackled and then Wilder's familiar Scottish lilt filtered through the phone. Matt felt suddenly nineteen years old.

'Professor Hunter?'

'Yes.'

'Not our former student, Matthew Hunter?'

Wilder always did have an amazing memory with names. He'd said it was one of the finest skills any pastor (or politician) could have. 'You can learn all the Bible in the world,' he'd said one afternoon, in a lecture on pastoral skills, 'but I tell you, if you remember their names, they'll love you for it.'

'It's me,' Matt said. 'I'm amazed that you remember.'

'Don't be so impressed. I'm aware of your work. I read all the journals, you know . . . even the atheist ones. You're a provocative writer.'

'Yes, I er . . . I've . . .' he squirmed in the seat, 'moved away from some of my old beliefs.'

'Which is your privilege, of course,' he said, with no sense of reproach. 'You work with the police I hear?'

'More and more, I guess.'

'Good for you.' A short little clear of the throat. 'So how can I help?'

'Actually I need to ask you about a former student. I started in 2002. He was a year above me but I got to know him over that first term. Until he left at Christmas. His name was Chris Kelly and he—'

'Christopher Kelly.' There was a sudden gravity in his voice. 'I certainly remember him.'

'Brilliant. Then I'd like to ask you a couple of things about him. Firstly, do you still have his address on file when he was at the college? I know it was somewhere in Hemel Hempstead.'

'Well, I can't very well tell you that, can I?'

'Actually, this is a police matter. I'm assisting them. You can call DS Larry Forbes if you need verification. I have his number.'

Wilder seemed to wait, then he expelled a long flow of breath. 'I suppose my secretary Nikki can get that for you. Is Chris in some sort of trouble?'

He tried to put it into police-speak. 'They just want to eliminate him from their enquiries.'

'I see. Then what else do you want to know? Chris wasn't a particularly good student, grades-wise. And I must say that he wasn't very popular with the other students, either. Though I remember the two of you got on. Still, it was sad that he had to leave the way he did.'

'I take it you know why he stopped coming to college?'

'I know a little. A family tragedy. His wife died. She was called Lydia as I recall.' He waited, then cleared his throat. 'Yes ... yes ... that sounds right. Chris decided he couldn't study once it happened. Understandable, I suppose. I did feel very sorry for the chap.'

'Do you know how Lydia died?'

'No. But I did speak to her once. I called his home because I wanted to talk to him about one of his assignments. Something that troubled me . . .' Wilder paused.

'Can you elaborate on that?'

'Well, I remember Chris Kelly quite vividly actually, because his theology was rather unique for a college like ours. He seemed to lean towards the . . . how can I put this . . . the ritualistic. Far more than the college was teaching. What I mean to say is that he had an obsession with Holy Communion. And baptism, in particular.'

'He still does.'

'Well, that's a real shame. He seemed to think that the water actually washed sins away. I mean literally. The college view is that it's more of a symbolic act. He really wasn't in step with us.'

'You have an amazing memory for all of this.'

'Don't flatter me. I remember this because of what happened when I called him. It was pretty hard to forget, to be honest with you. Lydia, his wife . . . she was the one how answered.'

'And how was she?'

'Antagonistic, confrontational, offensive. When she heard I was from the college she told me to never call again. I distinctly remember this because I've never heard such foul language. She said I was an "effing parasite", and that Christians were "weak-minded—" Well, I shan't repeat the word. Anyway she sounded very upset and ranted that the virgin birth meant that God was a rapist. Quite memorable, really.'

'Did you get to speak to Chris?'

'Oh, he was there. In the background. He was pleading for her to stop abusing me on the phone. He kept saying, "Lydia, Lydia. Don't say those things. He's my teacher." But she hung up and that was that.'

'Did you ever speak to either of them again?'

'Not really. He came in late the next day but seemed very distant. I gave him space. I thought he might be embarrassed by the phone call. Then he left early and went to the pub, as far as I know. I never saw him again. We learnt later that his wife had died.' He suddenly paused. 'You don't think Chris had something to do with her death, do you? Is that why you're asking me these questions?'

'I'm assisting on a different case. This is just background.'

'I see.' He didn't sound convinced. There was a ruffle of papers. 'Listen. I'll get Nikki to hunt out that address. I know we keep them on file. Though you're sure it's for the police?'

'Yes. Listen, I appreciate this.'

'That's quite alright. Now, I'm afraid I have a lecture to give and I really must go. Models of the Atonement . . . perhaps you remember sitting through it yourself?'

Matt laughed. 'Actually yes, I do.'

'Correct answer . . . Stay on the line so that Nikki can get your details. And best of luck.'

'Thank you.'

'Oh, and Matt?'

'Yes?'

'I hope you find what you're searching for. In everything, I mean.'

Matt held the phone to his head but didn't say anything.

'Take care.' With a click he was gone and Nikki came back on the line. She told him the address and he jotted it down on a pink Post-it note that was lying in the glovebox. Then he planted it on the dashboard and pressed it in place.

119 Kellaway Heights, Hemel Hempstead

After he hung up he put the phone in its holder and leant across the steering wheel to tap in the postcode. Just as he was finishing the phone suddenly buzzed.

Incoming call: Sergeant Terry Miller

Matt snapped his hand back from the phone, like it was on fire. Ever since he'd walked out of the crematorium he'd wondered if Miller might suddenly spring from behind a bush and nab him. But he'd never considered a simple phone call. He felt his mind lock down into tunnel thinking. He just stared at the phone. Pulsing its light, playing theme music from *Jaws*. His new ringtone was definitely not helping the mood right now.

He refused to touch it. Miller would probably be asking where he was, acting all normal and asking him to pop in and chat about the fox. If that was the case then Matt wasn't biting. He needed more time. Instead he just pushed the car into first and lurched out from behind the bins, heading for the iron gates that led out of the crematorium.

And the ringing kept going, sounding like some manic funeral march. His. And when it didn't stop ringing he slowed the car.

A superficial quadrant of his brain – largely educated by TV cop shows – insisted in a New York accent that he just grab the phone and throw it out of the window so they couldn't trace him. Better still, stow it on some other moving vehicle so he could hide his trail. But how dodgy would that look? Them finding his phone abandoned and stuffed in the tarpaulin of a long-haul Tesco truck. And besides. He might need it.

Oh shit, this was turning into a mess.

When the ringing finally stopped he waited for Miller to leave a voice message, but he didn't. Which somehow felt a lot more ominous than if he had. In his rear-view mirror the chapel chimney reflected back. A tiny low cloud hung above it, looking different to all the others. Like the last belch of smoke from Reginald Arthur Keech's body had somehow got stuck in the Hobbs Hill sky.

'I know how you feel, Reg,' Matt whispered nervously under his breath and pushed the accelerator into the floor.

CHAPTER FORTY

It felt good to be out of Hobbs Hill. Very good. Rat-out-of-a-cage good, even as Google barked out dispassionate, female robot commands as Hemel Hempstead grew closer. *Take the first exit! Turn left onto Willow Way!* At one point, he was sure the satnav lady said: *Turn yourself over to Miller and stop running away, idiot!*

He just slammed his foot harder onto the pedal and swung back into the fast lane.

What the hell was Chris playing at? If he'd requested Wren to come to Hobbs Hill because he hoped to convert Matt again, bring him back into the fold . . . well, *that* he could believe. Christians could be tenacious and cunning in their quest for spiritual conquests. But to set him up . . . *why?* If it was punishment, then punishment for what? Did Chris hate him, for some reason? Was he jealous of him having a wife with a pulse? Or was there something else?

And then there was the thought that brought long cold waves running through his skin. Did Chris actually kill those women? An image of Chris popped into his head, kneeling on the floor, both hands gripping a pair of pliers stuffed into a fourteen-year-old's mouth. The loud crack of teeth breaking off.

He winced.

Don't you realise, Nicola Knox . . . that God gets very, very angry?

He shuddered then quickly shook his head. No, no, no it was way too early to say that. The evidence was . . . how do they normally say it? Circumstantial?

But still . . . something felt distinctly wrong about Pastor Kelly. Too many ragged edges. And there's only so many times your nose can twitch before you have to admit that *someone* has shit on the floor.

Thankfully, Wren had texted. Unaware of Miller's suspicions of Matt, she and the girls were largely still in that blissful kingdom called 'normal life', having fun in Oxford. He wanted to call her and tell her about the golden tooth and about possibly being set up. But it would take up time and freak her out. And what would be the point, anyway? Better to leave her out of it, at least for now.

They were seeing a film tonight in the city centre, and it started at 8 p.m. Amelia was apparently buzzing that she was being allowed up so late, thinking of it as a treat rather than what it actually was: a 'keep everyone away from the dodgy cottage' tactic. At least for today.

He checked his watch. It was just after 12.40 p.m. That gave him plenty of time to nose about in Hemel without worrying that they'd come back to find themselves alone at the cottage.

Of course he knew full well that driving there might be pointless. But if Miller really was gunning for him since the gold tooth discovery, then he needed all the evidence he could get that something wasn't right with Chris Kelly. And since the word Hemel seemed to push his buttons, Matt wanted to find out why.

The satnav told/ordered him to leave the motorway and he obeyed with a click of the indicators. The voice was starting to distort and now sounded like a premenstrual dalek. Then the drone of the motorway grew quiet, and the roundabouts began.

It didn't take him long to get into the centre of Hemel, and just as the dalek announced that he'd reached his destination, he could already see the tower block he was looking for against the dull, grey sky.

He turned a few corners, headed down a backstreet then pulled up outside and killed the engine. A few fat raindrops started to slap off the windscreen, so he reached into the back seat and pulled his jacket through. He grabbed his phone and checked the address again.

119 Kellaway Heights, Hemel Hempstead

He stepped out as a few teenage girls squealed in the rain and ran past. They pulled their jackets tight over their heads, hobbling like a bunch of Quasimodos. The cold drops were growing more frequent now, bouncing off his face, so he held his hand across his eyes and looked up.

Kellaway Heights loomed over him, about thirty floors up by his guess. There were no balconies, just sheet metal and grimy windowpanes. It was yesterday's vision of the future. There were *a lot* of satellite dishes.

He could smell the damp pavement under his feet.

Admittedly the place didn't look particularly rough or dilapidated but the birdsong paradise of Hobbs Hill had warped his perspective. This place looked like the east wing of a concentration camp.

As the rain grew heavier he pulled his collar close and rushed in through the double doors made of blue peeling metal and reinforced glass. He expected to smell urine, but someone had been cooking curry instead. It hung so heavy in the air that he might as well be rubbing his face in turmeric.

He pressed the green plastic button on the lift and a few seconds later the brushed silver doors scraped open, like an abattoir meat locker. A young guy wearing headphones stepped out, hands thrust into the tiny pockets of his jeans. He pushed by Matt as if he weren't even there.

Matt took his place in the lift and the doors drew together. He glanced at the list of flat numbers, then found his button.

110–124

The metal felt sticky when he pressed out 119, but he chose not to lick his finger clean. It was only as the lift began to rumble and rise that he pictured Chris with his guitar, back in 2002, coming in late at night from the station after a day in Bible college and a few drinks at Monday Pub Night. He glanced around at the graffiti and read it all. Who knows, maybe Chris may have scrawled something here on one of those late nights.

Hey! One day I'm going to frame the perfectly innocent Matthew Hunter. Just sayin' Signed by Christopher Kelly.

But there was no such illuminating graffiti. Unless Chris had written *Muslims Out*, there wasn't anything to see.

Flat 119 was at the far end of the corridor. The fluorescents above him were certainly bright enough, but most had an almost imperceptible yet constant flicker to them. It made the place look like the inside of a faulty fridge.

'Money' by Pink Floyd rumbled loudly through a door. The music stopped dead on the word 'caviar'. Just as he walked past it. He picked up the pace.

He reached the end of the corridor, looking back nervously. He tapped a knuckle against flat 119.

And waited.

Eventually, a muffled voice came from inside. 'Just a sec.'

Matt reached into his jacket and pulled out his university ID while a key cranked inside the lock. Finally it swung open.

'Yes?' The man was probably in his early twenties with a huge swept-back fringe and tight beanpole jeans. His red and white striped top and horn-rimmed glasses were supposed to make him look trendy and alternative. Just another fake-nerd hipster type, but Matt felt like telling someone to stop the clock, because he'd finally found Wally.

Matt flashed the ID at him, long enough to show the general official looking outlines, but not enough for the man to actually read anything. 'I have some questions.'

Wally visibly stiffened. He stepped out onto the landing and closed the door. A familiar gingery odour wafted out with him. The guy stretched his neck and Matt heard it click. 'Actually, my girlfriend's sleeping right now. Do you mind if we talk out here?'

'Look. I can smell the cannabis—'

'It's medicinal!' Wally blurted out, panicked. His eyes shot back up the corridor. Then he said in a whisper, 'It's medicinal alright? I've got MS.'

'Is that right?'

'Well. Suspected.'

'Calm down. That's not why I'm here. What's your name?'

'Rob,' he frowned. 'Rob Bennett.'

'I want to know about a previous tenant of this flat. How long have you lived here for?'

It took a moment but eventually Rob started to relax, leaning back on the wall. 'Three years.'

'And do you know who lived in the flat before you?'

'Some Chinese guy. Student I think. I remember his name because it made me laugh. Ding Dong or something like that. That is quite funny, don't you think?'

Matt nodded. There was no denying it.

'Anyway Ding Dong wasn't here long,' he laughed again.

'Actually I'm curious about another man who lived here, up until about four years ago. Would you have any idea—'

'That's a year before I got here. The turnover in this place is crazy. It's like a conveyor belt. I'm one of the long-termers, me. But next door was an old lady who lived here since forever. Edna. She might have known something but she died like, last Christmas. Shame. She made me a cake once. A lovely, normal cake.'

'Did she ever talk about past tenants? She ever mention a man called Christopher Kelly?'

'That rings a vague bell, actually.'

'Or a woman called Lydia. Lydia Kelly?'

Rob's mouth fell open.

'You recognise that name?'

He nodded. 'Edna *definitely* told us about her.'

Maybe it was the low-rent fluorescents but the guy's face looked suddenly pale.

'What do you know about her?'

He puckered his lips, like he was about to kiss the air. 'Only that she slit her wrists in my bath.'

CHAPTER FORTY-ONE

A sleeping cat lay stretched across the hallway.

'That's Justin. You can step right over him.' Rob led Matt down the hall and started to call out, 'Anna? Anna?'

The living room door creaked open and a young woman, clearly stoned, opened the door, her head tilted against the frame. She was wearing a Superman t-shirt and a tiny pair of 70s-style shorts. Bright yellow, with a rainbow trim.

'Hey, hey,' she said, looking Matt up and down and beaming. 'Whose the fitty?'

'He's a policeman,' Rob said.

Her stunning smile dropped instantly.

'Don't panic. He's here about our ghost.'

'Actually . . .' Matt held up his hand. 'I'm not a policeman. I'm a university professor.'

Rob looked confused but Anna's eyes flashed excitement. 'What, like you mean you investigate the . . . the supernatural and stuff?'

'That's one way of putting it. Yes.'

'Niiiiiiice.' Anna was nodding. 'So you know about Lydia?'

'A little bit. But I have some questions.'

'Do we still have that newspaper clipping?' Rob said, clicking his fingers. 'That Edna gave us?'

'Yes!' Anna clapped her hands together. 'I'll need to hunt it out. Ohmygod this is cool.' She raced into the other room and started pulling drawers open.

Rob piped up, 'Can I just point out that I don't believe in this stuff? But she does.'

'You should believe it,' she called through. 'Because it's true. We've got all the classic signs, Professor. Place feels cold sometimes. The bedside lamps flicker on and off in the middle of the night. And there're puddles of water in the bathroom. Unexplained. I've seen enough episodes of *Most Haunted* to know there's something up. We get orbs whenever we take—'

'Don't be daft,' Rob said with a dismissive swish of his hand. 'I used to keep telling her it was all down to crap heating and plumbing.'

'But?' Matt said, sensing there was more.

'Well, then Edna gave us this article. Spooked us a bit. Now Anna reckons the place must be haunted.' He turned to her. 'But it isn't.'

'Can I see the bathroom?' Matt said.

Rob pushed his elbow against the door he'd been standing against. 'Voila.' It creaked open and he stepped aside to let Matt in. 'Don't you need equipment or something? A little box with flashing lights?'

'That won't be necessary.'

It was a bathroom. No more, no less. A small one at that, with grimy-looking tiles and black specks of mould in the corners. The toilet had a pile of old *Empire* magazines stacked right next to it. They were damp and curling, either from shower spray or wayward urine. Probably both.

'That might explain your unexpected puddles,' Matt said, pointing to the sealant where the bath touched the wall. It was brown and peeling away. Then he knelt by the bath, unsure of what he was looking for. There were no broken tiles like Tabitha's house.

'Is this the same actual bath?' Matt asked. 'Sometimes after a suicide the council changes it.'

'That's what Edna reckoned.' Rob pushed his glasses back up his nose. 'I'm a bit more cynical. I bet they just squirted a bit of Mr Muscle on it and that was that.'

Matt stood back up and glanced around the tiny bathroom, at the rusted mirror over the sink where years ago Chris and his young wife Lydia probably brushed their teeth and squeezed their spots. And the toilet, where they would have taught Ben how to poo the big-boy way.

Anna stood in the open door, waving the newspaper clipping like it was a flag. She looked more stoned than ever. 'Found it.' But before handing it over she looked at it, then seemed to shiver with an obvious sense of thrill. 'I just *love* spooky stuff. I swear death makes you feel . . . alive. Don't you reckon?'

'You've got problems,' Rob said.

Matt reached out for the paper but she clutched it tight to her chest. 'I'll read it to you. *Then* I'll give it.'

Matt sighed. 'What's the date on it?'

She looked down. 'December 2002.'

The month when Chris stopped coming to college.

Anna cleared her throat as Matt sat on the side of the bath. The plastic panel groaned a little but it felt sturdy enough.

'Here we go . . . local woman commits suicide.' Anna had assumed a weird sort of telephone voice. 'Lydia Kelly, thirty-two, committed suicide by cutting her wrists in the bath in Kellaway Rise, Hemel Hempstead. Her husband, Chris Kelly, twenty-seven, said she was close to death when he found her, early on Sunday evening.' Anna trailed off. 'Are you getting creeped out yet?'

'Give me the paper, please,' Matt said.

She stuck out her tongue. '. . . Chris Kelly, twenty-seven, said she was close to death when he found her early on Sunday evening. He had returned home with local church caretaker Seth Cardle but despite their best—'

Matt looked up, 'What did you just say?'

'Ooooo,' she smiled. 'You're feeling the vibes, aren't you?'

'Read that last bit again. The name.'

'He had returned home with local church caretaker, Seth Cardle . . . What, do you know him or something?'

Matt let out a long heavy breath. 'Keep reading.'

'Despite their best efforts, neither could save her. Kelly said that his wife of seven years passed away peacefully in his arms, "her eyes filled with heaven".' Anna stopped reading to look at her boyfriend. She had a slightly goofy but earnest look of affection for him, as though there were a tragic romance to it all. 'The final verdict: self-inflicted death, brought on by massive loss of blood . . . that's it.'

'Give me the paper,' he said.

She handed it over, reluctantly, like it was a cherished photograph of someone she loved.

He read it over to check what she said was right. It was.

'I'll need to hang onto this, but you'll get it back,' Matt said. 'And thank you. You've been very helpful.'

'Hang on,' Anna said. 'Aren't you going to exorcise the spirits or something? I might get a kick out of this stuff but I still don't want some creepy dead lady watching me take a piss.'

'Sorry. Call a priest.'

At that point, Justin the cat wandered in, which somehow shut everybody up. He slinked himself against Matt's legs. They all watched him spring up onto the bath and then jump down inside it.

'Get out of there, Justin!' Rob shouted, as the cat lay on its back, paws in the air like it was being petted. The purring seemed very loud.

'Whoah. Look at him. Maybe Lydia's *stroking* him.' Anna's tone was utterly serious.

'Don't be stupid,' Rob said.

'Eerie though . . . isn't it?' She pointed at where the cat was now writhing on its back. 'They say that animals know these things. Maybe he knows someone topped themselves. Right here.'

'You know,' Rob said quietly, 'my granddad used to tell me that suicides go to hell.'

Anna gave him an odd look. 'That's harsh.'

'*They all do,*' Matt whispered, suddenly realising he'd said it out loud.

Anna frowned and pulled her head back a little, as if she'd decided that she didn't like Matt any more. 'You actually believe that?'

'*I* don't,' Matt said, 'but I know someone who does.' He pictured Chris ranting at him that morning in the crematorium, paranoid about the eternal fate of Isabel Dawson at the bottom of the falls.

And that desperate shout, *Suicides go to hell! They all do!*

For a moment they just watched the purring cat squirming against the bathtub. But Matt wasn't really seeing a cat at all. It was a woman called Lydia who was no fan of Christianity, arching her back in the throes of a self-inflicted death.

So the article said she was close to dying when they found her. He considered that and wondered if Chris and Seth had sat on the edge of the bath, the toilet or the floor when it happened. And how would their belief systems have coped, he wondered, as they watched his wife wheeze and bleed and slide herself down the long red road to hell?

CHAPTER FORTY-TWO

Rob may have been stoned, but he turned out to be right about the turnover here.

Matt knocked on every door on that floor and all of the tenants were fairly fresh arrivals. None of them lived here when Chris and Lydia Kelly were in the building. He even tried the floor above and below, just in case, but after his knuckles started to hurt he decided to give up. Without anyone else to help, he certainly didn't plan on knocking on all 144 flats in this block. He'd go to the next stage in the plan, such as it was.

He headed back down to the car and typed the word 'library' into the satnav. He found the place in seconds. Before moving off he sent Worthington and Larry a quick text message, asking them to check with Hemel police to confirm whether someone called Lydia Kelly had killed herself in that flat. Maybe the files mentioned details that the papers didn't.

He also asked them to pull out the records for Seth Cardle. Matt had no idea that Chris and the old man had such a long and dramatic history.

The library was just off the main high street near the courthouse, so he swung the car into the parking bay, leapt out directly into a puddle and hurried across. The rain was furious. Big sheets of it flung against him and rattled his jacket. In the eleven seconds it took him to run from the car to the library entrance, he might as well have run directly through Cooper's Force.

He shook a hand through his hair as he stepped inside the library where a plump older lady stood behind the counter. She looked at him with the sort of disgusted pity reserved for beaten-up pensioners or three-legged kittens. 'Well aren't you a mess. It's the proverbial drowned rat.'

'It's insane out there,' he laughed.

She held a bent arthritic-looking finger up. 'Noise? *Hello?* It's a library.'

'Oops, sorry.' He unzipped his jacket, now thick and heavy.

She set some books onto a trolley as he approached the counter.

Her badge said Maggie Baines. She *really* reminded him of an old art teacher he once had, with her huge golden hoops dangling from ears that poked out under a swoop of shipping-rope thick grey pigtails. Except his art teacher had been a lovely walking cuddle, who said his bloated papier-mâché model of Big Ben was 'charming'. Even while the rest of the class were pissing themselves laughing at how the clock face was slowly sliding off.

Maggie, however, looked so furious with the world she appeared to have been recently hit by a shovel. She had a black t-shirt with a garish, airbrushed wolf's head and a Red Indian's face blended into starlight. It was a truly horrible design. She raised a suspicious bushy eyebrow just before he spoke, which made her large, golden-framed glasses rise up. She could tell that he wasn't looking for books.

'Do you keep any local newspaper records here?' he said.

'Of course we do. They're digitised on the computer.'

'Excellent. Then I'd like to look through some newspapers from around 2002. Do they stretch back that far?'

'Young man, we stretch back to 1801 and well before that.'

'Cool. So can you show me to the computers, please?'

She tapped her glasses down her nose and looked over the frame. 'May I finish putting these books on the shelf first? Or would twelve extra seconds irreparably ruin your life?'

Matt wanted to say *quite possibly*, but he bowed and said, 'Sorry. Go ahead.'

A depressed-looking young guy with a beard (but weirdly no moustache) walked past, pushing a book trolley. Maggie caught sight of him and narrowed her eyes. She leant over the counter and whispered in his direction, 'Are you on death row, Ryan?' Then she pointed at her own face and the forced, unpleasant smile she was trying to assemble there. A forced grimace the likes of which the Queen did after her Christmas Day speech.

Ryan sighed, and gave a bitter smile back.

'That's better,' she tutted and turned back to Matt. 'Come on, then.'

She led him to a room with two computers in it. Vintage maps and photos of old Hemel hung on the walls. 'If we don't have what you need on the system, then I can request the microfilm. That takes a few weeks, though. Or you could try contacting the papers themselves, but I wouldn't hold your breath.'

'Got it.'

A Dell computer monitor sat chained to a desk. She clicked the silver button in the corner and the light on it turned from blue to green. 'You'll be able to search the system with keywords, or by date.'

He sank into the blue operator's chair. 'This is really helpful . . .' He looked down at her badge '. . . Maggie.'

Using her name was supposed to make him look friendly but she looked down at her chest, like he'd just read her private diary. 'Printer's over there if you need a hard copy. Twenty pence *per* side.' She raised a finger. '*Per side*, not per page.'

'I reckon I can manage that sort of price.'

'Would you like tea?' she said.

He was shocked, 'Wow. I'd love some.'

'Pound.' She headed out of the door and over to the little room opposite. She clicked a kettle on and dumped some Jammy Dodgers out onto a plate. He heard them clink. She grabbed one and ate it herself in two gulps.

Rain rumbled hard against the window. It poured fast down the glass, making huge arches of water, while the gutter outside rattled and shook. He thought of Hobbs Hill and the falls. And for a moment he saw the faceless ghoul from the bottom of the waterfall this morning. Isabel Dawson, falling from the clouds like every other raindrop. He turned back to the screen. The cursor blinked, awaiting his command, then he typed in the name Christopher Kelly.

Within seconds he was looking straight into the man's eyes.

CHAPTER FORTY-THREE

The name Chris Kelly brought up two different references. One from the year 2000 and the other from 2002.

The first article was the one with a photograph on page 17 of the *Hemel Hempstead Gazette*. The headline had the sort of excessive alliteration that was typical of bored local journalists: *Believer Busted for Busking*. He checked the date. It was the issue leading up to Halloween of that year.

Matt read it through. Just a story about a young man called Christopher Kelly who was playing Christian songs on his guitar – *all day long* (their italics) – outside Boots the Chemist in Hemel Town Centre. He hadn't applied for the correct licence so he'd been moved along by the police. Apparently he kicked up a stink about freedom of speech and the demonic dangers of All Hallows' Eve but he quickly shut up when the officers threatened to arrest him. There really wasn't much to the story but Matt had hit print anyway. He noted the date. It was a year before Chris would have started Bible college. Fighting the demonic realm, even back then.

The other was the same report of Lydia's suicide that Anna had read to him back at the flat. The whole grim tale of Chris and Seth finding her dying in the bath. Frantically ringing for an ambulance. He printed that out too, as a backup. He scrolled through for a few minutes but it soon became clear that there were no more references to Chris Kelly in the database.

So Matt tapped in the name *Seth Cardle*. Three new items came up and he clicked eagerly on every one, sipping his scalding-hot tea as he scrolled through them.

The most recent one was about a farm that Seth had helped manage just outside of Bovingdon, not very far from Hemel itself. Apparently Seth ran hands-on farming workshops for underprivileged kids, the whole, *'stick a cow-teat in a kid's hand instead of a gun and they'll appreciate life'* type of thing.

The article also mentioned that Seth was the caretaker of a small Christian chapel in Hemel Hempstead in his spare time. But it went on to say (and this was the point of the story) he was moving on to a village in Oxfordshire, called – *drum roll* – Hobbs Hill, where he planned to 'expand his farming business with the acquisition of a new holding'. There were no plans for any more youth work.

A picture of Seth gazed out of the screen, as the windows rattled with rain. He was standing by a tractor, with one wellied foot planted on a shovel sticking deep into the ground. Lots of kids stood with their thumbs up behind him. He had a tight-eyed Bugs Bunny beam to his face, a wooden cross dangling over his Barbour.

Matt clicked 'print'.

As the machine started to buzz into life another article caught Matt's attention. It didn't have a great deal of relevance to the case, but Seth was part of it so he read it anyway.

He'd been invited to say prayers at the funeral of a local boy who drowned in Hemel's Grand Union Canal one winter morning. He'd come along to one of Seth's farming workshops, 'and thoroughly enjoyed it'. The family asked him to pray at the funeral because he was the 'only churchgoer they really clicked with'. Matt made a note of the date: 2002. It had happened a few weeks after Lydia's suicide in the bath.

It was a very depressing read. The type of article you stumble across when you're relaxing in the coffee shop on a Saturday afternoon. When you decide to read the paper cover to cover and 'get informed' about the world, only to be reminded that the world is pretty shit and you wish you had bought *Viz* instead.

The kid had crawled out alone onto the ice to retrieve the Spiderman glove he'd accidentally dropped from a bridge. But he was too heavy, and the ice cracked beneath him. Apparently two elderly ladies were walking and saw him scrambling to escape, clawing at the ice, but then it collapsed and swallowed him completely. The horrified women didn't know what else to do. They had no mobile phones. So instead they called for help as they followed the red smear of his ski jacket as it slid on the current down the river. There was one chilling little detail. 'At one point we saw his little hands, still under. One with a glove on, one without, banging and pushing on the wrong side of the ice. But it was too thick for him to push through. I've had nightmares about that, and I reckon I always will.'

Other than call down a jogger with a phone there was little the ladies could do, except walk along with that red smear and watch. The boy finally surfaced half a mile down, where the ice had thinned out. He bobbed up on his back, face looking up. Dead and blue-looking. He floated a few more metres before the hood of his parka jacket got tangled in the branches of a low-hanging tree. It kept the corpse there until help arrived. A dog-walker tried to reach for him, but it was way too far, and the jogger told him to stop; that people die when they jump in. So they, and the ladies, watched him floating there for a full five minutes until help came.

So the family invited Cardle to the funeral, to say a few words and pray. There was no picture of Seth in this, though. Just the boy himself, alive and upright. Matt rolled the mouse near the kid's little face. It was a school photo, with the requisite awkward smile. The dead boy was only seven years old, but old enough to be self-conscious about showing his teeth. He kept them covered with puffed-out lips.

Matt sighed and took a sip of his tea.

Print.

But it was the final article, at the bottom of the list, that stopped Matt crunching through the Jammy Dodger in his mouth. It was from March 2004, a couple of years after Lydia's suicide. Interestingly it was another drowning, but one far more connected to Seth himself.

Caretaker Cleared of Drowning Church Cat

Farmer Seth Cardle, and part-time caretaker of Hemel's Light of God Christian Church, has denied accusations from a congregation member that he drowned Jinx, the church cat. Bessie Major (77) claimed to police that she arrived at the chapel at the end of January to arrange the flowers when she saw Mr Cardle (50) wrapping the deceased wet body of Jinx in a plastic bin liner. She accused the widower of drowning it, on account of the splashing and animal screams she claimed she had heard. Cardle insisted that the cat had fallen into the open baptistry and drowned after snagging its collar. He had been filling the baptistry pool for the Sunday service.

Another member of the congregation backed up Mr Cardle's account and eventually Bessie Major withdrew her accusation. She wrote an apology letter to Mr Cardle last week and was keen to set the record straight. In it she stated that she had been depressed about an upcoming doctor's appointment on the night the cat died. She suggested that her raised levels of stress had contributed to her confusion that night. Cardle accepted the apology with good grace, and the curious case of Jinx the cat has finally been closed.

Matt sat staring at the screen.

The only noise in the room was the rattling gutter, the pounding rain and the sound of his own breath growing quicker as he read the article again. Then he read it a third time. Matt leant back in his chair and blew out a long low breath.

Print.

The door creaked open and Maggie leant in. 'Have you found what you're looking for?'

'Quite possibly, yes.'

The printer buzzed its mad rhythms. He pulled out a sheet and swung his chair in her direction. Over her shoulder he saw Ryan, the miserable librarian from before. He was in the kitchen opposite, slowly turning his spoon in a plain white mug of coffee, staring down into it for much longer than necessary.

'Don't you dare go using all the milk again, Ryan,' she called back over her shoulder.

'I just need one more favour,' he said. 'Do you keep records of the books people borrow?'

'Um, yes. We're a library.'

'Ha . . . quite right.' He threw her a charming smile, which seemed to bounce right off her concrete face. 'How far back do those records go?'

'Decades. Longer.'

'So if I was to give you some names, you could tell me if they were members of this library and, more importantly, what books they borrowed? It might be worth a pop . . . while I'm here.'

She frowned at him, 'Are you a policeman?'

'No. I'm not.'

'Then what are you?'

'A university professor. I teach at Goldsmiths in London. And this is actually some very important research I'm doing here. So I really appreciate you helping me out like—'

She tutted in such a loud, mocking, derogatory way that it cut him off dead. She'd been perfecting that *cap gun snap* sound for decades, no doubt. He spotted the wedding ring on her finger and had a vivid picture pop in his head. Of him and Ryan sharing a pub beer with Maggie's husband. Putting a hand of commiseration on his shoulder and telling him to *hang in there, mate*. She said, 'No, no, no way.'

'Just a couple of names. It's important.'

'Don't you have the Data Protection Act in Higher Education?' she said. 'Do *not* ask again, because it's *not* happening. You're an academic, so you should know better. Now, are you finished with the computers?'

Matt hesitated then nodded at the half-eaten biscuit. 'Not just yet.'

She shrugged. 'Suit yourself.' Then she marched back out to the main library, but not before leaning into the kitchen and whispering, 'Do not leave crumbs, Ryan. Do you hear me? *The ants* . . . remember?'

Ryan waited till she was long gone before he emerged, cup in hand.

'Fun is it . . .' Matt said, trying his luck, '. . . working for Hitler?'

Ryan smirked and set his coffee back on the counter. 'So tell me . . . which names do you want to look up?'

CHAPTER FORTY-FOUR

Ryan tapped the computer keyboard with machine gun speed, while Matt hovered near the door on lookout. It didn't take him long for Ryan to spin his chair around. 'Okay. There's nothing on Seth Cardle. He was never a member with us.'

'Fine. Try Christopher Kelly.'

'Address?' Ryan said, as he span back.

'119 Kellaway Rise, Hemel.'

The keys clicked again as Matt watched an old man with a hump slowly passing the corridor, shuffling toward Non-Fiction and wincing a lot.

'Got him,' Ryan said. 'Take a look.'

Matt grabbed a chair and rolled it over.

'Right . . . there's your man,' Ryan started waving the mouse cursor around. 'It says here that his card's still active.'

'So he's still using this library?'

'Not necessarily. Do you cancel your library card when you move?'

He thought about it. 'Never.'

'Exactly. He hasn't taken anything out, in' – he squinted at the screen – 'four years.'

'That makes sense. That's when he moved from here, I think.

And you have a list of what he borrowed?' Matt wasn't entirely sure why he was asking this. But he was in a library, with books on the shelves, and he'd been working in the university long enough to know that the books students borrow could often give unique glimpses into their character.

'I can't see *Mein Kampf*, if that's what you're thinking, though I guess Maggie has that on permanent loan.' Ryan's laugh sounded like a series of awkward sneezes. 'But I'll print them out. You'll have to pay for the paper, though, or she'll probably slit my throat.' He clicked a button and the printer started again. He pulled the sheet and handed it to him. 'The ones that have an "O" symbol next to them means we had to order those in from the bigger libraries. For the most part, though, it seems like he was into biographies.'

Matt ran his eyes down the list. Chris might have lived in Hemel for over ten years, but there weren't many books on there. A few cookbooks, *Slow Cooking the Easy Way*, *100 Things to do with Chicken*, *Budget Grub*. He also must have been swatting up on some theology, long after he'd left college, because one of the more recent, ordered-in books was *St Augustine's Confessions*. Heavy.

Matt remembered reading that in the second year of Bible college. Sitting on the sill of his room late into the night, wading through the sticky drag of the writing style then suddenly falling into its flow.

But Ryan was right. Most of the list was made up of biographies of famous people.

Matt started to read them out, sounding like an announcer at a very weird and eclectic party. 'Oscar Wilde, John Wayne, King Charles II, Emperor Constantine and . . . Wallace Stevens? Dutch Schultz?' Matt frowned. 'I don't recognise those last two names. Do you?'

'Wallace Stevens was a poet. American I think. Died in the 50s.'

'And Dutch Shultz?'

'Cartoonist maybe? Let me Google him.' He started clicking

again and the answer flicked up instantly. 'Okay. He was a New York gangster. Died in 1935. A bootlegger. Organised crime. That sort of stuff.'

'That's a bizarre mix of people,' Matt said. He leant into his chair, staring at the printout.

Oscar Wilde? That was an especially odd choice. It was pretty safe to assume that Chris was still against homosexuality. He certainly had been at college. *God made Adam and Eve not Adam and Steve!* he once said, as if a rhyming couplet was enough to close the case on the matter. So why would he be reading the biography of someone so blatantly in that lifestyle?

Ryan suddenly looked up from the screen. 'Found it. They do have a link.'

'And what's that?'

'They're all dead.' The squeak-sneeze laugh was back.

Matt gave a sarcastic smile. 'I was hoping for something a little more specific.'

'I *can* dig a bit deeper into these people, if you like. See if there's a link between them.'

'That'd be great, but I don't want to get you in any—'

'I'll help you because that's what librarians do,' he said. 'Plus she wouldn't want me to. So I will.'

Matt checked his watch. 'Tell you what. Here's my card. I'd appreciate you looking into them. It's probably pointless. But sometimes it's worth pushing any door that comes your way. And Ryan . . . thanks for this. It's actually very important.'

He took the card from his hand and flicked it with his finger before slipping it in his pocket. 'I'll do my best.'

Matt left the room and headed back through the library. The old guy with the Quasimodo back was reaching for a book at the top shelf, gasping, so Matt leant over and grabbed it for him. A doorstep-thick overview of the career of Benny Hill.

'Much obliged,' the man said, licking his lip.

Maggie was sticking loose pages into a pile of kids' books at the counter. Matt slapped a ten-pound note in front of her. 'For the ink and the biscuits . . . and for your kindness.'

Maggie didn't answer him. She was too busy holding the ten pounds up to the light to check if it was fake. Then she counted his pages, sighed and pushed the tenner through a slot in a black tin. When she handed him five pounds and some change back, he couldn't resist lifting the note to the light and checking to see if it was legit.

'Can't be too careful, these days,' he said.

She glared at him.

He smiled and headed to the door and almost immediately stopped smiling as soon as he stepped outside.

No running this time, Matt.

It was time to go back to Hobbs Hill, and to the police that were searching for him. If he spent too long away he really was going to look like, as his mother put it, a *dodge-pot*. Besides, he wanted to talk to Seth Cardle and hopefully Chris again, before he called Miller.

He headed outside into the rain, clutching the printouts that spoke of drowned cats, bathroom suicides, bootlegging gangsters and Oscar Wilde. And for one desperate second he could clearly visualise Miller sifting through all these documents and laughing right into his face. In the murder evidence Top Trumps, old biographies of Emperor Constantine had seriously fewer points than a missing girl's golden tooth showing up on your drive, inside a dead fox's throat that you happened to have killed.

But still, Matt kept the papers tight and close under his jacket as he rushed to the car, refusing to let them get hit by a single drop of rain.

CHAPTER FORTY-FIVE

Matt once worked with a psychology lecturer called Roy Hansen who insisted that reactions like disgust were driven purely by the mind. Once he'd excitedly pulled Matt into his office and opened up a plastic sandwich tub on a small uncluttered desk he'd set up. The tub was filled with something brown. Roy pushed it closer to Matt and told him to 'sniff deep the smell of dung'.

'Clear your mind of all negative thoughts,' he'd said, eyes closed. 'Now imagine that you're smelling a hot plate of lasagne. I mean, *really* visualise it. Go all Saint Ignatius on it. Now . . . tell me that your reaction doesn't change. It's sort of a nice smell, when you think about it that way.'

Now that Matt was back near Hobbs Hill, drawing close to Seth Cardle's farm, the fetid stench seeping through the cracks in the car was already starting to turn his stomach. And no amount of positive thinking was making it smell like anything other than dirty cow shit.

At least the rain hadn't followed him from Hemel. Back here the sun was still sharp and on duty, firing down its vitamins.

He spotted the sign for Helston Farm on the hill.

When Matt turned the car, his phone slid off into the footwell but he didn't stoop to grab it. He didn't care much for being near that thing, right now. There had been one more missed call from Miller but, again, no message. The printouts fell off too. The newspaper reports, the library books, the web search he did on Seth Cardle so that he could find the exact address of his farm. It was located about two miles out of Hobbs Hill, in the navel of a huge green belly of curved fields. Not that far from Tabitha Clarke's house, he noticed.

Larry had been in touch to confirm the suicide of Lydia Kelly in that cold little bathroom in Kellaway Rise. But the coroner's report had an extra bit of information that the local papers didn't mention. They'd found bathwater in her lungs. It was put down to her struggling in the bath, accidentally swallowing as she writhed about. Whatever the case, she'd been under the water.

That cracked tile in the old farmhouse suggested that Tabitha Clarke had probably been under too. Then there was this business with Jinx the cat, dead in the baptistry and of course the little kid who drowned in the canal. He couldn't get the idea of it out of his head.

'Water, water everywhere,' he whispered to himself. When he finally ran into Miller again, he'd suggest (like Taylor had) that they send a team of divers into that lake, if they hadn't started already. That and check those crematorium records.

Larry also said that Chris Kelly had come back with no criminal record. The odious youthworker Billy Stephenson also turned out to be similarly clean. Seth Cardle had a string of traffic offences but, other than that, nothing of any major concern.

The road to Seth's farm was made of packed-in dirt from all the lorries and tractors that must have pounded up and down it every week. He'd planned on visiting Seth to get some answers but what he didn't expect to see was a gang of about twelve protesters. They stood by the huge wooden gate, looking lobotomy-level bored. As soon as they spotted his car they sprang to their feet. Placards with miserable-looking pigs and squashed chickens flicked up everywhere. They started to punch the air with the images.

'Stop the Helston Horror! Stop the Helston Horror!'

Matt slowed the car as they all zombie-swarmed around it. He buzzed the window down and was sorely tempted to tell them that, yes, he'd love his windows washed, but he had the feeling they wouldn't take the joke. One of them had a ginger beard, but brown hair. How was that even possible?

'I need to get through.'

'Not until you know the sort of business you're supporting,' the beard guy said. 'Charlotte? Get over here.'

A young woman with vintage sunglasses perched in her bleached blonde hair came over. She licked her thumb to pull out a leaflet.

'Actually,' Matt said. 'I'm not here on business. I'm doing some work with the Metropolitan Police.'

A few of them heard that and shared glances that were hard to quantify.

The man scratched his beard then leant into the window, suddenly intrigued. 'Are you lot finally bringing this place down?'

'We're working on it. But for now, I need to speak to the boss in there. Got to build the case.' Matt held up his fist in a sort of fight the power way.

The bearded guy waited for a moment.

'Do I look like a farmer?'

He laughed and shook his head, 'Nope, you look like a policeman.' Then he waved his hand at the rest of his friends. They parted. 'Let him through.'

It wasn't exactly a huge place, but he could spot at least three barns and two tractors. Seemed like a pretty substantial set-up to him. As he pulled into the courtyard and stepped out of the car he was shocked at the animal noise. Not the presence of it; it was a farm, after all. But the *level* of it. Pigs squealed, cows roared and somewhere something that sounded like a chicken squawked as if it was being boiled alive. The screech of it all merged into one long wail. Hellish.

The ground was uneven, with muddy tyre tracks caked hard in

the sun. Evidently the rains of Hemel hadn't made it to Hobbs Hill at all. But then hadn't Cardle always said it was the promised land?

On the side of one of the barns was a painted wooden sign that said OFFICE. He headed over and knocked on the half-open door and waited for a few moments. When no answer came he pushed the door open all the way. 'Hello?'

'Yup?'

He turned to find a tight-faced, stocky man in green overalls. He had a smear of something Matt hoped was mud across his cheek.

'My name's Matt Hunter. And you . . . ?'

'Dale Jennings.'

'Well, Dale. I'm looking for Seth. Is he here?'

'Was, an hour ago, but I reckon he must have popped into town. I know we needed teabags. Can I help?'

'I'd really hoped to speak to Seth. It isn't actually a business call.'

'You from a newspaper? You look like you're from a newspaper.'

'Ha, no. Definitely not. I know him from church.'

At that, the man's eyebrows drew apart to a less intense distance. 'Oh, right. Maybe you should try him at home, then?'

Matt looked at the protesters, over on the other side of the wooden gate. They were settling themselves down with phones and iPads. Checking their Tinder until the next visitor. 'How's Seth handling all this attention?'

'From them wasters? Doesn't phase him a bit. Those lot are on a mission to turn everyone veggie, that's all. Probably employed by Quorn or something to bring the meat industry down. That's my theory, anyways. You eat meat?'

'Like a Viking.'

He smiled, 'Then you're alright with me.'

'Are they affecting business?'

'Bit, yeah. But it's the supermarkets who are really kicking us in the nuts. This lot are our best mates compared to Tesco. You know how much we have to drop our prices to get our eggs in their store?'

Matt shook his head.

Dale looked to the left, trying to work it out. 'Well, I can't remember the exact figure off the top of my head. But it's a lot. A hell of a lot.'

Somebody must have stepped on one of those pigs, because a horrendous yelp suddenly came from one of the barns. It made Matt jump, probably because it sounded so human. But then the fox howls had already shown he wasn't exactly an expert at working out what was human and what was animal.

'Hey. Feel free to look around if you like. You can see how much these protesters exaggerate. Anyone who comes up here, I always tell 'em . . . look around. I keep saying to Seth, we need word to get out. Let people know that we're not monsters like them lot think.'

'You know what, Dale? I *will* have a look. Thanks.'

'Good, and spread the word. Just don't feed any of the animals. And if one of the pigs bites you in the testes, then that's *your* hassle, not mine. Got it?'

'I'll bear that in mind.'

'Well, don't mind me . . . I'm off to clean shit off a cow's face.' Dale headed off to the field, grabbing a bucket with some bright-yellow gloves hanging over the rim. Living the dream.

Matt turned and went in the opposite direction, to where the psychotic pigs were crying out. He'd do each barn in turn but he wanted to get those hogs with human squeals out of the way first.

CHAPTER FORTY-SIX

He saw what he expected to see.

Straw, grain and a whole lot of death row animals. Did they snort *Dead Swine Walking!* as the others wandered to their fate? Probably not. He wasn't vegetarian. Wasn't particularly an animal lover, to be fair. But seeing them gazing out through the wooden panels with that resigned, *yeah-we've-worked-this-out* look was kind of depressing. He'd seen documentaries about barbaric farms where artificially fattened pigs gasped for space in minuscule holding pens while they waited for the bolt gun. This was hardly as cramped as that. There was room for the animals to wander, to lie down.

But not much.

Matt had no idea how much floor space the current regulations prescribed but as he glanced from pen to pen he kept thinking, Seth Cardle, you are pushing it.

There was one other thing he did notice, though. Something unexpected but important, and the knowledge of it opened up a whole new route of possibilities. Most people would walk into a place and think they were seeing it, but normally they weren't seeing even half. Mostly, folks spent their life looking through tubes, paying little attention to what was around them.

Matt had always been good at taking the tube away. It was one of the few things he remembered his dad teaching him. *Notice stuff, boy. Notice it!* It was probably the reason why religion came up so wanting . . . because he had bothered to observe it in extreme close-up. One of the reasons Larry Forbes kept inviting him along to crime scenes these days was that he had a habit of spotting stuff.

And so his eyes searched every corner, every beam of those barns. And when the curve of something odd, nestled in a joist up near the roof, caught his gaze he pulled over a bale of hay and stood up on it. He had to push up on his tiptoes, making the bale wobble, to see exactly what that curve was.

It was a little webcam, with an almost imperceptible black wire pinned to a beam, running up to the ceiling and out onto the roof. To a solar power cell?

It wasn't easy to find but he noticed another in the next barn, but not in the third. Either Cardle had put these cameras up for security reasons or maybe they'd been placed here by someone else. People who wanted to keep an eye on the conditions here. He smiled and headed out into the sun.

The final barn was away from the others and it took a minute to reach it. As he walked towards it Matt spotted Dale over in the field. He was running after a cow shouting, 'Bungle! Get back here, you ponce!' His bucket of water was sloshing over the sides, splashing his overalls and turning them dark green. Matt almost stopped walking just so he could watch Dale potentially fall over. He could do with a little light relief.

Instead he moved towards the final barn and immediately started to notice something strange. His nostrils were drawing in a different smell, unlike anything he had experienced so far at the farm. He tilted his head back and took a long sniff, like he often did whenever he walked into a baker's shop.

The odour was both familiar and unfamiliar at the same time but with every step closer he knew that what was creeping up his nose and through the pores of his skin wasn't anything like warm bread. It was death.

The barn was wooden, with a corrugated metal roof. He couldn't see any windows, just a set of double doors with a Keep Out sign, painted in white on the back of what looked like a baking tray bolted to the wood. He pushed at the door expecting it to be locked, but it swung slowly open with an unsettling, human-sounding moan. Like a fairy tale witch was in there, waiting. The old wood looked damp and the place was dark. But the sun started to seep in as he opened the door and stepped inside. It picked out the golden dust dancing in the air. Some long shafts of light shone through the cracks in the roof, like rods of light. Over on the barn wall he saw a wooden table, and above it, a rack of metal tools hanging from rusty hooks.

He slapped his cheek as a fly whizzed past and escaped out into the fresh air. On the floor, two huge grooves ran through the mud and straw and at the end of them, in the very centre of the barn, was something utterly bizarre.

It was a stainless-steel box, more like a windowless room. The sunlight didn't stretch far enough to light it all up but the sun did fall on the bottom half, making it gleam. Set against the ancient-looking barn the metal contraption looked like a spaceship, and he half expected some alien to waddle out and say, *Don't fret about the missing women. They're TEFL teachers on our planet now.*

The thing was fixed to some industrial-sized trolley, and a tow bar stuck out from it. The type you'd find on a caravan. But while the box was a similar size, this wasn't something anyone would want to take a holiday in. The metal pipes that sprouted from it like fingers made that clear enough. That and the small but thick-looking door with a submarine-style wrench wheel and a row of gauges with tiny arrows, all set to zero.

He leant in closer and saw that the markers were in both Fahrenheit and Celsius.

'Gets up your nose, doesn't it?'

Matt's body jerked in surprise and he spun his head.

Dale was hovering in the doorway. 'You'd think you'd fry up a pig and you'd get a bacon smell. But it don't work that way. Worst smell in the world, that. But I just rub a bit of that stuff under my nose and it helps.' He pointed to a tub of Vicks Vapour Rub on a wooden shelf.

'So this is one big oven?' Matt said.

'Incinerator. Farms use them all the time to get rid of livestock that get ill. You can't exactly just dump a dead hog in your wheelie bin, can you?'

'I guess not . . . so this is permanently here? Do you get *that* many dead animals?'

'Nah, Seth hired it for a few months. It's one of the smaller ones, so we use it for pigs mostly. We use it for our own animals now and again but to be honest we mostly have it for other farms round here. We pick up their livestock and get rid of it for them. For a fee. Seth's thinking about hiring something bigger so we can do cows.'

'Do you make a lot of money doing that?'

'Not really. I'm not even sure if it covers the cost of hiring the kit, but Seth's got a vision. Says it might be our best bet against the supermarkets. Every little helps.'

'And what do you think?'

Dale laughed. 'I keep telling him Tesco are probably going to start installing these bad boys in their car parks soon. They do everything, anyway. Give it twenty years and you'll probably be able to chuck pensioners in these things, and still get the clubcard points.' He pressed his lips together, in a vain attempt to keep his own laugh in.

'Is it easy to operate?'

'Piece of piss. Though one time I forgot to rip off the ear pin of a pig and the bloody thing got stuck in the grille. Took me forever to get it back out. So you take any pins or collars off.'

Matt had been pacing around the machine. But this made him pause. 'So you take all metal off the animal.'

'Course. Stops it getting caught up in the machine. You open the doors and slam the pig in like it was a pizza. When it's done it's just ash. Takes a bit of sweeping out. But I make sure it's cleaned every week.'

Matt started to nod, picturing a pile of ashes with two pre-removed golden teeth in a jar alongside it. Spider sense, tingling.

Right. It really was time to call Miller.

Dale was about to say something else when there was a sudden commotion from outside. The protesters were getting excited about something.

'*Bloody students.*' Dale jogged out and Matt followed him, glancing back for one more look at the incinerator.

Slam them in like a pizza.

He thought of someone trying to stuff Tabitha Clarke or Nicola Knox in there. Alive or otherwise. But he could see that it was just too small for a human body to naturally fit.

That fact did not put him at ease. Bodies could be made to fit. And didn't have to go in as one piece.

By the time he got out, Dale was already down at the gate as a white van tried to push through the protesters. He felt a jolt of tension that this was Seth coming back. It wasn't.

'That's my pig feed, you dopes. Let 'em through!' Dale shouted. 'Pigs gotta eat, too, you know.'

Eventually, the protesters let the van past. On the side, it said *Brolin's Farm Supplies*; a grumpy-looking woman with a grey ponytail was sitting behind the wheel rolling her eyes at the delay.

'Hope you catch Seth,' Dale said, and waved. 'Like I said, try him at home.'

'Thanks for letting me look around.'

'No probs. Just tell those lot that we're running a decent farm here. And tell everyone else who ever asks you. See ya.'

Dale stood in front of the van and swung his hands towards the pig barn, like he was guiding a 747 along the runway. Matt headed in the opposite direction, straight for the protesters.

'You probably didn't see much in there today.' The guy with the ginger/brown hair combo came trotting over. 'They clean their act up a bit when they know we're here.'

'So who's in charge of these protests?'

He scratched the end of his nose. 'We're not into hierarchy.'

'It's you, isn't it?'

'Well . . . I co-ordinate the campaign.'

'What's your name?'

'Paul Mears.'

'Can I have a private word, Paul?' They wandered along the dirt road, away from the farm, until they were out of earshot. He checked his watch and was shocked to see how the day was vanishing. It was just after 7 p.m. 'What's your strategy to bring the farm down?' Matt said. 'What's the plan?'

'We're raising awareness locally. We're lobbying for the right inspections but, like I say, these toads are good at putting on a front when it matters.'

Matt pressed the tip of his shoe into a ridge of dry mud, and it crumbled away. 'How are you gathering the actual evidence of cruelty?'

'I'd rather not say. But we're building it up and are going to go public with it in the next few weeks.'

'Paul.' Matt held his gaze for a moment. 'I know about the webcams.'

He visibly gulped and looked back over his shoulder at the others. When he turned back he spoke in a sharp little whisper. 'How the heck do you know about those?'

'I just had a wander round and I spotted them.'

Paul threw up his hands and shook his head. 'Bloody amateurs. They're supposed to be covered up.'

'Don't worry. They're well hidden. Most people wouldn't notice them but I'm a bit anal like that.'

Paul shrugged. 'So, okay. We've got cameras.'

'And is the feed working on them alright?'

He nodded. 'Like I say, we're building a case. Slowly. But it takes time.'

'Are you storing what they record?'

'Obviously.'

'Then I'd like to see those camera feeds.'

Paul swallowed. 'What do the police want with our cameras? Do your people finally believe in the Helston Horror?'

Matt wriggled his nose. A sour breeze had swept across the field. 'You could say that.'

CHAPTER FORTY-SEVEN

Seth could feel hay digging into him as he sat on the pile of bales. It clawed into the bare skin on his back where his shirt had pulled out and ridden up. It always did that when he came up here. He'd reach to push up the hatch and nine times out of ten his shirt would stretch and pop from his jeans. He didn't feel like tucking himself back in.

He liked the hayloft.

It was a good place to reflect and God seemed to speak louder in here. It was private and out of the way, especially when he pulled the ladder up behind him. But it was still in spitting distance of the pigs. If there was an issue, like if one of them puked or tried to copulate with the electric fence, he could rattle down the ladder and sort them out. For the most part, though, he could sit and pray and watch the fields through the grimy windows.

But there were other sights to see out there today. He leant back a little, just to make sure he wasn't in a shaft of light, and watched the protesters. It was the end of their day and they were packing up their banners, flinging the dregs of their expensive-looking flasks into the mud.

Professor Matt Hunter stood off to the side, talking with one of them. He'd been wandering around the farm just a few moments ago. Looking at the animals. Now he was ducking into his car while one of the protesters got into theirs. The rest of them clambered into a white van, which to Seth looked far *too* clean. And when the car and van pulled away, Matt's car followed.

Good old dependable Dale was down there shifting the pig feed. Heaving lips together and puffing out his thick heart-disease cheeks. Seth felt guilty about not helping. But there were other things now. Bigger issues crowding all possible light out. Like when Neil Armstrong stood on the moon, blotting the earth out with his thumb. It felt like that.

He shifted himself around and the Bible on his lap almost slipped off. He grabbed it with his left hand, tearing one of the tissue-thin pages.

'Dammit! Bloody!'

He stilled himself for a moment, caught his breath, then read the story of Jesus's crucifixion one more time.

At his feet, Tabitha Clarke's painting lay flat. He'd folded the bedsheet it was wrapped in, so that he could see it fully. It showed a large lady with huge quaking breasts that insisted on going their separate ways. The curl of a tree branch was coiled around her ankle, helter-skeltering up her legs, vanishing into her crotch. She had her eyes closed, and above her a storm cloud was gathering.

The picture made him consider something he hadn't ever before. Was Eve screwing the serpent, even before she bit the apple? Is *that* why she was so eager to please him and do what he asked?

As he reached down, the bale of hay groaned underneath him. The shift of his weight made it tip forward. With a start he thought he might tumble off and fall headlong into the picture. If he did that, he might never climb out again.

But he stayed upright and didn't fall. He just pushed the bed sheet to one side then grabbed the piece of paisley material from under it. He ran it across his fingers. Soft. Perhaps not silk, but something close. Karl, a friend of his, had cancer once. A baptised believer who would be in heaven right now. Karl used to wear one of these headscarves around his head for months during the chemo. Seth pushed it to his face and sniffed it, just to see if cancer had a scent, common to all sufferers, male or female. Then he was suddenly aware of the tears rolling down his cheeks.

He didn't want to get Tabby's headscarf wet so he set it onto the picture. It slid across it, covering up Eve's nakedness, stopping just at her neck. She looked less like a succubus now and more like just a sleeping girl, tucked up under the covers.

He needed both hands to press the tears away. Then with a short prayer he closed the Bible and folded the corners of the bed sheet back into place. Tabby's picture and headscarf were covered again.

It was time.

He grabbed the ladder from the hayloft floor and wheezed a little as he lifted it. He slipped it into the metal runners then slowly lowered it to the ground floor below. It still rattled loudly when it hit the dirt down there. Then he picked up the painting and wedged it under his arm. Tight. Eve and the serpent felt ice-cold against his skin, like their cold little tongues were licking him frantically through the sheet.

The ladder groaned as he climbed down, and his pensioner knees groaned louder. When the pigs spotted him they squealed and yelled. They often did that when he walked in. He liked to think that it was because they recognised him. A sort of *look-daddy's-here* sound. But today there was a jagged edge to their tone which he didn't like.

Unsurprising, really.

He tried to avoid the bead of their eyes watching him. One of them hissed at him. And he had to look away from their stare.

They're whispering to each other. Because they know.

When he finally looked over at them, they just looked sad. They pitied him.

'And he did maketh his home with the swine,' Seth said to himself and shuddered. Then he headed off towards his office, face pointing down, set like flint.

'Bloody hell, boss.' Dale pretty much spasmed in surprise when Seth appeared round the barn door, nearly dropping his bag of feed. 'Where'd you spring from?'

'I'm sorry. I didn't mean to startle you.'

'I thought you went into town. Where've you been?'

'Thinking.' Seth tried his best to smile but such skills seemed beyond him now. 'Praying.'

'Right, well a friend of yours was here just now. Sorry I thought you weren't—'

'That's alright. I'm sure I'll catch up with him later.'

Dale looked at the sheet-covered thing under Seth's arm and frowned. 'Called himself Matt Hunter. Said he was a friend from the church. I let him look around for a bit.'

'I noticed.'

'You don't mind, eh?'

A moment of silence. 'I'm going to make a phone call now.'

'Are you alright, Mr Cardle? If you don't mind me asking, like.'

Seth set his shoulders back and lifted his head, noticing that the pigs were quiet now, listening for his answer. 'I'm not alright, actually.'

Before Dale could speak Seth was already walking to the office. When he was inside he set the wrapped picture on the paper-strewn desk and closed the door tightly. Through the smeared window he saw Dale looking over, pushing himself up on the balls of his feet. Seth yanked the blinds cord and they shut with a dust-cloud snap.

Seth sucked in a survival breath and grabbed the phone from the desk. Pressing the number was the hardest part. Each digit like a step towards the edge of some hideous drop. The phone rang four times and after that, the world started to fall.

'Hi, this is Chris Kelly.'

A pause.

'Hello? Is anyone there?'

'Chris, it's me, Seth.'

'Hey.'

'Are you alone?'

'I am.'

'Then we need to talk.'

'Sounds ominous.'

Silence.

'Well, you can come straight over if you like. I'm at home. I'll put the kettle on.'

'No, we need to talk right now.'

Chris waited before speaking, and when he did his voice was lower. 'What do you want to say to me?'

'We need to talk,' Seth said, as he stared at the covered painting. 'We need to talk about what we did.'

CHAPTER FORTY-EIGHT

Animal protester Paul Mears curved his Toyota Prius round the country roads at a stately pace, with Matt following behind. At one point they reached a set of lights and there was room to draw up alongside him. Matt wound the window down and called over, 'You don't have to break the speed limit but do you mind if we get a move on?'

Mears smiled behind his beard then he saluted Matt and buzzed his window up. When the lights changed he wheel-span out of there and Matt, shaking his head, lurched the car forward to catch up.

Country roads flashed by the car while in the fields farmers were climbing down from tractors, finishing for the day. They looked timeless, apart from all the Samsung Galaxys pressed to their heads.

Twenty minutes out of Hobbs Hill and the fields grew smaller, less frequent. They were replaced by villages, a town, then an industrial estate and a leisure park. Matt looked at it through the window and felt an overwhelming desire to go bowling, not because he was into bowling, but because it was normal and banal and innocent. He spotted a family peering at the menu in the window of Pizza Hut and part of him despised and envied them simultaneously. That the biggest issue in their lives right now seemed to be deep-pan or thin.

Right on cue the image of the pig incinerator flashed up in his brain again.

– slam them in like a pizza –

He winced the vision into nothingness. Thank God Wren and the kids were in Oxford today. It was 7:40. They'd be settling down for in the cinema right about now, stealing each other's popcorn.

Mears eventually pulled his car into a huge grey brick of a building. The sign said it was one of the halls of residence for Oxford Brookes.

They parked up. Got out.

'The hard drive's in my room,' Paul said.

Matt followed him across a courtyard lined with pretty, skinny trees. In the centre was a piece of metal art that looked like a giant wasp, hovering. Paul pushed through blue-painted doors and headed up a few flights of stairs. The walls were brick, all painted a sickly yellow.

Term didn't start for another couple of weeks. So he only spotted one or two overseas students who couldn't afford to go home for the summer holidays, and a few British ones who just didn't want to. Quite a few of these latter types pottered around Goldsmiths too, where Matt worked. Sometimes he'd buy the especially lonely looking ones a coffee and chat about random stuff on the University lawn. Maybe Paul Mears was one of these guys. The students that seemingly had nowhere else to go.

His room was on the top floor.

'These rooms are prison cells pretty much, aren't they?' he said as Matt stepped inside.

'At least you have a coke machine.'

Paul flashed a sharp, sarcastic smile.

He'd done his best to cover the yellow-brick walls with posters. Either the guy liked irony or he had some 'interesting' tastes, because in the centre of the wall was a huge *My Little Pony* poster. The rest were of bands Matt had never heard of, vintage French movies, multiple photographs of David Hasselhoff and quite a few newspaper clippings on animal rights issues. He couldn't decide if the right word to describe it was eclectic, ironic or swivel-eye weird.

'What are you studying?' Matt sat in the creaky wooden chair. The only seat in there.

'International politics. But it's less impressive than it sounds.' He reached under his bed and dragged out an old-looking MacBook, then an external hard drive. He put them both on the desk. 'Pass me that power lead.'

Matt handed it over and Paul poked the USB cable in. He tapped the power switch. The hard drive started whirring and the lights flickered.

'What are you looking for, exactly?'

'For now,' Matt said, 'I only want to see the feed for one of the barns. The one with the incinerator in it.'

'Oh, you mean the KFC room?'

'The what?'

'Sorry, that's what we call it. The Kill, Fry and Crumble room. And no we're not being irreverent, before you say anything—'

'I don't care what you call it,' Matt glanced at his watch, 'just show it to me, please.'

'Don't be pushy.' Paul swept a few textbooks off his desk to make room. They fell in a heap on the floor. 'So do you have a particular time frame in mind? Because we have a lot of stuff to go through.'

Matt pulled up some notes he'd made on his phone and flicked to the dates of disappearances. 'Go from July 7th, up until now. Just the KFC room.'

'Okay. And by the way, don't expect moving images. This webcam's old school. It takes a new shot every five minutes. It's enough to get a feel for the conditions in there, but don't be expecting Ultra HD. Alright?'

'That's fine,' Matt said. He just hoped that any potential evidence didn't fall in the gaps between when the stills were taken.

'Give me five or so minutes to get it all ready for you. Might be longer.' Paul drummed his fingers on the desk while the Mac booted up. 'Man, do I need a new machine. This thing's getting clogged.'

It took longer than five minutes. Enough time for Matt to sit there and realise that he was actually starving. Those Jammy Dodgers he'd had at the library were not nearly enough for his groaning stomach.

'Paul . . . I'm going to grab something to eat. You want anything?'

'I refuse to use that machine. It stocks Nestlé.'

Matt shrugged and wandered down the corridor. The corporate monolith hummed and glowed in the corner. It had Dr Pepper written on the side with the picture of a young Chinese guy looking so transfixed by the sugary taste that he might as well have been witnessing the birth of the universe.

He threw some coins in it and pulled out a Peperami, a White Nestlé Crunch Bar (screw it, he needed the sugar) and a strawberry milkshake. Nice to see that students were so health-conscious these days. Next to the vending machine was a large open window looking out onto an empty field. He took a few swigs of the milkshake and looked over at the sun. It hadn't started to sink yet, but it was prepping itself. Making itself a cocoa and checking the news for an hour before it would slowly trudge down the stairs to bed down. A pink looking cloud was passing it and for a moment the light seemed to dissolve so it threw finger shadows from the trees, across the concrete pavements outside. By the time he was done here and drove back to Hobbs Hill, it'd probably be getting dark. That's pretty much an entire day rushing around the shires, avoiding Miller's call. This was not good form, at all.

He gulped at the inevitable. His heart was beating so quickly he thought it might scamper up the shaft of his throat and flop up into his mouth.

Just do it.

With a quick breath he grabbed his phone and finally switched it back on. It had been off for the last couple of hours. He waited for the signal bars to show and then dialled.

'Hello? Terry?'

A moment of silence. A swish of activity. Matt pictured old TV cop shows where a flurry of officers gathered around a single phone, plugging in headphones and tracing the call. Miller's voice was all friendly. *Uber*-friendly. 'Matt. Finally! Where've you been? I've been calling you.'

'Sorry, I was in Hemel.'

'What? Why?'

'I was looking into Chris Kelly. Listen, I think there's something odd going on. I've got a lead which I'm following up right now.'

'A lead? Well, how about you pop down and fill me in. There's some stuff I want to talk to you about, anyway.'

'You could tell me on the phone.'

'Well no, I'd like to see you, really.'

'Any progress with Isabel Dawson?'

When Miller breathed through the earpiece it sounded like hard static. 'The fiancé got in touch. The one who stood her up at the altar. Turns out Isabel left a message on his machine last night recording the whole thing. She was crying and said she was a bad person and just threw herself off the waterfall. The phone must have landed in the water because it's nowhere on the rocks. His machine managed to record most of the screaming.'

'What about the dog collar that PC Boyd found?'

Miller sniffed and seemed to pause.

'Well?'

'Yeah, I checked that out and it's a no-go. It wasn't a dog collar at all.'

Matt felt a bubble of disappointment pop in his gut. He was hoping that if Chris or Seth really were involved in this, that might be a concrete link. 'What was it then?'

'Her wedding garter. She'd raked it off on the barbed wire fence and cut herself.'

Matt sighed hard and didn't attempt to disguise it.

'It wasn't frilly or anything so I see why Boyd thought it. But then *you* were the one to suggest that to him, remember? That it was a vicar collar . . .' He waited. 'Oh, and one other thing. A big thing. Chris has an alibi. The fiancé says he got Isabel's message just before midnight. So we know when she jumped. Chris was at some midnight prayer vigil at the time. There were three other people with him up at the church.'

'Which people?'

'Seth Cardle, from the church. The youth worker, Billy. Another man, whose name I forget. I wrote it down.'

'I see. And what was the vigil for?'

'They were praying we'd find Nicola and Tabitha . . . and Isabel.'

Matt took another sip. 'Is that it?'

'There was one other thing. It turns out that Isabel Dawson can't swim. I asked her mum.'

'Meaning?'

'Well, I thought it might explain why she jumped onto the rocks and not the water. Because she was scared of it.'

'Terry, she was killing herself.'

'I know, I know. But suicides aren't always thinking straight at the time. Why else would she not want to die in the water?'

'I have a theory,' Matt said.

'Oh, do you?' Miller barely hid the beat of suspicion in his voice.

'She was supposed to be baptised in that lake on Sunday morning, wasn't she? But she kills herself on the rocks instead.'

'And your point?'

'I think it was defiance. A rejection of being baptised. I think she resented it being forced on her and she wanted to die. So she jumped on the rocks and not the water.'

'Well, that's a frigging bizarre theory.'

Matt pondered the thought of it and watched the clouds. 'Unless she just didn't think she deserved forgiveness.'

'Look, the bottom line is that it's almost definitely suicide. So that just leaves Nicola and Tabitha,' Miller said. 'So how about you come in and we rattle this out? I'd appreciate your help.'

'Give me an hour.'

'No, now would be ideal for—'

'Give me an hour. Just to test a theory . . . after that I'm all yours.'

Miller paused. 'Where are you?'

He thought of hanging up just then. Not even hissing pretend interference into the phone as if they had a bad connection. Just a straight hang-up . . . but then he thought about it some more, as the silence ticked between them, and said, 'I *will* be coming back, Terry. And by the way, I swear I've done nothing wrong in this. I'll show you that . . . somehow.'

A pause. 'Matt, I think—'

Click.

He hung up and slid the phone back into his pocket, then he hurried nervously back down the corridor. He began peeling the foil from his Peperami. The smell wafted up and he shoved it in his mouth for a quick bite.

'You ready yet?' Matt hovered in the corridor, calling through Paul's open door.

'Two minutes. Soz, but this thing's ancient.'

Matt was mid chew when he spotted a poster on a black door that led to a kitchen. It was the typical thing he saw back on his own campus. The sort of *we-so-clever* joke that students like. The poster had the Latin phrase *Carpe Diem* written on it, with the words 'Seize the Carp!' written in bold next to it. Under it was an eagle carrying a carp fish off and up into the air.

Oh please, Matt thought, a rim-shot clicking in his mind. *You're killing me.*

350

He was about to groan at the way they'd given the Latin two meanings when he suddenly stopped chewing.

He gulped, in fact, then reached into his back pocket and yanked the folded A4 sheet out that Ryan the librarian had given him. He pulled it out so quick he almost tore it.

'Mr Hunter?' Mears called through. 'It's ready for you.'

'Two seconds . . .' He ran his finger down the sheet of paper to the book he was looking for. *St Augustine's Confessions*. Then he jabbed at the title a few times, like it was some sort of button, opening up some dusty old door in his subconscious. With his mouth still full he whispered the word, '*Verecundus*.'

That Latin phrase fell from his mouth and back into his ears. But when he heard it there was a much different ring to it now. Another meaning. 'Verecundus'.

Finally, it sounded right.

That feeling of déjà vu when he first read that phrase in Tabitha's text message made sudden sense. Because *Verecundus* may well have been a Latin phrase meaning shy or shameful, but it also had another meaning.

It was also a name.

And he could almost picture himself back at Kimble Bible College, sitting on the fat window sill of his room, listening to Jeff Wayne's 'War of the Worlds', reading *St Augustine's Confessions* because Principal Wilder insisted it would be worth it. Chris had read it too, according to Ryan's library sheet. Heck, hadn't they even discussed that book, over a pint one night?

The fragments of that work flickered awake in Matt's memory.

The part where Saint Augustine complained of toothache. The part where he shared the turmoil he had felt at age thirty-two when he couldn't decide if he should convert to Christianity or not. But it was the other moment that sank in now. One which had been bubbling in his subconscious ever since he'd seen that word lurking in those two text messages.

351

He recalled an old painting from the centre pages of that book: a halo-headed St Augustine baptising his friend, a non-Christian called Verecundus, just moments before he died. And how Augustine wrote how good it was, how desirable, for that young man to have died so soon after baptism.

Because that way, he had no time to lose his faith. No time to be polluted. He had died pure. And when Verecundus opened his eyes again, he would open them on heaven.

And there was another picture beyond that, long forgotten, but really just tossed into the outer rims of his subconscious – or was it just his imagination? It was hard to tell which. But he could see it, clearly. A picture of him and Chris discussing that chapter over a beer and Chris so, *so* animated, with froth on his lip, hands gesturing, saying, 'Wasn't that noble of Augustine, Matt? Don't you think that was wise? To baptise someone just before they die? He did Verecundus a wonderful favour. Heck . . . and eternally speaking, maybe it'd be more loving to baptise everybody alive then kill them straight after. That's a fast track to paradise, that is.'

Matt suddenly realised he was leaning against the wall, hand scraping through his hair as he stared at the paper. He couldn't think of any better way to say it. 'Holy shit,' he said. 'Holy shit.'

CHAPTER FORTY-NINE

Matt sat back in the creaky chair, heart tapping a frantic little rhythm in his chest. Despite the generous sloshing of milkshake he'd just gulped down, he was conscious of the utter sandpit dryness in his throat. There was an entire section of his personality that wanted to walk out of the room and avoid what might be the truth. To run from this. That Chris Kelly's twisted obsession with baptism might have led to murder.

Not like these pictures might show anything . . . but still.

'You okay, Mr Hunter?' Paul said, blinking a lot.

'Just show me the pictures. Quick.'

'Okay. I've lined it up for July 7th. But like I said, the camera takes a shot every five minutes, so that's 288 pictures a day.' Paul ran his finger up and down the wheel on the mouse. 'Just scroll through them and it shouldn't be too hard to spot anything out of the ordinary.'

'How often do you check these?'

He pulled a face. 'To be honest with you, I stopped checking the KFC room months ago. Once they brought that incinerator in, there wasn't much point. You can't really build a case of cruelty to *dead* animals. People barely give a damn about the live ones. So we've been concentrating on the other barns.'

Matt took the mouse in his hand and pulled it nearer to him.

'Oh, and it'll be quicker to go through than you think. Remember half of those shots are going to be jet-black once the lights go out. I can't afford night vision. So you'll probably only have about 144 shots to check on, for each day. Just skip the black ones.'

'Understood. I'll get started, then.'

Paul went to lie on the bed and pulled out a book called *The Economics of Killing*. 'I need to read this for a seminar. You don't mind music, do you?'

'Not at all. Go ahead.'

Paul leant over to the speaker dock by his bed and hit shuffle on his iPhone. 'Everybody Knows' by Leonard Cohen started up while Matt tore the wrapper from his chocolate. He broke a huge chunk of it off in his teeth, like he was a mountaineer setting off on a long, undesirable journey. Then he started to scroll.

He couldn't help it, but after a while he was pulling those pictures down to the beat of the song. At least it was slow enough to let him get a decent look at each picture.

For the most part the barn, or rather the KFC room, was empty. Yet every now and again there'd be a busy day, when Dale Jennings would reverse a flatbed truck into shot. It was odd seeing time jump in five-minute increments. In one picture the back of the truck was bulging and covered in polythene. Then in the next the plastic was gone and voila. Pile of pigs! Sometimes three, maybe four. One by one they vanished from the truck.

There was some sort of harness attached to the incinerator. In a few of the shots Matt saw the oven door wide open like a hungry black mouth. Trotters (what a truly hideous word) stuck out as Dale stuffed the bodies in with his bare hands. Matt could imagine the feel of those muddy hooves, scraping his palm.

A few scrolls on and the truck had been moved away. Then Dale was on his knees with a brush. Then standing, wiping his forehead. Next. Cleaning the gauges. Next. Scrubbing the truck.

354

Next. Nothing again. Just that hungry spaceship sitting there like something from Area 51.

He could speed up during the nights when the shots turned into solid-black squares, and after a while he developed a decent rhythm.

The phone moved to a new song, then another. As the scrolls went on Matt had to force his eyes to concentrate. He used all his energy to resist the voice in his head: *What the hell were you expecting?* A little black flower of paranoia was growing in his gut. Unfurling. *Get back in your car and see Miller and talk to him about Chris Kelly. Do it now! Because you've been away for way too long, Matt. Cos what's that phrase? Absence makes the heart grow . . . suspicious as fuck.*

Johnny Cash started singing the *Nine Inch Nails* song, 'Hurt', and the sheer melancholy power of it made Matt want to stop scrolling and rest his head on the desk. But he didn't. He couldn't. And just as Cash sang that first line, Matt spotted four light-coloured squares whizz by under his fingers, in amongst the constant parade of black ones.

His index finger started to push instead of pull, scrolling back up to those shots that he'd just missed.

He froze.

Almost yanked his hand back from the mouse.

Matt sat up so quickly in the chair that he almost sent his milkshake flying across the desk. 'Oh, no.'

Cash was singing that the only real thing in life was pain.

'No, no, no . . .' He ripped his phone from his pocket and it slipped to the floor with a bump. He grabbed it.

'Er . . . what's going on?' Paul sat up onto his elbow.

'I'm impounding your computer and the hard drive.' He jabbed at the keys on his mobile, searching for Sergeant Miller's number.

'Like hell you are. I've done nothing wrong.'

Matt clicked on the number and nothing happened. 'Dammit. Where can you get a signal in here?'

'You'll need to go back out to the window on the landing, by the vending machine. We get dropouts in the rooms. It's the bricks—'

'Are there *any* other members of your team receiving this feed?'

'A few. But just the live shots. I'm the only one with the archive. And, like I say, we don't check that room any more.'

'Then I need you to make multiple copies of the pictures on the screen right now and any others like it that you find.' Matt sprang to his feet. 'On printouts, on whatever memory sticks you have, on the Cloud. We *cannot* lose this.'

Paul was about to say something but once Matt got out of the way he started staring at the screen with a wrinkled look of confusion on his face. 'What's the big—' His eyes stretched wide with shock. 'Jesus Christ, is that what I think it is?'

'Whatever you do. Do *not* delete it.'

Paul's hand flew to his face, and when he spoke his voice seemed to fluctuate in pitch. 'Oh, my God. That's hideous.'

'Make copies, now. And then start scrolling for more.'

Before he left the room Matt thought for a moment and held up his phone just in case. He took four quick shots of the four separate pictures on the screen, all from the same fifteen-minute period.

The first was just the empty incinerator room, but with the main light suddenly on. The time code read July 22nd, 3.03 a.m. The next shot was a figure pulling an odd-shaped bag, his back to the camera. The third: the figure again. Half in shadow, cupping his hand around his mouth, obscuring his face but showing clearly that he was calling back to someone else, out of shot.

And then there was the fourth picture, the money shot, that had Paul wanting to gag.

The camera quality may not have been perfect but this robotic click of a webcam had managed to catch a horrendous moment in time. It was obvious what it was. Matt just knew, from the baldness of what was being held, as sure as he knew who it was that was holding it.

In front of the gaping mouth of the incinerator, two hands held what looked at first like an odd-shaped pumpkin ready to carve. But a couple of blinks reprogrammed the brain and showed the reality of it. Just Tabitha Clarke's hairless, staring head. And in the splash of the light bulb, the gentle eyes of Chris Kelly's son, Ben, who gazed down lovingly at it. He was crouched by the incinerator like a mad monkey with its prize, as both faces glowed in the light of the flames.

CHAPTER FIFTY

Matt wasn't asthmatic but right now he genuinely felt like one as he breathlessly waited for the bars on his phone to stack up again. He hung out of the open window and then, finally, caught one bar of signal. He kept the phone completely still and quickly called Miller. Outside the sun had finally drifted lower in the sky.

When Matt told him what he had just seen on the computer, Miller had to ask him to repeat it.

'I'm telling you, Terry, it's his son. It's Ben Kelly.'

Miller said nothing for a moment. 'Why don't you come down and we'll talk about—'

'Dammit, Terry, I know you found Nicola's teeth in the fox. And I know why he ripped them out. They'd have gotten caught in the grille of the machine,' Matt snapped. 'I have no idea why they were dumped on my drive but I swear to you I had nothing to do with that. Or the emails. Or *any* of this.'

'Then come back and we'll talk—'

'I am! I'm coming right now. But you need to find Ben Kelly, because I'm not the one you want. When you see what I've seen you'll—' He broke off.

'Matt? Matt? Are you still there?'

'Right. I'm going to hang up, and then I'm going to text you the

358

pictures. Then you'll know.' Matt was about to press *End call* when he stopped. 'Wait, I forgot. There's something else. In one of the shots, Ben's calling back to someone out of the frame.'

'You're saying someone else was there, helping?'

'That's exactly what I'm saying.'

'You think it might be Cardle?'

'Maybe. It might even be Chris. Both even? I just don't know. But he's definitely calling to someone.'

'Send me those pictures. Now. Then get back to Hobbs Hill,' Miller said. 'And I swear to you Matt. If you're not back here within the hour, I'm going to issue a manhunt for you. Do you understand what I'm saying?'

'You mean you haven't already?'

Miller paused. 'Just come back, now.'

'I'm on my way. Stay by your phone.'

Matt quickly texted the pictures, thumbs shaking as he did it. Then he raced back to Mears's room and grabbed some of the paper copies and a memory stick that he'd already made. 'Good. That's good. Have you got a bag?'

Paul looked so traumatised that he could barely speak. He just nodded to a Nike backpack on the bed.

Matt grabbed it and folded down the MacBook. He stuffed it inside, along with the hard drive. 'Don't worry, you'll get this back.'

'It's got my coursework on it,' Mears said, then gave a grim laugh at how trivial that sounded.

'You'll get it back,' Matt said again. 'And thank you. You may have just saved my life.'

He raced down the stairs, jumped the last few steps and ran towards the car, holding the backpack tight with one hand and clicking his key-fob in the air like a laser gun. His car blinked its welcome-back eyes and Matt climbed inside. He slotted his phone into the holder and put the car into hard reverse. Just as he pulled away he thought he saw two of the campus security guards talking into their walkie-talkies and pushing through the door of Paul Mears's building.

He wondered if they were looking for him.

He kept his lights off until he reached the main road then the phone rang again. Rigged up through the stereo system, Miller's loud voice boomed into the car.

'Bloody hell, Matt.'

'You got the pictures?'

'Yes. We're heading over to Ben Kelly's house now.'

'Good. I'll meet you there.'

Miller paused and Matt knew that his initial reaction would have been to tell Matt to stay away. Yet he'd clearly just seen the fact there *was* someone with Ben in the photograph. Who's to say it wasn't Matt? So Miller was choosing to keep him close, no matter what.

'Yeah, good,' Miller said. 'Meet us there. It's the big house on Ashley Hill right at the top. You won't miss it. It's got a neon cross on the roof.'

'Okay.' Matt clicked the phone into dial mode. He tapped on Wren's name and waited for her to answer as he hugged the curves of the road.

'Matt?'

'Wren, hi.'

'Why's your phone been off? I've been calling.'

'Sorry. I've been busy.'

'Great. Did you finish your chapter?'

'Wren, listen . . . you should stay over at Oxford tonight. Go to Premier Inn or something.'

'Huh? Why?'

'I can't talk right now, but I'm okay. I just don't think it's safe here tonight.'

'Matt . . .'

'Go anywhere. Stay at a posh place, whatever. Just don't—'

'We're here. We're already at the cottage.'

For a second he drifted, and saw the lines in the middle of the road rumble under the car.

'Your policeman friend, Miller . . . he called me up and asked if I'd come back early. He wanted to ask me some questions about that fox we hit the other day.'

He closed his eyes.

'I've been trying to call you. Now tell me what's going on.'

He felt a breath catch in his throat. 'Don't freak out.'

'I'm already freaking out. I want you back here, now. And I want to know what's going on with you.' She suddenly sighed and when she spoke again her voice was small and uneven. 'Plus me and Lucy have had this huge fight.'

'Wren. Listen to me. There's a manhunt on tonight in Hobbs Hill and I don't want you or the girls there. Get in the car and get away from that place. Drive to a Travelodge or something. Drive back to London if you have to. But get away.'

'You're scaring me.' Her voice had a clear tremble to it and when he went to speak he realised his had too.

'It's going to be fine. Just get the car and get going. Don't pack.'

'Okay,' she said quickly. And then, 'Who are you looking for?'

He took a breath. 'We're looking for Ben Kelly. I think he dumped that fox on our drive last night. And he's certainly involved in the murder of Tabitha Clar—'

There was a shuddering yelp from the phone. It sounded loud and weird and wrong.

'Wren?'

Silence.

'Wren? Are you still there? Wren? Wren?'

The white lines on the road, swerved again.

There was the sound of sudden movement on the other end of the line, a swishing of material and the clomping of feet.

'Wren? What the hell is going on?' he shouted and suddenly

361

remembered again that he was driving a car. The intensity of the conversation was making him slow down. He slammed the accelerator into the floor and sped forwards down a long, straight stretch of road. He shouted at the phone as it hung in its plastic holder. 'Wren! Dammit, answer!'

An agonising few seconds passed, then she came back on the phone.

'She's gone. Amelia's there but Lucy . . . she's gone.' Another rush of movement. The sound of what seemed like a window creaking open. The rushing stomp of feet across the landing and the shout of Lucy's name. Up and down the stairs again. All through the speakers of the car. It was like he was listening to some obscure and badly recorded radio play. Wren's voice came back loud, falling into a desperate breathless panting. 'The church. The youth group. She told me today that she met with Ben.'

'And what happened?'

'She met him at that youth group pizza thing after the big baptism. She said she and him walked in the woods. She was upset about the fox and so she showed him where we buried it . . .'

Something collapsed in his chest.

'She was angry with you but he defended you. He said that you killing it was a good thing. That you were a merciful person. Then she said he prayed for her. She said she wanted to meet him again,' Wren swallowed a frantic breath. 'I told her he was too old for her. She got upset and said me and you were anti-religion. She wants to be baptised.'

'Call the police.'

'. . . I'll kill him.'

'The police, Wren. Call them now.'

'Yes . . . yes, okay.' The phone clicked off.

The car plunged into silence and he tried to contain the lurching nausea in his gut. He gripped the wheel tightly, as if it might suddenly spin uncontrollably out of his hand.

Someone made a desperate moan in the car and he realised that it was him.

Outside the sun was finally going down, grabbing all the darkness it could muster and flinging it like a sheet across the world. Across Hobbs Hill. And in the distance, the now-growing sound of the waterfall sounded nothing less to him than a thousand little girls, screaming.

CHAPTER FIFTY-ONE

When they converted the Bethesda Healing Centre, Chris Kelly oversaw the whole project. Not the nuts and bolts building stuff; he wouldn't have the first clue on all that. But the important part – the *vision* for the centre. The idea of how it would be spiritually fuelled. So he specifically requested that as many windows as possible could see the waterfall. It was the *water* that he wanted to see. He knew it wasn't weird to want that either, because everyone he'd ever known liked to look at water. Walk along a crowded beach and you'd see families pressing the legs of their deckchairs deep into the sand and anchoring a position so that they could look *out*. Never back at the shiny promenade, no matter how enticing the arcades and shopfronts.

Never.

When it comes to chair layouts by the sea, there are only ever lines and curves. There are no circles or squares. Water is the show and people will pay a surcharge to watch it from their hotel windows, to sleep to its whispering. He knew it wasn't just because it looks nice, either. Something revelatory is at work in water. Water could cleanse, water could birth. Water could be the living presence of the divine.

Even in the dark tonight, he could see Cooper's Force glowing like long curtains fluttering into a big black disc. Churning, constant, unchanging and strong.

Watching the falls gave him hope. That was why he chose to come here tonight, to kneel at this window, because if Seth's phone call wasn't a mistake then he needed the water very much tonight. It helped his doubts. It reminded him that God really was out there, pulling people's eyes in his direction, that no matter how dark things were about to get, there was always the chance of light.

'Give me the words,' Chris prayed.

He stood up from his knees and started to pace the floor of the Healing Centre. He was in the main ground-floor meeting room, with the panoramic glass. Through the doorway, he could see the main entrance, and the window that Matt had smashed the other night. Bless him. He was a silly, confused man, but he was only trying his best. Chris wished Matt was here right now. He could use a friend.

Earlier he'd pushed most of the chairs to the side, but he kept two in the middle facing each other, for him and Ben to sit on. But that looked a little confrontational, like a job interview, so he pulled a few of them back out again and dotted them around, cafe-style.

He knew it was trivial and would do little to help, but he scattered some Maltesers in a bowl on a little coffee table because ever since he was a kid Ben liked them more than any other chocolate in the world. They used to lie on their backs, the two of them, when he was little, when Lydia was alive, heads together on the lounge carpet, hovering the little brown balls on the breath from their lips until their giggling broke the flow and they'd try and catch it without choking. Lydia would be drying cups with a tea towel and giggling at them both.

A million years ago. Old Testament.

Chris stared at the chocolates in the bowl when he heard the front door clicking open and for a moment he was suddenly, desperately afraid.

Ben was in the foyer looking around.

'I'm in here, son.'

'Dad?' Ben pushed the door open. 'Hey, I got your message. Is everything alright?'

'I'd like to talk, if that's okay?'

''Course . . . hey, I heard about Isabel. Did she jump off?'

Chris nodded.

'But did she fall in the water?'

'No. She hit the rocks.'

'Oh . . . that's a shame isn't it? That it was the rocks, and not the water . . .' He rubbed his eye a little. 'You look down, Dad.'

Chris pulled out one of the chairs. It had a slot at the back for Bibles and hymn books, but it was empty right now. 'Grab a seat.'

Ben spotted the chocolate. 'Can I?'

'Go for it.'

He sat and grabbed one of the little Maltesers and started eating the chocolate off first, leaving a little, light brown ball to crunch on. His usual method. 'You want one?'

'No.'

'So, is that why you wanted me to come here? To talk about Isabel?'

Chris spoke in a tone as gentle as he could make it. 'Did you know Tabitha Clarke?'

People smile with their eyes, not their mouths, and the gentle reassuring look that had been on Ben's face for the past minute never flinched, never changed. But as her name echoed in the air Chris saw his son's eyes grow strangely fixed.

'Did you know her?' he said again.

The smile was fading.

'Did you visit her? You can tell me.'

An unbitten half-sphere dropped from Ben's hand and both of them watched it bounce on the floor, landing on the carpet like an earth-rise. An entire minute passed before either of them spoke again.

'I know her,' Ben said, not looking up. 'Actually, I was praying down here one night. She left a message for you on the answering machine but you were busy with your healing stuff, so I thought I'd meet with her instead.'

'Where?'

'In her house, up on the hill. She needed help. You should see how messy she has it up there.'

'And what did you do?'

A deep, throb of silence.

'Ben, you can tell me. What did you do?'

'I picked her up and I kissed her head. She was dying and falling into hell.' He looked his dad in the eye. There was no malice there. No deviousness, or madness even. Just a terrifying gentleness. 'I helped her.'

The carpet started to move and swim, and Chris had to blink to make it stop. 'She's dead?'

'She *was* dead. But she's not any more . . .' Ben cracked a smile that sent an instant creep through Chris's skin. 'She's more alive than ever now.'

He could hear the sound of his son's breath. Both of them seemed to be breathing in the same quick rhythm.

'Why are you suddenly asking me this, Dad?'

'Because Seth went into the hayloft to pray today and—' He suddenly couldn't speak. It felt like an invisible hand was clutching at his chest.

'Heeeey,' Ben sounded like a schoolteacher, calming a frightened pupil. 'You don't have to get upset about this.'

Chris closed his eyes, trying to fight the mad panic scratching and scraping his brain. He was trying *so* hard to be calm. 'I don't think Seth realised that you sometimes go up in the hayloft to think. And he found her . . . her things.'

'I don't know why I kept them. I shouldn't have, I suppose. I burnt the rest of her paintings. They were pretty sinful, Dad. But one of them was different and it reminded me of Eve in the Garden, so I kept it.'

'Do you really think God wanted this?'

For the first time, there was a flash of something fierce in Ben's eyes. 'I wouldn't have done it if I didn't think God wanted it.'

'But you killed someone.'

'She was dying.'

'You killed her.' Chris heard himself saying the words and the

367

sound of it sickened him. But there was some rabid morbidity in him that wanted to ask the details. How did he do it? Did it take a long time? Where was the body?

Ben's face grew cold. 'Sometimes, I think I'm the only Christian alive who understands the Great Commission.'

'Ben. Is it because of what me and Seth did? Is that—'

'Heaven's healing. Isn't that what you and Seth taught me? What . . . don't you believe in heaven any more?' Ben slowly rose to his feet. 'Tabby's there *right* now. With Jesus. I bet she's painting with colours we've never even heard of, now. And *I* made that happen.'

'And Nicola? Is she with Jesus now, too?'

'U-huh.' The way he nodded, slowly and with the smile of a child, froze Chris to the chair, clamped him to it with a horror and dread that felt utterly unreal. Like the walls were starting to quake and blur. Like the room was filled with water, pulling him back. When Ben slowly walked towards him and put a gentle hand on his shoulder he was unable to react to the insect prickle rushing through his body, so he just watched his son, standing there, and Ben's—

. . . chewing like a rat on his own thumb. Peering through the gap of the bathroom door, in 119 Kellaway Heights. While his mother writhes in the bath. Pink water is spilling over the edge, and darkening into red.

They have no idea that he's there, watching through the crack in the door. But he sees them. And there's Daddy, collapsing against the toilet, crying like a crazy person as he calls the ambulance on the cordless phone, white plastic splattered with red, trying to get the address of his flat out of his mouth and finding it impossible to remember the sequence. While Seth clamps towels against Mummy's wrists and throat, pressing against the hot and hopeless gush of blood. The white towel turns pink, red. He has to drop it to the floor with a slap, and grab another. There's too many cuts to cover up.

Then the blood stops jetting out, and it's slowing to a pulsing trickle.

'It's too late, Chris.' Seth's weeping voice. 'She's lost too much blood.'

'She can't die. She doesn't believe any more.' Daddy flinging himself to his knees and cupping his hands around the splitting seams in her wrists and throat. Hands sliding all over. And this shuddering, sobbing voice, that sounds like an animal. 'Suicides go to hell. They all do. We have to help her!'

Mummy's gasping body in violent spasm, bubbling for a few seconds before Seth finally does it. He plants a hand on her forehead, and though he speaks through tears, he says the words loud. 'Lydia Kelly. I baptise you in the name of the Father . . .'

A pause, to say – should I do this? – then a nod from Chris to proceed.

And down she goes.

Daddy and Seth say it together the second time. 'And the Son.'

Ben sees Mummy's naked body, the curve of her knees, and the bulge of her hip. She looks so vulnerable. She goes under white and comes up pink.

And then they speak the final time, only this time, Ben's tiny, little, unbroken sparrow voice joins in with them. 'And the Holy Spirit.'

Daddy spins his head round first, then Seth. And for the first time the two men see a seven-year-old standing in the corridor. Door now open, watching the whole thing.

Then everyone's aware of each other. Father, son and friend. Ben even thinks Mummy has opened her eyes a tiny fraction, to see him before she leaves. Looking down her cheeks at him.

Once they're all together in it, everything changes.

Because she isn't gasping any more. Her eyes close and her mouth's no longer twisted and deformed. She looks as at peace as any of them have ever seen her. The depression that dragged her down is now gone. The water isn't red now, either. Now it's filled with roses that are falling and scattering across the steps of heaven to guide his mummy home. He's never seen anything more beautiful in his life. It's the moment he knows God exists.

'Heaven is healing,' Daddy says with the voice of a madman.

Laughing or crying, it's impossible to tell which. Then he rushes over to fling his wet arms around his son—

'Heaven is healing,' Ben said.

Chris could feel the chair he was sitting in. As if his body had its own gravitational pull and was dragging things toward it. Tugging his ribs inward.

'I know I'm going to get caught. In fact, God told me I would,' Ben said, matter-of-fact. 'But it's okay. Because you brought Matt here. He knows the police and he understands what I'm doing. I've been sending him clues. Signs.'

'What signs?'

'He'll tell them that I'm not a bad person. They won't listen to you Dad, sorry, but they will listen to him. People are going to ask where the girls are and he can tell them. They're in paradise now.'

'Where . . .' Chris could barely bring himself to say it. 'Where's Tabitha's body, son?'

'Oh, she's all gone.'

'How?'

Ben waited for a moment before answering, 'Stephen took care of it.'

Chris frowned. 'Who?'

Another pause. 'I said Stephen took care of it.'

'Stephen?'

'You haven't forgotten about him, have you?'

'*Stephen?*' That was the moment, really. The second when all resolve truly dropped through his body and Chris slipped right off his chair and onto his knees with a crack. The plate of chocolate tipped and fell to the floor too, rolling like marbles on the carpet. And Chris Kelly started sobbing like a child, completely unrestrained. He covered his face with one hand and reached out like a blind man for Ben with the other. He grabbed his boy's hand, pulled him down to the carpet and cradled his head against his. 'Oh Ben, my son. My poor, poor son.'

CHAPTER FIFTY-TWO

Matt's car lurched to a stop and he stepped out into the glare of flashing blue lights. They made the edges of Chris and Ben's house flicker against the trees. It was a huge beast of a home, with withering vines clawing at the walls. The neon cross shone against the now-black sky, like an ecclesiastical McDonalds.

By the time he ran up onto the wooden porch, Miller and Taylor were already kicking the door in. Each impact made a groaning creak against the wood.

'Good. You're here,' Miller said before pounding his boot again. 'Any news on your daughter? Your wife and little girl came to the station.'

'I know. She says Lucy's bike's gone.' There was a desperation in Matt's voice that he made no attempt to disguise. 'Is he inside?'

'There's a light on upstairs and we thought we just heard a voice.'

Just as Miller said that, the door crunched in its frame under his boot. With another kick from Matt, it splintered itself open.

'Shouldn't we wait for help?' Taylor said, which was pointless. The other two were already in the door.

CHAPTER FIFTY-THREE

Chris pulled his head away from Ben's then pushed himself back up onto the chair again. He never let go of his son's hand. 'Ben. Stephen's gone.'

He frowned and shook his head. 'What a peculiar thing to say.'

'He's dead, son. He drowned in the canal. You remember?'

'Yes.'

'So he's dead.'

'Yeah, but he's *around*. You've always known that.'

Chris pushed his fingers deep into the corners of his temples. He thought of all those times that Ben had spoken about Stephen, the seven-year-old dead boy who wasn't even at his school, boys who shared nothing more than being the same age and living in the same town. A kid who was trapped under ice and dragged down the Grand Union Canal, until he was caught by the trees, dead. Drowned two weeks after Lydia's suicide.

Those weeks after Lydia killed herself were horrendous. The inquest, the funeral. The bathroom refitting where those council men turned off the water and unhooked the death-bath. Then they carried it on its side and scraped the walls with it, while Ben sobbed and told them to put it back, put it back!

And those terrible nightmares Ben had about his mother, where she'd crawl on all fours from the bathroom, naked. Her split wrists dripping, searching for his room. Calling for him. Those dreams only stopped when his invisible friend turned up one morning. It was as though Ben's delicate psyche had sent down a helper, a friend who pored over his homework with him and played with him in the park. It was the only thing that calmed Ben after that terrible night of blood. And didn't all kids have friends who weren't really there?

A sudden thought hissed in his brain, in Matt's voice: *Isn't that what your God is, Chris? Isn't that exactly what he is? An imaginary friend.* For a dangerous moment, that sounded very plausible.

Back then, God help him, Chris went along with it for a few months. At dinner, Ben said, 'Stephen wants the salt,' and Chris passed him the salt. 'Budge up, Dad, Stephen can't fit in,' and Chris would shift up the sofa to make room, so all 'three' of them could watch *Power Rangers* on TV.

And even when they sat in the kitchen one night in those cold months after Lydia killed herself and they ate Pot Noodles (which Chris had poured out onto plates to make the meal feel more special), when Ben said that his friend was the little boy with the red jacket who used to live where the water was coldest, Chris just sat there with his fork stuck in his mouth putting two and two together.

The boy who drowned in the canal, the one Seth knew from the farm's youth programme who he'd prayed for at the funeral: that boy was called Stephen.

Chris remembered saying the words, 'It might be better not to play with invisible friends,' but it was the only time such a sentiment ever left his lips because as soon as the suggestion was out Ben's mouth began to tilt and his chin contracted, started to tremble. Then he just stared at the scrapes on the walls where they'd removed the bath, shaking his head because he couldn't handle any more loss.

So it just felt easier to go along with it.

It seemed to work itself out, too, because when winter left, so did Stephen. Like Jack Frost he vanished with the thaw of the ice. When winter came back, the following year, Ben was eight and different. Older. And he never mentioned Stephen again.

As far as Chris knew, the dead boy was gone. Or perhaps, and this was the thought that had always chilled him most, perhaps this wasn't an imaginary friend at all. And certainly not a ghost. Because didn't the devil sometimes send his demons out, *masquerading* as the ones we have lost? The dark presence that had ruined Lydia's faith. What if it had slipped out of her body after the baptism, and settled its eyes on Ben instead? Or was Stephen all in his mind?

These questions. they were overwhelming.

'We need to get you some help,' Chris said.

'Huh? I don't need help.'

'I think you need to talk to someone.'

'I talk to you, Dad.'

'I . . . I mean someone qualified.' Chris's heart, like a wine glass deep inside his chest, started to break. A tear trickled down his cheek. 'Maybe there's anger there about your mum leaving us, that they could help you with—'

'I am getting my anger *out*,' Ben snapped. It made Chris blink. Ben had half-cocked eyes and there was something accusing about it. 'Isn't that the way? Don't you always say we have to externalise our pain? Purge it from ourselves?'

'Yes. It helps, but Stephen's not real . . . and . . . well I never meant externalise your pain as . . . as a person. Is that what Stephen is? Is he . . . is he your pain?' Chris started weeping again.

Ben looked at him like his dad had completely lost his mind.

'We'll get you some proper help,' Chris said.

'But he does the bits I don't like.'

'Don't. Please.'

Ben suddenly looked back over his shoulder at the door. Then he turned back and pushed a finger up to his lips. 'You mustn't tell Stephen about the emails.'

'What emails?'

'And the fox. He'd be furious.'

Chris started to press his fingers into each side of his temples again, but harder this time. Like he might break skin and bone.

'Matt *will* help me, won't he? He'll tell them I'm a good boy. You said the police listen to him. You said he's a decent man. That you brought him here for a reason. To show the police that I was saving these girls, not—'

'I brought him here so that he might believe in God again. That his family might believe. That's all.'

Ben quickly looked back at the door again. 'I know . . . Stephen wants to help with that part.'

'Stephen doesn't exist! He's dead!' Chris shouted, with a fury directed only and purely at himself. There was a crackling anger at the fact that he hadn't spoken like this back in that kitchen, fifteen years ago. 'He's dead, son.'

'Do you honestly think that?' Ben said.

'Of course I do.'

'Really?'

'Yes, really.'

'Then why . . .' A sudden ripple of a grin. 'Then why is he standing behind you, right now?'

The ice Chris felt on the back of his neck might as well have been a little boy's cold fingers touching and caressing him. He spun on his foot but of course there was no one there.

Stephen wasn't behind him.

At least not any more.

Because when Chris turned back, Stephen was standing right in front of him, glaring at him through the eyes of his son, filling Ben's lungs with air, his arms with strength. Like someone had slit the boy down the back and crawled inside him like a costume.

Chris tried and failed to hide his terror. 'I'm going to get help, alright?'

Ben was standing utterly still, his body rigid, while his lips moved in swift, silent whispers.

Chris turned; walked to the door and left the meeting room. He rushed to the office and shut the door behind him. But his hands were trembling so much he could barely work the lock on the door. After a few attempts he heard it click into position. The door had a poster on it that said, *Don't Just Sit There, Pray Something*. Seeing it made him suddenly laugh. He pressed his hands together hard, genuinely wondering if he might have just completely lost his mind. That this was a mad fever dream. For Ben's sake, he longed for that to be true. For the sake of those girls . . .

He grabbed the phone from its cradle and pressed the '9' key three times.

There was no dial tone. The line was dead.

He looked back at the door and, through the porthole, saw his son, but not his son, looking in. The phone's base unit was in his hand and he threw it behind him, its frayed cord whipping through the air.

Then Ben just dropped out of sight. Chris's first thought was that he must have fainted. But then a chair suddenly appeared in the porthole and the metal leg slammed into it. The force of it popped the glass like it was made of sugar.

Chris moaned in horror.

A long arm suddenly pushed through the hole, dragging skin across shards of glass teeth, slashing and quickly drawing blood.

Chris shot forward to push Ben away but it was too late. He had already reached down and grabbed the lock. He turned it.

Click.

The door swung open. Ben's chest was heaving. Mad tears glistened in each eye. 'It's what you've always wanted. To be with Mum in heaven. To be a new creation.'

376

'Son, please don't do this. *Please.*'

'I'm going to help you, Dad,' Ben said. He was crying now. 'The lake's ready.'

'The lake?'

'Let me baptise you, Dad.'

'I already am.'

'The lake's ready.'

'For God's sake.'

Ben frowned at that, and when he spoke again his voice was different. Lower. And the crying had stopped. 'I know it's painful, Mr Kelly,' Stephen said. 'But then birth always is.'

CHAPTER FIFTY-FOUR

At the top of the ridge, Lucy watched the handlebars of her bike dip up and then down. Her backside came off the seat.

'*Shit. Shit. Shit.*' The slant of the dirt track shot her speed up and the pedals spun without her, smacking hard into the soles of her trainers. Finally she clamped her feet back on and got control of the handlebars. The front wheel stopped shaking and she leant forward so she could push ahead.

The black shape of the church was vanishing behind her as she pelted down towards the Healing Centre. The lights down there were on and spilt out onto the car park. They tossed a glowing sparkle out onto the lake.

When she called Ben earlier she said she needed to talk, but he'd told her that he couldn't meet her. He had to go down to the centre and see his dad about something. She had no idea if he'd still be there but even if he wasn't she was making a statement by doing this. By taking the initiative and riding a mile and a half on her bike. She was telling her mum something.

That this was different. That she could make her own decisions now.

When her mum said this afternoon that she shouldn't get too close to Ben Kelly, she knew mum had read the situation all wrong. Mum just heard he was twenty-two and assumed that was the international codeword for some leering perv, eager to get her pregnant. Mum just had this rabid distrust of most men. Understandable, perhaps, but did Lucy really want to see things through the same sort of constant filter as she did?

She'd spent time alone with Ben once, big deal. A walk through the woods after the youth group pizza session. They'd sat by the fox's grave, tearing leaves into neat little pieces and talking about eternal life. They were together for, what, thirty minutes?

And they didn't even do anything wrong. That was the clincher. No kissing, no hand holding. Nothing even *approaching* that. They just pondered deep things, no matter how much her mum assumed otherwise. Lucy had said she was interested in God, and he'd given her his mobile number.

That was it.

Yeah, he was good-looking but so what? The attraction to Ben was spiritual and philosophical. For the first time in her life, she'd met someone who made her wonder if there might be something else out there. Something watching out for her and making the bad things good.

So in some ways this was more an issue of religious freedom than anything else. It wasn't her fault that her parents were so pissy about God. Especially Matthew—

Dad. Just call him Dad again, you idiot.

She was halfway down when she saw a pair of red lights blinking over by the waterfall, at the far edge of the lake. A car was pulling up to a little barn where, presumably, the cows were housed at night.

The car moved around the back, out of sight, and then she saw a rectangle of light opening up in the side of the barn. The silhouette she saw was Ben's.

She reached the bottom of the hill. The door of the Healing Centre was wide open, with light streaming out. She ignored it, turned her handlebars and raced the quarter of a mile to the barn, along the shore of the lake.

Her tired legs pumped the last of the energy she had into the wheels.

Ben would understand. He seemed good like that. He'd realise that she needed some space and if her mum and dad freaked out they'd take it easier on her because Ben's dad would be here too. He was a vicar. Maybe he could even answer all those questions that were buzzing around her head. Like why did God say let there be light on day one but not invent the sun till day four? And why did he not stop her real dad from smacking mum's head on the kitchen worktop, when she specifically, frantically and tearfully prayed so many times that he wouldn't?

Point was, there'd be another adult here, so it wasn't like she was being *completely* reckless.

Ben must have heard her coming because he came from the back of the barn and stood in the puddle of light on the grass. She skidded her bike to a stop right in front of him (instantly aware of how cool that looked), then she let the bike drop to its side, one wheel still revolving, slowly. She bent over to breathe, glanced over at the churning waterfall, which was very close.

He was little more than a sparkling shape against the harsh light of the barn but she saw enough glow around his cheeks to see his shock. 'What are you doing here, Lucy?'

She put her hands on her hips, chest rising and falling with her breath. She saw his eyes flick down her body and then back up again. It felt nice. 'Why are you so wet?'

'I've been in the water.'

'Yeah, I worked that out. Where's your dad?'

'In the barn.' She heard an animal moan inside the barn. Sounded like a cow. The surprise at her arrival softened. He slicked his fringe back with his wet palm and a smile flashed out of nowhere. 'Have you been thinking about what we talked about? About God?'

'A bit. Yes.' She tapped her forehead. 'He definitely seems to be in there. Lurking about.'

'And you want to know more? Are you still interested in baptism?'

'I'm not promising anything, but you have got me thinking. So yes, I've got questions.'

She thought that might please him, that she was interested in hearing more, but his face turned crooked, and he spoke not to her but to the sky. 'I don't know if I can handle all of this . . . not all at once.'

'Pardon?' she stepped forwards.

'I think God must be planning a party in heaven tonight and getting lots of guests.' Even as he said it there was a jittery look in his eyes as if he wasn't quite sure what he was talking about. He used his other hand to wipe his now-wet hair again, and for the first time she saw the cuts on his arm.

'Whoah, what happened?'

'I cut it on some glass.'

'Jesus, you need to go to a hospital.'

'Lucy. It's fine.'

'Don't be a tool, you'll bleed to death. Go get your dad.' She called out towards the barn door. 'Mr Kelly?'

No answer.

'Seriously, you need to get that cleaned up.' She took a few steps to the right, so she could see through the gap of the door and called out again, 'Mr Kell—'

It was as far as she got.

She saw the head and shoulders of Mr Kelly through the gap in the barn door. He was on his stomach, cheek pressed against what looked like blue plastic, stretched across the hay-strewn floor. His neck was black and his tongue bulged like a bloated purple worm was crawling out across his lips. Gravity pulled it to the floor. His eyes weren't alive, but they were open. Glassy pupils swivelled down at his tongue. Like Ben, his hair and clothes were wet, but much more so. He looked drenched.

Lucy had a vague sensation of turning and running. Of the heel of her trainers skidding to avoid the bike she'd dumped. And there was the feeling of the breeze from the lake running through her hair and lifting it up. Bringing it high, then tight, then pulling it backwards in a sharp yank.

She noticed that the front wheel of her bike was still spinning. She must have clipped it when she ran past it. The six of diamonds playing card she'd stuck in the spokes rattled like it always did. And oddly it was that sound more than anything else that made her burst into tears, as he dragged her back to the barn.

CHAPTER FIFTY-FIVE

'Dammit.' Matt clenched his fist to stop himself from slamming it hard into Chris Kelly's TV. The voice Miller thought he'd heard from inside was just this Christian channel playing. A woman with a deep voice was talking about the Ten Commandments.

Behind him, Taylor appeared in the doorway, panting. 'I've checked the other rooms. There's no sign of Ben or Chris.'

'Then we try Cardle's house,' Miller said.

'Or Helston Farm.' Matt's heart instantly plunged at the hideous implication of that statement. Of his daughter possibly being up there.

Slam them in like a pizza.

His entire body jerked when his phone vibrated in his pocket and he grabbed it quickly, in case it was Lucy.

1 Voicemail.

He tapped the phone quickly and listened to the recorded message as he rushed down the stairs.

Hi. Professor Hunter. This is Ryan Goldsmith.

Who the heck was Ryan Goldsmith? He was about to throw the phone back into his pocket when he stopped.

The library guy.

He pressed the phone hard against his ear, listening to the recording as he hurried through the house.

'Well, I've been having fun on Wikipedia. I found a link between all those biographies we looked at. Oscar Wilde, Charles II, that gangster Dutch Schultz and the rest of them. Apparently they all converted on their deathbeds. Most of them were supposedly baptised into the church just before they passed away. Bizarre, but I hope it helps. Good luck.'

His feet slowed on the steps, held there by an image of Ben reading his dad's library books. Or maybe the two of them reading them together, discussing the fear of hell and the power of baptism on a so-called sinful life. He had an image of Ben slipping one of his dad's clerical collars around his neck to give him some spiritual gravitas.

'I know why he's killing them.'

'What?' Miller sounded frantic.

'He thinks he's saving them. He thinks he's sending them to heaven.'

Just as he said that, Taylor called out from the far end of the hall. 'Sarge. There's an answering machine here.'

Matt raced down the hallway to the table in the corner, which had a little black phone lying in a base unit. A red digital display showed the number 1. It wasn't flashing, so if this was anything like Matt's phone at home, the message must have been listened to already.

Miller was standing by the open front door, bending the radio on his shoulder strap up to his mouth. He was instructing some of the extra police that he'd called in from the surrounding towns to scramble to Cardle's house and the farm.

Matt jabbed the button on the machine.

Message. Received. Today. At. Nineteen. Twenty. Four.

A short click, a slight hiss.

Then Chris Kelly's voice suddenly buzzed out of the machine and they all turned to stare at it. His voice sounded weird, a little shaky.

384

Hi, Ben. It's Dad. Listen, I couldn't get you on your mobile so when you get this message can you come to the Healing Centre? I need to talk to you. It's important, so I'll be here all night. And son? I love you. I love you very much.

Matt could just about hear the machine click itself off as they ran out of the door towards the cars.

CHAPTER FIFTY-SIX

This is happening.

This is actually happening, right now.

The water in the animal feeding trough was bitterly cold. Freezing in fact. It shot up Lucy's nose and down her throat as Ben slammed her face under and back up again. He was spouting words she couldn't understand because her ears were so blocked with water. Her nose stung as if she were snorting battery acid.

At one point she thought she heard a voice other than Ben's. Somebody with him. Lower and angry-sounding, but she was so delirious, so disorientated that she really didn't know what she was hearing.

She lost track of how many times her face went under. Three, four. Maybe it was ten. Frankly it was impossible to concentrate when all she could hear from her subconscious was,

And this is the final experience of your life. Brace yourself.

Soon she was aware she was in the water and not coming back up again. All sound vanished in a pop. She closed her eyes tight and gulped out an air bubble filled with her vomit. It flickered against her face and rushed up to the surface.

Not coming back up was strangely desirable because Ben was up there, in the dry world. Better off under, in the quiet water, where she could hold her breath and think.

But unexpected thoughts came. In fact she knew she must be going delirious because she started to see her real dad, everyone's favourite wife-beater, Eddie Pullen. He was way down at the bottom of the trough, looking up at her. Fading in. Tiny but getting bigger and more substantial. Swimming the long, long way up toward her with his cold, greedy eyes.

Hey love! Me, God and your mum arranged that when you died you'd come and move in with me. Down here. Okay? Good . . . good . . . now hold my fucking hand . . .

And as her body started to convulse she could see Dad getting closer, clearer, but now it was through the memory of a gap in the bedroom door. She turned her head to the right and it was Thursday night. She was four. He was 'scary drunk', straddling her mum on the bed, pushing a pillow into her face in utter silence. Holding it there until her limbs went limp and still. It took ages, but finally the repulsive twitching in her mum's body stopped. Then, content that he'd finally killed her, he pulled his hands from the pillow and slid to the side, passing out on the bed, crying.

She remembered being frozen to the spot and watching her dead mum for a whole minute. Enough time for her to figure out how she was going to run away (bus) and where she would live (Blackpool at first, because that was far away) and how she would cope (block out an hour a day, and no more, to cry.)

But just as the plans started to crumble in her mind, her mum suddenly moved an elbow. Her trembling hand reached up silently and pulled away the pillow.

Lucy was about to fling herself to hug her but the thing that came out from under that pillow didn't look like a human being any more. It had purple swollen eyes and a mouth dripping long strips of something horrible. Its shoulder was lined with gashes and its red ear was stretched and ragged where an earring had been torn out. And all Lucy could think of was that her mum was now the troll from 'Billy Goats Gruff', creaking its broken ribs over the edge of the bed and tiptoeing to the phone so it could finally call the police.

– *Trip trap, trip trap.*

Mum played dead, and it worked, Lucy thought. So I will, too.

– *Trip trap.*

She let her limbs go limp and felt the edge of the trough start to dig into her neck. Almost instantly she could feel the pressure of Ben's hand easing on her head. And then he let go completely and she flopped up and out of the water. She slid hard, slumping onto the floor, sharp with straw.

For a second she literally had no idea if she had convinced him that she was dead, or if she actually *was* dead. The latter could have been true. She'd read in the back of a school textbook once that a severed head still sees for thirteen seconds after it's been chopped off. She strained to feel her own heartbeat. Maybe she was witnessing the last few seconds of her life before her brain fully shut down.

But neither was right. She wasn't dead. And Ben didn't think she was, either.

Because he started to gently slap her on the side of the face. A fountain of dirty water erupted from her mouth and he clapped his hands together. It was muffled but she thought she could see his lips saying, 'Thank you, Jesus.'

She couldn't speak; her lungs were too busy trying to heave wheezing breath back into her body. It felt like someone was dragging heavy furniture directly across her nerve endings.

Then the water in her ears crackled and opened and she could hear the cows again. They were looking at her, idly chewing.

'I'm so sorry,' Ben said.

You're sorry? You're SORRY? *You think that covers it?*

She could feel the physicality of her brain, pulsing against the skull as it racked up a thousand furious insults to say to him. But her mouth was impossibly weary and desperate for air, so she couldn't articulate them. The closest she got to speech was a peel of her lips to say, *I'll kill you.* But the sound never came out.

She squinted against the hanging bulb and suddenly noticed thousands of little red dots across Ben's face. Especially up his neck, under his chin. She knew it was blood. Tiny spatters of it, which she hadn't been able to see outside in the dark, but could see now under the light.

Then she looked at Mr. Kelly, lying on the floor. Earlier, she'd only seen his head through the crack in the barn. But now she saw the rest of his body.

She screamed.

'I'm sorry,' Ben nodded to the water trough. 'I know I'm letting you down but I can't finish it for you. I just can't.' He ran a trembling hand through his hair. 'They're coming for us.'

He looked frantically over his shoulder towards the barn doors and she realised that what she had thought was a ringing in her ear was actually a police siren.

Her heart started beating again. 'Give yourself . . .' she whispered, 'up . . .'

'What?' he leant closer. 'I can't hear—'

'If you're sorry. You'll give . . . yourself up,' she said.

He shook his head and pushed his hands up and into her armpits. Both of his thumbs, she noticed, were drenched in drying blood.

'What are you doing?' The floor peeled away from her and she felt a new stab of panic. 'Where are you taking—'

'Shhhh.' His left arm slipped all the way around her throat like a snake and he pressed her into a headlock.

By the time she felt the strength to kick out against him, he'd already grabbed a butcher's knife from a black plastic bucket. He brought the blade higher.

She stared at it, as it came. Closer. Closer.

Petrified, she saw it come close enough to go out of focus.

The sudden touch of cold metal pressed hard and flat against the top ridge of her right cheek, right under her eye. She blinked once, and actually felt the lashes skim against the tip of the blade.

'Lucy, don't struggle. It's dangerous.'

Petrified, she forced her eyelids wide open, terrified to blink.

'I hate how this has turned out,' he whispered.

She believed him, which made her even more afraid. 'What are you going to do?' Her voice now, an old woman's.

'I'm sorry, Lucy, this was supposed to be me helping you.' With the knife wedged firmly under her eye and with wet lips pressed against her ear, he whispered, 'But now you're going to have to do something for me.'

CHAPTER FIFTY-SEVEN

'Empty,' Miller slammed the Healing Centre door back open in frustration.

Matt and Taylor rushed to join him on the gravel outside. 'There's been some sort of struggle in the office.'

Taylor nodded. 'The glass to Chris's office is smashed. And there's . . . there's blood in there.'

'Shit, shit!' Miller said. 'Where the hell is he?'

'Who cares?' Matt shouted. '*Where's she?*'

The field was flashing with the blue light of the patrol car. Matt's gaze raced up the grass, up to the church, across to the falls, and especially along the shore of the lake, all the time fighting the fierce, acidic fire in his stomach. In passing, he caught a horrible sympathy in Miller's eye.

Condolence.

It was the sort of breath-holding look a doctor gives to a mother whose kid just died on the operating table, the sort Matt had given to hundreds of mourners at funerals, to old ladies weeping in doctors' waiting rooms after the test results.

Matt had to pull his eyes away from that desperate gaze, before it overtook him.

He felt God's cruel lips pressing at his ear.

Little Lucy dead and gone.
And Killer Kelly carries on. Ha!

He could drop to his knees right now.

Taylor grabbed his radio to check where backup was and for a few hideous seconds Matt felt at an utter loss as to what to do next. But while his mind began to panic, his eyes kept on working. He suddenly caught sight of something over at the far edge of the lake.

'Turn the lights off.' Matt nodded toward the patrol car.

Taylor looked over, a little confused.

'I said turn the bloody lights off!'

Miller reached into the car. The flashing blue, which shimmered across the lake, suddenly stopped and things turned black again.

But not everything.

'Over there. Near the falls.'

A thin, solid line of yellow light stood horizontal against the shadows, near where the field reached the water.

'It's the cowshed,' Miller said. 'Someone's in there.'

Before he'd even finished the sentence, they were inside the car with Miller at the wheel. The car heaved forward, spitting gravel as they went.

It took seconds to get there. Just seconds. Tyres tearing up the grass of the field as the black lake sped past. But it was enough time for the swing of the headlights to catch something that solidified everything. Up until now, Matt could still have this notion: that Lucy had realised how stupid she was being and had just headed home. But the moment he saw her bicycle wedged in the dirt, that hope fell away.

He couldn't take his eyes off it: her Apollo Endeavour Mountain Bike. He could picture him and her trying to fit it into the boot at Halfords car park when they bought it last year, Lucy barking at him that he was going to bend the handlebars.

He thought he might vomit.

The car skidded to a stop. Matt flung the door open so hard that it bounced on its hinge and almost sprang back against him, crushing his leg.

Cooper's Force roared into the lake, louder and more threatening than any other waterfall in the history of the world.

'Ben!' Matt called out as they moved towards the glowing yellow slit of the barn door. 'It's over now. The police are here. You don't have to do this any more.'

They waited for an answer.

They got nothing.

'Listen. I'm going to open the door now, okay?'

The line of light was maybe an inch wide so he curled the tip of his fox-killing shoe into the crack in the door and slowly creaked it towards him. Electric light crept up his body like quicksand. Up and around his legs, up his waist, up to his chest and finally over his face until he was squinting his eyes and stepping into the brightly lit barn. He blinked a few times.

Once they all understood what they were seeing, the reactions came. Taylor froze and the stale coffee breath from his lungs blew out all at once. Miller put a fist across his mouth and started to back away.

Ben wasn't there. And neither was Lucy, from the looks of it.

But Chris Kelly was. Or rather, most of him.

He was stretched out in a wet puddle of dark blood on a huge sheet of blue polythene. He lay on his stomach, face snapped to the side. One of his legs was completely missing and was now seeping. Matt could see the tip of something dark and glistening in a tin metal bath just next to the plastic.

His other leg was still attached but a hacksaw held by some invisible hand was stuck hard in the groove, just under the buttock, wedged into bone. The handle was sticking up in the air in the same way a lumberjack might leave a saw stuck in a log when he went on a break.

The Reverend Chris Kelly, downsized for the pig furnace. His own father.

'Lucy?' Matt said, staggering forwards, speaking in nothing more than a whimper. He said it again, louder. 'Lucy?'

At the sound of his voice the cows swung up their heads. They were moaning and shouting as if Matt was intruding and spoiling their fun. He hated them for it.

'Matt!' Taylor's shout came suddenly from outside the barn. 'Bloody hell, Matt, get out here.'

By the time he joined Miller and Taylor outside he could already hear the shouting. It echoed as if it was coming from everywhere at once. But he could see it was actually from only one place. He craned his neck to look up at the pounding water of the falls, to the very top where he picked out a shape in the moonlight.

Two figures tangled together, as if they were one person. Ben Kelly and Lucy Hunter, struggling at the very edge of the ridge. The leaping point Miller said suicides normally chose to jump from. The two shapes were grappling against each other, stumbling towards the edge.

A logical chip in his brain promptly sent a message down to his heart to say, it's over. All you need to decide now is if you're going to keep your eyes open or closed when she hits the water.

But the weird acoustics of the place meant that words as well as images were tumbling down those falls, pulsing around them even over the roar. And the things he could hear were odd and unexpected.

It was Ben.

And he was shouting, pleading, begging her. 'Lucy. Do it. For God's sake. Push me over!'

CHAPTER FIFTY-EIGHT

The roar of falling water shook the night air as Matt ran across grass that led to the ridge of Cooper's Force. There were picnic benches and plastic litter bins shaped like huge squirrels. He even spotted the exact patch of grass they'd all sat on the other day when they came up here to admire the view.

But it all looked so different up here, in the dark.

There was a wind from the north, which shook the trees on the other side of the river up here. The side where Isabel Dawson had wept and run and jumped through barbed wire. Just so she might learn the true meaning of entropy.

But Lucy and Ben were on this side, which had no barrier at all. They were standing horribly close to the edge, a few feet from where the river rolled over the side. The churning spray in the air made it look like a swarm of flies was constantly at Ben's side. He had Lucy by the wrist. One sharp yank would send her over the side.

A knife glinted in Ben's other hand.

Matt slowed down, panting, and started to walk slowly. He raised his hands to show he had no weapons.

'Who's there?' Ben said, squinting into the darkness.

'It's Matthew Hunter.' He started waving. 'I'm over here. Just by the river.'

Ben strained his eyes. Then he saw Matt emerge from the shadows. 'Mr Hunter.' He looked . . . relieved. Pleased.

'I can't really hear you with the water. Let me come just a little closer, okay?'

Finally, Matt could make out Lucy's face. The shadows were painting her as much, much older. Her eyes bulged at the sight of him and she opened her mouth to speak, but didn't. Her face just twisted into a tight ball of tears.

Seeing her like that made the clouds slow down and the wind stop. What would it feel like for her if the knife went in, if she went over? What sort of terror would race through her body as her hair fluttered in the wind? He was almost floored by his fear for her.

'What you did for the fox,' Ben called over. 'That was a beautiful thing.'

Lucy closed her eyes.

'It was struggling,' Ben said. 'And you released it.'

Matt waited before answering, 'Yes. I did.'

Ben's shoulders seemed to relax. 'I knew you'd understand. I knew it was right Dad brought you here. I dug it up and put Nicola's tooth in it.'

'Why?'

'So everyone would know.'

'Know what?'

'That they were . . . the same. The fox, the girls. They were the same . . . And I want people to know that *we're* the same, too. Things were dying, so we set them free. And they're in paradise now because of us. That's where Nicola is. That's where Tabitha is . . . Paradise. God's promise.'

'The rainbows,' Matt said, closing his eyes.

'Exactly. I knew you'd understand them.'

Matt gave a weary shrug. 'I do now.'

In the book of Genesis, God supposedly made the first ever rainbow in the sky as a promise to the world. It meant that after the Great Flood, he would never, ever do it again. The idea of that always used to unsettle Matt. Like God was this abusive partner, insisting he'd be 'better' in the future. But none the less, a rainbow meant that the time for water was over.

'I sent them to you so you'd know. That they're healed now. No more suffering or pain, no more being under. At first I just hoped you'd understand, but after the fox . . . well I *knew* then, didn't I? That we are exactly the same, you and me. We find the dying and we give them life.'

'By killing them . . .' It was almost impossible, but Matt tried to speak as calmly as he could. 'How about you step away from the ledge? Just a few feet. Then we can talk.'

'When I die you'll be able to tell the world that I was helping those girls. Read them the texts and the emails. I was releasing them. I thought that maybe you could teach about me in your classes. Write a book, maybe. I think I could inspire people.'

Matt took another slow step closer. 'What are you going to do?'

There was about twenty feet between them now but they still had to shout to be heard over the roaring water.

Lucy suddenly spoke. 'He wants me to push him over.'

'Just a little nudge,' Ben nodded. 'And then she can come to you.' He said it as if it was the simplest favour in the world. Just the lend of a pencil, a push on a swing. Faint clouds hovered above them, still and false-looking against the full stretch of Hobbs Hill countryside.

Miller and Taylor's footsteps suddenly came pounding along the grass from behind. Matt quickly held up his hand. 'Wait. Give us some space.'

They stopped and held back.

'Alright, Ben. Let her go.'

'I need her to push me. I can't jump.'

'I know you can't.'

'It's not that I'm scared.'

'Oh, I know you're not scared. Because death doesn't scare you, does it?'

'No.' He smiled at Matt, as though there was finally somebody who got him. 'It doesn't scare me at all.'

'Because death's got no victory, has it? It's got no sting,' Matt took another step. 'But it's what comes after death. Now that's a different story . . .'

Ben turned his head a little, to look back over the edge. 'I can't jump.'

'I know. Because suicides go to hell, don't they? They all do.'

For the first time, Ben looked panicked. 'I can't go there, Mr Hunter. I just can't. I won't. Not after all I've done. I wouldn't belong . . . in hell. I belong with my mum and dad. And with the girls I've helped.'

'But if you jump you might as well be throwing yourself into the lake of fire.'

'So I'll make her push me. Then it won't be suicide at all. . .' Ben's lips twisted in desperation. He shook his head and his attention flipped to Lucy. Yanking at her wrist and pulling her a little closer to the edge. 'Listen, Lucy. Just think of me as your real dad. I'm Eddie. You told me how bad he was. How you want to kill him.'

Matt took another slow step forwards.

'Think of him when you push me. And for God's sake hurry.' Ben's eyes flicked to the rushing river next to Matt. Something had caught his eye, something in the hurtling water. But when Matt looked there was nothing there.

'Lucy. Do it. And when I go over, it'll be *him* going over. It's the only way your nightmares are going to stop. So push. Push him! Push!'

'Get your hands off me.' She dragged herself away from him so he gripped her harder and raised the knife.

Ben's eyes darted to the river again but this time when he looked at the water they grew wider. And he seemed to gulp in a breath. His chest filled out and, when Ben finally spoke, it was someone else's voice that they heard. 'Push him over, you dirty bitch. Do it. Push him or I swear to Christ I'll cut your fuckin' eye out. Now do it!'

Lucy screamed as Ben yanked her towards the edge.

She's going over.

'Verecundus!' Matt shouted.

The struggling stopped. Lucy fell to her knees on the ground.

Ben grabbed her hair and yanked it back, but his gaze was on Matt.

'Verecundus,' Matt said again. 'You've baptised Nicola Knox and Tabitha Clarke. But who's going to baptise you?'

Ben's eyelids flickered. 'What did you say?'

'I said, who's going to baptise you? How are you going to prepare yourself?'

'I'm already baptised . . . when I was younger.'

'But think of all you've done since then. All that blood needs cleaning off, don't you think—'

'You're confusing me.'

'I'm just saying it's better to be cautious about these things. You should be baptised.'

'Then I'll do it myself. I'll say the words and she can push me into the water. Watch.'

'Don't you know *anything*?' Matt said.

Ben didn't reply. The wind whistled around them for a moment.

'You can't baptise yourself. It's impossible. Someone else has to say the words.'

'God's going to understa—'

'Ben! *Jesus* didn't even baptise himself. He had to get John the Baptist to do it. Are you saying you don't need anyone else? Are you saying you're superior to Jesus?'

'Of course I'm not. Don't say that!' He lowered the knife, and held it by his side. His jumpy hand made it skitter against his jeans.

'So, I've got an idea. Why don't you let me do it? You know I'm an ordained minister.'

'Dad said you left the church.'

'I know. I shouldn't have done that. It was a mistake. But Ben, I'm back now.'

'You are?'

'Yes,' he lied. 'I've repented. Since coming to Hobbs Hill I've turned back to God. Your emails helped.'

'Really? I prayed they would.' Ben suddenly sniffed back a tear, his face a jumble of amazement and regret. 'Did you tell my dad? Did he know that you've changed?'

'I didn't get the chance.'

Ben's face screwed itself in pain. 'You should have. It would have meant so much. That's . . . that's why he brought you here . . . said God was calling you back to him. And your family. How you were a good person. That you understood people who were . . . were different.'

'Well your dad was right. I've answered that call. Which means I'm the only one who can do this. Lucy isn't even a Christian. At least not yet. So it won't work if she does it. You won't go to paradise. Let her go, then I'll say the words and I'll push you over myself.'

Ben started to bounce on one foot, then the other. It reminded Matt of a little kid about to wet himself. 'How do I know you'll do it?'

He said the words slowly, precisely. 'Because as God is my witness, I promise I will say the words, and I promise I will push you over. Just let her go. It's the only way, son.'

'Swear it.' His voice was smaller. Younger. He was a child. 'Swear it to Jesus.'

Matt looked at the sky and called out words loud enough to bounce off the clouds. 'In the presence of the Father, Son and Holy Spirit. I swear I will do this.'

Ben's hand opened and Lucy wriggled out of it. She ran towards Matt, trainers slamming into the grass, flinging her arms around his waist as she tumbled at his feet. Her grip was tight and he dropped so they could hold one another, as if the wind was going to blow them off the edge and it was the only way to stay safe.

She turned back to Ben, face filled with hate. 'You killed your own dad, you sicko.'

'Lucy,' Matt said. 'See those policemen, back there? Up by the benches. Run to them now. Run to them and don't look back.'

She shook her head and gripped him tighter. 'I'm staying with you. He's crazy, you might need me.'

'Dammit, Lucy, for once do what I say.'

She brought her head back and looked at him. An odd sound came out of her, somewhere between a sob and laughter. 'Okay . . .'

She pulled her hands away, and ran.

'Alright,' Ben said. 'I've done what you asked. Now come closer so you can push me.'

'Drop the knife, first.'

'Oh, I'm not going to do that. Just come here and push me, please.'

'Okay. But just one question before I do it.'

'What now?'

'Other than Tabitha and Nicola Knox . . .'

'Yes?'

'Have there been any more? Have you sent any other people to heaven?'

His eyes closed halfway, and the edge of his mouth rose up a notch. 'Some.'

Matt felt his skin tighten. 'How many? What are their names?'

'Not telling.'

'Then tell me this. Who was helping you? I know you weren't alone in this.'

Ben stood straighter, looking suddenly proud. 'Stephen helped me.'

'And who's he?'

'A friend. Now do it.'

'Who's Stephen?'

'No more questions,' he shouted. Then more gently, 'And I'm sorry I couldn't save your daughter. Maybe you could baptise her for me, one of these cold nights. Just don't let her up after.' The wind ruffled his hair. 'So do it. Say the words, and push me over. God says it's time. Can't you hear him shouting?'

Matt took another step forward. 'Are you ready?'

'I think so.'

'Are you scared?'

'A little.'

'You know we don't have to do this. At least not tonight.'

'Ah, but we do.' He turned his head and looked back out over the edge and down across the lake. He aimed his voice towards the glow of Hobbs Hill and shouted, 'I am the world's last evangelist!' The echo made it sound like there were other young men down there, saying the same thing. When Ben turned back a tear was running down his face. 'This calling hasn't been easy for me, you know.'

He nodded, 'I know.'

'Then I'm ready. God bless you for this, Mr Hunter. Tell others about what I've done. Show them the fox. Show them the emails. And put a rainbow on my gravestone. Then they'll understand.'

Matt lifted his right hand in the air, finger's raised in blessing. 'Ben Kelly. Do you confess Jesus Christ as your Lord and Saviour?'

'I do.'

'And forsaking all others, do you promise to follow him as long as you live?'

'I do,' Ben said. 'Come closer. You can't reach me from there.'

He took another step forward.

Eight feet away now. Matt could see the water from the lake, sparkling in the moonlight below.

'Then, Ben Kelly. I baptise you, in the name of the Father . . .'

Ben started to whisper prayers under his breath. Mostly it sounded like the words, thank you.

'In the name of the Son . . .'

It would only take one hard push to send him over the edge. Ben closed his eyes and opened up his arms. The wind ruffled his shirt. 'Finish it, please.'

The moon looked beautiful in the sky. The stars were like angels' cameras catching the sacred moment. The cosmos itself was waiting for Matt to complete the ritual.

Screw the cosmos.

Matt glanced at the sky, turned and started to walk back the way he came, leaving Ben with his arms open and eyes closed.

He'd taken seven or eight steps when Ben must have opened his eyes. 'Hey.'

Matt kept walking.

'Hey, where are you going?'

He glanced back over his shoulder, to make sure Ben was still at the edge but he still ignored the question. He picked up the pace.

'Hey, don't leave me. Don't . . . hey! Don't leave me here. What are you doing? You haven't finished it.'

Matt started to jog up the little ridge to where Miller and Taylor were standing. 'Start walking.'

They turned and the three of them headed in the same direction.

'Damn you!' Ben shouted after them. 'You promised. You swore before God!'

Matt could see a line of police and the flash of the paramedics van. They were racing through the picnic benches to get to Lucy. And with them he saw Wren, clutching Amelia yet running faster than anyone towards her daughter.

By the time Matt had reached the plastic squirrel bins, there was a hundred-foot gap between them and Ben on the cliff edge.

'Okay, that'll do,' Matt said and turned again.

Ben was still there, calling out 'liar' in one breath, and begging him to come back in another.

Matt cupped his hands around each side of his mouth, and started to call out, 'Ben. Listen to me. Can you hear me alright?'

Ben stopped speaking.

'Suicides go to hell. You know that. And even if you try to accidentally fall, it's not going to be an accident, is it? So you need to know something . . . *nobody* is going to push you off there tonight. You hear me? Nobody. So drop the knife and give yourself up.'

Ben said nothing; he just turned his head and leant back a little. Gazing over the edge and down into the water. He looked petrified.

'Maybe God wants you to live a while longer. To tell your own story.'

'You think he'll jump?' Miller whispered, coming up behind him with Taylor.

'He can't. Not by himself.'

'Then what do we do? We just sit here all night?'

'As long as he's near that ledge, then yes. If we try to pull him back he's going to stab someone, or pull them over.'

'Let the bugger jump, I say,' Miller said quietly.

'And if we do that we'll never know how many others he's done this to. Or who helped him. So we wait.' He looked back towards the line of police where Lucy was. 'Look, I'm going to check on—'

'Sir?' Taylor said suddenly. 'Look. He's doing something.'

Matt turned.

Ben was still at the very edge but now he was lifting the knife. He seemed to look at it for a few seconds then he flung it over his shoulder. It sparkled in the air before dropping into oblivion behind him.

'He's going to turn himself in,' Miller said. He called back to a few of his men. 'You four. Follow me.'

'Wait,' Matt held up his hand. 'Just wait.'

'Why? We need to get down there.'

'Something's not right.'

Ben started to raise his arms again.

'What are you on about?' Miller said. 'He's dropped the knife, and now he's surrendering.'

Ben started waving his hands towards himself. Beckoning. There was something about it. Something weird and wrong.

Miller spat out a breath in frustration. 'He's calling us over. I'm getting down there before he changes his mind.'

'Look at him,' Matt said. 'He's not calling us over. He's not even looking at us.'

They started to walk back towards Ben, slowly down the ridge.

'He's spotted someone by the river,' Miller said. 'He's calling them. Have we got any men down there, Taylor?'

They quickly broke into a run, towards the edge. With every

step, Matt could make out the growing smile in Ben's face. Then a wild, giddy laughter. Ben was staring at the river, waving someone close. But Matt couldn't see anyone. Just the swirl of water rushing to fling itself over the edge.

'Ben,' Matt shouted. 'Wait! Just think about what you're doing.'

But now Ben had opened his arms wide and was tilting his head to the side.

They ran.

Twenty feet away now, and Matt started to cry out, 'Ben, for God's sake. It's still suicide!'

But Ben wasn't listening any more.

His eyes weren't even on the water. Instead they were scanning the side of the river. He saw something, someone, that nobody else could see. Running towards him.

Ben's eyes flickered.

They were twenty feet away from him.

Fifteen.

Miller's voice. 'He's going to jump.'

Ten.

Ben suddenly closed his eyes tight to brace for impact. Anyone else would have assumed it was because he thought Matt and the others were about to plough into him.

But Matt knew. Ben wasn't even aware of them. He was seeing someone else.

Four feet.

Matt reached out his arm, Miller did too. He tried to grab Ben's shirt.

'Do it, Stephen,' Ben whispered. 'Do it!'

It was so dark that Matt couldn't see Ben's lips move at all. But he *did* hear another voice. Which sounded like Ben, but somehow wasn't. And it whispered the final words that he'd been longing to hear. 'And in the name of the Holy Spirit.'

Matt, Miller and Taylor grabbed at thin air.

Ben fell backwards. Silently.

Eyes closed. Arms outstretched, he had became one final, Hobbs Hill crucifix.

The three men stumbled to the ground, a couple of feet from the edge, expecting to hear a scream but there was none. The wind whistled in Matt's ear as he grabbed the grass and peered over the edge to watch Ben fall. Cooper's Force fell with him.

Ben seemed to drop slowly. Shirt, hair, clothes, flapping in the wind. His face was framed with an infuriating serenity. And when he hit the water, there was no wail of agony or pain. No yelp of shock at the snapping spine.

Just a dull splashing sound that echoed around the rock walls.

They watched for what felt like forever. Matt started to wonder if the body would ever come back up again. Then Miller spotted something, twenty feet away, towards the centre of the lake. It was the mound of Ben's back and the wet curve of his head bobbing up out of the water. The force of the impact must have ripped his shirt away.

Miller spoke first. 'So, Professor. Do suicides really burn in hell?'

'Hell isn't real.'

'Shame,' Miller brushed the dirt off his jacket, 'because I bloody well hope it's real for this one.' He turned and started to walk back along the river.

After a while, Taylor turned as well. But before he did, for some reason he said, 'Don't look for too long, Matt.'

Matt wanted to go with them, but his body wouldn't let him. He just stood up and watched the glistening lump drifting through the water.

Despite Miller's hopes of hell, Ben didn't look like he was burning at all. Perhaps when they pulled him out they might see that Ben's expression had changed in those final moments from joy and peace to the sheer desperate, hopeless terror he probably deserved. But though Matt couldn't see anything from here, he somehow knew that Ben's face would show no fear.

Asleep, and happy in that final baptism. Dreaming of heaven in death. In his final moments Ben would have felt hopeful and, most cutting of all, innocent. Forgiven. Maybe in God's scheme of things, killers like Ben Kelly and Ian Pendle would get matching heavenly mansions.

Matt stood utterly still for a minute, feeling like the clouds might suddenly swoop down, wrap themselves around him and race down his throat to make him choke. He fought a hot, gushing urge to burst into mad screams at God, which at first felt like bitter rage but was more truly, he knew, a sort of heartbroken bafflement. A desperate, gasping tug at a cosmic collar, spitting out tearful questions like, *If you're there, then . . . why is it like this? How can this be right?*

How could God, in good conscience, earmark Matt and his wife and his beautiful daughters, and every other non-believer for hell while below him, another forgiven killer was floating gently and peacefully toward the lapping shores of paradise?

How could anyone not reject a belief system so twisted? Then for a moment – a small, heart-stopping moment – he heard a voice behind him, and he thought it might be Ben's accomplice until he smelled that odd stench that had drifted from Arima Adakay.

Mama neeeeeed

He span round, half expecting to see her crouching on the hill, lettuce hanging from her mouth, all demonized. But he saw nothing. He only heard the rattle of something, which sounded too much like the low buzz of laughter in the shadows.

Then there was nothing, and the laughter was gone. All that was left was his family on the hill, hugging one another.

He hurried back towards them, pushing past the police. Wren, Lucy and Amelia were in a heap on the grass, crying with relief and gratitude. He swooped his arms around them and for a while they wept and hugged and shivered in the moonlight.

CHAPTER FIFTY-NINE

Matt stood at the coffee machine with his tired head resting against the glass. His breath fogged circles onto it and he watched the mist grow, only to vanish again. He yawned, stood up straight and ran his finger down the buttons. He jabbed the one marked PG Tips. Tea gurgled into a brown plastic cup, which stung his fingers when he grabbed it.

A nurse almost collided with him as he turned. She rolled her eyes and pushed through the double doors, trotting loudly down the stairwell.

He set his tea on the little plastic tray. Wren and Lucy's coffee sat next to it, with a carton of apple juice for Amelia. Then he carried it back down the corridor to Nelson Ward, yawning as he went.

He glanced at the clock on the wall.

2.22 a. m.

It was only as he was pushing at the ward door that he heard the lift doors slide open. There was a squeak on the shiny floor, loud enough for him to stop and see who had made it.

Seth Cardle stepped out, with a huge tray of chocolates under his arm. A balloon bobbed from his other hand, pink with yellow smiley faces on it, saying, 'Get Well Soon'. Seth's eyes were hollow, devastated. He walked slowly towards Matt, lifting his limbs like a grim marionette.

Matt set the tray down on the arms of a chair.

'How's Lucy?' Seth's tone was softer than usual. Thin.

'Shaken up, obviously, and quite bruised. The doctors are going to keep her in to get some sleep but they think she'll come home later today.'

'And psychologically?'

It seemed like an intrusive question, but Matt answered it anyway. 'That's impossible to know.'

Seth pushed the chocolates forward. 'I won't come in. It's late and she'll need some space. Just tell her the church are asking after her.' He set them down on a chair by the ward door. He hovered for a moment, not speaking.

'Are you going to be alright, Seth?'

His eyes glistened with tears. 'Tonight I've lost two people who were very dear to me.' Seth pursed his lips. 'I met Chris and his family at Hemel church. Became friends. I liked him and Lydia very much. And the little one . . .' He paused on that. Swallowed something sharp. 'A while after I'd moved down to Hobbs Hill, I found out that the church needed a new pastor. I asked Chris if he and Ben wanted to join me. I thought this place would make them happy.' He dabbed his tears away with the heel of his hand. 'I genuinely thought that.'

'I want to ask you something. About the night you found Ben's mum in the bath.'

Seth's eyes suddenly grew fixed on the floor. 'How did you know about that?'

'Why did she kill herself?'

He looked up. 'She was depressed. Clinically. And the pills seemed to make her worse. She'd always had such a strong faith.' Saying that made him bite his lip, quite hard. 'But when her brain went wrong she turned angry with God, said life had no hope and that she just wanted it to be over, as if life can ever truly be . . . over.'

'What about the bathwater in her lungs? Did you and Chris baptise her that night?'

409

Seth sucked a breath in, but he still nodded. 'She was pretty much dead already, from the cuts. We just wanted to give her peace. It was . . . her last rites.'

'Do you think it worked?'

'I like to think so.'

Then Matt asked the question that had been gradually climbing out of him, ever since he read that article in Hemel Hempstead library. 'Ben saw it, didn't he? He saw you do it.'

Seth took a long moment before speaking. 'We thought he was in bed. We did it all so quietly. I had no idea he was watching.'

A hospital porter suddenly appeared at the doors, pushing a trolley filled with dirty towels. He passed them and headed towards the lift, pressing the button.

'I know we're partly to blame,' Seth whispered, 'for Ben's state of mind. But only partly.'

'You didn't think to get the boy help, even when he drowned a cat in church?'

'The cat had a tumour. The boy thought he was saving it. Well . . . its soul, I mean. We didn't get help because Chris was learning about counselling. He wanted to sort Ben out himself.' Seth tilted his head. 'We were wrong.'

'Yes, you were. The boy was schizophrenic.'

'I know but . . . I just keep thinking about the main culprit behind all of this.'

'And who's that?'

'Satan, of course. He's been pulling the strings all along.'

'Well, isn't that a very convenient way to abdicate responsibi—'

'How *dare* you say that?' Seth took another marionette-step forward. 'How dare you? I know full well I contributed to this, but listen to me. There are darker forces at work in this world. I mean just look at what happened with that possessed woman you tried to save in London.'

'I *did* save her.'

'You haven't seen the news?' Seth frowned. 'She walked out in front of a tube train tonight.'

The skin on Matt's arms. He felt it tighten.

'Her and her boy, killed instantly.'

His whole body slowly flinching.

'So you see the dark is still working. Behind every murder and rape and death. Just as God's behind every kind word and every sound of laughter,' Seth seemed to shiver. 'They say she was singing when she did it.'

Matt didn't say a word for a very long moment. And didn't breathe much either. His mind flooded with images of Arima and her son and the peals of 'Amazing Grace' bouncing off the tunnel. He shook his head and looked back up at Seth. 'You actually believe that, don't you? That life is binary. Good and evil.'

'I most certainly do,' he said, then his eyes softened. 'Matt. I asked you once if you believed in God. But let me ask you something else. Do you believe in the Devil?'

'Nope.'

'Even after all the things you've seen?' He frowned. 'Or how about I put it this way. Do you believe in evil?'

Maybe it was because he was so shattered, but for one brief moment Matt could see his mother over Seth's shoulder. She was standing by the lift, opening her lipless mouth to scream.

Matt rubbed his eyes. 'Sometimes. Maybe.'

'Well,' Seth said, 'at least that's a start. Please give Lucy my good wishes.'

He turned and headed for the door.

'Seth, the police are going to need to talk to you about all of this. They'll need a statement.'

'I've already been in with Sergeant Miller,' he said. He stopped at the lift door and turned. His eyes were glistening with tears again. 'He won't let up, you know.'

'Who? Miller?'

411

'The Devil. He'll keep making himself known to you. I can sense that about you. You interest him, I think.'

'I thought Satan preferred people not to believe in him. To give him the advantage.'

'Maybe it's different with you. Don't you ever wonder why you left the church and seem to be drifting towards the police? All this death . . . all this horror . . .' Seth tugged at his earlobe. 'Maybe it's because you *want* to see the Devil. Maybe you're drawn to see the things he does.'

'And why on earth would I want to do that?'

'Because in its own way, it's the proof you want, though you don't admit it.'

'Of what?'

'That the night exists. And if the night exists then . . . who knows . . . maybe the morning does too.' Seth nodded in his direction. 'Keep on hunting, Professor Hunter.'

Seth stepped inside, and before he had a chance to turn around, the lift door slid to a close.

Thoughts of Arima and her son kept rushing in but he shut them down quickly. Pulled up the shutters of his psyche. Instead, he hugged the tray of drinks into his side and scooped up the tin of chocolates from the chair. He grabbed the ribbon from the balloon between his teeth. With arms full, he pushed the door of the ward open with his foot.

The place was quiet. Lights dim, people were snoring. Someone at the nurses' station was wrapping their hands round a mug of tea and was squinting at something on a computer screen.

It was an NHS hospital but tonight they'd put Lucy in one of the private rooms. Number 23. He slipped in and set the drinks down on the long window sill that looked out across the lights and the black shapes of Oxford city centre.

Wren was sat on an armchair with Amelia perched on her lap. Her scrunched up face was nestled into Wren's neck, and both of them

412

were sound asleep. Lucy was too, her head on the side, flat out on the bed. Her hand was still clasped in her mother's, stretched across the bed to the armchair like a bridge. One of them was snoring but it wasn't easy to tell which.

He felt desperately tired.

Lucy's chest was rising and falling, and the sense of relief at seeing that made him feel suddenly unsteady on his feet. So he turned to the window and rested his arms on the sill.

It was raining, and it kept pelting the glass for a very long time. At one point it turned so heavy and angry that the glass shook, like the pane might shatter. But it didn't. So he just sipped his tea and watched the water pound hard against the window, waiting for them to wake up.

ACKNOWLEDGEMENTS

Years back, I was walking in a field with my wife when a seemingly random thought popped into my mind: write a novel. The time between that day and this was filled with words and ideas, but most importantly it brought people.

So thanks go to my brilliant agent Joanna Swainson. Her cheerful and constant support is the key to this book being in your hands. And also to agent Broo Doherty, who made me think I wasn't crazy to try. Thanks go to Genevieve Pegg at Orion, too. She gave me a little water in the desert once, and it lasted for longer than she might imagine.

To my publishers Allison & Busby I say a giddy, grateful thank you. For Susie Dunlop, Daniel Scott, Kelly Smith and especially to Lesley Crooks. Her January 'yes' turned the colours back up. My laser-eyed editors Sophie Robinson and Fliss and Simon Bage were great. They came to Hobbs Hill, walked in its woods and managed to get out alive. Best of all though, they took notes. And to Christina Griffiths, who designed the cover. When I saw it I gulped – in a good way. This book is better because of you all.

Thanks to all those who read the early drafts when it was at its cruddiest (and most disgusting). And to all who scrolled through a million neurotic emails from me, charting my quest to scale Mount Published. It must have made for a very samey read, but I always felt like you listened. Thanks for your support and prayers, particularly those from Russ and Judy Taylor. I also want to thank Ken and Anne Dwight. Ken made a joke about baptisms and snipers once. I never forgot it, and neither, it appears, did the Hobbes Hill killer. Moreover I thank God, without whom this book – and I – could not have been written.

To every barista, bar staff and monk who has poured the vital Earl Grey which has fuelled this novel, I say cheers. I hope the incessant tapping of my keyboard hasn't made you want to stab me with a dessert fork. And an extra special thank you to Jan Evans, whose uber generous childcare freed me up to get the book done.

A massive thanks go to my family. Especially to my incredible mam, the poet, who has always loved words and made me love them too. To a great sister Julie, a thoroughly decent human being who thinks I hum when I eat. I hope she's wrong. And to my brother Norman who still seems just that little bit cooler than me. To Dad too, and all those Hammer Movies we watched together. None of these four people laughed when I said I wanted to be an author, it was thumbs up all the way. That stuff matters.

And finally, like a reality show contestant, I'd say that this book has been 'a journey'. But those closest to me know it really, really has. Yet to share it with the loves of my life, Joy, Emma and Adam, has made it a wild and wonderful climb.